RELENTLESS

SUSPENSE SERIES - BOOK FOUR

KAYLEA CROSS

Relentless

*** * * * ***

Cover Art by
Sweet 'N Spicy Designs

*** * * * ***

ISBN: 978-1494878436

Dedication

For the weasels. Thanks for your help researching this one, and I'm sorry Spiderman didn't make it into the final draft. I'll keep him in mind for a future book.

And also for Katie, because you're a sweetheart.

Author's Note

This is the fourth book of my **Suspense** series, and it features the quiet controlled Sinclair twin, Rhys, and Neveah. You know what they say—the bigger they are, the harder they fall. I can't wait for you to see Rhys brought to his knees in this story!

Also, you'll be happy to know that Luke and Emily's story is coming up next. This one's gonna break your heart (in a good way).

Happy reading,

Kaylea

Chapter One

Walter Reed Army Medical Center, Washington, D.C.
Tuesday afternoon, mid-November

He was a walking miracle.

No one had expected him to make it. They'd all told him that, from the doctors and nurses to the PT staff and the people who'd brought him his meals. He shouldn't have survived his injuries, yet he had. Now? He couldn't wait to get the hell out of the place that had been his prison for the past eight weeks.

Slinging his heavy duffel over his right shoulder, Rhys Sinclair headed up to the ICU to say goodbye to the nursing staff there. Least he could do was say thank you, since they'd brought him back from the dead.

Well, them and Neveah, the American surgeon he and his CIA-sanctioned team had gone into the Afghan mountains for, to rescue her from the notorious terrorist Farouk Tehrazzi and his evil minions. Right before everything went to hell.

That's all Rhys remembered from the op, but he was aware of the rest of the story and the irony of it. He'd freed Neveah from her vindictive captors, and hours later she'd wound up saving his life when he hit the landmine. Was it only two months ago? It seemed like it had all happened in another lifetime.

Tugging on the brim of his twin's cherished Red Sox ball cap, he pushed the steel door open and stepped out of the stairwell. Behind the nurses' station desk, the fiftyish head nurse looked up from her paperwork and broke into a huge smile. "Hey, handsome."

A grin tugged at his lips. "Hey, Gina." He walked over and leaned a forearm on the countertop above her desk.

"Come to say goodbye?"

"Yep. I'm officially outta here, thanks to you and your staff."

She waved his thanks away. "Trust me, you have yourself to thank for making it through. I've never seen anyone with such incredible will." She laced her fingers together and laid her hands atop a file with his name on it. "I was just going over all your paperwork. Bet Doctor Adams is pretty thrilled with your recovery, huh?"

Rhys stilled. "Doctor Adams?"

"Yes, don't you know her?" Gina gave him a confused look.

Neveah, crouched on the dirt floor of the filthy hut when he'd burst through the door. Her lips peeled back from her teeth, a feral snarl of warning issuing from her throat. Her long hair lying in greasy disarray around her shoulders. Her eyes glinted with a wild fear. In one bloody hand she held a rock she'd pried from the wall. She hunkered in front of her helpless colleague to defend him, and her deadly expression made it clear she would attack if he came closer.

Rhys shook away the stark memory. Yeah, he knew her.

"She was real involved with your progress while she was here."

His lungs seized for a moment. She'd *been* there? When?

"And when we moved you out of the ICU, she insisted the floor nurses and PT staff update her personally each day." Gina frowned. "I thought you knew."

"No." God, he'd had no idea Neveah would go to such trouble for him, especially after what she'd been through. He glanced down at the file on the desk. "May I?"

Gina hesitated for a moment, then handed him the binder with a conspiratorial smile. "Just between us, okay?"

"You bet." A funny sensation bloomed in his chest when he flipped the cover open and glanced at the recorded entries. He read about his status upon arrival from Germany in the Medevac; the meds he'd been given to reduce the intra-cranial pressure and swelling in his brain for the eight days he'd been in the coma; and finally, the visitors log. His eyes skipped over the list of names, sticking on one in particular. *Sweet Jesus…*

When he studied the dates, he couldn't believe it.

"Better give that back before I get caught."

Rhys closed the binder and returned it, caught off guard by what he'd just seen. He couldn't figure it out. It didn't make any sense. "Thanks again, Gina."

"My pleasure. Come back and visit us anytime."

He shook his head, but softened the rejection with his version of a smile. "No offense, but I don't plan on coming back."

Once he'd said the rest of his goodbyes, he headed back down to the physical therapy area with its bland beige paint and smell of stale sweat. He'd shed gallons of the stuff in here over the past six weeks, putting in countless physically and mentally exhausting hours, biting back grunts of pain while his muscles strained under the burns scars across his back and shoulders. All in all? He was damned glad to be leaving the place behind forever.

He'd just stepped inside when Ben, his six-minutes younger twin brother, appeared through the far door. A swell of affection hit him. "Hey, punk."

"Hey, hard-ass." In a way, the familiar Southie accent soothed Rhys. Ben grinned as he strolled over, a former Army Ranger just under six-four, chomping on his Big Red gum. His pale green eyes sparkled with mischief, their color emphasized by black lashes and brows. "Check you out." He ran an approving gaze over him. "You look like a million bucks."

Yeah, well, compared to how he'd looked when he'd first arrived, that wasn't hard, was it? Rhys pulled off the Sox cap and ran a hand over his skull trim. The newly grown hair covering his surgical scars on the right side was soft against his palm. "Here. Think it's time I gave this back."

Feigning horror, Ben recoiled. "Jesus, put it back on. You think I wanna walk out of here with you looking like a freaking Frankenstein?"

Rhys's lips tugged upward. His brother was the master of talking smack. "Just take it."

"You sure? I don't need it back yet. Maybe it's still got some magic in it."

"I think it's done me as much good as it's going to."

With a shrug, Ben pulled it on and clapped a brotherly hand on Rhys's back. The cinnamon scent of his gum hung in the air between them. "Damn, it's good to see you in your civvies. Gotta tell you, there were times I thought I'd have to bust you out of this place in order to take you home."

Tell me about it.

He'd thought of busting out a few times as well, and his years as a Delta Force member had given him plenty of creative ideas about how to make that happen.

Rhys shifted the duffel higher on his right shoulder, then decided to place it over his weaker left one to give it more work. Hard as he'd pushed himself, his left side was still weaker than the right. And while the right was stronger, he wasn't as coordinated as he wanted on that side.

That's what happened when you suffered a penetrating wound to your right parietal lobe.

Not that he should complain. He was one of the lucky ones. A lot of the veterans he'd met here had it way worse than him. The not-so-lucky traumatic brain injury patients at Walter Reed were still up in the neurological ward. Some in comas, others little more than drooling vegetables. Every single day he counted his blessings that he wasn't numbered among them.

"You're gonna need some new threads, there, Superman."

Rhys glanced down at himself and swept a palm over his black button-down silk shirt. It was too tight across the chest now, the placket puckering from the strain.

"What'd you put on, like ten pounds of muscle in the last two months?"

"Eight." And it still wasn't enough to make him as physically strong as he'd been before his injury. That bothered him. As far as he'd come with the rehab, he wasn't sure if he'd be able to go out into the field again. His chances of making it back into the Unit were pretty much nil now. If it turned out he couldn't, he had no idea what the hell he was going to do with the rest of his life.

"What does that make you, like, a double XL?"

"Nope. Plain old XL, same as you, only taller." He'd never pass up the opportunity to jab his brother about being vertically challenged.

Ben scowled. "Whatever, by like, two inches."

"Still makes you shorter, doesn't it?" He flexed his fingers around the straps of the duffel hanging off his shoulder, a surge of restlessness coming over him. "Let's go."

Ben followed him out into the underground parking and unlocked the shiny black F-150 he'd parked close to the elevators. Rhys was damned glad to get to it. How many times had he sat in his hated wheelchair behind the plate glass window to watch his twin climb into the cab and drive away, back to real life, while Rhys had returned to his sterile room to stare out the tiny window?

Too many to count, and the pure frustration of having to stay in the hospital and wait for his body to play catch-up with his brain had been hell.

With a sense of liberation, Rhys opened the passenger door and slid onto the seat, still conscious of a lingering hesitation in his right arm and leg. No one would notice the delay unless they were a rehab specialist, but *he* knew it was there, and it drove him crazy. He expected one hundred and ten percent from himself, in everything he did. Period. Brain injury or not.

As Ben settled behind the wheel and started the engine Rhys glanced over at him, the long overdue thank-you crowding his head. He wasn't one for sentiment. He'd rather face enemy fire than talk about his feelings.

And while words weren't easy for him, sometimes they needed to be said regardless of whether he was comfortable with them or not. This was one of those times. His twin's face had been the first thing he'd seen when he'd come out of the coma. Three units of Ben's blood ran through his veins. His brother had served as his cheerleader and drill sergeant every single day he'd been in the hospital. At first when he'd been too weak to do more than turn his head, Ben had even bathed and dressed him. Now *that* hurt a big brother's ego.

Rhys took a deep breath and cleared his throat, searching for the right words. "So, I uh… Thank you. For everything," he said, drawing a startled glance from his brother. He tamped down the discomfort of feeling stupid and kept going. If a severe head wound hadn't killed him, words wouldn't. "I don't think I'd have made it without you. I want you to know I appreciate everything you did for me." He even laid a hand on Ben's sturdy shoulder and squeezed once, as touchy-feely as he ever got.

Ben hurriedly glanced away, but not before Rhys caught the sudden sheen of moisture in his twin's eyes. Little punk had always been the more emotional of them.

Ben shrugged. "Whatever, man. You know there's nothing I wouldn't do for you, so's all good," he said, his voice a bit rough. He cleared his throat. "Besides, I think the medical staff deserves most of the credit. I was just happy to ride your ugly ass for a change."

Man, had he ever, Rhys remembered fondly. As always, Ben hadn't understood the concept of quitting while he was ahead, so those rehab sessions had been…interesting. If looks could kill, Ben should have keeled over dead hundreds of times over the past six weeks. "Hope you enjoyed it, because it won't happen again in this lifetime."

"Oh, I did. I've committed all my favorite parts to memory. Like when I beat your sorry ass two out of three times with the Rubik's cube—"

Rhys rolled his eyes, remembering the unspeakable frustration of not being able to make his hands obey his mental commands. When he'd first woken up, he'd struggled to even hold a damn pen.

"—or when I won two out of three arm wrestles last week. Trust me, I won't forget."

And he wasn't going to let *him* forget, either. That was Ben for you. A smart-mouthed punk ready with a snide remark in any given situation, a demon in a fight, and the best damn friend anyone could ever ask for. He could also be a severe pain in the ass, but Rhys considered himself lucky to have Ben at his back.

With the mercifully brief sappy moment behind them and the weight of it lifted from his shoulders, Rhys stared out the windshield as they exited the parking lot. Ben turned onto the busy street and stopped at a red light.

A light rain pattered on the windshield amidst the swish of the wipers. The sky overhead was bleak, kind of like the curiously empty feeling inside him. He was alive and healthy again, but with an uncertain future looming ahead, he felt almost…lost. Aside from Ben and their folks, he had no one.

"So, where to on your first day of freedom?" Ben asked. "To get you some shirts that fit? And don't you dare say the gym. I'd say you've had enough of that for a while, and since you're the guest of honor tonight, Sam'll kill me if I don't get you to our place for dinner on time."

Sam was Rhys's future sister-in-law and a total sweetheart, as well as a top CIA communications contractor. "What's she making?"

"Like you have to ask. Turkey dinner with all the trimmings, because it's your favorite."

Rhys was glad things had worked out between her and Ben despite the rocky start they'd had to their relationship while working together in Afghanistan. Well, maybe rocky wasn't quite the right word.

After Rhys had his head blown open, Ben had actually accused Sam of sabotaging the mission and setting the team up to die in order to secure her cousin Neveah's release. To this day Rhys couldn't understand how his twin had come to that harebrained conclusion, but then, Ben was known for flapping his face first and thinking later.

Right after Rhys had come out of the coma, Ben had gone off with his tail between his legs to beg Sam for mercy, and she'd actually given it to him. Rhys had to smile. His brother might drive her crazy, and at some point Sam was guaranteed to want to kill him, but Ben would love her with everything he had for as long as he breathed.

The thought brought Rhys's solitary existence into sharp focus, and the sudden flicker of loneliness caught him off guard. What was up with that? He'd always known he'd spend his life alone. He wasn't cut out for relationships, let alone one that ended with happily-ever-after. "You guys set a date yet?"

"Not yet. Though I'm sure she and Mom will hammer out the details within an hour of us flying into Boston tomorrow."

"Good, because if you do anything to screw you and her up, I'll beat your ass into the ground."

"Only if Dad didn't find me first. Or Neveah, for that matter. Now that is one female you do *not* want to piss off," Ben said with a shudder.

Rhys hid a smile. Neveah wasn't just Sam's cousin, she was like her sister and best friend rolled into one. She was as strong as she was beautiful, and that was saying something. Her absolute confidence in her abilities and in herself shone out of her vivid blue eyes and showed in her body language. It was sexy as hell, and the first thing he'd noticed when he'd met her in Paris six months ago after the job he'd worked with Sam.

He'd thought about Neveah a lot since then. Probably too much.

While they drove Rhys considered what he'd seen in his hospital file, and became aware of a dull ache in the center of his chest. "Sam heard anything from

Neveah lately?"

Ben shot him a quick glance and went back to staring through the windshield while he navigated through traffic to get to the freeway. "They talk every few days. Why?"

Rhys tried to think of how he could broach the subject without showing how preoccupied he'd become with her. "I owe Nev big time." He laid his palms on his thighs, careful not to fidget but irritated he had the urge to. He was usually more contained. "Did you see her?"

"See her where?"

"When I was in the coma."

Ben frowned and shoulder checked before pulling onto the on ramp. "I told you I did in Kabul. She left the day after Sam."

But not since then. Interesting. Nev was close to Sam, yet she'd been here in D.C. to see him and not contacted her cousin. Why all the secretiveness? She would've been welcome in the ICU, both as one of the doctors who had performed his craniectomy, and as someone who'd just come through the gates of hell with the rest of them. Ben would have let her stay. So why didn't he know about her visits?

"Spill it," Ben demanded.

Rhys folded his arms across his chest and hoped the gesture didn't seem defensive. "She was at Walter Reed."

"What? When?"

That's the interesting part.

"She was in town back when they debriefed her at Langley," Ben continued, "but I never saw her. You sure she was at the hospital?"

"Yeah." The dates matched perfectly, but for the life of him Rhys couldn't figure out why she'd tried to hide it. Because he didn't want Ben to know how much it mattered to him, he changed the subject. "So you said you had some news."

"Sure you want to hear it now?"

"Hit me." After everything he'd been through in the past two months, he figured he could handle anything.

"Luke called."

Jesus, except that. Rhys turned his head and stared at Ben. Whatever their special ops legend ex-boss wanted, it had to be serious and business related. "And?"

"He wants us to provide extra security at his son's wedding next weekend in Vancouver."

Which could only mean one thing, and it wasn't good. "Tehrazzi?" Rhys guessed with a frown. "Last I heard he was dying from the knife wound his bodyguard gave him."

"Yeah, well, apparently he's damn hard to kill. Some recent chatter surfaced that he might've intercepted an e-mail back in Afghanistan about the wedding. Luke's concerned enough to call in backup."

Major understatement. If Luke was worried enough to warrant calling them in, the threat to him and his family must be pretty damn big. If not imminent. Thing was, Rhys wasn't up to that kind of operational standard anymore. Not yet. Maybe never again. He squeezed his hands into fists. "What'd you tell him?"

"I said I'd get back to him once I talked to you."

"You in?"

"If you are."

"What about Sam? I thought you didn't want her involved with this anymore."

"She'll stay with Mom."

Oh, so Ben would up and leave his fiancée behind just to keep him company in Vancouver? Like hell. Rhys shot him a hard look. "I don't need a babysitter." It irked him that Ben thought he needed to keep watching over him.

Ben shook his head. "Luke wants all of us. Dec,

too. He'll already be there with Bryn, since she's a bridesmaid."

Rhys let out a slow breath, the wheels turning in his head. Dec was the SEAL who'd rescued and was now engaged to their good friend Bryn. They'd known her for years. Ben had been head of her father's security team, until Jamul died from injuries sustained in a bomb blast Tehrazzi set up at the US Embassy in Beirut. Bryn had nearly died, too. Then Tehrazzi had gone after Sam and Neveah. After what he and his friends had suffered, Rhys would love nothing more than to nail the son of a bitch, but…

"Does Luke know I'm only at ninety percent?" He wanted to cringe, saying that out loud, but it was the truth. Ninety percent at most.

"Hey. Your ninety percent is a hell of a lot better than most people's hundred and ten."

See? When the punk came out with shit like that, Rhys couldn't help but love him. Still, he wasn't sure he was ready. "I'll think about it."

"You do that." Ben changed lanes and the truck picked up speed with a powerful surge. "Oh yeah, almost forgot."

Like hell. Ben never forgot anything. Rhys raised an eyebrow.

"There's a medical conference in Vancouver that same weekend. Nev's the keynote speaker."

Rhys's heart leapt against his ribs. Fighting to keep any emotion from bleeding through his bland expression, he looked back out the windshield at the tanker truck ahead of them.

If Luke thought Tehrazzi might be making plans for an operation in Vancouver, Rhys didn't want Neveah anywhere near there. Hell, he didn't want her in the same hemisphere until the threat was over. "That right. She up for that already?"

"No idea, but she's doing it anyhow. You could bring her to the wedding as a date," he added with a sly grin. "Luke mentioned wanting to tighten security for her, too."

His head cranked around so fast to stare at his twin that the muscles in his neck twinged. "He thinks Nev needs security?" Christ, maybe Tehrazzi was targeting her again, just to make a point.

"Whoa, chill, dude. He said it's just a precaution."

The hell it was. If that bastard Tehrazzi knew about Luke's son getting married, then for damn sure he knew Neveah would be in the same city to give a keynote speech. And Luke had to be well aware of that, too.

"Has anyone told her?" Rhys asked.

Ben shook his head. "No, and that's the way Luke wants it for now."

Rhys fought back the dread in his gut. He couldn't stand the thought of anything happening to her, especially because she'd already survived Tehrazzi once and had to still be suffering the aftereffects. Rhys owed her something in return for what she'd done for him, and providing protection was the least he could do. But Christ, could he even hit what he was aiming at if he fired a weapon now? Or move fast enough to avoid a blade in a fight? He didn't know.

As the minutes dragged out along the freeway, his guts clamped up tight. "Forget the shirts. Let's find a gun range and see what damage I can still do." If he was going to seriously entertain the idea of taking this job, he wanted to be damn sure he still had what it took. He would never place lives in jeopardy if he wasn't sharp enough, and that went double for his brother's and Neveah's.

Ben shook his head and sighed. "God, you're a relentless bastard."

Yep. And that's exactly why he wasn't still flat on

his back in his hospital bed.

"Fine. I'll give you an hour, but we're not showing up late for a meal it's taken my fiancée two days to make. Unless you want to see my head on the platter instead of the turkey," he added dryly. "You know how Sam is about punctuality."

Oh, how the mighty have fallen. "Pussy-whipped already, huh?"

Ben shot him a glare. "Bite me. Your time will come, and then we'll see who has the last laugh over that one."

Not freaking likely.

"I've already reserved you a seat on a flight first thing tomorrow, just in case."

Rhys withheld a sigh. Like there was any doubt he'd be going now?

He was still mulling over the situation with Neveah when his cell phone rang. Grabbing it from his belt, he recognized Luke's number in the call display and sighed. He must want them bad.

Meeting Ben's questioning glance, Rhys gave him a sardonic grin. "Speak of the devil."

****

New York City

Neveah opened her laptop to check her itinerary one last time. Her open suitcase lay next to it on the foot of her four-poster bed. She had a million things to do before leaving for the airport the next morning, and a mountain of laundry waiting to be folded in the basement of her building.

She hated being so disorganized, but she'd worked an extra shift in Emerg, and a gunshot victim had come in ten minutes before she was due to go home. She and a thoracic surgeon had spent more than four hours putting him back together and stabilizing him, so she'd only gotten home twenty minutes ago. She was in desperate need of sleep, but she had too many things to take care of first.

Covering a yawn, she glanced around her bedroom while she waited for the laptop to start up. Her studio apartment was quiet and cozy, and the view of Central Park made it worth every penny of the rent that cost two-thirds of her paycheck. Opening her e-mail, she checked her messages.

The Pan Pacific in Vancouver confirmed her reservation for the next five nights, and the chair of the conference outlined the timing for her speech and other functions she was expected to attend.

At least she'd be busy, so she wouldn't have time to dwell on her stubborn PTSD symptoms that wouldn't go away. The panic attacks and insomnia were lessening, but she was still far from functioning optimally. Sometimes she questioned whether she was ready to take on something as big as the conference, but she refused to let fear rule her life. She was determined to get past the anxiety that threatened to cripple her ever since her traumatic experience in the Hindu Kush Mountains of Afghanistan.

To her mind, the best way to get over it was by forcing herself to keep going on with her life the way she had before her captivity. Before the day Rhys Sinclair had kicked down the door of that soiled hovel and carried her out. Before the vehicle he'd been driving had hit the land mine and blown the side of his head wide open.

She still saw it happen when she tried to fall asleep. The images were burned indelibly into her mind. Only exhaustion could extinguish the sight of those flames devouring the wreckage of the truck and Rhys leaping from it, on fire as he hit the snowy ground. Sometimes she woke up with his name clawing out of her throat, just like it had on the mountainside.

Except in her dreams, she didn't reach him in time. Ever. Instead he writhed in agony in the snow while the flames ate him alive. His navy blue eyes always locked with hers, full of terror, silently begging for help. But she never got to him.

She'd woken up in tears more times than she could count, reminding herself over and over that she *had* gotten to him in time. She *had* doused the flames, and *had* pressed that filthy shirt against the gaping wound in his head. She *had* assisted the US Army neurosurgeon who'd been at the base hospital at Bagram and helped stop the bleeding.

Without question the emergency in-situ flap craniectomy had saved Rhys's life. That was the only thing that made the memories bearable. Well, that and the fact she'd been able to see him herself at Walter Reed, though he'd still been in a drug-induced coma while they waited for the swelling in his brain to diminish enough for them to bring him out of it.

That was her guilty secret, and something she didn't want him or anyone else finding out. The last thing Rhys needed was to know the traumatized woman he'd rescued had developed an unhealthy obsession with him. Hell, it wasn't something she was proud of either, but it didn't change the fact that she thought about him every free moment.

He'd been released today. They'd called to tell her.

His meteoric recovery was nothing short of miraculous, but he'd worked damn hard—harder than any patient she'd ever seen. Whenever he'd hit a plateau in his progress, he'd personally upped his rehab sessions by fifty percent until he reached the next goal, pushing himself to the wall every time, no matter how much the staff tried to get him to slow down. It gave her goose bumps just thinking of it. She was easily his number one fan, and though she understood the psychology behind it, that didn't mean she was comfortable with her feelings. She wasn't.

He'd come to her rescue, so it was natural for her to be attached to him, and because she'd operated on him the bond was even stronger for her. Trouble was, she was pretty sure the connection was one-sided. As far as she knew, Rhys didn't do emotional attachment, let alone relationships.

For God's sake, Nev, get a grip. She crossed the room to her tiny closet and pulled out clothes to pack, thinking about when she'd first met Rhys. She'd gone to visit Sam, who'd just finished working a job in Paris for the CIA along with Rhys and his team. Her cousin had brought him with her on their first night out together. Nev had expected to hate every moment of his company while she'd waited at the café to meet the knuckle-dragging, government-trained assassin Sam had invited.

The reality of Rhys had been so completely opposite to that, she'd been stunned into staring at him. Her first impression was that he was drop-dead gorgeous, and *quiet*. Not at all the arrogant, look-how-dangerous-I-am predator she'd assumed he'd be. But then her cynical side had kicked in and pointed out that she couldn't let his looks or civilized demeanor distract her from what he was. A trained killer.

Throughout the night he'd continued to surprise her. He hadn't said much, but what he had said was shockingly intelligent. He'd known more about Parisian history and the paintings in the Louvre than she did, and spoke almost fluent French. Sam had laughed at her stunned expression when he'd conversed with the waiter at the restaurant he'd chosen for them.

Looking back, Nev was ashamed of how she'd

dismissed him as uneducated simply because of his vocation. Whatever else Rhys was, he was extremely intellectual. Unfortunately for her, that combination of brains, confidence and looks made him a thousand times sexier than any other man she'd ever met. He'd been a total gentleman, guiding her and Sam through the busy streets with a solid hand on the smalls of their backs, or acting as a human icebreaker to lead them through crowds. They'd hit a club later and he'd stood guard, watching over them from a distance. When she'd met his eyes across the room, it had felt like a hand reached in and squeezed her heart before he glanced away.

Placing her favorite pale pink skirt suit into her suitcase, Nev frowned at the memory. She'd sensed a silent yearning in him at that moment. As though he wanted to get close, but didn't know how to.

She jumped when her phone rang. Stepping over the pile of clothes beside the bed, she checked the display. *Sam.* She crawled up onto the mattress and answered. "Hey, cuz."

"Hey. Bet I caught you packing, huh."

"Yes." She gazed around the torn apart room. Sam would *die* if she saw it this messy. "Somehow I don't think you'd approve of my method."

"Well then I'm glad I'm not there. Listen, just wanted to wish you luck with everything. You feeling okay about it?"

Nev laughed softly. If she had a panic attack on stage in front of all her medical colleagues, she had only herself to blame. But hey, look at all the first responders she'd have standing by. "Not really, but I figure it'll be better once I get there."

"I guarantee it. Know why?"

Nev rolled onto her back to survey the pile of clothes mounded up at the foot of her bed. "Why?"

"Hang on a minute. Someone wants to say hi." She

waited on the line, expecting to hear the flattened vowels of Ben's Boston accent.

"Hi, Nev."

Her stomach did a terrified back flip as she scrambled into a sitting position. She would never mistake that voice. Deep and calm, devoid of the accent his twin still carried, the timbre resonated in her ears like the perfect pitch of a cello in the hands of a master. "Rhys?"

"Yeah. How are you?"

Butterflies fluttered to life in her stomach. She swept a hand over her hair, which was ridiculous, since he couldn't see her. "Fine, good." Damn, her heart was racing like she'd been running for a half hour. "What are you doing there?"

"I got released today, so Sam had me over for dinner to celebrate."

"Oh." Would have been nice if Sam had warned her before putting him on the phone. The butterflies continued their frenzied flight in her belly as she scrambled for something sensible to say. "How are you feeling?"

"Great. Almost good as new."

Almost. But knowing how hard he'd pushed himself, he wouldn't be happy about his remaining strength imbalance. "I'm so glad." She hated that she couldn't think of something better to say, and that she felt so awkward. For God's sake, she'd had her hands in the man's cranial vault, which was way more intimate than anything she'd ever done with another man. Why was she so nervous?

He picked up the thread of conversation for her. "So, I hear you're flying to Vancouver tomorrow."

She toyed with a lock of hair that had slipped over her shoulder. "Yeah." *Great dialogue, Nev. He must be spellbound.* "For a conference. I'm giving a speech on

Sunday."

"I heard that. Sam tell you I'll be in town, too?"

She nearly swallowed her tongue. "What?"

"Ben and I have a wedding to go to Saturday afternoon."

"Oh." Odd. Sam hadn't mentioned anything about going to a wedding in Vancouver.

"Thing is, I need a date, and Ben's not all that attractive. I wondered if you'd go with me, if you're not too busy."

Her jaw fell open. *If*? Was he kidding? "I—yes, that would be fine."

"You sure? I know it's short notice."

"I'm sure." She wasn't going to miss an opportunity to see him, let alone go on a date with the man she'd been fantasizing about for over six months. Even spending time with him in a platonic way was reason enough to skip Saturday's agenda at the conference, and besides, her speech wasn't until the Sunday brunch. "Sam didn't mention anything about this. Isn't she going?"

"No. It was a last minute thing, so she's already committed to spending the weekend with our mom in Boston. I'm flying to Vancouver tomorrow, and Ben's going to meet me there Friday."

A last minute invite to a wedding, yet he was going three days early? Weird, how they were going to be in Vancouver the same time as her, and at the last moment. She narrowed her eyes as a sickening possibility took root. "Does Sam or her work have anything to do with this?"

"Well, sort of. It's Luke's son's wedding."

Was it. "And he just happened to invite you and Ben at the last minute."

"Right."

"As guests, or security?"

"You sound like a reporter," he said on a chuckle that stirred her insides. "Luke knew Ben wouldn't go unless I was out of the hospital, so when he found out I was released, he called and invited me along."

Her gut said he was keeping something from her. As far as she knew, neither of the twins had even met Luke's son, so the only reason she could think of for the invitations was because something scary was up. She swallowed, battling an onset of nerves. "Is there something going on that I should know about?"

"No, not at all."

"Would you tell me if there was?"

"Of course."

Yeah, right. If it involved her directly, he might, but probably not even then. He'd been with one of the world's best covert units and was used to hiding things. He had the poker face thing down to an art, plus as Sam's future brother-in-law, he wasn't going to say anything that might worry her or her beloved cousin. Nev took a deep breath and made herself let it go. "Okay. Good."

"Where are you staying?"

"The Pan Pacific. You?"

"Not sure yet, but I'll get in touch with you when I arrive."

"Sounds good." The thought of traveling to a new city alone used to be exhilarating, but now it filled her with dread. At least she'd feel safe with Rhys. That was something to look forward to. She hadn't felt safe in forever.

Sam's earlier comment came back to her. "Sam said something about guaranteeing I'd feel better once I got into town. She must have meant because you'll be there, too." When he didn't say anything, she swallowed. "I can't wait to catch up."

"Yeah, it's been too long. Have a safe flight."

"You too." He said goodbye and handed the phone back to Sam.

Nev heard her cousin speaking, but didn't really hear what she said. Her brain was preoccupied with knowing that she had a date with Rhys Sinclair in four days' time.

****

Peshawar, Pakistan
Wednesday morning

The two-inch knife wound in his gut had almost killed him twice now.

Too exhausted to open his eyes, Farouk Tehrazzi laid his hand on the layers of bandages covering the new surgical incision on his lower left abdomen, where the doctor had removed a section of his bowel.

A fly droned somewhere close to his head. Peeling his lids apart, he found it above him and fought to summon the strength to lift his arm and wave it away. His skin was bathed in sweat from the fever breaking, but the pain was still there. Deep. Consuming.

Peritonitis was a dangerous condition, and not conducive to living on the run.

Two operations and three courses of IV antibiotics hadn't repaired the damage done to his intestines by his former bodyguard's blade on that frozen summit in Afghanistan. Beneath the dressing he lifted, the row of staples holding his ravaged flesh together seemed obscene against his pale skin, the raised edges red and swollen. Every breath he took was its own separate torment.

But the physical suffering was nothing compared to the frustration eating at his soul.

The laptop his men had recovered from his

teacher's command post in the Hindu Kush lay on the table next to his bed, disabled and free of tracking devices so long as it was shut off. He was too paranoid to let it out of his sight.

With the help of an IT student from Islamabad to break the encryption, he'd found a personal e-mail from his teacher's son about the upcoming wedding. After that, finding the location and date wasn't hard. This coming weekend in Vancouver, his teacher's son would be married. Bryn McAllister was a close family friend. She would undoubtedly be there, as would his teacher's beloved ex-wife.

Tehrazzi would bet his immortal soul his teacher would be there also, regardless of the complex family history.

He let his head drop back onto the pillow and closed his eyes with a sigh, the motion pulling on the staples. Gritting his teeth, he pressed a hand against the bandages and coughed. Mucous rattled in his lungs. The violent jarring of his incision covered him in another film of sweat.

After the spasms passed, he collapsed onto the damp pillow taking slow, cautious breaths as the waves of agony ebbed. How ironic that he couldn't partake of the limitless supply of opium poppies he controlled in Afghanistan.

He refused to take pain medication because he couldn't afford to have his mind dulled while he was at the safe house. He might have to move at any time to avoid detection. Besides, physical suffering brought him closer to Allah.

Gradually the fog of pain lifted, clearing his mind as he focused on the simple act of breathing. No matter his conviction about what must be done, there was no way his body could make the journey to kill his teacher. Even if he managed to slip past all the security agencies searching for him and make his way to Canada, he was too ill to carry out this mission. Was this Allah's will? That he send someone else to do His work?

Someone knocked on the door.

He schooled his features into a calm mask so his visitor wouldn't know how much pain he was in. Showing weakness was even more dangerous than the infection ravaging his body.

"Enter," he called in Urdu, shifting so he could reach the loaded pistol hidden beneath his pillow if necessary.

The young IT expert, Mahmoud, came in, glancing at him cautiously out of too-innocent brown eyes framed behind round glasses. "You look much improved. Are you feeling any better?"

"I am," he lied, motioning for him to sit in the single chair placed next to his bed.

Mahmoud sat. "You asked to see me?"

"Your uncle. I understand he is very much involved in our cause."

The man's throat bobbed. "Yes, sir. He is a most passionate advocate of yours."

Was he. "Tell me, is he a loyal man?"

"Oh, yes. Extremely loyal. And intelligent, as you already know."

Scholastic intelligence was one thing. Practical intelligence was another entirely, as was the will to go through with the act. And the man they spoke of had yet to be tested. "Do you have some further information for me?"

Mahmoud blinked. "I traced phone and e-mail records from the doctor you asked me t—"

"Doctor Adams."

"Yes." He cleared his throat. "I thought you'd want to know... She is the keynote speaker at a medical conference in Vancouver next weekend."

After an initial moment of shock, a slow smile spread across Tehrazzi's feverish face. *How perfect.*

Allah was exercising His divine will once again, using him as the instrument. A rush of excitement surged through his veins. He could wipe out his teacher's family, Bryn McAllister, and Doctor Adams in a single operation. And hopefully, his teacher also.

He could erase all his past mistakes within the space of a few hours. The whole world would know he did not tolerate failure, and that no one could escape his reach once he'd marked them for death.

Urgency clawed at him with sharp talons. He had to move soon. It wasn't safe to linger here much longer, but he must act now to ensure everything was handled properly.

When he drew in a breath to give the instructions, his congested lungs spasmed. He struggled to stop the coughing attack, but lost the battle and braced himself for the onslaught of pain. It tore through him, cruel and sharp. He fought not to cry out at the searing pain in his gut. When it finished, he lay on the bed gasping, soaked with his own sweat.

Gathering his waning strength, he sought the young man's wide-eyed gaze and pinned him with an intense stare. "Tell your uncle to expect my call," he rasped, regretting only that he would not be the one to deliver the final blow to his teacher. "I have an important task for him to complete."

Chapter Two

Vancouver, Canada
Wednesday

The drizzle had stopped long enough for the sun to peek through the heavy layer of clouds rolling off the water when Rhys parked outside the Hotel Vancouver. The distinctive verdigris copper roofline caught the weak rays of morning sunlight as he climbed out of the Escalade Luke had provided for him, and surveyed the place. Nice digs, he thought as he dragged his suitcase out of the back hatch and shut it with a slam. So far this job was worlds better than anything else he'd undertaken.

After checking in under a prearranged alias, Rhys forwent the elevator and took the stairs to the eighth floor. By the time he swung the door open to the main hallway, his damn left leg showed signs of fatigue. It pissed him off and made him question again what in hell he was doing taking this assignment, though he knew damn well why he had.

A gorgeous five-eleven surgeon named Neveah.

In his two-bedroom suite, he unpacked everything

neatly in the closet and eyed the luxurious king-sized bed he'd be crashing in for the next few nights. Beat the hell out of the places he usually bedded down in when he was working. Plus with Ben in the next room, Rhys wouldn't hear him snore all night.

Next to the mound of snowy white pillows against the headboard, a red light blinked on the phone sitting on the nightstand. He picked up the receiver and accessed the message from Luke, telling him to come to his room once he'd checked in. Nothing like cutting to the chase, Rhys thought with a smile, but he liked the way Luke worked.

He'd first met the former-SEAL-turned-CIA contractor after signing up to protect Bryn when Tehrazzi targeted her for the second time in Iraq. When that plot didn't work out for him, the terrorist mastermind had gone after Neveah to garner Sam's cooperation, guaranteeing Luke's involvement in the process.

The bitter hatred between Luke and Tehrazzi was the root cause of all that shit. As a CIA operative, Luke had inadvertently made Tehrazzi into a major threat to the western world during the Russian-Afghan war. Over the years, the young mujahedin had somehow mutated into America's worst nightmare, thwarting every effort to capture or kill him. Luke had been trying to nail the bastard for years now. He'd come close a few times, but despite his best efforts, Tehrazzi was still out there. And more dangerous than ever.

He jogged up the remaining flights of stairs to the top floor and found Luke's room, standing with his back to the wall as he knocked to maintain his lines of visibility. Some habits just couldn't be broken.

"What's the password?" came the familiar Louisiana drawl.

One side of Rhys's mouth lifted. "The Black Hawk

flies at night." Well, it did in their world.

A second later the door opened and Luke stood in the threshold, a wide smile on his dark-bearded face. He'd trimmed it so it was tidy and respectable, but Rhys understood why he'd left it on. No telling when Luke would have to go back overseas to a country where Islamic law dictated that men wear beards. A country that no doubt ended in "stan."

Luke appeared to have fully recovered from the head injury he'd suffered during a friendly fire incident in Basra, and his dark gaze was sharp as ever. The guy might be fifty and have a head of hair sprinkled with gray, but he was still in damn good shape and the best operative Rhys had ever met.

He held out a hand and gripped Rhys's. "Glad you could make it."

"Thanks for the invite." He looked past his boss and whistled at the elegant suite. "Who's payroll are we on this time?"

"Mine. Figured you could use some TLC after the goatfuck that went down last time you worked for me."

"Nah, I got your flowers." They shared a grin. Luke had sent him an enormous bouquet of roses in the hospital, with a card saying *Sorry about that mine*. Gallows humor. Prerequisite of the job. "Careful you don't spoil me."

"Not worried about that," Luke said, turning away to lead him inside. "It's your brother that might be a problem."

"Oh, guaranteed."

A laptop sat open on the desk next to the window where a stunning view greeted him. The downtown core spread out below, and to the north the sparkling waters of Burrard Inlet and white-capped peaks of the North Shore Mountains lay in the distance. "I could get used to this."

"Yeah. Too bad the Muhj don't think much of luxury accommodations."

No, the mujahedin weren't big on anything but fighting to the death to rid their homeland of infidels. Rhys faced him. "Going back soon?"

Luke dropped into the chair, the furniture way too dainty and feminine to suit its occupant. "Just waiting on some sources to pan out."

Rhys glanced at the laptop screen and noticed his boss was in the middle of reading e-mails. People thought Rhys was hardcore, but Luke made him look like a slacker by comparison. "So where's Tehrazzi right now?" *Don't say Vancouver, don't say Vancouver...*

"Pakistan."

Thank God. Half a world away from Neveah. Just the way he liked it. "That the best they can come up with?"

"Pretty much," Luke admitted with a wry smile. "Last known sighting was at a house in Islamabad, but he's long since disappeared from there. Word is he's not doing well. Our informant said he's suffered complications from the knife wound Assoud gave him, so if he's mobile it'd most likely be by vehicle."

"And how reliable's the ISI going to be with trying to root him out?" The Pakistani intelligence agency was notorious for playing both sides of the field in a futile attempt to back the US-led war on terror while protecting the people who waged it.

"You know how it is. The new government's doing a delicate balancing act between keeping the populace safe from terrorists while maintaining a front of independence from the US."

Nothing new there.

Someone knocked on the door. Luke got up. "What's the password?"

"SEALs rule."

With a chuckle, Luke opened the door and Dec McCabe stood grinning at them, a muscular dark-haired SEAL an inch or two taller than Luke. Another well-built man around Luke's age stood behind him.

"Hey." Dec shook Luke's hand, then came over to grip Rhys's and slap him on the shoulder, golden-brown eyes glinting. "You look better than I thought you would," he said with a smirk.

Rhys cracked a smile. "Important thing is, I feel better than I look." He admired and respected Dec because the guy was a total pro in the field. Plus, they had history together. Not only was Dec engaged to Bryn, but Rhys had hauled him out of a burning chopper when it crashed in the desert outside Basra after he and Luke were caught in the blast of that wayward missile. Two other SEALs on board hadn't made it.

Luke motioned at the stranger behind Dec. "Rhys, this is Nate, the RCMP contact I told you about. He served with the Marines in Beirut during the Lebanese civil war. He knew Bryn's father."

"Good to meet you," Rhys said, liking the keen intelligence in the other man's gaze.

"Likewise. I've always wanted to meet Luke's boys."

I'm not one of his boys. He'd do his job, but truthfully he was here for two reasons only: to watch his brother's back and protect Neveah. Rhys glanced over at Dec. "You get cleared for duty?"

"Yep. Going out on deployment in a few weeks."

Luke arched a sarcastic brow. "Ball and chain letting you go back to work?"

Dec gave him a very male, very satisfied smile. "My ball and chain is awesome."

Yeah, she was. "Where is Bryn, anyway?" Rhys asked.

"I dropped her off at the bride's place. Some sorta

chick slumber party where they paint each other's nails and shit." He shrugged his wide shoulders, appearing as fit as ever. Like he'd never suffered severely broken ribs and a collapsed lung that had almost killed him.

Rhys's gaze slid to his boss, who tapped at his mouse pad on the laptop. He wondered if Luke still suffered from his own symptoms, because sure as shit he hadn't gotten treatment for them. Rhys would bet a year's pay on that.

"Ben joining us?" Dec asked him.

"Yeah. He's coming in tomorrow."

"Good times," Dec commented.

Rhys half-smiled. "Yep." With Ben around, things were always interesting.

"Okay, boys, enough socializin'," Luke said. "Let's go over the intel and security plan for the rehearsal and wedding, then we'll tackle the reception."

"And Neveah?" Rhys asked, careful to keep his tone neutral.

"Is a separate issue that you, Nate and I will take care of. You two can pick her up from the airport and take her to her hotel, then later on meet with the rest of the security team posted there for the conference. Her flight comes in at thirteen hundred."

Two hours earlier than originally scheduled. Rhys frowned.

"I got her on an earlier flight," Luke explained.

"She know you did it?"

"Nope, the airline called to offer her a seat on the flight, and that's the way the story stays. For everything and everyone involved with this weekend. You all understand how my presence here puts everyone at the wedding at risk, because we think Tehrazzi knows about it. That information goes no further than this room."

"Understood."

Dec came over to take a look at the laptop. "So?

What's cooking in Tehrazzi's sick little world now?"

"Depends who you ask," Luke said, tapping a few keys to bring up a new screen. "This is a blog the agency's been following. Word is they think a sleeper cell here in Vancouver was activated by a larger cell in Montreal, on direct word from Tehrazzi. They're still looking into possible connections."

Rhys glanced over at him, his mind stuck on part of the blog entry he'd just read. *The American female doctor who survived her captivity in Afghanistan will soon taste the fires of Allah's retribution.* Scary shit. "Sam involved with any of the analysis?"

"Not since coming stateside. She's already torn up about Tehrazzi's people stealing the laptop, and with Neveah and the rest of us involved..." He shook his head. "She's too close to everything. The agency's denied her security clearance." He gave a wry smile that Rhys understood perfectly. Sam was one of the most brilliant computer geeks in the world. Being denied access by the CIA would only slow her down a bit.

Rhys bet her staying in Boston with his parents had as much to do with taking her mind off the situation as it did with planning the wedding. Ben wouldn't want her involved in this any more than she was already. "What kind of threat are we talking about here?"

Luke leaned his shoulder against the wall. "Could be anything. Chemical, biological maybe."

Rhys's stomach tightened. "For real?" Nasty, nasty shit.

"Anthrax, botulism, and nitrogen fertilizer are the most feasible possibilities, but it could be anything. Weapons are tougher to come by up here because the laws are stricter, but we can't rule that out either."

"Police and CSIS have any leads yet?"

"We're following up on some right now," Nate said from near the French doors. "The CIA, FBI and

Homeland Security folks have all been alerted and are working with CSIS. We get whatever filters down from them."

Bureaucracy was a beautiful thing. Too bad that tangle of red tape always cost lives.

Luke straightened. "Nate and I've already gone over the basics of what we need for security at each venue. My paramount concern is that we not take any possibility of a threat lightly. If something doesn't feel right, check it out, and I'll deal with any toes we step on later. Whatever we find, it goes no further than our team." His dark eyes held a fierce gleam, and Rhys felt the strength of his resolve. "No one finds out about us, and no one at any of the venues gets any clue that we're there in a security capacity until after the fact. Understood?"

"Roger that," Dec replied as Rhys nodded.

Luke's shoulders seemed to lower a few inches. "Okay then. Let's get to work."

****

Vancouver International Airport

Neveah followed the stream of passengers up the Jetway to the gate with a buzz of excitement in her stomach. The lounge was full of people waiting to board the plane she'd just come off, so she found an out-of-the-way spot to set down her carry-on luggage and glance around for the man Luke had arranged to pick her up.

Standing in the middle of the busy terminal made her nervous. Her eyes automatically scanned the crowd for possible threats. It was something she couldn't control, and by now did it without thinking. After what she'd gone through, it would probably never go away.

At first she didn't spot anyone who matched the description Luke had given in his e-mail, but then an attractive middle-aged man started toward her and gave a friendly wave. She smiled back politely and picked up her bag.

"Doctor Adams?" he asked when he got within earshot.

"Yes. You must be Nate." She offered her hand and shook his firmly, maintaining eye contact. A firm handshake was important to her because it conveyed confidence. No matter how nervous she was, she always made sure she projected an image of strength. It had served her well during her years as a resident surgeon. "Thanks for coming to meet me."

"Not at all," he said easily, taking the bag from her over her protest.

She followed him through the terminal and down an escalator to the luggage carousels. He strode straight over to number four and set her bag down. She couldn't hold the question back any longer. "So. Any developments I should know about?"

Nate's deep brown eyes twinkled. "Luke said you were a tough cookie."

Good, because she was. "I'd like to know what's happening."

Nate shrugged. "I'm just here as a favor to an old friend, and as a precaution. I understand you went through a lot in Afghanistan, and my job is to make sure you feel safe while you're here."

She had to smile at his charm. "Well, I appreciate the gesture." Not that she needed it. Unless a credible threat against her existed that she didn't know about, she was quite capable of taking care of herself. Above all, she was determined to live as normal a life as possible. "I have a…friend who worked with Luke, and he's supposed to be coming into town. His name's Rhys

Sinclair—do you know if he's in yet?"

"Why don't you see for yourself," came a baritone rumble behind her.

Nev whipped around and found Rhys smiling at her. A beautiful six-and-a-half-foot wall of muscle encased in snug jeans and a black leather jacket. Her heart did a somersault. "Hi." Her voice sounded all breathy and feminine, even to her own ears. The blood rushed to her face as she struggled to stay the impulse to rush over and throw her arms around him. He looked amazing.

"Well," Nate said dryly, "I'll leave you in his capable hands." He handed her a card, which she took distractedly. "That's my cell number. If you need anything, call me, but I'll be in touch."

"Thanks." She barely noticed him leave, her eyes all for Rhys.

His rare smile warmed his cool navy gaze and softened the harsh landscape of his face. "Hi."

Her throat was too tight to speak, so she smiled back. Inside her suddenly too-small ribcage, her heart pounded like a drum. He towered over her. The sheer size and breadth of him took her breath away as she scanned starved eyes over him. He'd always been jacked, but now he was *huge*, like a heavyweight fighter in prime condition.

The skull-trim looked good on him, and the surgical scars would be barely noticeable once his thick black hair grew in a bit more. Seeing those scars took her back to the night she and Ben had fought to staunch the flow of blood streaming from what should have been a mortal wound. Her gaze tracked lower, over the dark pink burn scars that covered the back of his neck. She knew they extended over his right shoulder and halfway down his thoracic spine.

The sting of tears had her blinking hard, and a wave

of embarrassment washed over her. Damn, the first time she'd seen him since he'd come out of the coma, and she was about to cry like a loser.

"Do I look that bad?" he asked, and before she could get herself together, gathered her close for a hug.

"No, you look incredible." Hard to believe that just a few weeks ago his right parietal bone had been hinged open, his brain swelling out of his skull beneath the loose surgical dressings. They'd had to turn him every two hours to make sure he didn't develop pressure sores, all the while keeping him off his back so the burns could heal. She'd imagined holding him like this a thousand times.

And he felt incredible, too. Hard muscle and enveloping heat stole into her bones, making her legs go weak. The subtle, dark spice of his cologne wrapped around her, warm sandalwood and sharp evergreen. Electric currents zinged along her skin from each point of contact they made. Fighting her devastating response to him, she bit back a moan and wound her arms tighter around his neck. More than anything in the world she wanted to just hang on, simply close her eyes and savor the feel of him, warm and strong and healthy against her. But after a moment he pulled back to look down at her.

"It's good to see you," he said, gaze roving over her face. He couldn't have missed the sheen of tears despite her efforts to stem them, but he didn't embarrass her by saying anything.

"You too." Her voice sounded strangled. She'd thought she'd been prepared to see him face to face, but being caught off guard like this had her on the verge of falling apart. "I didn't think I'd get to see you until Saturday."

"Wanted to surprise you."

"Best surprise I've had in years."

A half-smile curved his lips. "Let's go get your

luggage, then I'll take you to your hotel."

"You don't have to."

He met her eyes. "I want to."

The words sent a flare of warmth though her veins, then he slid a protective arm around her waist and guided her through the throng of passengers milling around.

Nev followed him without a second thought, something else that shocked her. If anyone else had tried to be proprietary and invade her personal space like this, she'd push away and make it clear she hated being manhandled. But Rhys made her feel safe and protected. Through her emerald cashmere sweater, the heat of his big hand singed the curve of her waist. His forearm was hard as an iron bar across her lower back. Everything female in her gave a delirious sigh. Never in her life had she reacted so strongly to anyone, let alone with such intense physical awareness.

Once Rhys pulled her suitcase off the carousel, he hefted it like it weighed no more than a sack of flour. With that steadying hand on her back, he ushered her outside into the crisp autumn air. She took a deep breath, catching the faint scent of exhaust fumes. She'd always wanted to visit Vancouver. Too bad she wouldn't be seeing much of it, with the conference and all.

Rhys took her to a shiny black Escalade parked at the curb and opened her door before helping her in, then put her luggage in the trunk. He came around to the driver's side and paused a moment or two, looking for something, but then popped the door and climbed behind the wheel. He did a quick survey of the dashboard, and a sinking feeling in her gut told her he was looking for something far more serious than an indicator light.

He must not have found anything that worried him, because he started the ignition and the big SUV's engine roared to life. He surprised her by glancing over with a smile. “Check-in’s not until four,” he said as he put the truck into drive and pulled away from the curb. “Got any plans or commitments for this afternoon?”

“No, I’m free.” The only thing she’d planned was falling into her bed and staring out the window until she got a call saying her friend Mike had arrived from LA. “But I thought check-in was at three?”

“At the Pan Pacific, yeah. But you’re not staying there.”

“What?”

“You’re booked at the Fairmont Waterfront, across the street.”

She gaped at him. He’d changed her reservation without her consent or knowledge? “Why did you do that?”

“Not me. Luke.”

Like that was supposed to make it okay? “Fine, why did *Luke* put me in another hotel?”

“He’s just looking after you.”

Her heart tripped. “He said there was nothing for me to worry about here.”

“Right.”

Rhys seemed completely at ease. Was he telling her the truth? She leaned against the seat and fought back the worry burning its way through her annoyance. “Am I still Neveah Adams?”

The side of his mouth quirked upward. “Not at the Waterfront.”

Why was she not surprised? She licked her lips, studying his profile. “Seriously, Rhys, am I in some kind of danger?”

He shook his head. “It’s just Luke’s way of letting you know you’re being taken care of while you’re here. That’s all.”

Well, his way seemed pretty heavy-handed and only reawakened her fear there might be a threat against her.

Rhys merged into traffic and flicked a glance in her direction. "How about we drop your suitcase at your hotel and then I take you out to see the city for awhile?"

That perked her up. Time alone with Rhys so she could get to know him better? *Sorry, Mike, but you might be eating solo tonight.* "Sure, sounds great, but I didn't pack any outdoor clothes."

"No problem, we'll pick you up some." He seemed utterly at home behind the wheel in a new city.

She had to admit she admired his navigation skills. He'd only come in today, and yet he got on the bridge to Vancouver like he drove the route every day. Must come naturally to him after mastering land navigation skills in the service. Something to be said for a well traveled, confident man.

Glancing at his hand on the wheel, she gasped when she saw an ugly, deep blister that had torn the skin off the web space between his thumb and index finger. It was almost two inches across and nearly as wide, and when she checked his other hand, she saw another one in the same place. "What did you do to yourself?"

He examined the wound on his right hand with a cursory glance. "Nothing. It's fine."

They looked awful. And painful. "Did you at least put some antibiotic ointment on them?" All that raw skin made a great opportunity for necrotizing fasciitis to take root, or MRSA.

"No. It's nothing. Happens all the time."

"Pardon?"

He shrugged. "It'd been awhile since I hit the gun range, that's all. Normally I'd have thick calluses to protect the skin there, but since it's been so long…I just have to toughen them up again."

Nev tried to imagine how many bullets he would have to fire to work up that kind of a blister, not to mention a callus. "How many rounds did you shoot?"

"Not enough." He glanced over and caught her watching him. "You're not afraid of heights, are you?"

The question threw her off balance. *Uh-oh...* "Why?"

He shrugged. "Just wondering."

****

Just over an hour later she was in a tram hanging from a cable, holding a steaming hot tea from Starbucks in her hand as they traveled up the side of Grouse Mountain, one of Vancouver's most popular ski hills. The ground dropped away hundreds of feet below them, covered in patches of snow that thickened as they climbed.

"Not scared, are you?"

She looked over at Rhys, leaning against the side of the moving car, holding his coffee. He wasn't teasing her. His expression was dead serious, and she was touched by his concern. "No." A little nervous, maybe, but not scared. Not with him beside her. Even if the cable snapped, she was sure he'd find a way to get them down safely. That's how much trust she had in his abilities.

Gazing at him now, she wondered what sort of person he was under that cool exterior. She really didn't know much about him, other than what Sam had told her and that he kept to himself and worked a lot. She might daydream about having Rhys all to herself in a committed relationship, she knew better than to think it would actually happen. He was a loner and a soldier to the core, and Sam had warned her.

Forcing her gaze away, she studied the tops of the tall, snow-covered cedars and hemlocks below them in the enveloping dusk. It was only four-thirty, but already the sky was darkening. "So what are we going to do when we get to the top? I haven't skied in years."

"Hill's not open yet, and neither are the snowshoe trails. Be another few weeks until the snow's deep enough up here."

She looked over her shoulder at him. "So what else is there to do at the top?"

"There's a lodge. I thought we'd take a walk or something. The view is supposed to be amazing, especially when it gets dark."

She smiled at him. Under different circumstances, it would sound downright romantic. "I'll bet." Staring out the tram window, she took in the spectacular sight of the city and surrounding waters revealed by the tram's climb. Nev studied the passing scenery to fill the void that followed. A subtle tension took root between them. She knew he wasn't used to making small talk, but if he was so uncomfortable with that, why had he asked her up here in the first place? Why not just drop her at the hotel until the wedding on Saturday?

Rhys shifted against the frame of the tram. Facing her, he cradled his cup in one large hand, arms crossed over his wide chest. She knew from firsthand experience how magnificent that chest was underneath his shirt and jacket, and was thankful he couldn't read her thoughts. The gleam of humor she saw in his eyes startled her. "What?" she asked, lips curving in response.

"I'm not good at this," he admitted with a chagrined expression. "Never have been."

She took a step toward him. "At what?"

"Conversation. Trying to make people comfortable. Ben got all the social genes, I'm afraid."

"That's not true." She'd seen the warmth in him, and the compassion. And if she wasn't mistaken, she'd also seen longing and maybe even some heat in his gaze all those months ago in Paris. "Maybe you're just rusty, in which case I can help. Warming people up is one of my specialties." She might be somewhat of a loner, but she was good in a social setting. Had to be, because of her work.

He gave a half chuckle and gazed out the window. "I know it is."

He did? "The trick is to find something that interests the person you're talking with. So, tell me one of yours."

"I doubt you'd be interested."

She raised a brow, trying not to be insulted by the way he'd dismissed her so easily. "Try me."

He took a breath and glanced outside again, almost as if he was struggling with his response.

"Okay. Why don't you tell me what you're thinking about when you're looking out the window right now?" she suggested, wanting to know how his mind worked. She'd bet it was fascinating.

He turned his head, and she saw the shadows moving in his eyes. Pain. Regret. A pang of grief hit her square in the heart. She was a healer by nature, but his pain *hurt* her. More than anything she wanted to sweep those dark clouds away from his eyes and fill him with peace and happiness. She wanted to make him smile and feel less alone. He had to feel alone living the kind of life he did, and it bothered her. Didn't he ever get lonely? Tired of keeping everyone at arm's length? "Well?"

"I was thinking about how the wind gusts and velocity of the tram would affect trajectory, and the odds of someone hitting us if they took a shot from the top of the mountain with a sniper rifle."

Something went cold inside her. *That's* what he'd been thinking about while she'd been enjoying the scenery? She was glad the other passengers hadn't overheard his quiet statement.

"We're not in any danger," he added quickly when

he saw her expression. “I wouldn’t have brought you up here if I thought it wouldn’t be safe.”

Oh, damn. Knowing he was looking out for her turned her into mush inside, despite his grim view of the world.

Rhys gave a tight shrug, the gesture almost belligerent. “You wanted to know.”

She forced a playful frown. “Yeah, I did, but man, we’ve got to lighten you up.”

Another chuckle, this one with an ironic edge. “You sound like Ben.”

When the tram finally stopped at the station on top of the mountain, she got off with Rhys right behind her. She glanced at him. “So? Where to?”

“This way.” He took her elbow in that protective way of his. The gesture seemed out of place considering his build and hard expression, but his touch was gentle and sent a flutter of warmth through her belly. Keeping her close, he led her through the cozy lodge, past the restaurants and out the rear doors. Their boots crunched in the snow as they walked toward the ski lift and past it. She stayed silent while he led her away from the inviting lights and down a well-trod path to a bench that overlooked the city.

The sky was a mysterious blend of purple and indigo, its first few stars winking to life overhead. Lights of skyscrapers and other buildings twinkled in the growing darkness, sparkling over the water.

“Wow,” she breathed, taking in the panoramic view.

“Like it?”

“Yes, it’s beautiful.” She shifted onto the bench beside him, berating herself for being nervous in his company. For God’s sake, it wasn’t like she was afraid of him.

Well, maybe a little if she counted the threat he

posed to her heart.

Watching her reaction to the view, Rhys admired the way the wind played through the ends of her long sable hair. Loose strands danced around her face and over her shoulders. Her cheeks and nose were pink from the cold, and her stunning lake-blue eyes were alive with pleasure as she gazed out at the glittering city below them.

The warmth of her spirit was so strong Rhys felt like he could almost touch it. Her innate curiosity and zeal for life were like a tantalizing beacon in the bleak landscape of his existence. Even after her horrific experience in Afghanistan she was still able to enjoy life, and it amazed him.

He tried to imagine what she saw in the city lights. They might be staring at the same view, but he knew they weren't seeing the same things. He was hardened. Jaded. What would it be like to look at the world with such wide-eyed wonder? Had he ever been that carefree? If he had, he couldn't remember.

Witnessing Neveah's enjoyment eased him inside. His own awkwardness was a small price to pay for such a gift. Cynical as he was, he had to admit the view was spectacular.

Nev took a sip of her steaming tea and tipped her head back. Eyes closed, a little smile played on her full lips. He had the passing thought that if it started snowing she'd probably open her mouth and try to catch snowflakes on her tongue.

Her deep sigh of contentment filled the silence. "I needed this." After a moment, she righted her head and looked at him. "How did you know this was just what I needed?"

"Lucky coincidence."

"I don't believe in coincidence anymore."

"No?"

"Nope. Too many things have happened to me to make them coincidences. I don't know the reasons behind them, but I do know it's not pure chance. It's a mathematical impossibility." Shifting her gloved hands around the paper cup, her stare grew thoughtful. He could watch her forever and never get bored. Then she huddled up on herself.

"Cold?" He'd wanted to sit outside instead of in the restaurant because it made him feel less cramped, but he should have found her a blanket or something before bringing her to sit out here.

"No, I'm fine."

"We could go into the restaurant and get something to eat while you warm up."

She shook her head, a dark wave of hair sliding over the back of the bubblegum pink, down-filled coat she'd bought. It matched the gloves he'd insisted on buying for her. "I should wait until I'm back at the hotel. I promised my friend Mike I'd eat dinner with him when he got in. You remember him—he was the other hostage you..."

"I remember." Where she was concerned he remembered everything, from her date of birth to her social security number and that she was allergic to kiwis. Most of what he knew came from the file Luke had compiled on her before her rescue, but the rest came from Rhys's own research and memories of her. But at the mention of Mike the happy expression had completely vanished from her face, and he couldn't blame her. Hard to ignore memories like that when they resurfaced. To distract her he slid closer, until his thigh pressed against hers. "Want my jacket?"

She shook her head. "I'm not that cold, honest, and you know I'd never take your coat."

He wanted to slide his arm around her and pull her

into his side, but was worried she'd take it as a come-on and didn't know how she'd react. She beat him to it though, and snuggled right up against him. His whole body went hard and his heart gave a curious leap. Angling his torso to cut the light wind for her, he allowed himself to drape an arm around her shoulders and hoped it seemed casual enough.

"Thanks," she said softly, wriggling in with a sigh. "That's much better."

This close to her he was tortured by the firm imprint of her body against his and the deliciously clean smell of the shampoo she'd used. He had to clench his hand into a fist to keep from stroking her hair, something he'd wanted to since the first night he'd met her. So long and shiny, the waves fell around the delicate oval of her face and slim shoulders. Not at all how it had been when he'd seen her last in Afghanistan, right after he'd pulled her out of that filthy prison. He pushed the brutal image away.

A lock of her hair swept over the back of his hand, the slight wind making it dance across her temple. She pushed it back and tucked it behind her ear, her gloved fingers brushing lightly against his. An almost electric charge rushed up his arm. Her profile was classically beautiful, almost like a cameo in the faint glow of light from the distant city. All he had to do was lean down a few inches and his cheek would brush the silky fall of her hair, putting his mouth right next to her ear. He imagined nuzzling her there. Gently, breathing in her scent before pressing his lips to the delicate hollow beneath her earlobe.

He squelched the urge to move in closer.

She was off limits to him, and anything beyond friendship would only complicate the hell out of an already complicated situation. For one thing, in probably less than a year they'd be related through marriage. For another, any move on his part would be a one way ticket to a one-night stand, and that could only end in disaster. She'd been through enough shit already without him hurting her more. He didn't do relationships well, so he didn't do them at all. He had to be damned careful not to send her mixed signals. Strange, though. When he was with Nev he didn't feel the suffocating sense of claustrophobia he usually did with other people.

She didn't make him uncomfortable or chatter about stupid things. She was smart and confident, which made her company enjoyable because he could just *be.* No need to wrack his brain for meaningless filler to plug the gaping holes in the conversation the way he had to with all the other women he'd been with. No need to build her up with compliments and flattery designed to boost her self-esteem. She was too sharp and would see through all of that anyway. Not that there weren't a million things he could compliment her on.

Sitting beside her like this, he was relaxed for the first time in recent memory. He still watched everything around them, but he wasn't on alert for a sniper or someone charging out of the trees at them. Which was why he'd brought her up here in the first place, to decompress. God knew they'd both been under a lot of stress lately. Up here away from everything and everyone, it could just be the two of them, without the worry that Nev might be in danger.

That would change the instant they went back down the mountain, however. His anxiety wouldn't stop until the conference ended and she was back in New York, safe and sound. He intended for her to get there without incident, and hopefully, without her ever knowing she was at risk. After that? He'd figure out a way to ensure her long term safety. He was good at planning covert missions.

Neveah settled even closer against him and tipped

her head back to give him a gentle smile. "Thanks for picking me up and bringing me here."

He allowed himself to glance down at her briefly, but then focused on the view and the surrounding area so he wouldn't be further tempted to cross the line and kiss her. He didn't know which worried him more, the possibility that she'd push him away, or that she'd kiss him the way he'd fantasized about. "You're welcome." The ensuing silence that blanketed them wasn't awkward. She seemed to understand, or at least respect his need for quiet, and he was grateful.

He tried to identify the burgeoning feelings taking life inside him. Something about her made him want to get close. Without even trying she opened the door to the lonely place inside him that cried out for warmth. He'd lived so long without it. Being around her made the emptiness all too sharp and though he didn't want to admit it, he needed the connection with her to reassure himself he wasn't cold to the core as everyone assumed he was. To prove the blackness within him hadn't taken over yet.

Not so long ago he'd come face to face with the ugliness inside him and been forced to take a long, hard look at himself. What he'd seen had scared him enough that for a long time he'd truly believed he was dead inside. Until he'd met Neveah.

Now that she'd awakened the yearning, he couldn't shut it off. Like it or not, he wanted someone to sit with like this and let his overactive brain take a rest. He wanted someone to smile at him with genuine warmth because they liked and even admired who he was, despite the darkness he struggled to keep at bay. He wanted someone to hold when the night was too long and the memories were too much. Wanted to feel those accepting arms around him in return and the press of a warm, scented body against his. Neveah held the power to give him all of that and more. She could banish the unseen monster he fought every single day.

With her cuddled into him, Rhys wished things could be different. If only she'd see him as a man instead of a medical specimen she was particularly proud of and intrigued by. He thought he'd caught flashes of feminine interest on her part throughout the afternoon, but not enough to dispel the lingering doubt.

Another shiver rippled through her and his arm cramped with the need to wrap her up close. "We should go," he said gruffly, the startled glance she gave him making him feel like a brusque asshole. "It's only gonna get colder," he added to soften the abrupt words. "I'll take you back to your hotel so you can warm up and meet Mike for dinner."

He didn't like the thought of her having dinner alone with the other doctor, but he had no right to feel territorial or jealous. She could have dinner with, go out with, and have sex with whomever she wanted. It was none of his business, despite the thought of her with another man being enough to make him feel like growling.

Chapter Three

Ahmed shut the master bathroom door behind him with a sigh and began unbuckling his belt, eyeing the newspaper laid on the counter beside the toilet. Lily had placed it there for him as she always did, knowing he would come up here to unwind and read when he got home. She was downstairs, engrossed as usual in one of the many reality TV shows she was addicted to.

She barely noticed when he came home anymore, though he had to shoulder some of the blame. Besides taking on extra shifts at work that had him away some nights and the regular meetings he attended with some men from his mosque taking up others, he hadn't made much of an effort to reconnect with her as a husband.

The thought saddened him. Not so long ago, Lily would have met him at the door with a hug and a kiss, telling him how much she'd missed him. Now, she acknowledged his presence with a mumbled hello and didn't even glance up from her show. How had they grown so far apart in three years of marriage that had begun so happily?

While he went about his business in the bathroom,

Ahmed thought of the last meeting he'd attended. The group he belonged to had grown increasingly radical in their ideology, but he strongly believed in their cause. The very existence of Islam was in jeopardy if America and the western world succeeded in their tyrannical wars in the Middle East. Too many innocent Muslims had died defending their faith. Ahmed and his friends felt they had to do something to help their suffering brothers and sisters overseas.

There'd been recent whisperings that something big was about to happen, and that it involved Farouk Tehrazzi. It was said he might contact Ahmed's group for help with a specific operation, so he and the other members had been careful to safeguard their privacy these past few weeks in case the police or CSIS had spies planted amongst them.

And, of course, the secrecy kept their wives from finding out what they were involved in. Lily had no clue about any of it and Ahmed was glad. She would be appalled and never understand why he'd chosen his path.

When his wife called his name, saying he had a phone call, he shifted on the toilet seat and set down his paper on the granite counter. "Tell them I'll call back," he shouted so she could hear him downstairs.

"It's long distance!" she yelled back, clearly annoyed her show had been interrupted. "Pakistan!"

A chill snaked down his spine. Could be relatives, but…it could also be something imminently more dangerous.

Ahmed finished up and washed his hands before walking out of the en suite into the bedroom. After a moment's hesitation, he picked up the extension. "Hello?" He heard Lily hang up, then a man's voice came on the line.

"Do you have a pen and paper?"

He frowned at the brusque command and unfamiliar

voice speaking Urdu. “Yes, hold on.” He rifled through the drawer in the bedside table. “All right.”

“Call this number in exactly five minutes, and make sure the line is secure.”

Copying the number, Ahmed’s heart thudded in his chest. Was this the “something big” they’d been expecting? He hung up, then retrieved a pre-paid cell phone and waited the remaining three minutes before dialing the number. His hand shook as he waited for the call to go through.

When it connected, a second’s pause filled the line before a soft, well-modulated male voice answered. “Ahmed. I have heard good things about you.” His English was flawless.

He gulped. *Holy...* “Mr. Tehrazzi. I’ve been expecting your call.” Dreading it, would be more accurate.

“Everything secure on your end?”

He glanced around, but of course he was still alone. His wife was no doubt deep into her program again. He didn’t have to worry about her overhearing or eavesdropping. The prepaid phone meant he couldn’t be traced. “Yes.”

“I have a matter of some importance to discuss with you.”

He held his breath.

“My sources tell me you are resourceful and reliable.”

His hand tightened on the phone. “I’m honored they think so highly of me.”

Tehrazzi gave a noncommittal grunt. “There are two events happening in Vancouver this weekend. The medical conference you are aware of, but there is also a wedding. I need you to make some last-minute arrangements.”

Ahmed gripped the cell phone tighter in his left

hand and listened to the detailed instructions. With each one his stomach drew tighter and tighter. He didn't dare write anything down, so he filed it all away in his head for later. He had an excellent memory.

This was an enormous task, and one he was not comfortable with. Before tonight, he'd only donated money to the cause and attended meetings. He'd never been directly involved with a plot, and never dreamed he would be called upon to carry out something so heinous. He wiped his upper lip with the sleeve of his pinstriped Oxford shirt, already panicking about how he would get out of this. Or if he even could.

"I assume you understand everything?" Tehrazzi said, the eerie calm in his voice sending shivers over Ahmed's skin. To be able to order something like this without any emotion made him think the man had no conscience. Or perhaps he simply didn't value human life the way Ahmed did.

"Yes." He had three days to pull this off. But could he carry out the orders? Actually go through with the execution of it when the time came? A bubble of panic surfaced, threatening to overwhelm him. He forced it away.

Technically it wouldn't be him performing the deed, would it? He'd arrange someone in their group to carry out the tasks so he wouldn't have blood on his hands. And he'd make sure he had a reliable alibi, to protect himself. He mentally listed the possibilities. Above all, for this to work, he had to maintain his image.

He cleared his throat. "Anything else, sir?"

"I will make contact with you once the operation is completed." Tehrazzi paused. "I warn you now that failure to comply will not be tolerated. Dire consequences would result."

Ahmed's heart, beating so fast up until now, seemed to stop altogether. *Dire consequences.*

He'd heard stories… Stories about what Tehrazzi did to those who failed him, or worse, betrayed him. Pictures of their fate had circulated on the Internet. Was it already too late for him to get out? Did taking this phone call mean he had no choice? "I… I understand."

Before he could drum up the courage to ask anything else, the line went dead in his clammy grip.

****

Fairmont Waterfront
Thursday morning

She was so afraid. All the time, afraid. All her senses remained in a state of exhausted overload, her body sluggish despite the roar of adrenaline in her veins.

Neveah crouched in the snow, waiting for something. What was it? Couldn't remember. Rescue? Or her captors, coming to kill her?

She trembled in the cold while gentle snowflakes fell around her.

The mountains. She was in the mountains in Afghanistan. Why was she waiting here? She was free—she should be running away as fast as she could. But something held her there.

Her eyes and ears strained in the darkness. The icy wind whipped over her body and through her tattered, filthy clothes as though trying to clean her, but she'd never be clean again. Even if she lived through whatever was coming, she would always be dirty, tainted by what she'd seen and lived through.

She held her breath as the sound of an engine reached her. Rising from her crouched position, she stared down the mountain through the swirling veils of snow and remembered.

Rhys was coming for her. He'd taken her away from

the men who had imprisoned her and filled her mind with nightmares she would never be able to erase. The engine grew louder, coming closer, Rhys behind the wheel of the truck.

Stop! *She screamed the word in her mind.* Rhys, you have to stop!

The truck kept coming, and her heart filled with grief. "No," she whispered as tears welled up. He was too far away to hear her. She couldn't stop what was coming. She never could.

The truck appeared in the distance, in blackout mode with its headlights off. A gray Toyota pickup. Though she knew what was coming she couldn't tear her eyes off it. She had to see it, had to watch it happen so she could get to him. Sorrow tightened her throat as the vehicle struggled toward her, moving in slow motion along with the beat of her heart. It echoed in her ears. Hollow, like a drum.

Thump-thump... Thump-thump...

The sudden explosion knocked her off her feet. Rolling to her side in the snow, her eyes flew to the orange-and-yellow ball of fire rising into the night sky. To the flames engulfing the truck. And Rhys. He was burning alive inside it while she watched.

On a ragged scream, Neveah shot to her feet and raced down the hillside. The heat of the fire burned hotter with each step, and she saw the outline of Rhys's body in the blazing interior, his arms waving desperately as he tried to extinguish the flames. Sobbing, she ran until her thighs trembled and her lungs threatened to explode.

Burning. He was dying, screaming in agony as the curling orange-and-red tongues devoured him.

She cried out his name and reached out a hand. The door opened and he fell out. Fire licked over his back and shoulders as he collapsed face down in the snow and lay still.

Not again, *she raged.* I can't lose him again. *Nearing his prone figure, she threw herself over his back to smother the flames with her body. Her hands were like claws, raking up snow and dirt to throw on him, straining to turn him over. The skin on his neck was blackened and blistered. But his head. Oh, God, it was blown wide open on the right side.*

"Rhys, no!" she cried, placing her hands over the gaping wound while his life's blood stained the snow crimson. "Don't leave me. Please don't leave me..."

His eyes opened, a startling navy blue. A shiver of foreboding rocketed up her spine.

"Too late," he said, voice so calm it raised the hair on her nape. "You can't save me."

She could. She had to.

Over the hiss and crackle of the flames she heard the distant thump of an approaching helicopter's rotors. "Stay with me," she begged, holding his gaze. Help was so close; there would be equipment on board. "Please stay with me." The roar of the engine was loud now, a shrill cry in her ears.

But Rhys's eyes were already staring sightlessly up at her.

Nev's eyes flew open, her heart racing as the alarm blared its morning greeting next to her head. With a groan, she slapped at it and struggled to calm down, get her bearings.

Six in the morning. She'd lain awake until two, then fallen into a fitful sleep, waking twice with her heart hammering in her ears from various nightmares. They always happened in the first few hours after she fell asleep, and they always woke her in a cold sweat.

Sighing, she rolled onto her back and rubbed at her sore, puffy eyes. She needed more sleep, but if she tried now she'd probably sleep right through lunch and into mid-afternoon. Since that was out of the question, she resolved to have a hot shower and go from there.

After crawling out of bed, she pulled back the cream-colored curtain on the wide window, and soft rays of sunlight greeted her gritty eyes. Over the crisp white tops of the mountains to the north, the sun cast its gold and orange rays across the city and over the water, touching it with a million rippling sparkles. Despite her fatigue, a smile pulled at her mouth. November in Vancouver was notoriously rainy, but hardly a cloud marred the azure sky, promising a beautiful fall day.

Glancing the other way, in the distance she spotted people walking and jogging around the seawall in Stanley Park. Rhys had driven her through it last night on the way back to the hotel. The remaining leaves on the deciduous trees were ablaze in gorgeous shades of russet and amber, made even more brilliant by the backdrop of tall evergreen cedars, firs and hemlocks filling the park.

Back home in New York, she ran at least three times a week in Central Park. A run around the seawall breathing in the salty air and admiring the spectacular natural scenery Vancouver had to offer seemed like the best idea she'd had in a long time.

Opting to skip the shower for now, she washed her face and brushed her teeth, then changed into her workout gear and grabbed a banana from her purse. Swallowing the last bite, she was about to walk out the door when a nagging unease stopped her, something she carried with her now when she left her "safe zone." Just another souvenir she'd picked up in Afghanistan. Was it safe for her to go out for a run alone here?

The instant she thought it she rolled her eyes at herself. Vancouver was a hell of a lot safer than New York City, and if she could run in Central Park, she'd manage here. Still, she eyed the clock on the nightstand.

Pretty early, but maybe Mike was up. They hadn't met for dinner last night after all because his flight had been delayed by a few hours. Instead she'd taken a hot bath and climbed into bed to read her book on Delta Force. Three chapters in, a loud boom had sent the book flying and her heart leaping into her throat. Worried there'd been an explosion, she'd called down to the front desk and the woman who answered told her not to worry, it was only the nine o'clock gun sounding across Coal Harbor from the hotel.

Nev guessed the hotel must not have many guests suffering from PTSD like she was, or they might have warned her about it when she'd checked in.

Stretching up on her toes, she thought again of Mike. He was usually an early riser, and he liked to keep in shape, so maybe he'd run with her. Before she could change her mind, she picked up the phone and called his room at the Pan Pacific across the street. He accepted the invitation, sounding wide awake. She met him in the Pan lobby ten minutes later, dressed in yoga pants, a fleece jacket and her runners.

Mike smiled when he saw her, but his warm brown eyes looked tired. "Morning," he said, giving her a hug.

"Glad you could join me." She stepped back.

"Yeah, well, I sure as hell wasn't sleeping, so this beats staring at the clock."

"We could start a support group for insomniacs," she offered.

"We could," he agreed, "if that was our only problem."

"Good point." They both had major psychological hang-ups since Afghanistan, but Nev still thought she was recovering faster than him. "How are things, anyway?" she ventured.

Mike held the door open for her and they stepped out onto the sidewalk, breathing in the crisp, clean air scented with fall leaves and the overnight rain. "I'm…the same. You?"

"Better." She told herself that every day. Each day she got closer to returning to normal. At least that's what she was trying to convince herself of.

From the corner of her eye, she spotted a dark-haired man dressed in a light gray pullover approaching them. Something about him instantly made her uneasy. His features were Middle Eastern, maybe that's why he'd caught her attention, but there was more to it than that. He had shades on, so she couldn't see his eyes as he came abreast of them, yet she knew without a doubt he was watching her. And not in a friendly, curious way.

She barely repressed a shiver as he passed, and couldn't help glancing at him over her shoulder. She turned to Mike. "Let's go."

They took a cab from the hotel to the entrance of the park, and got out at the yacht club. Walking for a bit to warm up, she eyed the nine o'clock gun with annoyance as they passed it, then broke into a light jog, their shoes made soft slapping sounds against the damp pavement. The seawall was busier than she'd expected for this time of day, full of people out taking advantage of the mild fall weather.

At a steady pace, they wove through walkers, joggers, and people on Rollerblades. Cars swished past slowly on their left, along with cyclists. Beyond Coal Harbor to their right out in Burrard Inlet, freighters and tankers floated on the calm water, silhouetted against the rising sun. Ahead of them, the sharp points of the Lion's ears on the North Shore Mountains were tipped white with freshly fallen snow.

What a place to run. "Isn't it beautiful?" she said after a few minutes.

"Sure is," Mike responded. "Thanks for the invite. I needed this."

"Glad to be of service." A while later up the path they came to a statue of what she thought was a mermaid, but drawing closer she realized it was a girl wearing a wetsuit poised on a rock in the water, her bronze shoulders glimmering in the morning sunlight. Nev stopped a moment to stretch her right hamstrings.

"Keeps cramping up on me," she muttered. She set her heel on a bench and leaned forward at the waist, breathing into the stretch as she held it.

Glancing up, with a shock she recognized the man she'd seen on the sidewalk outside the hotel, lounging against the seawall up ahead. He was in profile to her, but she still sensed he was watching her.

The back of her thigh twinged in protest as she quickly dropped her leg. Her pulse leapt, gut instinct telling her something was off. Was he following them? Watching them?

"That's twice I've seen that guy this morning," she said to Mike. "He's giving me the creeps."

Mike peered past her shoulder, frowning. "What guy?"

"That guy," she said, exasperated, and turned her head.

He was gone. In those few seconds she'd turned her attention to Mike, he'd disappeared. Unease buzzed in the pit of her stomach. She pressed a hand over it, her banana squishing around uncomfortably. Whoever the guy was, he could be anywhere now.

"It's probably nothing," Mike said. "We're just both overly paranoid since we got home."

Maybe. She might be over-reacting. But she couldn't ignore her nervous system's innate warning. Some part of her recognized possible danger, and since Afghanistan, she'd learned not to ignore the subconscious messages.

If she was paranoid, so be it, but she wouldn't be

taken unawares again. Not like in Kabul. "Maybe we should head back."

Mike studied her for a moment, hands on hips. "You really that spooked?"

She stared back, lifting her chin. "I just want to be cautious."

"Okay. Let's go, then." They turned back and resumed their jog.

The whole way back to the park entrance Nev sensed the weight of a stare pressing against her spine, but by the time the conference got going at nine, she was on her third cup of coffee and feeling secure again. People filled the large banquet room, and though the crowd made her a bit edgy because she felt the constant need to scan for trouble, she hadn't glimpsed the man from the park once.

The opening speaker left her inspired and glad she'd chosen to come. Her experiences, though horrific, only served to underline how desperate the need for medical care in Afghanistan really was. Now if she could just get past the constant sense of unease that came from being on the lookout for possible threats, she might actually enjoy herself.

"Which lecture are you going to now?" Mike asked her during the break, rifling through his information packet in the bright blue binders they'd been given.

"The neurosurgery one."

He closed his binder and looked at her with a sigh. "Why, because you want to torment yourself with the possibility you didn't do something exactly right on your one and only neurological patient?"

She shrugged, trying not to seem defensive. "I just want to go."

"He's alive and functioning near a hundred percent," Mike said quietly. "I'd say you did everything right."

"I didn't do much of anything. The neurosurgeon did most of the work."

"Yeah? And who kept him alive during the flight to the hospital and operated the crash cart when he flat-lined—twice?"

She had, but that didn't matter. She needed know if there was something else she could have done or something she'd missed. Nev narrowed her eyes at Mike. "Let it go."

He didn't look away. "Right after you, sweetheart."

"Doctor Adams."

She stared at Mike for another second before spinning around to address the speaker, finding a conference organizer gesturing for her to come over. She went to him and the Middle Eastern-looking man standing next to him, scolding herself for the apprehension that gripped her. She would not be reduced to bigotry because of her fear.

When she got close enough, she held out a hand and put on a smile. "Hello."

The organizer accepted the handshake and nodded to the other man. "This is Doctor Shirani," he said. "I mentioned him to you when we spoke last."

Her smile brightened. "Yes, hello, Doctor. It's a pleasure to meet you. I was just telling my colleague how much I was looking forward to your lecture."

Shirani returned her grip and flashed even, white teeth. "The pleasure's all mine, Doctor Adams. I've been looking forward to hearing your speech since they listed you as the keynote." His eyes were a deep, rich brown, intense and full of intelligence. "We're grateful that you would honor us with your experience here at the conference. I'm only sorry you suffered such terrible things during your time in Afghanistan."

"Yes, well, I'm making the best of it."

Admiration filled his expression. "I'm glad. I've

heard from various sources that you gained some experience with a flap craniectomy over there."

"Yes, but I only assisted. It was a miracle the patient survived transport to the hospital, let alone that a neurosurgeon just happened to be at the base hospital."

"An amazing story. Did the patient recover sufficiently?"

"Almost fully." Though probably not to his satisfaction.

"Incredible." He gazed at her fondly, almost like an approving parent. "I'm sure he has your skill and quick thinking to thank."

"I'm afraid I can't take credit for that. I think some higher power was at work that night."

Shirani's eyes grew even more intense. "Yes, God works in mysterious ways."

Did He ever. If she ever got the chance to meet Him, she had a long list of questions to ask.

"Come have lunch with me after the lecture," Shirani invited, "and we'll talk more about it. I'm interested to hear more about your story."

"I'd like that." If he could assure her she'd done everything humanly possible to help Rhys, then maybe she could cut herself some slack.

As though reading her thoughts, Mike raised a mocking brow at her.

Shirani glanced at his watch and offered another smile. "I'll see you soon."

"You bet."

Mike clapped a hand on her shoulder as Shirani walked away. "Well there you go. You just got the nod from one of the top neurosurgeons in the world." His mahogany eyes were full of understanding. "Think you can quit beating yourself up now?"

Neveah smiled sweetly. "Right after you, sweetheart."

Chapter Four

Finishing up the last set of bench presses, Rhys's pecs were on fire and his triceps were screaming, from both the weights and the push-ups he always did when he got out of bed every morning.

He brutally ignored his body's protests and finished off all twenty lifts before setting the bar into the holder above his head, his left arm trembling slightly as he did so.

Sitting up, he wiped his face on the towel he'd draped over one shoulder, and stared at his left hand. He turned it over, studying the shape and lines of it, the healing blister Nev had noticed. It looked strong enough. Couldn't tell the difference in function between the left and right just by looking at them, but the remaining strength imbalance was painfully obvious to him. He flexed the fingers experimentally, watching as they curled tight into his palm. Amazing how swelling in the brain could affect the body so much.

You know you'll never be the same. Face it.

Rhys clenched his jaw and adamantly rejected the words in his head. He'd already come a hell of a long way in two short months. Maybe in time he'd regain everything he'd lost.

"Thought I might find you here," said a familiar deep voice.

Rhys looked behind him. Ben stood just inside the doorway of the gym with a chagrined smirk on his face. One of the punk's default expressions. "Hey."

His brother jerked his chin at him. "You about done?"

"Almost. Wanna join me?"

Ben made a face. "Nah."

"Why not?" He ran his gaze over his twin. Still incredibly fit, so he had to be getting some sort of regular exercise. "Want to spar instead?"

"Jesus, *no*, I don't want to spar. I'm hungry, and I just got off a red-eye from Boston. Not everyone is hard core like you."

"You gonna get all fat and flabby on me?"

"As if." His jade green eyes twinkled. "I get all the exercise I need at home. And then some." He waggled his brows.

Rhys cracked a grin. "Bastard. Rub it in."

"Be happy to. What do you wanna know?"

Shit. "Nothing." Ben didn't know the meaning of the word 'boundary.' Rhys got up and drained the last half of his bottled water. "Luke brief you yet?"

"Just came from his room. He and that Nate guy are trying to crack the sleeper cell using phone records and satellite links to cell phones."

"Good thing that's part of your specialty." If it had wiring or a computer chip, Ben could do damn near anything with it. All those misspent years of their youth where Ben had passed the time hacking into computer systems had paid dividends for him as an adult.

Ben snapped his gum, a sure sign something was on his mind. "See Nev yet?"

He hesitated. "Yeah."

"When?"

"Yesterday. I picked her up from the airport."

Ben seemed surprised. "How'd she look?"

Delectable. Strong. "Fine. Not traumatized or anything." At least, not so much that the average person would notice. He'd picked up on her hyper-vigilance a couple times, but only because he was aware she had PTSD. In all, she seemed to be handling everything amazingly well.

"Sam's not happy about Nev being here."

Who was? "Luke's got everything under control. Does Sam know anything?"

Ben wrinkled his nose. "Nah. More of a hunch, I think. She's aware this involves Tehrazzi somehow, but that's as far as it goes."

And Ben had actually been able to keep the info from her? Unbelievable. Setting down his water, Rhys wiped the towel over his face and neck. "You going to tell her what's happening?"

His twin gawked at him. "Are you nuts? She's been through more than enough without worrying about Nev. At least with me here she's relaxed a bit."

"But still worried about you."

Ben shrugged. "She's seen firsthand what we do. But she knows I've got you here to watch my back."

Damn straight. "And Luke and Dec."

His eyes brightened at the latter name. "Irish is here already?"

"Came in yesterday with Nate."

"Damn, can't wait to see him. What about Bryn?"

"Haven't seen her yet. She's staying with the bride for a few nights."

Ben frowned. "They've got security there though, right?"

"Oh yeah. You know Dec wouldn't even think of leaving her there without him otherwise."

The reassurance seemed to appease his brother. “Well? Can you drag your ugly ass into the shower so we can get some breakfast, or do I have to do it for you?”

“Keep it up, punk.”

“I intend to. It’s what I live for.”

No shit. “I’m going,” Rhys said, stretching his arms over his head as he stood. “Got a long couple of days ahead of us.” Whatever else happened, they had to make sure Nev and the others stayed safe throughout the weekend. Four days. That’s all they needed—four days without incident.

Unfortunately, Rhys knew shit could happen at any time between now and then.

****

After a morning of meetings with Luke’s security team at the church and a good chunk of the afternoon spent at and around the reception site, Rhys started to notice the effects of fatigue on his body.

Little things, like the emphasized hesitation in his right leg. It was more pronounced from climbing up and down staircases and the steep banks surrounding Seasons in the Park restaurant in Queen Elizabeth Park.

Ben shot him a sidelong glance as he drove the Escalade back to their hotel downtown. “You coming to the hockey game with the rest of us?”

“Nah.”

“The Canucks are playing Boston,” he said, in a tone that said it would be sacrilegious not to go. “You gotta support the Bruins, man.”

“Can’t tonight.” He didn’t like hockey anyway, and Ben knew it. His sport allegiance started and finished with the Red Sox, which Ben also knew.

“Don’t tell me you’re going to the rehearsal

dinner?"

Withholding a snort, he shifted against the leather seat, enjoying the luxury of the heater against his back and thighs. "No, Luke said they had plenty of help." And thank God. A rehearsal dinner was way out of his comfort zone.

His twin's eyes narrowed, and a knowing smile spread across his face. "You've got a date lined up, don't you?"

He had to laugh. "Don't know. Haven't asked her yet."

"Yeah, but you're gonna. Wow, look at you. Mister Tall-Dark-and-Remote looking for some action with Neveah."

Rhys rolled his eyes. "It's not like that."

"No? Then how is it?"

He aimed a hard glare at Ben. "It's just dinner, and don't talk about her like that. She's your future in-law for Christ's sake—show some respect."

Ben chuckled as he merged onto the Cambie Street Bridge. "Wonder how a surgeon plays doctor," he mused. "Could be hot."

He would *not* smile. If he gave the prick that much satisfaction, he'd never hear the end of it. "You're pushing your luck, punk."

" 'Course I am." Then he shook his head. "You know she's a Yankees fan, right?"

"Is she?" Lucky for him being a BoSox fan wasn't a make or break deal.

"Better think about it before things go too far. It'd be like sleeping with the enemy." After a minute, Ben slanted him a sideways glance. "It's driving you frickin' mental that you're not behind the wheel right now, isn't it?"

Damn right it was. "Actually, I was just thinking how much I'm enjoying the ride."

His brother snorted. “Yeah, right.” Then he smiled fondly. “Christ, I’ve missed needling you.”

Rhys had missed it, too, which was completely messed up. Brotherly banter and talking smack was one thing; it was just that Ben didn’t know when to quit.

“So, you gonna call her up, or what?”

“In front of you? Not likely.”

“Aw, come on, give me something. I’ve got the night off in a strange city, and my fiancée’s on the other side of the continent. At least let me in on this.”

“Forget it. You’re going to the hockey game.”

Ben threw him a sour look. “You’re such a fun-times killer.”

“Well, we can’t all be ass-clowns.”

Once he got into their room and Ben headed for the shower, Rhys called Neveah’s cell and was surprised when she answered. “Hi, it’s Rhys,” he told her.

“I know, I have call display. And even if I didn’t, I’d recognize your voice anywhere. How did your day go?”

An image of her bright smile took over his brain, along with a wave of relief that she sounded glad to hear from him. “Fine.” He rubbed the back of his neck. “So… Are you still free tonight, or do you have to be somewhere?”

“I already stayed to schmooze through a happy hour, so I’m free if I want to be. Why, you have something in mind?”

He smiled at the hint of challenge in her tone. “Feel like having dinner?”

“Just us?”

“Yeah.”

“Then absolutely.”

Tension he hadn’t even realized he was holding melted out of his shoulders. “Do you like Italian?”

“It’s my favorite.”

His, too. "Then I'll pick you up at seven."

"Sure. Want me to meet you in the lobby?"

"No." Call him old-fashioned, but he believed in picking up a date at her door and returning her to it when the night was over. Add in the possibility that she might be at risk for another kidnapping attempt or worse, and there was no way in hell he'd let her wait around an open lobby for him. "I'll come up and get you."

When they said goodbye, he set his phone down and stared at it with a thoughtful frown. The buzz of anticipation inside him was something he only experienced before an op. The stirrings of excitement inside him felt strange. He couldn't remember the last time he'd felt like this about anything, other than leaving the hospital. Damn, he was really looking forward to this.

Without tipping Ben off that anything was up when he passed him, Rhys went into the bathroom and started the shower. Pausing in front of the mirror, he angled his head so he could see the scars on the right side. They weren't as visible as they once had been. No one could tell by looking that a metal plate held his skull together. Once his hair got a little longer, he'd almost look normal again.

But you'll never be normal again.

Shoving the negative thought out of his mind, he stepped under the hard spray and scrubbed himself. His hand swept the soap over his chest and back, where the burn scars covered his skin, and thought of Neveah. The instant he did, his cock hardened. He ignored it, thought about her contribution to his recovery. Her hands had tended to him, first in the field, and later at the hospital in the operating room. That increasingly familiar pang of gratitude and longing started up again. The tangle of emotions he felt whenever he thought of her might confuse him, but he couldn't wait to see her again and looked forward to spending more time with her over dinner.

Rhys turned off the shower and grabbed a towel to dry off, rubbing a corner of it over the steamy mirror. When he pulled back and caught sight of his reflection in the circle he'd made, he stopped cold. He was smiling. For no other reason than he had a date with Neveah.

Staring into his own eyes, the smile broadened until the corners of his eyes crinkled. He looked…happy.

Goddamn. Maybe he was back from the dead after all.

****

Two hours after sunset, Ahmed pulled into the parking lot for the Stanley Park train and killed the engine. The sudden silence filled him with dread. He stared out the windshield at the people busily stringing miles of brightly colored lights and putting up displays of holiday decorations for the Bright Nights celebration due to open in the next few days. The firefighters put it on each year to raise money for burn camp. He'd taken his wife on opening night the past three years, and donated money to the fund.

Such a model citizen you are, a caustic voice in his head purred.

He wiped his damp palms over his wool trousers before pulling on lined gloves and exiting his vehicle. A flock of Canada geese honked overhead, winging their way south in a V formation. The stiff breeze, scented with cedar, rose up to pluck at his heavy wool pea coat and he hunched deeper under the collar to shut it out.

It wasn't the temperature or even the wind that made it so damn cold, it was the constant dampness. The chill of the moisture laden air seemed to seep into his bones, making it feel much colder than it really was.

To help disguise his face as he passed by the entrance, he pulled the collar up higher on his way to the trails across the road that wound through the heart of the park. The disposable cell phone lay in his left pocket, within easy reach should it buzz, but he hoped it wouldn't. He had enough to worry about right now without receiving another call from Tehrazzi. For starters, this clandestine meeting he'd set up.

The soft treads of his shoes on the loamy path and the wind in the trees were all that disturbed the silence as he slipped into the forest. Cedars and Douglas firs towered overhead, their dense evergreen branches moving in the wind like arms, beckoning him deeper into their shadowy embrace. A shroud of fog hovered above the damp forest floor, obscuring whatever lay ahead of him. Shoving his hands deeper into his pockets, he pressed on despite the growing sense of dread.

Never in his wildest dreams would he have imagined he would be involved in something like this. Meeting a self-proclaimed assassin in the middle of the woods in November. Like something out of a movie.

A branch snapped under his foot, making his heart jump. He paused a moment and listened for any noise that might alert him to the fact that he'd been followed, but heard nothing. Moving deeper into the dense network of trees, the uneasiness intensified.

What if this whole thing was a set up?

The assassin had agreed to the meeting over the phone, but who was to say they weren't an undercover officer looking to make a bust on their little group? And Ahmed couldn't rule out the possibility that his contact wouldn't shoot him dead out here and leave him for the scavenging animals living in the park.

The man had come highly recommended from someone in Ahmed's circle at the mosque, but Ahmed wouldn't be disappointed if he didn't show. The guilt was already eating at him. He'd seen Doctor Adams today in the flesh, and had looked into her pretty blue eyes. She'd survived horrors he didn't even want to imagine, and yet here he was, meeting with someone he had hired to kill her.

"That's close enough."

He gasped and froze, glancing about for the owner of the voice. Only swirling fog met his eyes.

"Put your hands where I can see them."

"I—I'm unarmed," he stuttered, half expecting a bullet to hit him.

"Show me."

Slowly, his stomach drawing tight, Ahmed raised his hands and held them above his head. This was it. His contact would either shoot him, or get on with the transaction.

"You bring the money?"

"Yes." He swallowed past the knot in his throat. "It's in my pocket."

"Get it."

Ahmed reached in and pulled out the thick envelope of American hundred dollar bills, withdrawn from his account a half hour ago. Then he paused awkwardly.

"Don't move."

He couldn't have even if he'd wanted to.

A shadow moved out of the tree line to his right. He squinted to make out the silhouette in the darkness. The man materialized out of the forest, dressed from head to toe in black with a knit cap covering his head. They were about the same height, but the other man was thinner and had a slighter build. He came within arm's reach and stopped. Ahmed couldn't tell what color the man's eyes were or what shade his skin was, but the lethal air he held was enough to make him glad there wasn't enough ambient light to see his face.

The man held out his gloved hand. Ahmed gingerly

placed the envelope in it. The quiet between them was unnerving.

"Still just the one woman?" the assassin asked.

He fought back a cringe. "Yes."

"I hear you've got more interesting targets lined up for Saturday afternoon."

His muscles tensed. "Where did you—"

"I'd be happy to take care of them for you for an additional charge."

Having it spoken aloud and so callously made Ahmed's conscience prickle like he had stinging nettles buried in his soul. "I've already arranged something." God, was that him saying those heinous words?

"Think your people will be able to take care of something like that without help?"

He nodded, afraid to go into details. The crew he'd assembled through his contacts weren't professionals, but they were unknown to the police and thus had a better chance of infiltrating the wedding crowd. He'd been assured they could get the job done and it was too late to change things now. The planning was in its last stages and he couldn't undo what had already been done at this point. Not without raising suspicion.

"Well. You know how to reach me if you change your mind."

A moment's doubt assailed him. This man was far better suited to carrying out the mission than the others. What if they didn't come through? What would Tehrazzi do then? He cleared his dry throat. "You'll contact me for the remainder after it's done?" he asked, referring to the balance of the payment owing.

"Yeah, don't worry," he said with a mocking laugh. "I'll be in touch." He stepped back.

After a few seconds Ahmed opened his mouth to call him back, but the man had already melted into the deep shadows of the forest. *Too late. No going back now.*

The return trip to the car seemed to take twice as long. The shadows were darker, the forest more ominous than before. He was cold to his marrow, and not from the damp wind tugging at his clothes.

The knowledge of what was coming triggered a memory of when he'd almost drowned as a young boy. He'd swum out too far and the current had gripped him, pulling him helplessly along as the water closed in over his head.

Then as now, he'd gone too far to turn back. All he could do was let the current carry him away and hope someone would be there to fish him out of the water before he drowned.

Forcing a cheery whistle out of his mouth to stop the thoughts in his head, he retraced his steps to the parking lot and past the point of no return.

Chapter Five

When the knock came, Neveah slipped her heels on. After checking the peephole, she opened the door for Rhys. Her heart gave a great thud as she took him in, all six-foot-six of him in a sapphire-colored dress shirt that intensified the blue of his eyes, and black dress pants that hugged his well-developed thighs. A black leather jacket clung to his broad shoulders.

Mouthwatering.

"Hi," she managed, doing up the top button of her wool coat. "Ready to go?"

"Yeah." He seemed surprised to see her standing there ready.

"Why are you looking at me like that?"

"I don't think I've ever gone to dinner with a woman who was on time. Or one tall enough to look me in the eye."

She flashed him a saucy smile. "Ah, but I'm not like any other woman you've been out with before."

One side of his mouth lifted in the semblance of a grin. "No, you're not." He offered her his arm as she stepped into the hallway. "Shall we?"

Touched by the gallant gesture, she slid her hand into the crook of his elbow and it nestled tight against the swell of his biceps. The jacket's leather sleeve was smooth and supple beneath her palm. Oh my, the man had sexual charisma. In spades. Coming from any other man, his actions would seem like a calculated move to be smooth. Not with Rhys. He was a gentleman to his core, and that made his treatment of her even more special.

"Hope you're hungry," he said as he escorted her into the elevator. "I asked around and this place is supposed to have the best Italian food in the city."

"Can't wait." She stole another glance at him as the elevator descended. "You clean up really nicely, by the way."

His lips quirked. "Thanks. I don't know what you've got on underneath that coat, but I'm sure it's beautiful."

She thought so. She'd specifically chosen to wear her take on the little black dress. Its super soft jersey knit felt like velvet against her skin, and it hugged every curve she had tightly enough that she couldn't wear panties. Besides her thigh-high fishnet stay-ups, she was bare-assed naked underneath the thing. She wondered what Rhys would think of *that*. His expression remained neutral, though. She could never tell what he was thinking, and suspected he liked it that way.

He led her through the lobby toward the glass doors, her spike-heeled black shoes clicking against the marble floor. He'd left the Escalade parked out front at the curb, and he hit the remote starter before he escorted her through the hotel door. A gust of cold wind stole her breath. She wrapped her scarf tighter around her neck to keep out the draft while he opened the truck door and handed her up. Her cheeks flushed with a delighted blush and from the chilly air. "Thanks."

"My pleasure," he responded, shutting the door and rounding the hood to climb in behind the wheel. As he slid into the seat, she caught the delicious scents of leather and spice.

"Where's Ben tonight?" she asked, doing up her seatbelt and settling back into the cushy leather seat.

"At a hockey game with some of the guys." He pulled away from the hotel and headed south on Burrard.

For no particular reason she was suddenly nervous enough to fill the silence with chatter. "Too bad Sam couldn't come here, but after all she went through, I can see why she'd just want some downtime."

"She's been looking forward to planning the wedding details with our mom."

Nev nodded. "Yes, and I'm glad she's got something happy to do for once." She looked over at him, pretending she was unaffected by being this close to him. "She's asked me to be her maid of honor. I assume you'll be the best man?"

"Wouldn't miss it."

"Well then I guess we'll be spending more time together next year."

He glanced at her. "That's a good thing, right?"

"A very good thing." She squirmed inside. Sometimes her direct speech put her at a distinct disadvantage. Rhys wasn't the type to wear his heart on his sleeve, and she had no idea what was going on in his head or if he even found her attractive. But he must at least like her enough, or he wouldn't have invited her to dinner, right?

"How's the conference going?"

The nerves eased with the change of subject. "Very well, thanks. People have been extremely helpful and supportive." And she was glad to be able to spend time with her friend Mike. He felt comfortable around her, and they stayed together during all the functions in a kind of co-dependency that worked just fine for both of them. Misery loves company after all, Mike had said.

Nev sighed as the warmth from the seat heaters penetrated her coat. "To be honest, though, I was really glad you invited me out tonight because I needed a break. I was starting to feel like a bit of a sideshow act to everyone." *Step right up! See the woman who survived a kidnapping and brutal imprisonment by terrorists in northeastern Afghanistan.*

"Honestly, I was surprised to hear you'd taken something like this on so soon," Rhys said.

She squeezed her hands together in her lap. "Well, I thought the best way to get over all that was to dive headfirst back into life." Her nails dug into her damp palms. "And I wanted to do something to honor my colleagues that…died."

Rhys shocked the hell out of her by reaching across the console and squeezing one of her hands. "You don't have to talk about it."

But she did. She desperately needed to talk about it to someone who understood what she'd gone through. Nobody knew the horrors she'd seen better than Rhys. Squeezing his hand as a thank-you, she forced a smile. "Okay. Kind of a downer for a date anyway, huh? I gotta tell you though, it makes it a hell of a lot easier that you know everything already."

"I'm glad." He didn't let go of her hand. His fingers wrapped securely around hers, and his thumb rubbed in wordless comfort. The swath of skin he caressed became violently sensitive, and within moments his touch radiated all the way up her arm.

The silence that settled over them should have made her edgy, but for some reason with Rhys she found it peaceful. Safe enough that she didn't feel compelled to fill the void with meaningless conversation this time. She could simply be herself because he understood her and what she'd been through, and because he was naturally quiet. Confident. Watchful. She subconsciously knew that no matter what happened, Rhys could and would handle it.

It was sexy as hell.

By the time they reached La Terrazza on Cambie at Pacific Avenue, Nev felt more relaxed than she'd been since her trip to Paris. With Rhys she could let down her guard. She didn't have to maintain the exhausting sense of vigilance tonight. She could turn back the clock and be a thirty-one-year-old woman out on a date, instead of a wary, traumatized surgeon who'd suffered unspeakable horrors two months ago.

Rhys offered his arm once more and took her inside. Removing her coat, she caught the male appreciation in his stare as he ran his gaze over her and was glad she'd chosen the dress. She paused at their table, cozily nestled into the corner and set for two, waiting to see which chair he'd choose. She assumed he'd want the one against the wall so he had a better line of vision.

He raised his brows. "All right?"

"Yes, I just thought you might want that chair," she said, gesturing to the one tucked into the corner, then lowered her gaze. Jeez, maybe she was being stupid. The last thing she wanted was to make him feel analyzed or embarrassed.

But his expression turned curious. "Why's that?"

She cleared her throat and said softly, "Because you'd feel more…secure with the wall behind you and the exit in front of you."

He grinned. "You do know me pretty well."

She smiled back, relieved, and allowed the maître d' to seat her. A waiter came over and took their drink orders. Nev looked across the table at Rhys. "Feel like wine? We could share a bottle."

The cleft in his chin smoothed out a little as he smiled. "I don't drink."

She blinked at him. "Ever?"

He shook his head. "But since I'm driving, feel free to drink as much wine as you like."

His teasing made her laugh. "I think I'll just start with a glass of red," she said to the waiter and agreed to the one he recommended. She turned her attention back to Rhys, tilted her head. "Are you allergic to alcohol or something?"

"No. Just don't like the taste."

Huh. "Did you have a bad experience when you were young?" Alcohol poisoning from a party when he was a teenager perhaps? A wild weekend leave during his time in the military?

"You could say that."

She waited, all ears.

He looked uncomfortable for a moment, then answered. "My birth mom was an alcoholic and a heroin addict."

"Oh, I'm sorry." Damn, how had she missed that critical detail from Sam?

"So yeah, I was just turned off the whole drinking thing at a real young age."

The waiter returned with her wine, but now she felt bad for having ordered it. "Makes perfect sense. But are you sure it's got nothing to do with the fact that you're a control freak?"

His eyes sparkled with amusement. "Takes one to know one, sweetheart," he murmured, the casual endearment making her heart clench. Raising his water glass, he held her gaze. "To healing. Cheers, Neveah."

She touched her glass to his. "Cheers." Taking a sip, she thought about his comment. "You think I'm a control freak, huh?"

The slow smile he gave her did funny things to her

insides. "Yeah. Aren't you?"

She shrugged. "Yes, but how did you know?"

"I'm observant."

And good at sidestepping questions, she thought, considering him over the rim of her wine glass. They ordered salads and entrees, and once again he surprised her by ordering a vegetarian meal as she had.

"Let me guess," she said. "You don't eat meat either because you're an environmentalist, or because it's too high in cholesterol and your tremendous discipline extends to your diet."

"I eat meat once in a while," he answered. "I just try to eat clean most of the time." He cocked his head. "What's your reasoning?"

She glanced away. "I uh… I haven't had much appetite for meat since I got back." She fiddled with the napkin in her lap. "I think it's got something to do with the fact someone slaughtered the animal I'm eating, and then I start thinking about how they did it, and… Yeah. Too close to what happened in Afghanistan, I guess." She'd always remember the sound of that knife cutting through her colleagues' necks. Like a butcher hacking up a side of beef.

Feeling raw and stupid, she reached for a piece of bread, but Rhys stopped her by placing a hand on top of hers. Swallowing, she looked up.

In the candlelight, his deep blue eyes gleamed, and the understanding in them almost made her tear up. "Nev—"

She pulled her hand away, embarrassed by how emotional she was feeling. "Wow. Bet you're glad you asked me to dinner, huh?"

"Very glad," he said, "but I hate that I just dredged up those memories again."

"Don't be silly, I can handle it." She took a fortifying sip of wine. It wasn't his fault. Everything seemed to make her think of Afghanistan. "What else should we talk about?" There were a million things she wanted to know about him and his job, but she'd already made him uncomfortable enough. "Ben and Sam are always an interesting topic."

His deep chuckle hit her square in the chest. "That they are."

Over their meal they shared stories about their respective siblings. Sam might not be her sister biologically, but she was in every other way that mattered.

In the middle of one story about Sam and her OCD tendencies, Nev even managed to get a laugh out of Rhys. Not a snicker or a chuckle, but an honest-to-God laugh that rolled up from deep in his belly. The sound filled her with warmth, and she wondered how anyone could accuse him of being remote and cold. He was incredibly caring and funny when he let himself be. She felt fortunate he was comfortable enough with her to let his guard down. She knew he didn't warm up to people easily.

Fascinated, she covertly studied him as he ate his pasta, impressed by everything about him. She loved how much he seemed to savor each bite. Few people took the time to enjoy the flavors of what they ate. "Bet it's good to be able to taste your food again, huh?" From her secret daily updates, she knew he'd only regained that precious sense a few weeks back.

"You have no idea," he said, laying his fork down. Then he frowned. "How'd you know about that?"

"Oh, it's typical for someone who's suffered your type of head injury." *Jeez, Nev. When are you going to learn to filter things before you say them?*

His manners were impeccable, reminding her again how wrong she'd been to dismiss him as rough and uncouth the first time she'd met him. The reality of him was just…incredible. “I bet you did really well in school, didn’t you?” she asked.

“Pretty well. Why?”

She cocked her head. “Because you’re really intellectual in your own quiet way. Did you go to college?”

“I earned a Bachelor of Science through the Army.” He shrugged. “Never went any further than that.”

She set her elbows on the table and rested her chin on her linked hands. “What was your major?”

The flicker of a smile crossed his face. “Physics.”

“See? That totally suits you.” And physics, how freaking hot was that?

He caught her staring while he twirled more pasta around his fork and smiled. “Want some?” Lifting a mouthful, he offered it to her across the table.

Maybe he didn’t intend for it to be a sensual gesture, but it was. Spellbound by the magnetic pull of his dark blue eyes, she leaned forward and grasped his wrist as he brought the food to her lips. She opened and he eased the forkful inside her mouth. Sliding the pasta off with her lips, she sat back again. The delicious flavors of roasted tomatoes and peppers burst in her mouth. She chewed slowly, savoring the taste, very aware of the way he watched her. Somehow she managed to swallow the bite.

“Good?”

Damn, was it her, or was it suddenly hot as hell in here? “Delicious. Thanks.”

“Want more?”

Boy, did she. But what she was hungry for unfortunately wasn’t on the menu. Or was it? Watching him closely, she tried to figure him out, but decided he was much too polite to proposition her over dinner. What a shame. “One more.” Where the hell that seductive tone had come from, she couldn’t say, but possibly her three glasses of wine were to blame. Still, she eagerly awaited the next bite he held out for her and even held his gaze as she took it.

Might have been her imagination, but she thought his eyes had a hungry gleam to them. And in that instant, she glimpsed the predator concealed beneath the carefully controlled exterior. A thrill shot down her spine, part excitement, part unease.

The waiter broke the spell when he came back and refilled her glass. She should be glad about that, she told herself, licking her lips to clean off the last trace of delicious sauce. At least he'd interrupted before she'd blurted out something stupid in her usual blunt way.

That hungry glint in Rhys's eyes was an important reminder that he was more than he seemed. Not that she was afraid of him. She knew with complete certainty he'd never hurt her. No, it was because he'd spent most of his adult life doing things she couldn't even think about. Things she couldn't imagine him doing. She'd had a firsthand glimpse of the violence he lived with on a daily basis when he was working, and the memories still had the power to paralyze her.

Throughout the rest of the meal, she kept asking herself the same question: How could she want Rhys when he was capable of such violence?

****

By the time they got to her hotel, nerves squirmed in her belly. Rhys had been quiet on the trip back, but her mind was in turmoil. Her chest was heavy with all the things she wanted to say and didn't dare. Her body was dying for his touch. Regardless of the inner conflict she battled, those things hadn't changed. If anything, her attraction to him had amplified as the night progressed.

He walked her up to her room, and she was still

deciding whether or not to invite him in when they reached her door. If she asked and he said no, it would make any further association with him awkward. If he took her up on her offer, things would never be the same between them.

But when she went to put the key card in the lock mechanism, Rhys stopped her by closing his hand over hers. She glanced over her shoulder at him, his touch and nearness stealing the air from her lungs.

"I'll do it," he said, taking it from her.

Do what? Oh, her door. Right. Biting back a retort about not needing him to take care of her, Nev stepped back and allowed him past her. Not that she had much choice. The set expression on his face convinced her any resistance would be an exercise in futility.

He slid the card into the slot and unlocked the door. "Stay here."

His high-handed attitude got her hackles up. She would've argued, but he was already through the door, so she folded her arms across her chest and waited for him to come back, which he did in a few seconds.

"Coast is clear."

She raised her brows. "Really?" What had he expected to find in her room? Assassins hiding behind the curtains? She strode in and shut the door, finding him studying the paperback about Delta Force she'd laid on the night table.

He met her gaze, amusement sparkling in his eyes. "Doing some research?"

She flushed guiltily. No way for her to deny it now. "I was interested in what you did, and thought it might help me get to know you better."

In the ensuing silence, his steady gaze made her want to squirm. Finally, he spoke. "If there's something you want to know, why don't you just ask me?"

She put her hands on her hips. "You'd tell me?"

“If I can.”

His answer startled her. “So anything I want to know, I can just ask you and you’ll tell me.” If he could. Barring the interest of national security and all that.

“Yes.”

Okay, then. She cocked her head, considering him. “Why did you join up?”

“The Army?”

She nodded.

His shrug was almost negligent. “Ben and I had it tough as kids. When we graduated from high school, neither of us had a clue what we wanted to do.” He ran his gaze around the room rather than look at her. “The Army seemed like a good place to keep us in line and it was a way to get an education paid for.”

“So you served out your time there and then went into the Ranger Corps?”

“We both served with the Rangers. I left when I was twenty-five to try for Delta.”

She couldn’t understand his decision. Did he like killing so much? “Why stay in when you had a Bachelor’s degree under your belt?”

He lifted his wide shoulders. “I was good at it. Delta was the next tier to reach after the Rangers, so that was the natural choice. I fit in well there.”

He was *good* at it? A lead ball settled in her stomach. Her brain refused to compute what he was telling her. Having read about the grueling selection process and the kinds of operations he would have performed, she couldn’t reconcile those things with the man she saw in front of her.

For God’s sake, the man had held her hand to comfort her after he’d pulled her out of her prison.

She struggled to put her feelings into words. “I guess I just have trouble believing you could live that way.” And do those awful things when he had to. She didn't think for a moment he would use lethal force unless it was absolutely necessary. No way would he relax his discipline, not even under extreme stress in the field. She would bet her life on that. Still, knowing he had killed and was good at it unnerved her.

He faced her. "Why's that?"

She wasn't the type to mince words. Her tendency for bluntness surprised people, but it was who she was. So she simply said what was on her mind. "You just don't seem like a killer."

A hard smile touched his lips. "I am when I need to be."

A cold shiver passed through her. Human life was the most precious commodity on earth. How could he take lives in the name of duty when she knew the other side of him, the kind, gentle protector? The disparity between the two halves of him baffled her, but his remorseless admission to having killed people frightened her.

With the two of them alone in the closed room, she became aware again of how big he was. Rhys was strong enough to overpower her with little or no effort, and he had the ability to kill her with his bare hands. She eyed them, tucked beneath the corded forearms folded across his muscular chest. They were big, the fingers long and the palms broad. He could hurt her so easily…and yet she knew in her gut he would never harm her.

Worse, his strength and total command of himself made her go all soft and shivery inside. He would be completely dominant in bed. The kind of dominant that left no room for awkwardness or embarrassment, but would simply burn past everything else and leave her limp with pleasure. The wicked thought sent a ripple of need through her. Nev had a sudden image of her pinned beneath him on the hotel bed, those powerful hands in her hair and his big, naked body poised over hers. A rush of heat pooled between her thighs.

"Having second thoughts about closing that door behind you?" he asked quietly.

She met his eyes, found him watching her carefully. "No. I'm not afraid of you."

"But you are afraid of what I'm capable of."

She swallowed, but didn't look away. His honesty deserved the same courtesy. "Yes." Mostly because he held the power to make her lose herself. "I'm not sure you'll understand, but after what happened to me, any kind of violence makes me panic."

He nodded. "That's understandable."

How could she feel so drawn to him? They were complete opposites. She was trained to save lives; he was trained to take them.

Efficiently. Violently.

Rhys tucked his hands under his armpits, the move emphasizing the muscles beneath the sleeves of his dress shirt. "If you want to talk about this some more, can we sit down? I feel like I'm being interrogated."

"Sure." A flush spread over her face and neck. She gestured to the leather couch set against the far wall. Going over to it, she sat on one end and he sank onto the other. "I didn't mean to make you uncomfortable."

He lounged back and rested one arm along the back of the couch, his biceps and triceps flexing noticeably beneath the fabric of his sleeve. "You didn't." He considered her for a moment. "I know the general public has this image of special ops soldiers being Rambos who shoot anyone who crosses their path on a mission, but it's not like that. You don't make it into the Unit unless you're highly disciplined. Out there our teammates and mission are the priorities. We do what we need to protect ourselves and complete the mission."

"Except when you do assassinations."

He went so still that she was suddenly afraid she'd

overstepped her bounds. *Too late to take it back now.* Holding her breath, she stared at him, not daring to move a muscle. His hand on the backrest of the sofa was squeezed into a tight fist. Kind of like her stomach. Oh God, why had she said that? It wasn't any of her business—

"Yeah," he said quietly. "Except then."

So he'd done that too. Swallowing hard, she wasn't quite sure where to look anymore. She didn't want to believe he could actually do something so cold-blooded.

"Look at me."

Startled, Nev swung her gaze up to his. She couldn't tell by his calm expression, but the bunched muscles in his arms and shoulders told her he was far from relaxed after her thoughtless comment. How mad was he?

"Sorry," she finally blurted. "I shouldn't have—"

"It's fine. Forget it."

Was he joking? How could she ever forget *that*? His muscles seemed to relax by degrees, and he maintained eye contact with her. "Anything else you wanna know?"

"No." She didn't want to find out anything else that would make the chance of getting together with him an impossibility, even if it only happened in her fantasies.

One side of his mouth turned up in a sexy smile. "Liar." He slid his hand over and gave hers a squeeze, then released it. "I can hear your brain whirring from here. Go ahead, fire away. You just…hit a nerve with that last one, that's all."

What nerve? she wanted to ask, but kept her mouth shut. She'd already done enough damage for one night. It surprised her he was still sitting there and willing to talk with her.

"Come on, say what's on your mind."

Oh God, he was gorgeous. All latent strength and

unshakable confidence sprawled out not three feet away from her, with a mind every bit as sharp as her own. Temptation personified.

She tugged at the hem of her dress. Rhys wasn't known for being talkative. Having a conversation this long with him was a surprise, and something she knew did not come naturally to him. Now, how to broach the topic she really wanted to discuss?

After pondering several opening lines, she went with her default setting and said it straight out. "I've been wondering if you remember anything from…that night. When you were hit."

His gaze was steady on hers. "The last thing I remember was going into the back room of the hut to get you."

Her stomach knotted. Damn. That *would* have to be the last memory he had of her. She'd been crouched on the dirt floor like an animal in front of Mike, ready to attack whoever came through the door. It made her skin crawl with shame to think of Rhys seeing her like that, filthy and primitive, out of control. Reduced to mindless terror and survival instinct. "Nothing after that?"

"No. The next memory I have is seeing Ben next to my bed at Walter Reed."

Nev lowered her gaze to hide the guilt she was afraid he'd see in her eyes at the mention of the hospital.

"What about you?"

Her head came up. "What do you mean?"

"You must have memories of that day."

Of course she did. "Some."

He wouldn't let it go. "Did you get help once you got home?"

She glanced away again, embarrassed to admit she'd sought professional help even though she knew she'd needed it. At the time, she'd told herself it was the most practical thing to do. Her job as a surgeon demanded she regain control of her emotions and master her fears. In the end, she'd jumped back into work as a distraction and to prove to herself she could do it.

She nodded. "I'm handling everything fine." For the most part. The rest, she'd overcome in time. She wouldn't accept anything less. "The first couple of surgeries were tough. I almost couldn't make the first incision." But she'd forced herself to, no matter how hard her heart pounded or how nauseous she became at the thought of slicing a blade into someone's flesh. Because she was a surgeon, dammit, and she'd fought long and hard to attain that status. No one, not even murderous terrorists, would take that away from her.

She cleared her throat. "I have a thing about knives now," she admitted. Didn't matter what kind. They all made her guts twist with fear because of the horrific memories associated with them.

"I worried about that."

Nev stared at him. Rhys, the remote, unflappable loner had *worried*? About *her*? "I'm fine." Her voice sounded very small over the heavy thudding of her heart. Of their own volition, her eyes strayed up to the right side of his head and the pink scars hidden beneath his closely-shorn hair. Just looking at them made her throat close up.

As if they'd been held back by a dam that had just failed, the words burst out. "I can't believe you lived," she whispered, near tears at the thought of how close he'd come to death.

Rhys reached over and took her hand. "Because of you."

She shook her head and looked deep into his eyes. "No. I don't know how you survived, but… It wasn't because of me."

"Yes it was."

She blew out a breath and swallowed the lump in

her throat. God, she wanted to touch him so badly, just run her fingers over the side of his head to assure herself that he was healed. A barrage of memories hit her, filling her mind. “You held my hand during the chopper ride to the rendezvous point.” She’d been on a stretcher on the helo’s floor and he’d stayed crouched next to her the whole time.

He smiled. “I’m glad.”

“Then Sam called on the radio and you ran down to get the truck. We saw the mine explode.” She pulled in a deep breath. “You were still conscious when I got to you.”

“Was I?”

“You were looking right at me.” He’d stared right into her eyes with a blank expression that chilled her to think about. Without warning, her body started trembling, though she tried to mask it. “You said, ‘I’m hit.’ ”

Hold on, Nev. Take a breath and calm down.

But the words refused to stay inside her. “The right side of your skull was wide open. There was no way you should have been functional, but you were talking to me.” She could still smell the stench of burning flesh whenever she thought about it. And that wasn’t even the worst part. “We got you intubated on the chopper to Kabul and you held on until we got to the hospital, but then you… You coded on the table in the OR. Did you know that?”

She’d almost lost it when he’d flat-lined. Bringing the defibrillator paddles down on his bare, blood-stained chest and then watching his whole body arc up off the table with the force of the electric current had put her in tears. “We had to shock you twice to get your heart re-started.” And all the while the blood had streamed out of his head wound, as fast as they could infuse him.

“Yeah. Ben told me.” He stroked his thumb over

her knuckles in silent comfort. "I'm sorry you had to see that."

Since he'd been the one going *through* that, his attempt to soothe her broke her heart. She was a trauma surgeon. She'd dealt with life and death situations dozens of times, but never with someone who mattered to her and her cousin, the only family she had. Never with someone who'd rescued her, and whose twin brother was in the next room giving units of his own blood for an emergency transfusion.

Her chest tightened painfully. Rhys had been unconscious the whole time so he couldn't have known how bad his injuries really were, but she would never forget those first agonizing, critical hours. "I don't know how you held on, I really don't. It was so damn close…" She pinched the bridge of her nose, pulled in a breath but the air caught in her lungs and wouldn't come out again. Her ribs jerked with the sob she fought to hold back. In a panic to get control of her emotions, she pulled her hand away and started to push up from the couch.

Rhys stopped her by snatching her wrist. "Hey."

She closed her eyes and shook her head. "Let go." She just needed some space, a few minutes to compose herself, alone.

He wouldn't release her.

"I have to…" She sucked in a sharp breath. "To get myself together."

"No need." Instead, he tugged her back down and pulled her straight into his arms.

Worse. Much worse. She resisted, her throat aching with unshed tears. "Rhys, no… I can't…"

"Shhh." He tucked her head under his chin and settled her against his wide chest so she could feel his heart beating steadily under hers, and stroked his hands over her back.

She shuddered in his arms and laid her palms

against the thick pads of his pecs, assaulted by the sensations of being pressed close against him. Warmth and hard muscles. The faint spice of his cologne mixed with the soapy scent of his skin, his body heat seeping into her. His touch on her back was gentle enough to make tears well in her eyes. She let out a hiccup.

"Shhh, baby," he crooned, his low voice caressing her senses. "I'm fine. Everything's okay now."

Baby. If any other man had called her that she'd have blasted them. But somehow from Rhys she didn't mind. He was so big he made her feel delicate and feminine. She nodded at his words, her cheek brushing over his left pec, right over the steady throb of his heart. She struggled for control. He must think she was such a loser, crying all over him at the mention of that day. It brought a watery laugh out of her.

Hands stilling, he angled his head toward hers. "What?"

"Nothing." She wiped her eyes. "I was just thinking of all the money I've spent on therapy, and that one hug from you was better than all of it combined."

Helping her sit back, he gave her an assessing look. "You always so direct?"

She blushed. "Blunt, you mean. And yes, I am. It's one of my biggest flaws."

"Assets," he corrected. "I've never met anyone like you."

"Trust me, it's not always a good trait. It's just that I'm a terrible liar."

He lounged back against the cushions, still holding her gaze. He had amazing eye contact skills, better than any man she'd ever met. But his next words sent a chill of foreboding through her.

"That's good, because there's something I've wanted to ask you, and I'm hoping you'll tell me the truth."

She stilled. This didn't sound good. "Okay. What is it?"

"You came to see me in the hospital, didn't you?"

Chapter Six

The side table lamp gave off enough light for Rhys to see his question steal the blood from her face. He was sorry to make her uncomfortable, but he needed to know why she'd hidden it, and counted on her innate integrity to tell him the truth.

Nev folded her arms across her middle in a classic defensive posture. "What do you mean?"

He almost laughed. She was a terrible liar. "At Walter Reed. You snuck into my room."

Her sharp inhalation echoed in the stillness. "Who told you?"

"No one. I read the visitors log in my file the day I was released."

"God." She dropped her gaze to the floor and started pacing aimlessly. He waited for her to continue, and in a moment she stopped and faced him again. If he wasn't mistaken, she jutted her chin out, almost in defiance. "I only came to check on your progress—"

"You came every day I was in the coma."

She nodded stiffly. "Yes."

"After hours, so no one else would see you." She didn't deny it. "And then the day I woke up, you stopped coming. Why?"

"Because then I knew you'd be okay."

Her answer didn't ease the frustration eating at him. "I don't buy it. Why?"

Her deep sigh filled the air. "Because I realized how pathetic and clingy it looked, that's why."

He frowned. Why would she—

"I didn't want to make the situation any harder on Ben or your parents, so I made sure I came in when they went down to the cafeteria for dinner every night. I'd check in with the staff about your progress, stay in your room for fifteen minutes, then leave before Ben came back for the night."

He ruthlessly pulled all that apart in his mind. "So you stopped coming in once I was awake because you didn't want me to know you'd been there?"

The pink flush still rode high across her cheekbones. "Visiting you under those circumstances was highly unprofessional of me. I was embarrassed about it."

Yet she'd done it anyway. More than her actions, her reasoning stunned him. She'd gone through her grueling debriefing at Langley, and then stuck around just so she could sneak fifteen minutes a night to sit with him. Didn't that say she had strong feelings for him? He pushed, needing answers. "What did you do while you were with me?"

Her gaze strayed to an ocean scene print hanging on the wall beside her. She swallowed. "I changed your bandages, held your hand and talked to you."

His heart squeezed. He could picture her there, perched next to his hospital bed, cradling his hand in her magical ones and speaking words of encouragement in her sultry voice. "What did you say?"

"I thanked you for rescuing me, and told you to hang on. That you had people who loved you and needed you to wake up." She shrugged like it didn't matter. "Things like that. I know it was dishonest of me to sneak in, but I wanted to see you and… Yeah, I'm sorry. I was being selfish, looking for closure that way."

Closure?

"You have every right to be angry."

"Do I look angry?" he asked, forcing himself to stay where he was and not march over to take her in his arms again.

"You must think I'm a stalker now."

"I don't think that at all."

She crossed her arms over her chest. "Don't you?"

"No." Rhys leaned forward and laid his forearms on his knees, edging closer without crowding her too much. He needed her to understand. "Did it ever occur to you that you might be the reason I came out of the coma? That I might have heard you?"

Swallowing, she turned her head and met his eyes. "That's not… You came out because they decreased your sedative levels, and because your brain had healed enough to allow you to resurface."

Bullshit. "You're a doctor, so you ought to know better than that."

"If you came back because of anybody, it's Ben." Her gaze dropped once more. "Well. Now you know what I did, and I apologize for any invasion of privacy."

"Dammit," he muttered, coming off the couch. Her eyes widened and she backed up a step, but he kept going. "You're not listening to me—I don't want an apology." Reaching out, he took hold of her upper arms and pulled her until her breasts touched his chest.

Her eyes were huge as she gazed up at him. "What—what do you want?"

More than he'd ever imagined wanting. He had no clue what to do with his feelings for her, but all he knew was they were getting stronger and weren't going away.

This was a whole new world of unknowns. "You had every reason in the world to go back to New York and put everything behind you, but you stayed. Not even to be with Sam, but for *me*." His eyes bored into hers, refusing to let her shrink away from the truth. "Tell me why you did it."

"I…" She licked her lips, staring up into his eyes.

"Because you operated on me? You felt responsible for me? What?"

"A-all those things," she whispered, then hesitated and bit her lip.

"So that's it?" He was ready to explode.

"You know it's not."

Yeah, but he wanted her to say it out loud so he knew he had it right. "Tell me."

She broke eye contact and stared at the base of his throat. "Because of my personal…attachment to you."

The whispered admission knocked the breath out of his lungs. "Nev. Look at me."

She hesitated, but then raised her head. Her eyes were wide and her heart thudded hard against his chest. Was she actually afraid he'd reject her or something? That he'd laugh at her?

He shouldn't touch her at all, but they were way past that now, and he couldn't keep pretending he didn't need this as much as she seemed to. It didn't matter that everything between them had been forged out of dramatic and emotionally charged circumstances that held no basis for a relationship. It didn't even matter that he wasn't good enough for her, or that he'd never been in a serious relationship before. All he knew was she was standing in front of him with her heart in her big blue eyes and he'd die if he didn't kiss her.

Moving slow so he wouldn't startle her, he took her delicate face in his hands. Nev was subconsciously wary of him, so he had to be careful not to crowd her. Keeping that firmly in mind, he leaned in to kiss her. Her sharply indrawn breath was her only protest as he brought his mouth down. He settled his lips against hers. A quiet brushing, to let her know that no matter how much he wanted her, he had complete control over his strength and would be gentle with her. In response, she slid her arms around his neck and returned the kiss, her lips soft and warm, tasting of spearmint as he slid his tongue inside to stroke hers.

She let out a breathless moan and wiggled closer, setting him on fire with the way her firm body pressed full length against him. The soft mounds of her breasts pushed against his chest. One of her knees slid between his, her thigh not quite touching his groin, but close enough to have him rock hard in his dress pants. And aching to pull up her dress, unzip his fly and push into her.

His arms went around her back, one hand coasting up her spine to cradle the back of her head in his palm to hold her as close as he could. The heavy weight of her thick, shiny hair spilled over his arms and shoulders, enveloping him in a luscious, scented cloud. His starved senses feasted on the sensory input. God, he'd been empty and cold for so long, and Neveah was the heat he needed to melt the core of ice inside him. The strength of his need shocked him.

Her fingers crept up to cradle his head as she angled her mouth for deeper contact, caressing the sensitive inside of his mouth. Her fresh, lemony scent enveloped him, swirling through his consciousness in another layer of sensation. She smelled good enough to take a bite of.

Tamping down his rising hunger, he took a little more, still in control of his needs. But the beast was inside him, prowling restlessly. Her mouth was so soft and inviting, the little moans coming from her throat turning his muscles to steel. The dark part of his nature wanted to push her onto her back on the floor and completely dominate her with his power.

He wanted to watch her eyes flare with arousal and a trace of unease as she realized how helpless she was, then take her apart with a well executed seduction campaign that left her writhing and begging him to take her. And then, when she was twisting beneath him and blind with pleasure, he'd thrust inside her hard and deep until she came over and over again. Christ, he could see it happening in his mind as he kissed her, fighting to stay mellow and be a gentleman.

Neveah arched her back and flattened her breasts against his chest, moaning as she rubbed against him with a feline motion of enjoyment.

God. Rhys tightened his hold on her hair and clamped down on his baser needs to pin her flat beneath his weight. Just kissing her was the most erotic experience of his life, but the driving need to dominate kept getting in the way. It scared him. He didn't want to do anything to frighten her or destroy the fragile trust she had in him, but if they kept this up he wasn't sure he could hold on. She awakened needs in him that no one else ever had. With Nev, he wanted more than he'd ever wanted before. He wanted to possess her. Literally, and with a power that shocked him. He wanted her submission and her surrender, her passion. God dammit, he wanted her *soul.*

Shaken, Rhys disengaged gently and moved back, gritting his teeth at the way she whimpered and reached for him. Wanting more. He closed his eyes. That's what he wanted: for her to need him with every cell in her being, and for her to feel empty without his touch.

What kind of a selfish bastard was he, to want that from her?

He sucked in a breath when she ignored the gentle pressure of his hands in her hair, holding her away, and leaned in to set her lips against his throat. Her tongue flicked out to tease his skin, making his fists tighten in her hair. She had no clue what she was doing to him. No idea what he wanted to do to her or how close to the edge of his control he was. Or what would happen if that darker side won out.

For a brief moment he allowed himself to feel the hot glide of her tongue, but then he set her firmly away from him. It was best for both of them.

Her eyes were so dark with longing the pupils all but swallowed the blue of her irises. "I don't want you to stop," she whispered, her lips rosy and swollen from his kisses. Her long hair was disheveled, framing her flushed cheeks.

He wanted to strip the form-fitting dress off her and see if the rest of her was just as rosy with that same flush of desire. Then he'd pin her arms over her head and make her sob with ecstasy while he feasted on her tight nipples and finally between her long, toned thighs. A low growl vibrated up from his chest.

"I want you so much," she said, stroking her fingertips over his face.

"I can't do this," he said gruffly.

She stilled, looking into his eyes. "Why not?"

"Just can't." Wouldn't. Even if his dick felt like it was about to explode from the unrelieved pressure.

Neveah cocked her head and studied him for a moment. "You're afraid of hurting me, aren't you?"

Christ, how did she do that? Crawl around in his head and find the answers to things he didn't even understand?

A gentle smile crossed her face, so full of tenderness and adoration he almost reached for her. "You would never hurt me."

"No." Not on purpose, anyway. He'd rather die. Accidentally? That was another matter entirely, and the possibility scared the shit out of him. He didn't want to ruin this. She meant too much to him to allow that to happen.

"You know what?"

He had a feeling he didn't want to.

"You don't need to stay in control all the time. That's the great thing about sex. You get to let go."

She had no idea what she was saying. She didn't realize the strength of the darkness inside him. He wasn't about to let her sacrifice herself to his inner demons to help him heal.

Keeping his touch gentle, he took her head in his hands and pressed a long, desperate kiss to her forehead. Then he let go and stepped back, grabbing his jacket and shoulder holster from the closet. He paused at the doorway, almost afraid to look at her.

She was still standing where he'd left her, her arms wrapped around her waist.

His heart lurched. *Walk over there*, the voice in his head commanded. *Walk over there and take her. You know she wants you to.*

Rhys ignored it. His hand tightened on the knob, fighting with himself. "Nev, I—"

"It's all right. I think I understand. I'll be fine, just disappointed and horny as hell."

His cock pulsed in his dress pants. Jesus, why did she have to be so frigging honest all the time?

She sighed, but put on a smile and waved a hand at him in dismissal. "It's okay, just go. I'll see you tomorrow."

He didn't feel right about leaving her alone, even though she might be safer if he left. "Call me if you need anything."

She arched a brow as he turned away, kicking himself for saying something so utterly stupid. Her voice made him pause halfway out the door.

"Fair warning, Rhys. I never give up on something I want."

He shouldn't have been surprised by the direct challenge in her voice. The dominant, aroused male in him almost turned around to stake his claim and show her just who was in charge of what lay between them. Thankfully the civilized part of him won out, but he still looked at her over his shoulder.

Her eyes gleamed with resolve and unfulfilled hunger. "I'm going to do everything in my power to change your mind."

Chapter Seven

Friday

Next afternoon once the lectures were over, Rhys picked her up to take her into White Rock where she would meet Bryn and the bride-to-be while he went to some sort of meeting. She knew better than to ask about it, and stayed quiet on the forty minute drive, grateful for the break from the conference.

A new tension existed between them now, and this one was as big as it was awkward. Nev still couldn't believe she'd let him walk out on her last night. For hours afterward, even though she'd taken a hot bubble bath and crawled into bed to get some sleep, she'd ached with unfulfilled need all night. The orgasm she'd been reduced to giving herself was a bland and ultimately unsatisfying substitute for what he'd have delivered, but it was all she'd had to keep from going crazy.

Casting a glance at him, she wondered what he'd do if she flat out told him about it. After toying with the idea for several minutes, she decided to let it go. She'd already thrown herself at him once and didn't care to be rejected like that again, even if he had done it out of a misguided effort to protect her.

"You sure you're okay with this?" Rhys asked as he parked in front of the gorgeous pale yellow Victorian-style house.

"Sure, I'll be fine. I've always wanted to meet Bryn." Sam told incredible stories of bravery about Bryn, like she was some sort of mythical Amazon woman.

Tugging at the hem of her snug pencil skirt, Nev peered out at the manicured lawn and beautifully kept yard full of neatly trimmed shrubs and hedges. More like a park than a yard. The place must be something in the spring and summer when all the flowers came out.

Rhys pulled the keys out of the ignition. "Meeting shouldn't take too long. I'll be back to get you as soon as I can."

She waved his concern away. "Take your time. I think I'm going to have fun, and this way I'll get to know the bride a bit so I'll enjoy the wedding even more." Plus it would give her a few hours of distraction from wanting Rhys so badly she could scream. She wasn't the screaming type, but suspected he might be able to make her if they ever got naked together.

Before she could climb out, he rounded the hood and helped her down with a steadying grip on her arm. As always, his touch never failed to wreak havoc on her neurological system, but she hoped it jolted him as much as it did her. Only fair that he suffered too, since he had called a halt last night.

His gaze lingered over her hips and her calves left bare below the hem of her skirt, the muscles emphasized by the four-inch pumps she wore. Good. At least she knew he wasn't unaffected by her presence.

He led her up the front steps onto the wide porch and rang the doorbell. Rushing footsteps sounded a moment later, and then the door swung open.

Nearly as tall as her, a woman with long dark brown hair stood in the opening and broke into a huge smile. "Rhys!" She leapt across the threshold and launched herself into his arms. Nev watched in awe as he caught her and returned the warm embrace with a chuckle, his whole demeanor relaxed and happy.

"Hey, little girl."

"God, you look fantastic!" Letting go, the woman turned that mega-watt smile on her. "You must be Neveah. I'm Bryn."

"Yes, hi. It's nice to meet you." She shook Bryn's hand, approved of her firm grip.

"I've been dying to meet you."

She grinned. "Well here I am."

"Get in here," Bryn said, grabbing her arm to drag her inside. "We'll take good care of her," she said to Rhys.

"I know you will." His gaze met Neveah's. "I've got my cell on if you need me."

"Okay. See you." He loped down the steps and Bryn closed the door.

Nev gazed around the cozy great room with its pale cream walls and warm-toned hardwood floors. The furnishings were homey but elegant, the kind that made you want to sink into the sofa with a good book. "Wow, this is some house."

Bryn laughed. "Christa's going to love you for saying that."

She followed Bryn into the kitchen, a gorgeous marvel of white country cabinets and pale granite countertops with every conceivable cooking appliance known to man. She caught the scent of rosemary and garlic plus something chocolaty and her mouth watered. "What is that heavenly smell?"

"Christa." Bryn went up on tiptoe to get two glasses out of one of the cabinets. "She and Rayne's mom have been cooking for two days together. They're ridiculous. Throwbacks, I swear. All they need are the '50s dresses and they'd both be fricking June Cleavers."

Nev smiled and took the glass Bryn offered, loving how comfortable Bryn seemed in her friends' house. Kind of like when Nev was at Sam's place.

"Red?"

"Please."

A jingling sound brought her head around, then a black-and-white dog with a lot of border collie in it trotted up, wagging its tail.

"You like dogs?" Bryn asked.

"Love them," Nev answered, bending to scratch the dog's ears.

"That's Jake, and he's a total mooch, so watch your food."

Nev patted the dog for another moment, then took her wine from the counter. With a full glass of cabernet, she followed Bryn into the family room. Passing a framed photo of who she assumed were the bride and groom-to-be, she stopped short. Setting her wine down, she peered closer at the image. She felt like rubbing her eyes as she stared at the groom.

"Rayne looks exactly like Luke, doesn't he?"

Nev glanced at her. "It's unreal." She picked up her glass. "I thought it was Luke when I first looked."

"Rayne's a few inches taller, built at bit bigger, and he's got hazel-green eyes. But if Luke dyed his hair to cover the gray, those are the only ways you'd be able to tell them apart."

Turning from the picture, Nev rounded the end of the loveseat and sank into it, already at ease. "Where is the bride, by the way?"

"She'll be down in a while. She and Emily are busy hanging *the dress*." She gestured to the bags of colored jelly beans and rounds of colored tulle on the coffee table. "This is the job I've been assigned. Wanna help me?" Jake flopped down at her feet and laid his chin on her toes.

"Sure." She knelt on the pretty woven rug and copied Bryn, adding a handful of candy to each piece of material and tying it off with a complementary ribbon, each with a tag that thanked the guests for coming to the wedding. *Today is the day I marry my best friend.*

Nev withheld a sigh of longing. Wouldn't that be nice?

"I was hoping Rhys would bring you out tonight," Bryn said as she set down one of the favors and picked up her wine, her long fingers curled around the bowl of the glass. "I've heard a lot about you from Sam." Her smile was warm and sincere. "She sure loves you a lot."

"The feeling is mutual," Nev said.

"She's already planning her wedding, I bet."

"Oh yeah," she said with a roll of her eyes. Sam was such a detail freak. "She's got colored folders and her labels for every topic. They're all alphabetized, referenced and cross-referenced too."

Bryn shook her head. "God, it makes me wonder how she wound up with Ben because it sounds so much like something Rhys would do." She took a sip of wine and let her head rest against the edge of the easy chair. "I still can't believe Ben's getting married."

"Believe it. If he did anything to mess up Sam's plans, she'd kill him."

"Yeah, that's why I like her so much. She doesn't put up with any bullshit."

Oh, Bryn *so* knew her cousin. "It's a family trait."

Bryn snickered. "So how's it going with Rhys?"

Going? It wasn't. She shifted in her seat. "He's been really nice."

Bryn opened her mouth to say something else but was interrupted by the sound of footsteps on the stairs.

Jake leapt up and raced to them, his tail swishing madly.

Neveah swiveled around as a young, pretty brunette came into view. An attractive middle-aged woman followed, her medium brown hair cut into a layered bob that ended at her chin. "Hi," the young one said, absently stroking Jake's head before rushing over to shake her hand. "I'm Christa, and this is Emily, Rayne's mom."

"Neveah," she answered, shaking Emily's hand. "Thank you for having me."

Christa waved her hand, the diamond ring on her finger catching the light. "You're welcome anytime. I'm sorry we didn't come down right away, but I wanted to hide the dress in case Rayne came home early. I don't want him to see it."

"Understandable."

Christa's friendly aquamarine eyes sparkled. "Are you hungry?"

"I—"

"Let's just get the food together and call them in," Emily said, heading to the kitchen. Christa and Jake followed, and within moments the air filled with the clatter of dishes and silverware above the feminine chatter.

Nev cast Bryn a questioning glance, feeling guilty for sitting there doing nothing. Shouldn't they offer to help?

"Leave them be," Bryn advised. "It's what they do. Trust me."

With a smile, Nev picked up her wine and nodded at Bryn's engagement ring. "A lot of Luke's employees seem to be popping the question lately."

The other woman's dark eyes laughed. "That they are."

"You planning your wedding, too?"

"What's to plan? I'm getting married on a beach, someplace hot. SEALs love the water, you know."

"I've heard that," Nev said with a chuckle.

"Have you met Dec yet?"

"No. I've only seen the twins since I arrived, in between functions at the conference. Just saw Ben this morning. They're keeping a very close eye on me."

"That must make you feel good."

"Well, truthfully I'd rather it wasn't necessary, but if someone has to look after me I'm glad it's them."

"Yes. You couldn't ask for a better security team than the one Luke's brought in."

"Ah, so that *is* the real reason they're here. I thought so." She didn't blame Luke for not taking chances with his family. In fact, she respected him for it.

Bryn gave a tight smile, telling Neveah she wasn't completely at ease with the situation. "Don't say anything in front of Christa or Emily. Dec would kill me."

"I won't." Neveah cocked her head, sensing an opportunity to learn more about Rhys. "So tell me, how do you fit in with everyone here?"

"I started out as Rayne's best friend, but got really tight with his mom, and now with Christa."

"And of course you know Luke now, too." Nev had heard bits and pieces of Bryn's ordeal in Iraq from Sam.

"Yes." Her eyes darted toward the kitchen before adding, "Though I already knew a lot about him from Emily. They've been divorced for forever, not that you'd know it from the way she pines over him."

How sad.

"I'm worried about her," Bryn admitted with a frown. "She doesn't look well to me."

"What do you mean?"

"I don't know, she's…exhausted. It's something more than being here for the wedding and having to see Luke again, but she just says I'm imagining things. She's been sleeping a lot since she got here, and that's not like her. Dark circles, low energy, fatigues fast."

Nev frowned. "Has she seen a doctor? Could be menopause or something hormonal."

"Yeah, I guess you're right," Bryn said, but her eyes were still filled with worry.

Nev resolved to take a look at Emily when she came back into the room and make note of anything that might be cause for concern. "I think it's neat that you have a connection with all of them."

"Actually, I'm even more connected with their family. My father knew Luke once upon a time during the civil war in Lebanon. That's where they met Nate. Have you met him?"

"Yes, at the airport. He and Rhys picked me up."

"Rhys picked you up, huh?"

She nodded. "Then he took me up Grouse Mountain. He even took me for dinner last night at a really nice Italian place."

Bryn set down her glass so suddenly the wine almost spilled over the side. "He took you on a date? I mean—two dates?"

Bryn stared at her like she'd just revealed the secret of life. "No, just for a breather on the mountain, and last night for dinner to…catch up." Nev carefully left out the kiss of course. Man, she wished there had been much, much more to it than that.

Bryn craned her neck to see into the kitchen, as if checking to ensure the coast was clear before facing her again. "Tell me *everything*."

It startled a laugh out of her. "Nothing to tell, really."

"Are you kidding?" Her eyes widened. "Rhys, on an honest-to-God date? I must know more."

"It wasn't a date." Well, it hadn't started off with that intent. At least not on his part, she didn't think.

"Oh. You think he just took up to enjoy the view

the night you arrived and then for a romantic Italian restaurant for kicks?"

She couldn't help the blush rising in her cheeks. "I think he needed the break."

Bryn gave her an "oh, come on" look. "Rhys doesn't take breaks. Trust me on this."

She sighed. "I don't really know him all that well." *But I'd love to know him better.*

"You met in Paris, right?"

"With Sam. Then our paths crossed again in…Afghanistan."

Bryn laid a hand on her knee. "I heard. And if it makes you feel any better, I went through something similar."

Strangely, that helped. "Sam told me about it."

"All of us," she said with a nod, indicating Christa and Emily in the kitchen, "have been through our own versions of hell. So you're in good company."

"Thanks. I know a great therapist back east if you're interested. We could get a group rate."

Bryn snickered into her wine glass. "Dec's better than any amount of therapy could ever be."

Yeah, she knew the feeling. Having Rhys's arms around her had made the memories go away. Bryn was great. She was so glad she'd come here. "You know the twins pretty well, right?"

"Oh yeah. I'm close with both of them—well, I am with Ben at least. Rhys… I guess I'm as close to him as anyone can be. Besides Ben."

"And Sam," Nev added. "He loves Sam."

Bryn smiled. "That's good. It's hard for him to get close to people."

"Why?" She was dying to hear Bryn's take on it.

"They had a really tough upbringing. Worse than most of the foster kids I see as a social worker."

"In Boston?"

"South Boston. In the roughest part. You know they're adopted?"

Nev shook her head. "Sam never told me and Rhys didn't say anything last night except that he doesn't drink because his mom was an alcoholic and drug addict."

"Well, he meant his birth mother, and she was way worse than that." Bryn folded her legs beneath her and picked up her wine, a frown marring her brow. "She was a prostitute and an addict, and when she was on a binge she forgot to feed them most of the time."

Oh, poor Rhys… Nev wanted to go back in time and punch his mother. She couldn't imagine him or Ben growing up that way. And to think that Rhys had turned out to be such an honorable man. More pressure filled her chest.

"The only reliable meals they got were at school, and even then only two meals per day during the week. On the weekends they either knocked on their neighbor's door, stole money to buy food, or went through dumpsters behind restaurants to find something to eat."

Nev put a hand to her stomach, trying to imagine two young boys having to scrounge through the garbage to feed themselves.

"By the time they were ten she had them living out of a beat-to-shit car, and the authorities finally came in to take them away."

"Thank God."

"Yes, but it wasn't easy. They bounced around from one home to the other, got in trouble with the police until their adopted parents stepped in when they were fourteen."

"Rhys got arrested?" She had trouble believing that.

"Let's just say he learned a few tricks of the trade he uses now, plus he had to clean up his brother's…messes. That's why he's so controlled all the time. I don't think he was ever allowed to have fun, and I know for sure he never had anyone to love him or trust in other than Ben."

Neveah closed her eyes. "Oh God, I just want to hug him."

"Yeah, I know how you feel. And if he lets you? That should tell you how important you are to him."

She gazed into Bryn's knowing brown eyes. "Really?" She wanted to believe that.

"Really." Her perfect white teeth flashed when she smiled. "Pardon the pun, but you're just what the doctor ordered."

A sappy grin took over her face. "We saved each other, you know. In Afghanistan."

"I heard that. Pretty amazing start, I'd say."

Yes. That bond was as powerful as blood to her mind. Like their souls were connected now because of it.

"Hope you're hungry," Christa said as she floated out of the kitchen bearing trays of food with Jake prancing around her. Nev couldn't believe how relaxed she seemed, and that she'd go to so much trouble looking after everyone else when her wedding was less than a day away.

Christa ordered Jake to lie down, then set the food out. She loaded the coffee table with lasagna and a spinach salad with all kinds of fresh fruit and nuts in it. A plate full of cheese scones hot from the oven followed, plus a platter with roasted red peppers, Bocconcini and sliced beefsteak tomatoes drizzled with olive oil and fragrant shredded basil.

"You grew this yourself, didn't you," Bryn accused as she popped a piece of basil into her mouth.

"Tastes better that way," Christa answered with a smile.

"Wow," said Nev, eyeing the spread. In Christa's situation, she'd have ordered in Chinese or something.

"Just wait 'til dessert," Bryn remarked, already helping herself.

"Emily made a coconut cake," said Christa, handing Nev a plate.

"It's a family wedding tradition," Emily said as she emerged from the kitchen with a white cake on a cobalt glass pedestal.

Neveah scrutinized her with physician's eyes as she approached. Beneath very tasteful and carefully applied cosmetics, there were indeed puffy and dark circles beneath her lovely green eyes. Her skin was a bit pale, but maybe that was normal for her. Short of taking her pulse or blood pressure, that's all Nev could tell for now.

Emily set the pedestal down with a flourish. Lying next to the couch, Jake lifted his head and gave a hopeful wag of his tail, but still wasn't invited to partake of the feast. "My great-grandmother's recipe. Every bride in my family has to have a coconut cake when she gets married."

When everyone was settled they dug in, and Nev listened to the banter passing back and forth, enjoying the cozy camaraderie between the women. All survivors, and all vibrant, interesting people.

"I was just telling Neveah that she's a kindred spirit," Bryn told the others. "We're all lugging baggage around too, and yet we're shockingly normal."

"I'll drink to that," Christa said with a smile, then winked at Neveah and refilled everyone's glasses. Nev noticed she was drinking Perrier instead of wine. "Cheers."

"Cheers," they chorused.

Their sincere warmth wrapped around her throughout the meal. They peppered her with questions and then tried to pry information out of her about Rhys. She gave them a mysterious smile. "I don't kiss and tell."

Bryn gasped and swatted her arm. "You *kissed*? You never told me that! Oh man, I can't wait to see the two of you together tomorrow night."

"Oh please, like you'll be able to look away from your hunk of a fiancé." Emily snorted. "If there's any spying to do, I'll do it."

Christa laughed at her. "You'll be too preoccupied by your gorgeous son and Luke in their tuxes to notice anyone else."

Emily sighed, not even bothering to deny her attraction to her ex-husband as she smothered a yawn. "I'd argue, but you're right. Damn, it's going to be a long day tomorrow."

Neveah glanced at Bryn in question, and the other woman waggled her brows as she lifted her glass. "But an interesting one."

****

Rhys showed up at Christa's front door at just after ten and rang the bell. The security personnel down the street had reported everything was tight when he'd checked with them partway through the meeting, and he was glad Luke had taken the precaution of making sure the women were safe while alone in the house.

He heard them laughing from out on the front porch and hoped Neveah was having a good time. He'd wanted her to relax and unwind, but he hadn't intended to be gone so long. Luke was clearly worried as hell about the wedding tomorrow, and they'd gone over all the contingency plans they could come up with several times to make sure they'd covered everything.

The door swung open and Bryn stood there with an almost empty glass of red wine in her hand. From the way her cheeks were flushed, he was willing to bet it wasn't her first. Or second.

"Hi handsome," she said cheerily, sweeping an arm out in invitation. "Come on in."

His eyes shot toward the sound of feminine chatter and laughter. He'd sooner take down a nest of armed Taliban fighters than be put in the middle of that. "Is Nev ready?"

Bryn raised one elegant brow, her eyes sparkling with mischief. "Is she ever."

Whatever that cryptic comment meant, Rhys was sure he didn't want to know. He peered past her shoulder. An instant later Nev appeared from around the corner, still laughing at something one of the others had said. She was so beautiful she almost hurt his eyes. Her raspberry satin blouse brought out the rosy tint in her cheeks and skimmed over the pert curves of her breasts. The snug knee-length skirt hugged every curve and made him think about having those amazing long legs wrapped around him. In her heels, she was only a few inches shorter than him.

"Thanks again for having me. See you tomorrow," she called out, shrugging into her coat. Then she gave Bryn a big hug, and the sight filled him with warmth. Nev, even taller than Bryn, displaying her obvious affection for his friend. "See you at the church."

"You bet," Bryn replied, meeting Rhys's eyes as the two women parted. "We like her," she told him. "You can keep her."

"Uh…thanks."

When they were outside and Bryn had shut the door, Nev startled him by going up on tiptoe to wrap her arms around his neck and snuggling in tight.

"Hey," he said in surprise, returning the embrace. She took a deep breath and exhaled, leaning against him. "What's this for? You okay?"

"Just wanted to. Do you mind?"

"No." He didn't mind at all. In fact, he loved it. He

was starting to crave any kind of physical connection with her.

She finally raised her head and gazed up at him with happy blue eyes. "I had fun. I like them, especially Bryn."

"I'm glad. Ready to go?"

"Sure." But she stayed where she was, looking up at him.

Damn she was beautiful with her cheeks all pink from her wine and her eyes sparkling like that. But he didn't dare take things further. He'd done enough damage last night.

"Missed you." Taking him off guard, she lifted her face and kissed him, gently but with enough hunger to make him tangle his hands in her gorgeous hair.

Acutely conscious of the fact they were kissing on the front porch under a carriage light for all the world to see, he toned his response down considerably. But the soft moan that escaped her made him want to get her somewhere more private so he could get his hands all over her and press his weight flush against her. Get inside her.

God help him, he didn't think he had the strength to walk away from her a second time.

Something thumped against the window.

He jerked back in time to catch a glimpse of three very curious faces pressed against the front window before they dropped out of view like he'd aimed a weapon at them.

The blood rushed to his face.

Neveah laughed and grabbed his hand, the sound so joyful and carefree he couldn't help but grin back at her. He felt like a teenager who'd just been caught necking with his date by her parents.

"Let's get out of here," she whispered against his ear.

Now that was a hell of an idea.

He helped her into the truck, gaze getting stuck on the tantalizing inches of bare thigh the skirt exposed as it rode up. When he looked up at her, he found a pleased smile on her lips. Brat.

Pulling down the long, curving driveway, he listened to her impressions of the evening, fascinated by the way she saw people. Nev truly made an effort to understand what made people tick, and her desire to help and heal were evident in the observations she made. "All of them have suffered, yet they haven't let their experiences cripple them. I admire that."

So did he. "You're like that, too."

The smile she flashed him hit him square in the heart. "Thanks. I'm trying hard." With a sigh, she leaned her head back against the headrest and stared out at the road. "Speaking of trying hard…" Her fingers trailed over his palm.

Uh-oh.

"You realize I was forced to take care of business myself after you left me hanging last night?"

His cock swelled to life in his pants. Christ. Was she trying to make him drive off the road? He had a sudden image of those elegant hands moving over her naked body, giving herself the pleasure he hadn't let himself.

"What do you have to say about that?"

Uh… "Hope it was good for you."

Her eyes narrowed. "It wasn't near as good as it would have been if you'd stayed."

Now that, he could guarantee. "Did you think about me?"

"*Oh* yeah."

Holy fuck that was hot. His hands tightened on the steering wheel. The beast inside him snarled and rattled its cage. "You'd better be sure you want what you're asking me for before you keep pushing me."

"I'm sure."

Keeping his eyes on the road, Rhys chuckled at her bluntness. He'd already made up his mind, but he wasn't going to tell her what his decision was. He'd rather show her instead.

This was gonna be a long-ass drive back into town.

Chapter Eight

By the time Rhys took her back to her hotel and checked her room to make sure it was secure, Neveah was fighting the need to throw herself at him. That calm, cool, collected routine of his was a total turn on. As was the efficient and decisive way he handled everything, like when he'd whisked her off the porch and into the truck after they'd been caught kissing.

After her bold declaration, he'd been extra attentive to her on the drive back, stroking her hand and her arm with his fingertips, the side of her neck. Add in the way he looked in his suit, and… God, how much stimulation was a girl supposed to withstand?

When he flicked on a lamp in the corner, she assumed everything was fine and took a step closer. "Can I come in?"

"Yeah." His deep voice caressed a place low in her abdomen that had lain dormant until that moment. "Coast is clear."

Slipping inside and shutting the door, she made sure to bolt it securely. The single lock and slide struck her as pathetically inadequate protection against a real threat, but she did have Rhys with her, and that was better than any reassurance she would ever get.

She took off her coat and hung it in the closet, then toed off her pumps. Looking behind her, she found him sliding his tailored jacket off his wide shoulders, exposing the gun holster criss-crossing his back and the black grip of the pistol beneath his left armpit. She swallowed, suddenly reminded that no matter how beautiful he was and how well he treated her, he was still lethal. The edge of unease came back to haunt her.

Stop it.

Meeting her gaze, Rhys shrugged out of the holster and set it carefully atop his folded jacket on the top shelf in the closet. He shut the sliding door so she wouldn't have to see it. As though he'd read her mind, he asked, "You okay with me being here?"

He was staying. Her heart started to drum in her ears.

"Yes. Thanks." She felt a hell of a lot safer being in the same room with him than if she were alone. Might even be able to get some sleep if he stayed, too. Or, if she was really lucky, no sleep at all.

She eyed the breadth of his shoulders and the swells of muscle beneath his dress shirt. He was the best reason she could think of to go without sleep, and she'd gladly sacrifice her precious hours of rest if it meant being alone with him. Especially if it involved being naked in bed with him.

Meeting her blatant stare, he arched a coal black brow. "Need something?"

Her eyes jerked to his while a hot blush stole over her face and neck. Where had all her bravery gone? "What?"

He seemed to be hiding a smile. She wasn't quite sure how she knew it, but something in his eyes warmed and flickered for a moment. Amusement? She hoped not.

"I asked if you needed anything."

"No, thanks. I'm good." She wasn't going to beg. He hadn't touched her since kissing her briefly in the Escalade when he'd parked in the underground, except for that gentlemanly hand on the small of her back on the way to her room. She wished they were still back in the shadowed confines of the truck so she could have more of him. Now, the comparatively bright light from the lamp across the room made her feel awkward about going to him. As did the remote vibe she sensed from him now.

Running her gaze over him longingly while he had his back turned, Nev withheld a sigh. Didn't he feel how strong the pull was between them? The magnetism was so powerful it sizzled over her skin and settled in her bones. Her lungs couldn't seem to get a full breath of air when he was in the same room as her. How could he just turn his feelings on and off like that?

To distract herself she picked up the remote and flipped the TV on to a sports show, figuring he'd appreciate that, and sank onto the couch. Behind her, Rhys turned off the lamp. She glanced over her shoulder, expecting him to come over and sit beside her.

But when he turned around and locked his gaze on hers, the little oxygen remaining in her lungs disappeared. Her stomach flipped like she'd just dropped three floors in a runaway elevator. Rhys had never looked at her like this. Everything about him radiated erotic promise.

She couldn't tear her eyes from his while he strode over and took the remote from her unmoving hand. Without breaking her gaze, he hit the power button to turn off the TV, plunging the room into sudden darkness before he leaned over and placed it on the coffee table.

Silence enveloped them. With him standing so close, invisible currents of electricity leapt across the empty space between them. As her eyes adjusted in the pale moonlight streaming through the window, she caught the stark hunger in his expression. She swallowed hard.

He watched her, waiting. He reminded her of a predatory animal, choosing its moment to strike. All she could hear was the thudding of her heart in her ears. She sat completely still, the muscles in her belly drawn so tight they hurt.

You wanted this. Little late to be having second thoughts now.

He closed the remaining distance separating them and stopped in front of her, taking her hands in his. The simple contact jolted deep in her belly.

Nev craned her neck back to meet his eyes, and the sheer desire revealed in them stunned a gasp out of her. No one had ever looked at her like that. Rhys's expression made her think he wanted to eat her alive. A shiver of anticipation rolled through her body.

When he tugged her to her feet, she obeyed without a thought, riveted by his focused expression. Before she had time to wonder what he'd do, he slid his hands up the intensely sensitive skin of her inner arms and over her shoulders, up her throat to her face. The seductive touch was completely at odds with the molten heat blazing from his eyes and set her heart pounding.

She'd sensed this in him, this volcanic heat beneath the icy exterior he showed the rest of the world. This was the real man beneath the cool façade. Some part of her had recognized this side of him the moment they'd met in Paris. Yet confronting the overwhelming power of him in the shadowed room wracked another shiver out of her.

Tilting her head and stretching up to meet him, she waited while he lowered his lips to hers. She was caught off guard when he moved aside at the last instant to ever so lightly graze his cheek against hers. His delicious scent enveloped her as the shockwave of warmth suffused her body. The five o'clock shadow across his cheeks and jaw rasped gently over her tender skin as he caressed her. The gesture was almost feline, like a huge lion nuzzling its mate. Her fingers automatically curled into the fabric of his shirt, famished to feel the bare skin beneath.

Rhys brought her even closer, until her breasts touched the wide wall of his chest and the front of her thighs brushed his. The rock hard length of his impressive erection against her lower belly set off an unprecedented wave of heat between her legs. She gasped, and at the same moment he covered her lips with his. Instantly she opened for him. He rewarded her with the slow glide of his tongue across her lower lip before dipping inside to stroke hers, the erotic caress making her womb clench. The damp glow between her legs intensified into a throb, as though her heart beat there.

Nev leaned further into him, wanting, craving more contact, running her hands over the mind-blowing swells and dips of muscle she found. His kiss was the most intense she'd ever experienced, and his almost lazy movements made the fire burn hotter.

In the space of a few moments he had her panting and clinging to him, little moans bubbling up from somewhere deep inside. The pleasure he'd already given her was unbelievable, and all he'd done was kiss her.

This was all wrong. This wasn't her.

With nothing more than a kiss, he'd turned her weak and pliant in his arms. She didn't *do* weak and pliant, especially when it came to sex. And she most certainly didn't do soft and submissive, either.

You do now.

The startling thought made her eyes fly open. How the hell did he affect her so much? God help her, but Rhys made her want to lie down and pull him on top so he could do whatever he wanted with her. She tried to come up with an explanation for it, but came up empty. Then he angled his head for a better fit with her mouth, and she stopped thinking altogether. Her lashes fluttered down on a sigh. *More*, she thought dizzily. She needed more of him.

With shaky fingers she found the top button on his shirt and undid it. She kept going until he released her to pull the hem from his waistband and peel it over his head, exposing the mouthwatering landscape of his muscular torso to her gaze and touch. She almost whimpered.

A dark scattering of chest hair narrowed to a thin strip that traveled down his ribbed abdominals and disappeared beneath his waistband. Her eyes followed the gorgeous lines of his lats as they fanned out from his ribs. She flattened her palms over the hot skin of his chest, ravenous to touch him, and turned her face up when he threaded his hands in her hair.

Rhys kept complete control of the kiss, never letting her take over, forcing her to meet his lazy rhythm. His fingers swept over her hair where it fell in waves against her throat and down to her breasts. Each light caress of his fingertips brought another wave of goose bumps racing over her violently sensitive skin, until she was arching her back to rub her breasts against his hard chest, seeking relief from the torture. In answer, Rhys let out an erotic purr and backed her up against the wall behind the couch, pressing her there with his body.

Neveah gave up all pretense of modesty and moaned aloud, letting her head fall back against the wall as his mouth moved over her jaw and down her neck beneath the collar of her blouse, unerringly finding the delicate spot where her neck joined her shoulder. He gently scraped his teeth over it, making her gasp, then soothed the slight sting with his tongue, warm and damp.

She cried out, knees buckling, and grabbed hold of his arms. Her fingers locked around the bulging curves of his biceps.

He caught her easily, holding her tight in his arms for a moment to steady her, one of his thighs wedged between hers. A low cry escaped as she rocked her hips, rubbing her swollen flesh against the steely muscles beneath it. Instead of hurrying things along, Rhys drew the pads of his fingers down the front of her throat into the deep V-neck of the blouse, pausing over the upper swell of her breasts.

Breathless, she stared into his eyes as he caressed her bare skin above the low cut neckline, gauging her reaction. He followed the curve of her breast with languorous enjoyment while her nipple beaded in anticipation, aching for his touch. When his thumb finally grazed across it, she groaned in relief, arching her back to lean into his hand, seeking more. She shivered. "Rhys…"

"Shhh." Rubbing his thumb back and forth, stealing deep, soul-shattering kisses, he slid his other hand down her back to her hips. Squeezing through her pencil skirt, he swept over the back of one thigh and lifted it, curling it around his hip while he moved deeper between her legs and brought the hard length of his erection firmly against the spot that wept for him. Her head snapped back with a throttled moan as he rubbed there, the heavy throb in her body intensifying into a desperate, uncontrollable ache that frightened her. She'd never been this aroused in her life, and he hadn't even undressed her yet.

"Clothes," she gasped, grabbing the taut cheeks of his ass to hold him against her, frustrated by the layers of cloth separating them. "Off."

"Mmmm," he murmured, running his fingers over the bare skin of her inner thigh, his other thumb still tormenting her nipple.

Oh, God, she needed much more than this, and she needed it right *now*. "Rhys…" She was going to lose it if he didn't do something to ease the terrible ache between her thighs. The bed was too far away for her liking. Right here against the wall was fine. His long fingers tugged at the buttons of her blouse, exposing the thin lace bra that encased her breasts. Shivering at the desire on his face, she watched him lower his head to nuzzle against lace and skin.

Without raising his head he pushed the blouse off her shoulders, then found the hooks at the back of her bra and undid them. The straps caressed her arms as it dropped to the floor. Biting her lip, Nev curled her spine in a shameless offering, bringing a flushed, taut nipple to his mouth. She heard his faint murmur of approval before he opened his mouth and took her inside, sucking so tenderly she automatically cradled the back of his head to hold him there. Tongues of pleasure forked through her body like lightning, making her writhe and whimper. She was so wet now. Hot enough to vaporize.

All on its own, her free hand slid over his taut waist and over his fly, finding the hard length of him and wrapping around it. She moaned at the feel of him filling her palm, dying to feel that part of him inside her. He moved into her hand with a rumble of enjoyment, turning his attention to her other nipple, one hand caressing the nape of her neck and the other trailing torturously up and down over her inner thigh, never moving up to where she wanted them no matter how she twisted and writhed.

Neveah was on fire, wet and ready for him, but he remained in complete control, driving her mad with need. When it came to sex, she always had to concentrate really hard to get aroused if she wanted a chance in hell at having an orgasm. With Rhys, it wasn't like that at all. She didn't have to think, and couldn't have if she'd wanted to. Her body was on autopilot, a setting she hadn't known she possessed. Everywhere he touched her sparkled, and those flickers coalesced into a glowing ball of heat in the pit of her belly and her throbbing core. This was sex on steroids.

But it wasn't *just* sex. The wild fluttering of her heart said so. And no matter what happened, she would have the memory of this night with him.

He continued to lavish attention on her breasts, pulling gently with his mouth, swirling his tongue over her electrified nipples. Growing frantic, she attacked his belt buckle and undid the button beneath it. The zipper made a soft buzzing sound above her panting breaths. Rhys didn't move, didn't stop what he was doing to her, content to let her open his pants and slide her hand into his boxer briefs to curl around the thick, hot length of his penis. He pulsed in her grip. Oh God, he was big, she thought giddily, her inner muscles clenching tight at the thought of him pushing into her. She couldn't fricking wait.

The clean, musky scent of his skin filled her nose, his erection kicking in her grip as she stroked him, up and down, swirling her hand over the swollen head until it grew slick.

His fingers moved, shifting up to lightly graze the soft lace covering her slick folds. She gasped, lids fluttering down, biting her lip as he caressed higher, higher. When he touched her clit through her thong she let out a sob and clung tighter. Rhys raised his head, leaving her taut nipple gleaming in the soft moonlight, and met her gaze. The breath caught in her throat at the raging inferno there.

His expression was so intense she couldn't breathe, his deep blue eyes burning hers. His jaw was clenched, the muscles across his shoulders bunched as he struggled to hold onto control. He was as revved up as she was, but still so gentle, so careful with her.

Staring down at him, her lips trembled. "Please," she whispered unsteadily. "I need you inside me."

In the half-light, something flared in the depths of his eyes like the blue flame of a match strike. He grabbed her by the waist and lifted her to straddle him. Raising her up, he pinned her flat against the wall while he caught her mouth in a ravenous kiss, tongue sliding, plunging deep, then withdrawing to play with hers. His hand slid up her skirt to her panties and smoothed them down her legs where it joined the rest of her clothes. When he reached for the zipper on her skirt, Nev whimpered into his mouth and wrapped her arms around his heavy shoulders, clinging tightly with her legs, rubbing that terrible ache against his erection.

Yes, now. Hurry.

The skirt hit the floor, then he pulled one arm out from around her and reached behind him. A moment later she heard the distinctive crinkle and rip of a condom being torn open and nearly sobbed in relief. She couldn't let go to help him, and her legs were already shaking with the strain of keeping her weight balanced.

Hanging on tight, she sucked in a breath when the head of his erection nudged the folds of her sex. The hard arm around her hips tightened as he positioned himself, sliding back and forth over her slippery, engorged folds and clit. When he finally lodged in the right spot she moaned a little, the incredible heat of him adding to the fire inside.

Seeking relief from the mysterious ache he'd created, she eased down, taking more of him into her. Her nails sank into his shoulders. God, he was big.

Kissing her hard and deep, Rhys wrapped his other arm around her shoulders to cushion her back from the cold wall and pushed slowly, inexorably upward, burying himself inside her.

Nev tore her mouth away from his at the unyielding breadth of him. “Oh…*shit*,” she breathed, trying to lever away from him with her hands.

He froze. Raising his head, he met her shocked gaze and lifted one hand to brush a wave of hair away from her cheek. His gentle fingers were cool against her flushed skin. “Hurt?”

Did it? Maybe. She wasn’t sure yet. “Just—just wait…” She couldn’t decide if the burning ache was painful or intensely pleasurable. The thick intrusion stretched her to her limit, making her feel impaled. She wriggled around to find a more comfortable position, but had nowhere to go, and no leverage to push away with.

As though sensing her plight, Rhys reached one arm back and dragged the couch toward them with a muffled scrape. Then he took her ankles and guided her feet to the top of the backrest. With the smooth, cool leather giving her purchase, Nev immediately extended her legs to relieve the incredible pressure of him wedged so deep inside her.

“All right?” he whispered, watching her eyes. She nodded and licked her lips, dizzy with pleasure. Her arms curled around his wide shoulders, holding him close.

Oh a sigh, Rhys wrapped both arms around her back and burrowed in tight, resting his face in the hollow of her throat. That he was staying so still to let her body adjust while holding her in a full length cuddle made tears burn her eyes.

She took several deep breaths and tried to relax, allowing her internal muscles a few moments to adapt to his invasion. Despite her efforts to stay motionless, they squeezed and fluttered around him, intensifying that pleasurable ache where his erection rubbed against what she surmised must be the G-spot she’d never found until now. When one of his hands slid between them to stroke her clitoris, she sighed and melted.

Heart pounding, she moved experimentally, just a tiny rocking motion, and moaned aloud at the incredible sensation it wrought. Her eyes flew open in shock.

He raised his head and stared at her, his muscular body held perfectly still. Waiting. Watching her reaction.

Oh, God, he *knew*. Knew exactly what he was doing to her, because she could read it in his glittering navy eyes. He wasn't moving solely out of consideration, but so that she could have whatever time she needed to explore the sensations.

Any control she had in this position was an illusion, of course. He was orchestrating this whole thing. Not that it made any difference to her body or her heart, for that matter. The damned thing rolled over in her chest as she gazed down into his eyes.

Trembling, she rocked her hips, helpless to stop herself. The pleasure magnified again, each short slide up and down his thick erection rubbing over the hot glow hidden inside her. Her body was full. So deliciously full. The ache grew stronger, melding with the intense pleasure. Strengthening it. Making her mindless. "Oh God, Rhys…" Her eyelids slid closed, lips parting in breathless ecstasy.

She'd read about this. She'd even heard about it from her girlfriends, but until this very moment she hadn't believed it was possible for sex to feel this good. It almost scared her, it was so amazing. Her body clamored at her to move harder, faster, greedy for more and the cataclysmic release she sensed was building. A whimper of need escaped her. God, she needed *more*.

Both Rhys's hold and gaze never faltered as she rode him, at first slowly, then with increasing abandon. Her rhythm grew faster, more demanding. Each movement coiled the new sensations tighter and tighter.

His thumb caressed slow and sure between her thighs. She was panting now, uncaring of how frantic she was or that he watched her, focused solely on the building orgasm that already eclipsed anything she'd experienced.

Through it all he remained silent, staring into her eyes, holding her rock steady, supporting her weight and allowing her to move how she wanted. The only signs of his intense arousal were his tightening expression and the muscles in his back and shoulders bunching under her grasping hands.

A long, throaty moan came out of her as the intensity of the growing orgasm increased. "Oh, *God…*"

Rhys's lips touched her jaw briefly, trailing soft kisses over her skin before he pulled back to watch her face. The intimacy between them in the shadowy, hushed room was as tangible as the sensations coursing through her awed body. She couldn't look away from him. The rapt hunger on his face pushed her even higher. Helpless, she stared back while the pleasure rose, and then rose some more. He was so thick, so hard inside her. That glorious ache built, as hot as the pleasure, and his fingers were stroking her trembling clit…

Her voice wobbled. "Rhys…" *Please let it be good for him, too.*

As she watched, his head snapped back on a strangled roar, the muscles in his neck and shoulders outlined in sharp relief from fighting to hold back and not move. He was heart-stoppingly gorgeous, every inch of him erotic perfection. Her body clamped down on him, the forerunners of ecstasy spiraling up, up.

She shuddered and closed her eyes, letting the orgasm take her, writhing and crying out in his strong grip as she died a little in his arms. The incredible pulses hadn't even begun to fade when he buried his face in her hair and thrust upward hard, once, twice, three times before arching and groaning with his own release. She held him close through the maelstrom, and when he finally stilled, wrapped her arms as far around him as she could. Gasping, she laid her head against his damp shoulder. She could barely breathe.

The room was so quiet now, disturbed only by their heavy breathing. Nev closed her eyes and savored the peace of the moment, shocked that her body was capable of experiencing such intense pleasure. She stroked her hands over his back and shoulders, up his neck to his head and trailed her fingers over his baby-soft skull-trim. Her skin was flushed and dewy, muscles filled with a heavy languor she now recognized as post-coital glow. So *that's* what all those books were talking about. She smiled against his cheek, kissed him there.

Rhys raised his head. "Okay?"

Her smile widened. "Oh, yeah."

He gave her that endearing crooked grin and hooked an arm behind him to help lower her feet to the floor. Her legs were so tired they wobbled under her, so Rhys gently disengaged from her body. He swung her up into his arms like she weighed no more than a child. Holding her securely, he carried her over to the king-sized bed. Pulling the covers back, he laid her down and tucked her in before heading to the bathroom.

Nev watched him walk away with a dreamy sigh, admiring the flex of muscle along his spine and buttocks and the incredible power of his long legs. The tattoo on his right shoulder blade lay unmarred amidst the burn scars covering most of his upper back. She stared at the half infinity symbol and upraised dagger, the mirror image to what Ben had on his left shoulder. One half of a whole. The eternal bond they shared as twins.

The last time she'd seen Rhys's tattoo had been at Walter Reed when she'd helped turn him and changed the dressings on the burns. Now, he was truly all healed. A spectacular anatomical specimen.

When he came back out a few moments later, her eyes devoured the front view of him. Wearing nothing but a smile, he crawled in next to her and rolled her into the cradle of his arms, tucking her head beneath his chin. She hugged him close and cuddled up to savor his warmth and strength, more content than she'd ever been in her life. Yawning, she closed her eyes, knowing she was perfectly safe with him watching over her.

Was it any wonder why she was falling in love with him? Tonight, for the first time in months, she was going to sleep like a baby.

Chapter Nine

Peshawar, Pakistan
Saturday

Tehrazzi hobbled into the stables at the edge of the property, bent over like an old man from the pain burning in his gut. His breathing was ragged— it was too soon for him to be up—but he refused to lie in bed any longer. He was not dying, and so he must continue to carry out Allah's will. His purpose had not yet been fulfilled.

With every breath he wished he could be in Vancouver to carry out the operation. But he could not. As much as he loathed having someone else take care of it, he had no other choice at present.

Carried on the hot, dry breeze, the earthy scents of dust and horses mixed, transporting him back to when he was a boy and he used to race his father's horses across the Syrian Desert. The familiar smell always did that, just as it always brought the memory of the smell of blood and his beloved mare's shrill cries of pain when she lay dying. Her large, gentle eyes had stared into his as he'd cut her throat to end her suffering.

She had died because of his teacher and the SEAL now with Bryn McAllister.

He shook his head to clear the horrific memories and entered the dark building, soothing himself with the knowledge they would receive their punishment tonight.

The moment he stepped over the threshold a blessed wave of cool air rushed over his sweaty skin. Down the row of stalls, a horse stomped its hoof and another snorted. Despite the awful ripping sensation in his belly where the surgeon had reopened his incision to drain away the pus the night before, he forced himself to straighten. Moving slowly, Tehrazzi crossed the well-tended paddock to the stall at the end of the row. Whistling softly, his heart gave a leap of joy when the animal put its head over the sliding door and pricked its ears toward him.

The coal-black Arabian stallion was a beautiful creature. Its large brown eyes regarded him with curiosity as he approached, lowering its ebony muzzle to sniff and whuffle over his palm when he extended it. Something eased inside him, yet at the same time the ache of his loss intensified. He had not allowed himself time to grieve the loss of his beloved horse, but now in this quiet, shaded stable he gave into a moment's need to remember her.

His hand trembled with a weakness he despised when he stroked the stallion's sleek forehead, down the white blaze that traveled the length of his nose to the black-as-night muzzle. In response, the animal heaved a groan of contentment and let its lids droop, leaning into his touch. A sharp twinge of yearning lit in Tehrazzi's soul.

This was his weakness. The one earthly thing his soul craved. A bond of trust with an animal whose loyalty matched his own, and the connection it provided. He stroked the stallion in silence for a long while.

At the sound of shuffling footsteps, he dropped his hand and stepped away from the stall. Carefully concealing his disappointment at being interrupted, he turned to the blinding rectangle of light that marked the open doorway. The black outline of a man's silhouette filled it.

"Sir?"

One of the servants. "What is it?"

"The master wishes to know if you would like to join him for tea in the garden."

The muscles in his upper lip began to curl and he stopped them before the sneer could form. He had no interest in spending time with a man who was loyal to the US-backed Pakistani government, let alone taking tea with him like they were old friends. They were not. Tehrazzi had no friends now. He'd learned that hard lesson over the past few months, and had made sure to repay his betrayers with death.

Just as he knew he'd betrayed the man he'd once loved like a brother. Like the father he'd never known.

The man he'd betrayed was now hunting him, half a world away. Sometimes between sleep and waking, he could hear his teacher's deep voice, promising he was coming for him.

Tehrazzi wasn't a fool. He knew how his teacher's mind worked. He would not stop until Tehrazzi was captured or dead. Death was vastly more preferable to captivity. That's why he'd made his peace with Allah some time ago. If He demanded Tehrazzi's life, he was prepared to give it.

Tehrazzi exhaled slowly and maintained his straight posture as he regarded the young aide before him. "I regret I must decline my host's generous offer," he told him in Urdu, almost choking on the words. "I will return to my room shortly to rest." And to plan his next move. He must leave soon.

The young man bowed and left. In the sudden silence, Tehrazzi battled the rush of exhaustion stealing through his ravaged body. With a last longing glance at the stallion watching from its stall, he, too, left the stable.

Outside, the force of the sun hit him like a blow, sucking precious strength from his muscles. By the time he entered the relative cool of the mansion where he was staying, he had to grip the door frame to stay upright. He forced his leaden legs to carry him to his bedroom at the far end of the polished parquet hallway in the guest quarters. Turning into it, he stopped so suddenly he swayed on his tired feet.

Mahmoud looked up from his chair with a smile of greeting, the captured laptop open in his lap. The computer whirred softly in the quiet room.

Tehrazzi's heart thundered in his ears. The blood drained from his flushed face, and his fingers curled around the jamb like claws. "What have you done?" The words came out a dry whisper.

Mahmoud's smile evaporated. A frown creased his forehead, as though he was confused by Tehrazzi's reaction. "I was checking for more information about—"

"I told you not to *touch* it." His icy voice sliced through the air like a blade.

The younger man's throat bobbed as he swallowed. "But I thought—"

Tehrazzi pressed a hand over his wound, fighting back a wave of nausea. His instincts urged him to flee, but he couldn't move. Fear all but paralyzed him. "They know where I am now."

Mahmoud blanched and flipped the lid shut, shaking his head as he set the computer aside. "Not possible. I made sure I disabled the security and tracking devices I found."

"You stupid fool!" He was trembling now, with

anger and trepidation. "You know *nothing*!" Tehrazzi stumbled over to the dresser and lifted the satchel he'd already packed, then retrieved the SIG Sauer from the top drawer along with the clips of ammunition he'd stored.

Mahmoud sucked in a breath and cringed in his seat. Tehrazzi had half a mind to shoot him then and there. He deserved it.

Ignoring Mahmoud's protests, he slung the heavy pack over his shoulder and hurried into the hallway, intent on getting to the door. The pain tore at his belly, but he ruthlessly ignored it. He should have gotten rid of the laptop. Why had he thought he could keep anyone from activating it?

He had to escape, now, before the CIA or other paramilitary teams his teacher had in place moved in. Gaining the exit, he burst into the midday sun, his skin chilled despite the scorching heat. The hair on his arms stood on end.

That one mistake could cost him everything. His teacher had found him yet again. Even from the other side of the world he was moving, setting into motion a chain of events Tehrazzi could not possibly hope to stop. The best he could hope for now was to escape and buy more time.

"Wait! I'm sorry, wait!"

He paid little attention to Mahmoud's entreaty, slipping unmolested out the guarded gate and into the streets of Peshawar. Fighting to control the panic eating at him, he climbed into a cab and told the driver to take him to a village near the Afghan border. The rage continued to build. To be found now, on the cusp of achieving his goal…

He glanced at his watch. Only a few more hours until the operation Mahmoud's uncle had planned. Tehrazzi sincerely hoped Ahmed was more reliable than his nephew. He'd been warned of the consequences if he failed.

For now, Tehrazzi had to flee. The border was close. He had followers throughout the tribal region who would take him in, hide him until he could get back across the border and disappear into the mountains that had swallowed foreign armies for generations. Including the Russians, whom his teacher had trained him to fight, and thus turned him into the threat he represented.

The vehicle hit a deep pot hole, and the sharp jolt jarred his wound. He hissed out a breath, squeezing his eyes shut while black spots swam behind his closed lids. More sweat broke out on his face. When he got his breath back and opened his eyes, the taxi was stopped. The driver was swiveled in his seat, staring at him with a concerned frown.

"Shall I pull over?" he asked.

"No," Tehrazzi growled. The driver turned away and turned up his radio.

Caught in the crush of midday traffic, the cab idled in the middle of the city. Tehrazzi glanced in the side mirrors and caught sight of another cab weaving through traffic toward them. As it came closer, he recognized Mahmoud's anxious face peering through the windshield at him.

Let him follow. If they reached the next safe house, Tehrazzi would have time enough to ensure there were no more mistakes made.

The hour of the operation was drawing nearer, and if something went wrong…Mahmoud may yet prove himself useful.

****

Vancouver

Cold. Damp. The earthen floor beneath her was clammy with condensation at the temperature dropped. Splattered on the floor and overflowing the metal bucket in the opposite corner, the stench of diarrhea nearly gagged her. Flies swarmed around the filth, filling the still air with a low buzz. She shivered against the mud brick and stone wall, staring into the darkness. No blankets to warm them. No light. Just eerie silence disturbed only by the shallow breathing of the other two men left in the room with her.

They all knew what was coming. Fear was a bitter tang on her tongue, filling her throat, so thick she could choke on it.

He *would come for one of them soon. The tall one with the light brown eyes and the scar bisecting his chin. His malevolence would drop the air temperature further when he approached the crude wooden door separating them from their captors.*

She twisted her fingers together and kept staring at the door, and the pale sliver of light escaping beneath it. Was she next? Her empty stomach rolled as she thought of how Gary had died the night before. Hacked to death, worse than an animal being slaughtered. She bit down hard on her lips to hold back a sob. She couldn't die like that, screaming and thrashing and fighting. How was she ever going to be able to withstand it? How long would it take?

Mike stirred a few feet from her, groaning as he shifted, miserable with the debilitating abdominal cramps they'd all come down with. Perhaps a parasite in the water they'd been given. Not that it mattered. They were all going to die here anyway, either from dehydration or by the tall man's knife. Every twenty-four hours he would kill another of them. Cool, sticky sweat beaded across her back and face, under her arms.

Then footsteps. Outside the door. She froze and held

her breath. Waiting. Please God, no more. Let us live…

They stopped at the door.

Every muscle in her body tightened.

Her heart sank when the door opened. She blinked in the beam of the flashlight, raising an arm to shield her eyes as the tall man stood silhouetted in the hellish outline. Walking past her, he hauled the orthopedic surgeon out, ignoring his pleas and struggles.

Unable to meet her colleague's terrified gaze as the man dragged him away, she turned her head and squeezed her eyes shut, nails biting into her palms hard enough to draw blood. Her heart slammed against her ribs like a trapped animal while she waited for the murder to begin. And it did.

Those bloodcurdling, inhuman screams of unimaginable agony started as the knife sliced through the tissues in his nape. She clapped her hands over her ears to try and block them out, her feral cries of rage and despair echoing inside her head. They went on and on, shattering her sanity until she wanted to rush out and have him kill her too, just so it would be over.

And then they stopped. Instantly. Because the knife had finally hit the spinal cord.

Her claw-like hands speared deep into her greasy, matted hair and squeezed hard enough to bring forth the tears that had been locked too deep inside. The hot rivulets trickled down her filthy face and over her trembling lips in salty streams.

Then the footsteps came back. No! No more. No more…

The tall man pushed open the door once again and aimed his flashlight at her face. She flinched and ducked her head, refusing to look at him. The warm, meaty smell of blood hung so thick in the air the bile rose up her throat.

"Look what I have," the psychotic murderer purred

in flawless English.

The flesh on the back of her neck prickled. She didn't want to see what he'd brought, but her eyes were already swinging his way. Blinking in the harsh beam of light, she tried to focus on what he held in his fist. Something round. The size of a melon.

A hand flew up to her mouth to stop the cry of horror and outrage. The blood drained out of her face.

The tall man held his victim's severed head by the hair, swinging it back and forth like a pendulum.

"Would you like to say goodbye to your friend before I throw him down the mountain for the vultures?"

A loud sob escaped her as she stared at the head, its sightless eyes half open and mouth stretched in a silent scream.

"No?" Assoud continued. "Then I wish you pleasant dreams. I'll be back again tomorrow for whichever one of you draws the short straw."

As she stared, the victim's lifeless eyes opened and fixed on hers. Navy blue. The face melted into another's, the one she'd been dreaming of for so long.

Rhys's eyes gazed back at her from within that madman's grip. "Neveah."

She jerked awake with a strangled gasp. *Shit!*

Watching her, Rhys came up on one elbow beside her. "All right?"

No. "Yep." She threw her legs over the side of the bed and bolted for the bathroom. Locking the door behind her, she hit the lights and laid her palms on the cool granite countertop at the sink and let her chin fall to her chest. God, she hadn't had that dream since right after coming back from Afghanistan, and never with Rhys in it.

She raised her head to look at her reflection in the mirror above the oval under mounted sink. Her face was white as the fluffy towels on the chrome rack next to the shower and she was shaking so hard her knees wobbled.

She closed her eyes and took a slow breath to calm her nervous system. But no, the nausea gripped her belly with a powerful twist, sending her to her knees before the toilet. This was way too damn familiar now. Mylohyoids and digastrics tightening beneath her jaw. Sublingual and parotid glands flooding her mouth with unwanted saliva. She fought it, desperately thinking of something else—anything else—to take her mind off it. Bracing her elbows on the rim of the toilet seat, she buried her clammy forehead in her trembling hands and debated shoving a finger down her throat just to get it over with.

After a few minutes she was reasonably sure the threat of throwing up was over, so she crawled over to the door and snagged the hotel robe from a peg on the back. She wrapped it around her shivering body. Resting against the edge of the tub, she laid her head back and took some deep, calming breaths.

"Nev?" Rhys called from beyond the door. "You okay?"

"I'm good. Be out in a minute." Thankfully he let her be. When she'd collected herself, she rose and went to the sink to run the water. The aftermath routine helped center her even more. Cold water on the face and the back of the neck. The bracing tingle of her mint toothpaste. The cool flow of water down her parched throat.

Setting the glass tumbler on the vanity with a soft clink, she took a hand towel from the rack and patted her face and neck dry, then used the facecloth to swab between her breasts, under her arms and between her legs where she was still sticky from earlier. She met her weary eyes in the mirror.

It's over, Nev. There was nothing you could have done. Time to get on with your life.

The one waiting for her right outside the bathroom in the luxury king-size bed. So resolved, she opened the bathroom door ready to face Rhys.

He'd turned on the bedside lamp and sat propped up against the headboard, naked chest and abdomen exposed above the snowy white sheets. His eyes held hers, no doubt scrutinizing every detail of her appearance and gauging how he should approach her. "Flashback?"

"Yeah." She scratched the side of her neck and crossed to the bed. "I'm okay, though." Last thing she wanted was to seem weak in front of a man who saw things like she had on a daily basis in his job. How the hell did he cope with it? She thought about asking him. A tip or two would be welcome right now.

When she came close enough, Rhys lifted an arm and she slid into his side with a sigh. He tucked her in tight so her cheek nestled in the hollow of his shoulder and kissed her forehead. His long fingers ran through her hair. Heaven, she thought, breathing in his clean, musky fragrance. He was the best cure she could think of for nightmares.

The way he held her soothed her on so many levels. It made biological sense because his arms were around her back and her front was pressed against his chest. All her vital organs were covered and surrounded by him. Her body knew it on an instinctive level, just as her brain and heart understood she was safe in his embrace.

Rhys's other hand sought out her left one, resting on the hard slab of his pec. He laced their fingers together, never stopping that heavenly motion on her hair. "Would it help if you talked about it?"

She tensed.

"No pressure. Just wanted you to know the offer was there."

If she could talk to anyone about her ordeal other

than Sam and her shrink, it was Rhys. He'd seen where they'd held her. He knew what had happened to the other hostages. And his job in the Unit had probably exposed him to things even more horrific than what she'd lived through.

Maybe she should tell him. She trusted him. And she could tell him without having to make eye contact, which was probably why he'd asked her after she'd lain down on him. He'd known it would be easier for her. Rhys didn't do things by accident.

She swallowed. "If you don't mind."

"I wouldn't have said it if I hadn't meant it."

In as little time as she could manage, she outlined the dream. "I haven't had this one in a long time," she finished, rubbing a hand over her tired eyes. "Usually they're about you. I never get to you in time to save you."

His big hand moved gently over her back. "You had a really hard time over there. It's no surprise your subconscious can't let it go."

At least he was there to hold her this time. Every other time she'd had nightmares she'd woken alone to face her deepest fears by herself.

Trailing her fingers over his chest, she gathered her thoughts. "Do you ever have nightmares?"

A subtle tension filled him. "Sometimes."

"About things you've seen?"

His chest expanded as he drew in a deep breath, then he released it. "And done."

She waited while the silence stretched out, but he didn't elaborate and she wasn't going to push him. Rhys leaned over and switched off the lamp.

Disappointed he hadn't opened up but not all that surprised, Nev curled up closer. "Anything help?"

"Time," he said, turning his lips into her hair. "In time they'll fade."

He sounded so sure of that. “I hope so.”

“They will. It’s just hell while they’re still fresh.” The wistful note in those words made her look up into his shadowed face. He stared up at the ceiling, a million miles away though she was pressed flush against him.

“You can tell me if you want to,” she told him. “You can trust me never to repeat it.”

He glanced down and met her eyes, an almost startled smile on his lips.

“What?”

“I’ve never talked to anyone about it. Not even Ben.”

Was he going to tell her? “Well the offer stands. If you ever want to tell me, I’m here. I tell you mine, you tell me yours. Free therapy.”

Rhys surprised her by rolling her on top of him with her thighs bracketing his, and wrapped his arms around her back. The pressure was at once fierce and protective, yet still gentle. It turned her inside out. There was such pain inside him. A lingering grief from his childhood coupled with whatever he was thinking about now.

“You’re such a sweetheart,” he murmured against the crown of her head.

“I care about you.”

He took another of those slow breaths, as though considering whether to tell her. “I’d tell you, but…”

“But what?”

He shook his head slightly. “I don’t want it to change how you see me.”

She closed her eyes against the ache beneath her ribs. Whatever he was hiding, the story was ugly enough that he was afraid he would lose her. She so desperately wanted to give him comfort. “I promise to listen and not judge. It won’t change how I see you.” It was all she could say to reassure him.

A few minutes passed. Just when she was sure he

wasn't going to say anything else, he finally spoke. "There was an op," he began, fingers sifting through her hair again. "Three years ago now, in the Balkans. When I was fairly new to the Unit."

Neveah kept her cheek pressed against his chest and listened closely to the words. She knew how hard it was for Rhys to reveal this part of himself to her, just like she also knew how much he must trust her in order to do it.

His voice seemed deeper than usual as he continued. "It was a targeted hit. Know what I'm saying?"

She nodded, afraid to speak in case it broke his rhythm. An assassination, he meant. From reading her books, she already knew Delta operators performed missions like that.

"He was an ex-soldier turned Mafia arms dealer, and stirred up enough trouble that the CIA put out a contract on him." Rhys's fingers paused in their soothing motion. "We were briefed and given a file, and my spotter and I went out."

Nev stayed where she was, determined not to tense up or do anything to make him stop, though she dreaded what he was going to say.

"I'd never done a hit like that before. Not on someone that wasn't a direct threat to me or my men." He seemed to gather himself, his muscles growing tighter beneath her. "He was with his family when it happened. At a resort with his wife and kids. They didn't see it, but I'm sure they found his body."

Nev bit her lip, glad he couldn't see her face. Those poor children.

"I did it with one clean shot, then packed up and walked away just like I was leaving the office after a day's work. I went back to the barracks and slept right through the night."

She tried to imagine it, but couldn't.

"The next morning I looked at myself in the mirror and saw a stranger staring back at me."

Oh, Rhys…

"I didn't feel anything, and not because I was in shock or denial or any of that. I'd just carried out an execution for the government and it didn't bother me at all." He gave a tired sigh. "How's that for a revelation? I really was the cold, remote shell people thought I was."

"Don't say that," Nev argued, unable to hold back. "If you really had no conscience it wouldn't have bothered you enough to think about it afterward. You did your job because you'd been trained to do it. Last time I checked, the military doesn't ask for your permission when they give an order." She came up on an elbow and turned his face toward her with her palm. He dropped his gaze, as though ashamed of what he'd just admitted. "You're not a monster, Rhys, and you're not a remote shell of a man. I'm living proof of that."

The muscles in his beautiful square jaw tensed.

"Know how I know?" She waited until he met her eyes. "By the way you look at me and the way you touch me." Lifting one of his hands, she laid her palm against his. "Look how big you are compared to me. Yet you've always been gentle. You came back to hold my hand when I asked for you in Afghanistan, and you kept holding it at the rendezvous point. You're not dead inside, Rhys, you're afraid to let people in. The wall you've put up to protect yourself is not the true reflection of the man you are inside. Don't ever confuse the two."

Rhys rolled into her, pressing his face into her neck. "God… I don't deserve you."

"Why the hell not?"

He chuckled at her show of temper. "I'm not…easy to get close to."

"Only because you make it that way."

A long beat passed. "Sure you're not afraid of me now?"

"Positive." She only wished she could help absolve him of the guilt he so obviously carried, but that was between him and his maker. "I wish you could see who you really are."

"But that part of me is still in there."

"We all have light and dark in us, Rhys. All of us." She knew he was afraid of losing control of that part of himself. "You saw that in me when you came in for the extraction." She would have killed the next person coming through the door to hurt her or Mike, or would have died trying. It still shook her to know she had that capacity in her. "What's important is how strong the light is."

"You're my light, Nev."

His quiet words shocked her, and she froze for an instant. Then she smiled, though he couldn't see her. "See? If your soul was dead you wouldn't say sweet things like that."

A low laugh rumbled through his chest, vibrating against her skin. He tugged her down so that she was cradled in his arms again and kissed her temple. "What's something you've always wanted to do but never had the chance?"

Surprised by the abrupt change in subject, it took her a moment to decide. Life was so precious to her now. There were so many things she wanted to see and do, to accomplish before she died. "I want to travel more. Maybe climb Kilimanjaro."

He pulled back and looked into her eyes. "Seriously?"

"Yep. Always wanted to. What about you?"

He stayed quiet for a moment. "I want to travel more too. As a civilian. Climbing Kili sounds like fun, though." His hand resumed stroking her hair. "I doubt

I'll ever be able to make it back to the Unit with my brain injury and all, but I'm definitely up for that trip. Want to go with me sometime?"

Her eyes widened. That was pretty long term planning for someone who didn't do relationships. *Don't read anything into it. He's just talking out loud.* "I'd go anywhere with you."

Rhys focused on her as her words sank in. "Yeah?"

"Absolutely. That's how safe I feel with you."

A slow smile spread across his face. "I'm glad." He kissed her softly on the mouth, a quiet *thank you*. "Ready to sleep now?"

She nudged the erection prodding her stomach with her hip. "Are you?"

He grunted. "Just ignore it and it'll go away."

"What if I don't want to ignore it?"

He squeezed her hip to make her stay still. "Just lie here with me and get some sleep. Long day ahead of you tomorrow." His low words came with him draping one leg over hers.

Neveah had so many things she wanted to say to him. Instead, she stroked his short hair and kneaded the back of his neck, reveling in his growls of enjoyment. For now, having him relaxed and trusting in her arms was going to have to be enough.

Chapter Ten

They pulled into White Rock early that afternoon with twenty minutes to spare before the ceremony started. Stepping out of the truck, Neveah pulled in a deep breath of the cold, salt-scented air.

The morning had been gray and overcast, but now the clouds were breaking up. Wide patches of cerulean sky showed through, and sunbeams arrowed down toward the earth. The faint cry of gulls rose from the beach down the hillside from the church. Its gleaming white exterior sat perched amongst well-manicured gardens, something the bride was sure to approve of. Shame there weren't any flowers blooming to add splashes of color to the evergreen shrubs bordering the steps.

Wrapping her black woolen shawl over her shoulders, Nev smiled at Rhys when he took her arm. He was a sight to behold in his black tux and crisp white shirt. The perfectly tailored jacket emphasized the breadth of his powerful shoulders, and the wraparound shades he wore made him look like a Secret Service agent.

"What?" he asked, sharing her smile.

"You look like a movie star with those things on."

His eyebrows swooped together. "What kind of movie star?"

"A badass action hero."

"Good. All the single guys will know to keep their hands off you."

She snickered. Like they wouldn't anyhow. With the size of him? Only a suicidal maniac would even think of it. And after last night, the simple memory of the pleasure he'd given her made her belly flip.

Nev squeezed his forearm with her hand, then ran a light caress over the steely muscles beneath the sleeve. My oh my, what a beautiful man he was. And hers, for now at least. It made her giddy to think she'd had all those muscles pressed against her naked skin the night before. She'd run her hands over his smooth skin long after he'd tugged the covers over them both. He'd purred like a contented panther the whole time, gouging out another chunk of her heart for himself. If it wasn't entirely his already.

He might appear to the rest of the world as being impervious to pain and the very human need for companionship, but the way he'd soaked up her affection last night proved how starved he'd been for it. The thought made her ache for him and want to make up for the terrible, lonely childhood he'd suffered. She wanted to hold him in her arms and caress him for hours or even days until he felt wanted and loved. Now there was a cause she could get behind.

Her throat tightened. Yeah, she loved him. The feelings inside her were too strong to be based on infatuation and gratitude. And as for the way he felt about her, she knew actions spoke louder than words for him. Judging from that, he must care about her a lot. Still, she had to face that Rhys might not ever be able to love her the way she loved him. It was possible he might never let himself feel that deeply for anyone but his brother, whom he trusted with his life.

Assuming Rhys was even capable of having a long term, committed relationship with her, could she be happy without an "I love you"? If she was honest, no, but she still held out hope that he would feel secure enough about her to acknowledge his feelings at some point in the future.

"Bryn's already inside," Rhys said, helping her up the concrete steps. His grip was firm but not overbearing, just enough to be able to catch her if she slipped in her high heels. The constant respect and consideration he afforded her was another thing she loved about him. One of so many, but telling him would no doubt spook the holy hell out of him. It was damn hard keeping the words inside, since she was used to telling it like it was.

For once in her life, the brain/mouth filter was working. Thank God.

An usher at the tall front door of the church opened it for them, and Rhys led her inside. A deep red carpet runner lay on the dark oak floor, leading through the foyer and into the main vestibule with its jewel-toned stained glass windows filling the room with shards of colored light.

"Oh," she whispered, taking in the huge arrangements of stargazer lilies and raspberry pink roses surrounding the altar.

"They're in there," Rhys said, gesturing to an office off the vestibule. "You okay with waiting here for a few minutes?"

"Of course." Before he could leave, she leaned up and kissed his cheek. Just a quick one, nothing too embarrassing for a man completely opposed to public displays of affection, but enough to proclaim her feelings for him. His lips twitched in a quick smile when he pulled back, but he gave her hand a squeeze before turning away.

Knocking on the oak door, she pushed it open when someone invited her in. She slipped inside and smiled at Bryn, a knockout in her navy blue bridesmaid's gown with her hair swept up in an elegant twist. "Hi."

Bryn already knew the boys were there to provide security, so all Nev had to do was keep that fact from the rest of them. Though she doubted either Emily or Christa hadn't figured out there was something going on.

"Hey," Bryn said, coming over to give her a hug. "You're just in time. We're about to put her train on." Rounding a partition, Neveah caught her breath at the sight of Christa, decked out in her ballerina-style white gown amidst Bryn, Emily and another bridesmaid whose heavily pregnant belly protruded beneath her gown. "Wow."

Christa turned and grinned at her. "Not bad for a ballplayer, right?"

"Not bad for a cover model."

Christa laughed and glanced at Bryn. "I really like her."

"So do I," Bryn said, coming over with a bouquet of flowers. "Here, hold this for a second, will you? This is Teryl, by the way."

Nev nodded hello to the pregnant woman. "Want me to hold yours, too?"

"That would be great," Teryl said with a smile. "I'm carrying enough weight around these days, if you know what I mean."

Nev took the bouquets, inhaling the heady sweetness of the stargazers. The things had to weigh five pounds each. Upon closer inspection, she found a softball tied to the bottom of each. "Nice touch," she said with a laugh.

Christa grinned. "Thanks." She pivoted so Emily

and Bryn could adjust the hooks on the train, and then Bryn lifted the armful of tulle and lace. She spread it out into a fan shape that trailed six feet behind Christa on the floor, and stood back to admire her while Teryl fussed with the veil.

"You're stunning," Nev told her, already getting choked up.

"We're so proud of you," Emily gushed, enveloping her in a hug. "I'm so lucky to be getting you for a daughter-in-law."

"Hey," Bryn ordered, clapping her hands. "No crying. I mean it. You'll ruin Christa's makeup, because once you start it's all over for the rest of us. Plus we've got an expectant mother here, and everyone knows they cry over everything." She glanced over at Nev. "Dec here yet?"

"Rhys went to find him and Luke."

Emily's head swung around. "Luke's already here?"

Nev saw the flicker of panic in Emily's eyes and nodded, not knowing what to say.

"Don't worry," Christa soothed, as though comforting Emily was more important than the fact her wedding was minutes away. "You won't have to sit with him and I bet you won't even see him until after the ceremony."

"Yeah," Emily said, a hand over her stomach as though she was fighting back nerves. She met Nev's gaze and forced a wan smile. "Haven't seen him in years. Not since the day he flew in from Louisiana to haul Rayne off to boot camp."

"What a day that must have been," Christa laughed, trying to brighten the mood.

"Oh, it was," Emily agreed with a wicked smile, making it plain something equally memorable had happened between her and her ex that day.

Someone knocked on the door once and then Ben popped his head in. "You guys ready to rock?"

They all looked at Christa, who gave them the most serene smile Neveah had ever seen. "Yes." Like a fairy princess with her train trailing behind her, she came over and collected her bouquet. "Thanks," she said to Nev, her hands rock steady.

"You're welcome. I'd wish you luck, but you don't look like you need it."

The woman's light blue eyes sparkled. "Please. After facing international-level pitchers and cheating death? Nothing could rattle me now."

Putting on a smile, Nev prayed that statement wouldn't be tested.

****

Outside the church door, Rhys stood with Luke and Dec while the guests passed into the foyer for the wedding. Considering he was the father of the groom, Luke didn't look too happy about being there. His dark brows were pulled together slightly above his wraparound shades, like he was deep in thought.

Or in a shitload of pain. Rhys watched him closely.

"Feeling okay?" Dec asked Luke, studying him with shrewd golden eyes. "You don't look so good."

"Yeah. Fine." He tugged at the collar of his tux. He wasn't fine. Rhys had never seen Luke so pale, and he doubted the thought of facing his ex-wife was the reason for his pinched expression. If he was worried about security, though, Rhys didn't blame him. Each of them carrying a single, concealed pistol to deal with the threat level confronting them was a joke.

Even with him, Ben and Dec here to add additional security, plus Luke's old buddy Nate and half the Vancouver PD prowling the grounds—not to mention that half the men inside the church were Emergency Response Team cops—none of it guaranteed everyone's safety. No wonder Luke wasn't feeling well.

"Everything's locked down tight," Dec commented, scanning the parking lot and grounds from their position.

The boss nodded. "Good."

Except it wasn't. No matter how careful they'd been in setting up their security, no amount of personnel and vigilance could prevent an RPG or a vehicle full of explosives from detonating close enough to take out the whole building. Or to stop a well disguised sniper hidden from view waiting to put a round through someone's head.

As Rhys watched, Luke pulled in two slow, deep breaths, clenching his jaw tight. Yeah. The guy was in serious pain. And maybe fighting not to puke because of it.

Rhys glanced at Dec, who looked at Luke closely. "You get your head checked yet?"

"Yeah, I'm tight." But when Luke turned his head to nod at the undercover officers making their way to the outer perimeter they had established earlier, he stopped as suddenly as if someone had shot him. Pressing his lips together, he put out a hand to grip the railing beside him and swallowed hard. Several times.

Rhys's stomach clenched in sympathy. *Oh, shit.* How serious was this? He debated getting Neveah, but held off because it would piss Luke off to draw attention to his condition. He decided to wait until after the ceremony and see how Luke was then, but hoped the hell whatever was going on wouldn't impede Luke's performance if something came up.

The concussion Luke had suffered in Basra on the night they'd gone in to rescue Bryn should have resolved sufficiently by now. When they'd gone into the mountains of Afghanistan to free Neveah a few weeks after the injury, the symptoms had landed Luke flat on his face in the middle of a firefight, and Sam had been forced to take care of business for him. After that, Luke had stayed busy tracking Tehrazzi plus dealing with the issue of proving Sam's innocence, and probably hadn't bothered to seek medical attention.

Rhys would bet his left nut Luke hadn't gone in because he knew damned well the doctors wouldn't let him out for at least a while. If that happened, he would've lost the tenuous thread he had on Tehrazzi's location and maybe not made his son's wedding. Both of those hadn't been an option, so Luke had carried on with his work and coped as best he could with his symptoms.

Maybe the flight to Vancouver had exacerbated them. Well, that and the stress of being here facing a likely threat to him and his family. That the pain was still there made it clear Luke was dealing with more than just a simple concussion.

Just then Bryn strode out, stunning and exotic in her clingy, floor-length navy bridesmaid's dress. Dec's hard face broke into a wide smile, dimples flashing in his lean cheeks. "There's my girl," he purred, curling a possessive arm around her waist and drawing her close to his body.

Bryn smiled up at him and then turned her gaze on Rhys and Luke. "They're ready to start. You should come inside now."

"Y'all go ahead," Luke told her and Dec. "Rhys and I'll wait by the back entrance."

Bryn frowned at him. "You're supposed to sit up front, with Emily."

Luke's eyebrows shot up above the tops of his wraparound shades, but when he opened his mouth to argue, she cut him off.

"They've left a spot for you in the first row. You're supposed to walk Emily down the aisle and seat her."

Her frown deepened. "It was a last minute change. Didn't Rayne tell you?"

Luke's hesitation was a clear no. "What about Alex?"

Rhys didn't know who Alex was, but he caught the sudden tension in Luke's shoulders as he asked the question, and figured it out fast.

Bryn gave Luke a sympathetic look. "Emily broke up with him months ago."

Drawing another deep breath, Luke forced a nod. "It's okay. I got it." Without looking back, he walked into the church like a man preparing to face a firing squad.

Behind him, Rhys exchanged a pointed look with Dec. Whatever the hell was going on here, they would both have to keep a close eye on Luke until this was over.

****

The ceremony made Nev's eyes sting despite how she kept part of her attention on Rhys, Dec and Ben, positioned around the church. They didn't move though, so that eased some of the anxiety swirling through her. Luke was up front, a few seats from Emily, and even without knowing all the details Nev could see the uncomfortable tension between them in their posture. With effort, she turned her attention back to the wedding.

At the altar in his red serge RCMP uniform, the groom took Christa's face in his hands and kissed her to seal the vows they'd made, and Nev's throat closed up. They looked so blissfully happy, and knowing the story of how Christa had barely escaped her deranged stalker only make their happy ending sweeter.

Their love for each other was so strong they almost

glowed with it. *This* was what life was about. To enjoy it to the fullest and appreciate every moment because you never knew which would be your last. And if you were incredibly lucky, you might find someone you loved to spend some of those moments with.

Too bad Rhys wasn't a happily-ever-after kind of guy.

On the lawn afterward, Nev watched Rayne pull his new bride close and whisper something in her ear that made her cheeks turn bright pink. Her pale blue eyes swung up to his face, brimming with laughter. Nev could not believe the striking resemblance between Rayne and Luke. It was uncanny.

"Not gonna cry on me, are you?"

Laughing, she leaned against Rhys's shoulder when he came up beside her. "No. I don't do it often, and it was during a wedding after all. You're safe until you take me to another one."

"Like next year?"

The question startled her, but then she realized he was talking about Ben and Sam's wedding and didn't necessarily mean he thought they'd still be together then. What would she do if they weren't? As practical and mature as she was, she didn't think she could stomach the thought of seeing Rhys under those circumstances without dying a little. "I'll work on it. That's all I can promise."

He threaded his fingers through hers. "Good enough."

Ben strolled over. "Let's beat the crowd and get down to the beach before all the parking's gone. Photographer is already on his way down there."

Rhys glanced down at her feet. "Will you be all right walking in those? We've got a couple hours to kill before the reception."

"Sure I can walk, if it's not for too long." He guided

her across the lush green grass and parking lot. The sun warmed her skin, making the air unseasonably warm. It felt lovely.

Helping her into the back seat with a firm grip on her hand, he shut the door and went around to the driver's side. Ben got in the front passenger seat. "Nice day for a wedding, huh?" he said, light green eyes hidden behind wraparound shades identical to his brother's. They looked more alike today than she'd ever seen them. How come all the men in Luke's circle were so damned good-looking?

"Beautiful," she agreed. "I wish Sam was here, though."

"Me too. We're great on the dance floor together." He tilted his shades down until she could see the pale green of his irises. "You'll stand in for her though, right?"

"Of course I will." Her eyes went to Rhys's reflection in the rearview mirror, but he didn't say anything.

"He won't be dancing," Ben said, correctly interpreting her glance. "Maybe you haven't noticed, but he's not really a party kind of guy."

"No need to be when you're around," Rhys remarked, pulling out of the lot and onto the quiet road. "You have enough fun for both of us."

"Yeah, because you're socially retarded."

Nev bit back a smile, but a pang of sadness hit her. She remembered at the club in Paris how Rhys had stayed off to the side of the dance floor, up against the wall as he kept a watchful eye on her and Sam to guard them from possible threats. At the time she'd thought he was just keeping his distance because he was working and didn't want to become distracted, but now she knew better.

After hearing about the twins' upbringing from

Bryn, Nev was positive he'd adopted that tactic deliberately as a way to shield himself. He'd probably developed the defense mechanism as a kid. Someone had hurt him terribly, and she bet it was his birth mother. Her betrayal had taught Rhys at an early age that even the people who were meant to love and protect you couldn't be trusted. It also explained the relationship he had with Ben.

Ben leaned forward to turn up the radio, and the big vehicle pulsed with bass for a few seconds until Rhys shot a hand out and turned the volume down. "Nev, tell him what prolonged exposure to loud music does to your eardrums."

"I would imagine it does the same amount of damage as prolonged exposure to gunfire and explosives," she said.

Ben laughed and punched him in the shoulder. "See? We're fucked either way, pal."

"Watch your mouth."

Pulling off his shades, Ben sighed and looked back at her. "Sorry. Good thing I've got the language police here to keep me in line."

She winked. "No offense taken. I've heard the word before."

His smile could melt chocolate at a hundred paces. "See why I love her?" he said to Rhys.

"Don't let your manners slip just because she tolerates you for Sam's sake."

"There's nothing wrong with my manners." He swiveled to face the windshield and let out a sigh. "Man, this is the best assignment I've ever been on," he said. "Nice place."

Nev agreed. White Rock was a beautiful seaside town nestled into the hillside. Its houses spilled down the slope to Marine Drive where the shops and restaurants lay. Even in mid-November the beach was busy on this sunny Saturday. People jogged and walked the brick paved promenade and down the long wooden pier jutting out into the water. She drank in the sights eagerly.

"Is that the Pacific Ocean?" she asked. Looked way too calm to be.

"No," Rhys answered. "Semiahmoo Bay."

She peered harder out the window at the slate blue masses of land dotting the water in the distance. "What islands are those?"

"The San Juans are to the south. They're American, and the Gulf Islands to the north are Canadian. The border with Blaine is right across the bay," he said, pointing for her. "And Point Roberts is that way." He gestured out Ben's window. "It's American, too. Forty-ninth parallel runs right across it."

The border between the U.S. and Canada. She gazed out the driver's side where a majestic snow-capped mountain rose in the east. "What's that?"

"Mount Baker. A pyroclastic volcano."

A volcano that erupted with ash, mud and gas, rather than lava. "Like Mount St. Helens?"

"Yeah, but dormant right now."

Ben faced her and shook his head. "Jesus, the two of you together are something else. A human Google link. One of you should see if you can get a spot on *Jeopardy!* —you'd make millions."

She took that as a compliment. She loved how knowledgeable Rhys was. "You'd be great to travel with," she told him.

He met her eyes in the rearview mirror for a moment. "Why's that?"

"Because you'd be the ultimate tour guide."

"I've traveled with him," Ben said with a shake of his head. "Trust me, it wasn't that fun."

She snorted. "To where, some godforsaken hole of a war torn country?"

"Well, some of those. But we've gone to nice places together too. Hawaii, for one. I had a great time, but I'm not so sure about him," he said, jerking his chin at Rhys.

Rhys shrugged his wide shoulders and pulled into a parking lot. "It was okay."

Ben looked back at her. "He's the best shot I've seen and he's a walking encyclopedia, I'll give him that, but he never lets himself have any fun."

"How about we change the subject?" Rhys suggested, parking the truck. He shut off the ignition and climbed out, but Ben was already opening her door and helping her down.

"Thanks," she said, smiling up at him. She had two of the hottest and most capable men on the planet flanking her, and it made her feel like a celebrity. Despite Rhys seeming unaffected by everything around him, even he couldn't have missed the appreciative looks women gave him when he walked by.

A warm glow lit inside her when he took her hand and laced his fingers through hers in a gesture of possession, because she knew how significant it was. A public display of affection! She caught Ben's approving grin and returned it, feeling on top of the world. Too bad they had hours left until she could get Rhys naked in her hotel room. On the plus side, though, the entire day was shaping up to be a foreplay marathon. By the time she got him alone later on, she'd be so primed one touch from him might send her over the edge. She looked forward to finding out.

Nev breathed in deeply of the cool ocean air, catching the sweet vanilla scent of fresh waffle cones and the smell of deep fried fish and chips. "Mmm, that smells so good…"

"Want some?" Ben offered.

One look at Rhys's face convinced her he wanted

no part of that deep fried gluttony, so she took Ben's arm. "Let's go."

They all walked across the street to a fish-and-chips place called Moby Dick's where a substantial line of patrons waited to pick up their orders. In her experience the best places to eat were the ones the locals frequented, and this had all the earmarks of a good one.

She hung back with Rhys while Ben ordered their food, and smiled at the people giving them curious looks. "Wedding," she explained, gesturing to their attire, and received several smiles. Beside her, Rhys loomed large and imposing. He and Ben would make a great good cop-bad cop team.

Ben turned away from the take out window once he'd paid and glanced down as he drew his phone out. The happy expression on his face left no doubt it was Sam on the other end.

Nev withheld a wistful sigh. The man she loved was standing right next to her, but she couldn't tell him. If she did, she risked losing him forever. For God's sake, Rhys had a hard enough time putting his arm around her in public.

After a minute, Ben walked over and held out his phone. "Sam wants to say hello."

"Hi, hon," she said when she put the phone to her ear, wandering a few steps away. She could feel Rhys's gaze following her.

"I have to make this quick," her cousin said without preamble.

Nev stiffened at the tense tone. "What? What's wrong?"

"Don't let them know I'm telling you this, or Ben'll kill me."

She deliberately relaxed her posture. "Okay. Go ahead."

"I don't know all the details because I don't have

security clearance, but I've managed to access some files."

Hacked into them, she meant. "Sam—"

"Just listen. Stay close to the boys, okay?"

The ominous warning made her skin prickle. "I will, but it's not like I have a choice. Rhys is on me like a shadow."

"Good. Let him do his job."

Nev's fingers tightened around the phone. Something bad had happened. Sam would never scare her like this otherwise. "Tell me."

A hard sigh came across the line. "There's chatter out there connecting Tehrazzi with a cell in Vancouver."

Her stomach rolled at the mention of his name. That's why Luke had brought the boys in. Unfortunately, it didn't come as a complete surprise. She'd known from the outset something important had brought the twins here. She swallowed, fighting to stay calm. "Okay. What else?"

"That's all I know. I just wanted to make sure you keep your eyes open."

"I will. You better not get your ass fired over this, Sam."

"Please," her cousin snorted in an insulted tone. "Like I'd let them find out."

Nev swiveled her head and met two stares pinning her, one navy and the other icy green. "Uh oh, the Secret Service is giving me the hairy eyeball."

"I'll let you go, then. Just tell them we talked about my wedding dress, and you can't give anything away."

"Will do. Love you."

"Love you too. Be safe."

Ending the call, Nev walked back and handed Ben his phone, doing her best to not look spooked. A possible link between Tehrazzi and a local cell did not mean there was a plot in the works, she told herself firmly, putting on a smile. "She's pretty excited about her dress."

"I'll bet," Rhys said dryly as he slid his shades back on, telling her he didn't believe a word of it. She almost flat out asked him what the situation with the local cell was, but knew damn well he'd never tell her anything. She couldn't betray her cousin by saying anything, and there was nothing more she could do to keep herself safe besides being alert and staying close to the twins. For now, she'd have to lock her anxiety away where it wouldn't show.

Just then, the lady at the takeout window called out their order number. Nev grabbed Ben's hand and towed him over. Despite the lingering tension in her gut, she was still hungry, and eating would help convince Rhys that Sam hadn't said anything she shouldn't have. "Sure you don't want any?" she called to him.

"No thanks."

"You're so pure," Ben called out to him over his shoulder. Together they drenched the fries with vinegar and got little cups full of ketchup and tartar sauce. On the first crispy, salty bite of fish, Nev let out a moan.

"Oh yeah," Ben agreed, popping part of the piece into his mouth.

Rhys shook his head at them in disgust. "That stuff will kill you."

Nev laughed. "One piece won't."

"My heart's stopped once already, thanks. Don't want to tempt fate."

His wry sense of humor, whenever he let it show, never failed to amuse her. "Oh come on," she teased. "Have one if you want it. Promise I won't tell." When he didn't reply, she went right up to him and leaned up so that her mouth was close to his ear. The delicious smell of his cologne drifted up to tease her. "If your heart did stop, I bet I could get it started without a defibrillator this time."

In response, he lowered his head until his mouth brushed her ear, sending shivers across her skin. "Baby, I know you could. But if it's going to stop around you again, it'll be because I'm inside you."

Chapter Eleven

After his brother and Nev polished off their revolting snack, they all walked down the brick-paved promenade past the famous White Rock, and down the length of the wooden pier while the photographer took shots of the wedding party. Boats bobbed in their moorings on one side of it, and on the other a group of children gathered around a crabbing pot to examine the catch just pulled from the water. Their delighted squeals made him smile.

At his side, Nev peered over the end railing at the purple starfish clinging to the rocks below the water line. Whatever Sam had told her didn't seem to have spoiled the day for her, so he left it alone. But Nev knew something was up. He'd seen the way her shoulders had stiffened at something Sam said. His conscience squirmed, but he ignored it. He still couldn't tell her what he knew, and hoped to God he wouldn't have to.

He went back to enjoying the view of the beautiful woman before him. The cool breeze played with the tendrils of hair framing her face. She was so damn pretty like that. Her enthusiasm and natural curiosity about everything around her was almost magical. She wanted to drink in everything she could about what she experienced every single moment, like a sponge.

Looking death in the face might be partially responsible for her outlook, but Rhys understood it was who she was. She loved to learn.

If they'd had more privacy, he would have dragged her up against him and kissed the breath out of her just to feel her go soft and pliant in his arms. Damn, he loved how she responded to his touch and that her eyes went dreamy when he kissed her. When he'd slid inside her they'd gone all smoky, and her expression of absolute rapture when she'd come apart in his arms…

Withholding a groan, he wrestled his hormones into submission and focused on enjoying her presence. They had hours left until he'd be able to do anything to relieve the erection shoving painfully at his fly.

When the call came an hour later saying the pictures were done, he and Ben walked her back to the Escalade and Rhys drove the forty-five minutes to the reception at Seasons. Helping Nev out of the vehicle, his heart swelled at the tender smile she gave him. But he wasn't here to have a good time, he reminded himself. He was here to make sure she and everyone else stayed safe. Just because the day had gone without incident so far didn't mean it would stay that way.

They walked her to the entrance. The grounds sparkled with strands of white lights wound through the greenery, and the tall panes of the glass conservatory glowed in the darkness. None of the guests would ever guess snipers lay concealed in the foliage at strategic points, or that undercover police were on hand to prevent any problems. And none of them *would* know, because that's exactly the way Luke wanted it.

Inside the restaurant, they awaited the arrival of the bridal party and then dinner was served. At their table positioned near the exit, Rhys watched Luke pull out his phone and check the screen. After a moment, his dark brown eyes swung up and locked with his.

Oh, shit. Nudging Ben discreetly under the table, he laid a hand on Neveah's silky shoulder, loathe to leave her but needing to take care of whatever situation was brewing. "Will you excuse us for a few minutes?"

Her gaze delved into his, wide and alert. "Is everything okay?"

He forced a smile. "Everything's fine. We'll be back shortly." He let his palm sweep over her upper back as he left.

Ben was right beside him, snapping his gum. "What's up?"

"Boss doesn't look happy."

"Does he ever?"

Luke strode toward them with Dec on his heels. He walked out the French doors at the back of the room without looking back, trying not to draw attention from the other guests and knowing his team would follow.

They got as far as the row of boxwood hedges separating the lawn from the gardens when Luke wheeled around. "Security's detained a young south Asian guy in a Lexus at the first checkpoint. We're going in to have a chat with him and strip the vehicle."

"Any weapons?" Rhys asked.

"Not yet, but he's got all the earmarks of a gangbanger."

"Let's go introduce ourselves," Ben said in the way of a man looking forward to the coming altercation.

They split into two teams, Rhys going with Luke, and Ben pairing with Dec. On foot they quietly made their way through the gardens the same way they'd rehearsed, and approached the checkpoint from behind. The suspect stood next to his low-slung silver sports car with his hands on his head, his arguments falling on the deaf ears of two undercover cops that had stopped him.

One of them nodded at Luke as he and Rhys appeared out of the bushes on one side. The kid jumped and cursed, eyes pinballing between them as if they'd just materialized out of thin air. Which was exactly what he was supposed to think. A second later, Dec and Ben appeared on the other side.

"Damn!" The suspect jolted again, one hand going to his chest.

"Hands on your head," one of the cops growled, and the kid did as he was told, his eyes goggling because he suddenly faced four big men who'd appeared out of the shadows.

"What've we got here?" Luke drawled.

The second cop nodded at the rattled suspect and handed Luke a thin black wallet. "Says he's here to pick up a relative working at the reception."

"My cousin," the kid said, looking at them nervously. "He works at the restaurant."

Luke glanced at the ID in the wallet, then handed it to Rhys and folded his arms across his chest. "Well then, you won't mind if we take a look in your car." A very expensive luxury car owned by a kid that couldn't be past twenty-one. Kind of hard to imagine him being able to afford it by working a regular job.

He stiffened. "You need a warrant."

"Not tonight." Luke nodded to the cops. "Thanks boys, but we'll take it from here." They both smirked and walked away toward the second checkpoint.

"Who are you guys," the kid blurted as the cops' footsteps faded away in the distance. "SWAT or something?"

"Or something," Luke answered, and nodded at Rhys. "Take a look."

Rhys went around to the passenger side and started in the glove compartment. The name on the registration matched the driver's license. "Car's his," he told the others, digging through the contents. Oh yeah. "Bingo," he said, lifting out a 9 mm Beretta.

The kid swallowed and backed up a step as though he was thinking about bolting, but Ben was right behind him to growl, "Don't even think about it."

Luke stared at the guy dispassionately. "Now what on earth would a nice kid like you need a piece like that for?"

His Adam's apple bobbed hard. "I…I have a permit."

"Do you."

"It's for protection! I need to look after myself and my peeps."

"Like your cousin."

The kid dropped his gaze to the damp pavement, the pulse in his neck fluttering visibly.

"Turn around," Ben snapped, grabbing the kid's shoulders and shoving him face first against the door. He kicked his feet apart and systematically frisked him. "Two knives," he said, dropping them onto the pavement with a metallic clang. He patted over the kids coat pockets. "And a throwing star." He leaned around to look into his eyes. "You a ninja or something?"

"I want a lawyer," the kid blurted.

"I'll bet you do," Luke said.

Rhys carefully went through the rest of the interior while Dec tore the trunk apart. Rhys pulled up the carpets to check for any hidden compartments and found one tucked inside the back passenger foot well. Holding a penlight between his teeth, he opened it up and felt his stomach clench. "Luke," he said, letting his grim tone speak for him. In three seconds Luke was standing behind him.

"What've we got?"

Rhys reached in and lifted out a grenade. "Four of them."

Luke's jaw tightened and his eyes darkened with suppressed rage. "Anything else?"

Like they weren't enough? "Two AK clips."

"Dec," Luke called out. "Appears our young friend has a fondness for Kalashnikovs."

Dec looked up at them from around the trunk. "You shitting me?" Rhys understood his surprise. This wasn't the type of hardware you expected a gang-banger to carry around, so it looked like they might have something significant to face yet.

"Unfortunately, no."

Standing up, Rhys aimed a lethal look at the kid as he thought of what could have happened at the reception if the cops hadn't spotted him. Christ, Nev and Luke's family were in there. He opened his mouth to start demanding answers, but Luke beat him to it, putting his face inches from the suspect's.

"Who the fuck are you working with?"

The kid wouldn't look at him. "Not saying anything else until I get a lawyer."

"No?"

This could turn real ugly in a heartbeat. Luke was on a hair trigger, and with the amount of firepower they'd just uncovered, the kid could have killed everyone at the reception. Twice.

Rhys looked at his brother, still pinning the suspect to the vehicle. "Ben, alert the others quietly, then go back in and make sure everything's secure while we get to the bottom of this."

Ben nodded and drilled the kid with a venomous look before giving him a shove and jogging away.

"Found it," Dec said, tossing pieces of the AK- 47 to the ground with a clunk. "Hid the pieces in the undercarriage and behind the spare tire."

Rhys could hear Ben's voice carrying to them as he gave instructions for the undercover cops inside the reception via his radio. A few minutes later, a police cruiser pulled up and Nate stepped out. "Hey. Heard you found some interesting hardware. He cooperating?" he asked of the suspect.

"Nope. Says he's here to pick up his cousin. Just happens to have grenades, a Beretta and an AK."

Nate's brows lifted. "That right? Well, you messed with the wrong people, kid. You might have noticed the size of these guys and their familiarity with weapons. I could tell you who that is," he said, nodding to Luke, "but then he'd have to kill you. I recommend you not piss him off any more than you already have. Start talking."

"I want a lawyer."

Nate stared at him pityingly. "You know what? I'm dying for a Starbucks right now. Maybe I'll take off for a while and come back after I've had my latte."

"You can't leave me with them!" the kid cried. "You haven't even arrested me or charged me with anything!"

"So remiss of me," Nate murmured, then in a quick move grabbed the kid's wrist to twist it up and behind him, while slamming him into the car again. Hard. The kid let out an "oof" and struggled up onto his toes to stop his shoulder from being wrenched out of its socket. "You have the right to remain silent," Nate growled and Mirandized him. Once the cuffs were on, he shoved him to his knees on the pavement. "Talk. Now. Last chance."

"Your cousin's name," Luke commanded, his drawl all but lost in his anger.

The kid swung his eyes up, all four of them towering over him with deadly serious expressions on their faces. Rhys's muscles coiled tight under his suit jacket. He thought about drawing his weapon to hurry the interrogation along, but the kid was now protected by civilian law. Damn shame.

"Has-Hassan," he finally stuttered, flinching when Rhys shifted his stance. "He's one of the wait staff."

Luke met Rhys's and Dec's gaze. "Get on it." Without a word they took off back to the reception, leaving Luke and Nate to find out if this was the threat they'd been anticipating, or if there were more to come.

****

Nev glanced at her watch. Twenty minutes and they weren't back yet. Something had to be wrong. Sam's warning kept playing in her head.

Tehrazzi. He's here.

The thought made her skin crawl. She rubbed her damp palms on the linen napkin in her lap and made a conscious effort to relax while she waited for Emily to return from the ladies' room. There couldn't be any imminent danger to her or anyone else in the room, or the men would never have left them. Whatever they'd gone to take care of must be preventative.

"Welcome to my world."

She glanced up as Bryn dropped into a chair next to her. "Where did they go?"

"No idea, but it must have been serious enough to warrant a firsthand look." She shook her head. "Someone would have to be frigging nuts to try anything here. The whole place is full of ERT members and ex-Marines, let alone our guys."

But radical militants *were* nuts, that's what made them so dangerous, and Bryn knew that every bit as well as she did. As for Tehrazzi…he was either insane or incredibly, scarily brilliant. Nev wasn't sure which of those options scared her worse, but she was betting he was a little bit of both.

Hating that she was sitting there when Rhys might be in danger at that same moment, Nev studied Bryn.

She was a survivor too, and now engaged to a man who risked his life each time he went to work. She would never know where he was or what he was doing, or when he'd be home again.

Nev shook her head. "How do you stand it?"

Bryn blew out a breath and met her eyes, not even pretending to misunderstand. "Truthfully? I haven't had to worry about him since we came stateside. Until now." Her fake smile was less than amused. "When he does go back overseas…I'll just have to suck it up and do the best I can."

Nev appreciated her honesty. "I don't know what I'd do."

"You'd better figure it out fast."

"What?"

Bryn rolled her expressive black eyes. "Please. Don't insult my intelligence by sitting there pretending you and Rhys are not ga-ga over each other."

For a moment, Neveah was speechless. It wasn't every day she met someone as outspoken as she was.

"It's always the biggest that fall the hardest," Bryn said with a grin.

If only that were true. What she wouldn't give for Rhys to fall in love with her. "You know how he is. I don't think he'll ever let himself be that vulnerable."

"Oh, he'll struggle with it," Bryn conceded. "But you already mean a lot to him. You're the reason he came here."

The bottom of her stomach dropped out. "I am?" He'd placed himself in danger specifically for her? Again?

Bryn nodded, making the lights glimmer in her sable updo. "He told Ben he wasn't sure if he was equipped to go back into the field, but the second Ben mentioned your name, Rhys was in. He likes working with the guys and all, but you were the coin that tipped the scales."

Glancing away, Nev put a hand over the suddenly hard ball of her stomach.

"Hey," Bryn soothed, grasping her hand. "They're the best, and they're careful. They'll be all right."

They were still flesh and blood, just like the rest of them, and their bodies were every bit as vulnerable to injury and disease. "That might mean more to me if I hadn't witnessed him dying already."

Bryn flinched, no doubt remembering Dec's own close call. "Yeah. Point taken."

The speeches had finished and the staff was busy getting the dance floor cleared off when Ben came back to the table. Neveah sighed in relief and waited for him to sit down, studying his face for any signs of stress, but his expression was calm.

Bryn beat her to it. "Well? What's going on?"

He helped himself to a forkful of scalloped potatoes from her plate with an impish smile. "Whaddya mean, sweets?"

"Ben," Bryn warned through clenched teeth, "do me the courtesy of *not* treating me like an idiot. What the hell is going on?"

Nev silently applauded her and added her own glare.

"Just had to clear up a thing or two with the staff," he said evasively.

She and Bryn looked at each other. Yeah, right. But whatever had made the four of them tear out of there must have been dealt with, because after another few minutes she caught sight of Rhys through the far door, approaching the entrance with Luke and Dec. Luke looked a bit drawn, but she couldn't see any overt signs of concern or danger so she let herself relax. Bryn jumped up and went to Dec, who lifted her off the floor and kissed her soundly. Neveah went to Rhys.

Ordering her heart to slow down, she gave him a big smile and was shocked when he came up and hauled her into his arms for a tight hug. Returning the embrace, she gave Ben a startled look over Rhys's shoulder but he just grinned and shrugged. When Rhys released her, she narrowed her eyes. "What's wrong? What happened?"

"Nothing. Just missed you."

As far as excuses went, that one was pathetic. She was about to demand an explanation when Ben came up to take her hand. "Dancing's about to start," he said, eyes alight with mischief. "I believe you promised me a dance." Neveah glanced behind her. Bryn was already making her way back to the table.

Damn she hated being kept out of the loop, but neither of them would tell her anything, so it looked like Rhys had just earned a reprieve. For now, she thought as she let Ben lead her to the edge of the dance floor.

Chapter Twelve

Against all odds, Rhys's heart rate was close to normal when Ben drew Neveah away. He made his way back to their table with Luke between him and Dec. They flanked him like bodyguards because they were afraid he might keel over. If their boss had been pale before the security incident, now he was downright ashen. Who the hell could blame him?

Rhys consciously slowed his breathing. Shit, that had been close. His whole body battled the adrenaline wave and the knowledge of how close the threat had come to everyone at the reception. Especially Neveah. The thought of anyone hurting her again galvanized him to do whatever he had to in order to keep her safe. In his heightened state, the loud music hit his eardrums like mortar rounds, so he could only imagine what it did to Luke's head.

At least things were secure again. They'd found Hassan in the back and Rhys had frog-marched him out to face Luke. After he'd refused to talk, they'd done a sweep of the kitchen first and then the rest of the place, quickly and efficiently without anyone taking notice of what they were doing. They'd found two more pistols, but nothing else. Luke had doubled security at each of the exit and entry points to the facility. They'd vetted each of the employees, and Luke assessed the threat to be over. For now. Hassan was on his way to the police station to meet his "cousin." Thing was, there had to be more members of the cell nearby, and they wouldn't necessarily be of Middle-Eastern descent.

Next to him, Luke squinted a bit as they came through the doors from the comparatively dim patio. The bride and groom were on the dance floor, swaying to the music in the traditional first dance as husband and wife. They appeared totally lost in each other, and happy as anyone could want them to be. Luke must have been relieved about that.

Thank Christ no one else knew about the foiled plot. The groom had to know something was up, because he was a cop and there were suddenly three strangers on the guest list. Two of whom just happened to be stacked twin brothers well over six feet tall, with special ops backgrounds. According to Luke, his son trusted his old man to look after everything and hadn't pressed him for details beyond seeking assurance they shouldn't postpone the wedding. Now, Rhys and the rest of the team simply had to make sure the newlyweds and everyone else in the place stayed ignorant about what had just gone down.

He and Dec kept pace with Luke as they walked over to their table at the edge of the dance floor. They were close enough to grab Luke if he needed it, but Rhys wouldn't dare touch him unless he was going over. He and Dec had enough respect for Luke to save him that humiliation, and they were more than capable of pulling off the acting job necessary to make everyone think everything was hunky dory. Another handy skill he'd perfected during his years in special ops.

Except for some reason, lying to Neveah made him

feel dirty. Not that he regretted it in this case. He'd continue to lie if it meant keeping her safe and happy.

When they finally reached their table, Luke all but dropped into his chair. Taking a seat next to him, Rhys ruthlessly got hold of his adrenal glands, slowing his heart rate, focusing on the happy newlyweds dancing before him and Nev waiting over with Ben. When they finished amidst an eruption of applause, the bride danced with her stepfather. By the time that song ended, Luke was in control enough to smile at his new daughter-in-law when she came up and did a curtsy in front of him.

"May I have this dance?"

Rhys hid a wince when the smile froze on Luke's lips. Rhys looked away, and in his peripheral vision saw the groom pulling Emily onto the floor as the music started again. Rhys pointedly avoided glancing at his boss in the awkward hesitation that followed the bride's invitation. Luke was *so* not in the mood for dancing.

But Christa's aquamarine eyes sparkled as she reached down to grasp Luke's hand. Probably because he didn't want to hurt her feelings or cause a scene, he rose and followed her. Rhys had to give the guy credit. If he hadn't known Luke so well, Rhys would never have guessed he was suffering. Luke even managed to chat pleasantly with her while they were out there. Like nothing had ever happened, and he wasn't in the kind of pain that would have most men curled into a ball on the floor and begging for their mamas.

Half of Rhys's attention was on the security team members posted about the room, and the other half was divided between Luke while he danced and Neveah, who was talking with Ben while waiting for the group invite onto the floor. The song finally ended, but when Luke kissed Christa's cheek and turned to leave, he stopped dead in his tracks. Completely froze, like he'd been paralyzed.

Rhys started to rise, thinking Luke was about to fall, but then he saw what had brought his boss up so short.

Emily stood right in front of him. Luke didn't even have time to cover his surprise before her warm smile slipped a notch.

Rhys kept watching in case Luke needed help, and saw him cover a wince when he shot a fervent glance behind him. The mother of the bride and the stepfather were dancing now. They were divorced too, and by all accounts not amicably. Rhys could almost hear Luke's thoughts. If they could keep up the pretense of getting along for one dance, then Luke would suck it up too. He was going to have to dance with his ex-wife.

By now, everyone watched them expectantly. Especially the groom, who threw his old man an "I-know-you're-on-edge-but-don't-be-an-asshole" look.

Covering the awkward lapse, Luke took Emily's hand and led her onto the floor. Glancing across the table, Rhys looked at Bryn, perched on Dec's lap. She had her hand over her mouth, her eyes wide as she stared at the couple. When Rhys met her gaze she immediately dropped her hand and smiled, but she couldn't mask the worry in her dark gaze.

He folded his arms and settled back into his seat. Whatever the history was between Luke and his ex, it had to be quite the story.

"Oh, man," Ben said in a low voice, staring at something past her head.

Nev peered around his shoulder. "What?"

"Luke's dancing with his ex."

"So?"

"Man, that guy's got balls of steel."

Nev scowled. "Actually, I think *she* does. She's the one that made the overture in the first place." After meeting Emily and learning a bit about her past with Luke, Nev was convinced the older woman had a spine of titanium to go through with this. Good for her.

But oh, man, they looked awkward. They avoided eye contact with each other, and Luke's mouth was a grim line in his bearded face as he stared straight out in front of him over Emily's shoulder. Nev's heart went out to her.

Tearing her eyes away from them, she went back to enjoying herself. She was *going* to have a good time, dammit. She'd earned it. Within moments her steps smoothed out.

Ben was fun and a great dancer, though she would have preferred having Rhys with her out here. Was it true he never danced? She peered through the dancing couples. He was still at their table with Bryn and Dec, but he was staring intently at Luke, like he was waiting for something. A signal, maybe. A fine tension took hold of her. Was something still wrong? Did it have to do with whatever had happened earlier?

Then Rhys turned his gaze on Ben and gave a subtle twist of his head in Luke's direction. Ben instantly began steering them toward the other couple.

Nev stiffened. "What are you doing?"

"Impressing you with my effortless skill?"

Despite her reluctance to intrude, he brought them up beside Luke and Emily, close enough that Nev could clearly see their expressions, but not close enough that they crowded them or overheard what they were saying.

Something was up. Nev did her own survey of Luke, checking if he seemed concerned. Instead, she saw a fine sheen of sweat on his forehead, though it wasn't hot in the room. And this close she realized he was past pale, into an ungodly shade of gray. She stopped dancing. "Ben," she began, worried Luke might get sick right then and there, and his steps suddenly faltered.

With her hand still resting on Luke's shoulder, Emily stilled, and Nev heard her over the music. "Luke?"

Luke blinked fast, barely moving now.

"Sorry," Nev heard him reply, and tugged out of Ben's grip. He might need her—

Emily pulled back a bit. "You're pale. Do you need to sit down?"

"I'm fine," Luke said.

Somehow he found his rhythm again, leaving Nev wondering when the hell the damned song would end. She glanced behind her for another signal from Rhys. At the table, Dec was laughing up into Bryn's face, still sitting on his knee, and Rhys had his arm across the back of the chair next to him. Watching Luke, but not on alert. Maybe he didn't realize how ill Luke was.

Ben took her into dance position again and moved them even closer, and Nev caught the way Luke winced and sucked in a breath when he turned. Emily peered up into his face with concern.

"He's hurting bad," Nev whispered to Ben, having trouble keeping up with the dance because she was more concerned with Luke.

"Yeah. That's why I'm over here."

"Is it his head?"

"Looks like."

Damn. What if he hadn't gotten himself checked out in Afghanistan?

Then Emily stopped again. "Luke, what's wrong?"

He'd stopped dancing, too. God, was he swaying on his feet?

Oh, shit, no… "Ben—"

"Luke?" Emily's voice was sharp with concern. She held both Luke's wrists.

"Fine," he rasped.

"No, you're not—"

Nev whipped her head around, searching for help. Ben wasn't jumping in, and she didn't want to embarrass Luke, but he was in trouble.

"Rhys," Ben called.

As though it was a predetermined signal, Rhys and Dec shot out of their chairs.

When she glanced back at Luke, he'd let go of Emily to spin around, and his knees crumpled. As Rhys swooped in, the last thing Nev saw was Emily's arms shooting out to catch her ex-husband as he went down.

At Ben's warning, Rhys jumped up from the table. Luke seemed to wobble, then Emily threw a panicked look over her shoulder. Rhys raced toward Luke. The guy's face was bloodless, eyes unfocused. Emily cried out and raised her arms to cushion his fall as he started to crumple, but Rhys leapt forward to grab Luke around the shoulders, controlling his descent and cushioning the back of his head with one hand before it hit the floor. Around them, everyone froze, watching the spectacle with wide eyes. Emily was already on her knees calling Luke's name, holding his face, taking his pulse.

She raised her head, eyes frantic. "Is there a doctor—"

"Right here." Neveah materialized beside them with Ben and crouched next to Rhys at Luke's side.

His lids fluttered, then lifted slowly, some of the color leeching back into his face as he gazed up at the wall of people surrounding him. "Shit," he muttered, lifting a hand to wipe damp his face.

Rhys looked to Neveah, who met his questioning gaze with a nod. Sliding one arm beneath Luke's shoulders, he glanced across the circle at Dec. "Let's get him up and out of here." Together, they hoisted Luke up and all but dragged him out of the ball room.

Dec spoke to Bryn on their way past. "Stay here

and do some damage control. Keep the bride and groom here with Emily. We'll be back in a minute."

While Bryn rushed off to intercept the newlyweds, already trying to make their way to Luke, Rhys and Dec walked him out with as much dignity as possible. Too late to save him the embarrassment of passing out in front of everyone, but at least they'd gotten him up and out fast, away from gawking spectators.

As soon as they had him outside and away from prying eyes, they set him down on a wrought iron park bench, then backed up to provide security while he got some air, both careful not to look at him. A guy deserved some privacy after an episode like that.

Nev glanced between Luke and him. "May I?" she asked. Rhys nodded, and she went past to sit next to Luke. She gazed at him in her frank way, all business. "You didn't get that CT scan in Kabul, did you?"

Luke's mouth moved in the ghost of a smile. "Busted."

She folded her arms across her chest, her serious expression telling him she didn't find anything about that amusing. "What other symptoms do you have?"

He shrugged. "The usual."

"Such as?"

"Headaches, dizziness, nausea, blurred vision."

"For how long?"

"Couple months."

Rhys winced. Uh-oh. Way wrong answer. Nev was gonna let him have it.

"Any behavioral changes? Memory loss?"

Luke hesitated a fraction of a second too long before answering. "Some."

Nice to find that out now, Rhys thought dourly. Beside him, Dec shot him an "Oh, shit" look, and set his hands on his hips.

"Want us to take you to the hospital?" Dec asked.

"No," Luke growled. "I'm fine. The symptoms were better until my flight yesterday. Must've been the altitude."

"You're not fine," Nev snapped. "You need to be admitted ASAP."

Luke shook his head, but stilled quickly and blanched, as though the motion had hurt him badly. "No way."

"Spare me the macho alpha male bullshit."

Luke's head jerked around to stare at her, and he flinched.

Rhys had to bite the inside of his cheek to keep from laughing. Luke's stunned expression was priceless. Probably the first time anyone had ever dared speak to him like that, at least to his face. Not many people could withstand Luke's glare, but Nev was holding her own.

When she spoke again, her voice was flinty. "You may be tough, but you don't strike me as stupid." Her eyes never wavered from Luke's, and Rhys was even more impressed. He'd seen special ops commandos wilt under that stare, but Nev seemed completely unfazed. "Sounds to me like you've either got a clot or a bleed in your brain, and it's likely in the occipital lobe, which explains your blurred vision and nausea. But the pressure could be compressing the cerebellum which—"

"Controls my balance and coordination," Luke finished. "Yeah, I've heard this already."

"Then you should understand how serious it is," she replied crisply. "If your intra-cranial pressure spikes high enough you could go into a coma. Just ask Rhys how much fun that is." She raised her lake-blue eyes to his, and Rhys felt that increasingly familiar ripple of awareness spread through him.

"And ask him how it feels to wake up and not be able to move one side of your body, or if you can, not well enough to do simple things like write or feed yourself," she went on.

Her gaze told him she understood exactly what he'd gone through, because she'd made sure to be updated about his progress. She'd cared enough about him to follow his rehab, and knew every single obstacle he'd overcome during his therapy. She'd stayed and held his hand, caressed him and talked with him even though he'd been unconscious.

The knowledge unfurled something deep inside him, a kind of yearning. The emotion was so strong it triggered an ache beneath his sternum.

She held his gaze another moment before looking back at Luke. "Go ahead, ask him. Because that's what's going to happen to you if you don't get this looked after—if you're lucky enough that it doesn't leave you in a vegetative state. Otherwise, it's going to kill you. Maybe not tonight, but at some point it will. And I think you know that as well as I do."

Luke didn't say anything, just sat there with his jaw tensed, staring in the direction of the reception room.

Rhys stepped in. "Let's just take you in for some tests and find out what's going on," he said in a reasonable tone, appealing to his boss' practical nature. "Dec and Bryn can stay here to make sure the bride and groom have a good time, and then we'll bring you straight back."

"If they discharge me," Luke pointed out. "Which y'all know isn't going to happen. If I go in there, they're going to want to open me up and then I'll be laid up for God knows how long."

And then he wouldn't be able to go into the field if he needed to. Luke hadn't said it aloud, but Rhys understood that's exactly why he hadn't had surgery before now. He was afraid he'd miss his shot of staving off disaster or eventually nailing Tehrazzi if the doctors wanted to operate. Rhys glanced at Nev for her opinion.

"If they need to do a craniotomy, you can be out in a matter of days, if not hours," she said. "It all depends on what they find when they go in."

Luke hedged. "Shit. Why tonight?"

"Stress amplifies the problem, as I'm sure you're well aware," Nev answered, and climbed to her feet. "Now let's go. It's way past time you took responsibility for your health. You're no good to anyone like this, so you may as well get it fixed and then you can go back into the field."

Rhys hid a smile as she breezed past him in a tangy lemon-scented cloud, and offered a hand to Luke. "Come on. Doc's orders—let's go."

With a resentful glare, Luke ignored the hand and stood on his own power, staying still a few moments until he got his equilibrium. He aimed a hard look at Dec. "Make sure they think everything's fine in there."

"Roger that."

"And Emily, too, or trust me, all of them are gonna wind up at the hospital."

"Consider it done," Dec said, already heading back to the dance. Then he stopped. "Which hospital you taking him to?"

"VGH, it's the closest," Nev answered, in the take-charge way of a woman who was used to being obeyed. "We'll call you with an update."

When she turned away, Dec raised his brows at him in amusement, then sauntered back to the party. Rhys waited for Luke to go ahead of him, just in case he had to step in and catch him again on the way to the truck. True to form, Luke threw him a dark scowl, silently warning him he'd better keep his distance.

With a weary sigh, the patient trudged along behind Neveah. Rhys eyed her swaying hips appreciatively as he followed. She was stunning in her midnight blue gown with her authoritative air wrapped around her like a suit of armor. Damn, she was sexy when she got all doctorly and took charge like that. He really should be paying more attention to his security role and not wondering whether she was wearing anything underneath that gown.

"Bet you intimidate the shit out of all the other surgeons," Luke muttered as he came alongside her.

Gazing straight ahead, Neveah smiled fiercely. "Yep. And that's just the way I like it."

Chapter Thirteen

When the call came in, Ahmed excused himself from the table and strode through the crowded dining room outside into the cold, clean air. The phone in his right breast pocket stopped buzzing, but the moment his shoes hit the damp pavement of the parking lot it started up again. He retrieved it and headed to the seclusion of his vehicle, parked nearby. When he saw the caller ID his hands grew damp. Though he'd helped plan the attack, part of him didn't want to hear about the deaths he'd caused.

Shutting himself in the leather interior and locking the door, he answered. "Is it done?" The words came out raspy.

"I—n-no."

His spine snapped taut. "What?"

"There was a problem. Our man was intercepted outside the location."

"What?"

"A group of SWAT members or something stopped him at a checkpoint, and then got Hassan."

Ahmed closed his eyes and pinched the bridge of his nose. "I thought you said this guy could handle it!"

"You didn't warn us security would be that tight."

He suppressed a growl of irritation. "I told you there could be some resistance, and that there might be military people involved—" He cut off the rest of his tirade and ordered his brain to focus on the task at hand. "What about the primary target?"

"The target collapsed."

"Dead?"

"No."

Ahmed ground his teeth together as his stomach turned inside out. This was a complete nightmare. "Then why are you calling me? Go after him and finish it."

A pause filled the line. "He is with two others. A huge guy that could be RCMP or military or something, and that woman doctor."

His pulse jumped. "Doctor Adams?"

"Yes. I've followed them to VGH. They just went inside. What do you want me to do?"

Wasn't it obvious enough? Damn, how had things gotten so out of control? He glanced at his watch in the light from the street lamps coming through his window. His dinner companions wouldn't think anything of him not returning, and as for two of the targets being at the hospital… Apparently he'd have to make sure nothing else went wrong personally.

"Stay there and wait for me at the Emergency entrance. I'll be there in ten minutes."

Ending the call, Ahmed grabbed for the keys and ignored the tremor in his hand as he fired up the engine. This wasn't supposed to be how it went. He wasn't supposed to be directly involved.

His heart beat faster as he pulled onto the street into traffic. He didn't want to have blood on his hands—not that kind of blood. But if the men he'd hired to commit the murders didn't follow through, Tehrazzi would blame him and then…

Ahmed didn't even want to think about what would happen after that.

****

An hour later, Nev walked through the emergency ward on her way to the CT area. Passing the waiting room, she did a double take when she saw Emily sitting on a chair, rubbing her hands over her arms.

She pushed the door open. "Hey. Didn't feel much like celebrating after that, huh?"

Emily shook her head, the pretty chin-length bob swinging against her jaw. "No." Her moss green eyes strayed to the window in the door. "How is he? Have you heard anything?"

"Not yet, I was just heading there." Nev angled her head. "Why don't you go back to the reception and we'll call you when we know something? Maybe it'll take your mind off everything for a while."

"Thanks, but I can't do that." She stood and wrapped her arms around her waist. "Is he having tests?"

"Yes. X-rays and a CT scan."

Emily met her gaze, looking agitated. "Is he in there already?"

"I think so. Why, what's wrong?"

She hesitated a moment before answering. "Luke's claustrophobic." She bit her lip. "Really claustrophobic."

He was? The idea shocked Nev. How in the world had Luke been able to get through SEAL training with a phobia like that? Didn't they have to lock out of subs and stuff? Tough to do if you didn't like confined spaces. Maybe Emily was looking for an excuse to be with him.

Emily shifted from one foot to the other. "Do you think… Would it be okay if I could maybe talk to him? It might help him relax."

Or it might put his blood pressure through the roof if it wasn't there already. "I'm not sure if—"

"I promise I won't say anything to upset him. I just…I want to help if I can."

How the hell was she supposed to say no when Emily was looking at her like that? "You really think he needs you to distract him?"

"He'd never admit to it, no, but…"

Nev narrowed her eyes for a moment as she considered it. She'd seen firsthand how much of an alpha male Luke was. And the rest of his team. Maybe Emily's presence would be a kindness. "All right. I'll get you in there, but if his vitals show signs of stress, you'll have to leave."

"Of course."

Emily followed her down the hall and into the CT room. Nev went into the booth where the technician was performing the scan and held the door for Emily. On the other side of the glass, Luke lay inside the sterile white tube of the CT machine with his eyes closed.

Repressing a sigh at the stubbornness that had landed him there, she motioned for Emily to approach the technician's place. "We've got an important message to deliver," Nev told the woman seated at the controls. "Mind if we say something to the patient?"

She smiled. "Not at all."

While Emily got situated behind the microphone, Nev thought about what was going on back at the reception, and wished the hell she could be sure something dangerous wasn't up. Dec, Ben and the undercover crew were still at Seasons. She knew Luke had the utmost faith in their abilities, but not being there in person to oversee the security must be driving him crazy. Add in the fact he was trapped in that tube with a possible bleed in his brain, and…well, maybe this was a good idea if for no other reason than it might distract him for a while.

Emily spoke into the mike. "Luke?"

He jerked slightly and his eyes flew open. "Yeah?"

"They're almost done here," she soothed in her soft Charleston drawl. "Just a few more minutes."

Even from where she stood Nev saw Luke's scowl. "What are you doing here?" he demanded.

"Well, it was either that or Rayne and Christa were coming down, so I figured this was the best option."

"Dec with you?"

"Yes, and Bryn. They're parking the car." Emily glanced over at her. "That fellow Ben stayed behind at the reception with Nate."

Luke grunted in reply and closed his eyes, but he gave no other indication of how Emily's presence affected him so Nev let her stay.

"I was just thinking of Rayne's Marine Corps graduation," Em said after a long pause.

He made a noncommittal sound, and Nev's heart swelled for Emily. What a sweetheart, to try and ease his anxiety like this. Add in the fact she'd been divorced from the man for two decades, and Nev was even more impressed. Few people had that sort of kindness in them. Without a doubt Emily was still hung up on him. Unfortunately for her, Luke didn't seem to reciprocate those feelings.

Nev wondered what had gone wrong in their marriage, apart from the obvious. Making a life with someone in the military was hard enough, but even more so when they were in special ops. Which begged the question, how was she going to deal with Rhys and his work if they stayed together? She really didn't know.

Nev tuned out while Emily kept talking to Luke, conferring with the technician about what the on-screen images showed. After another few minutes they were done, and Nev wanted Emily out of there so she wouldn't overhear something confidential. The whole night had been a mess, but Nev still had her patient's privacy to protect.

Chapter Fourteen

Ahmed ran a hand through his unkempt hair for what seemed like the hundredth time before entering the kitchen through the garage. Things were unraveling faster than he could fix them, and the people he was dealing with were every bit as dangerous as Tehrazzi.

He'd decided to stop at home before going to the hospital. Would be less suspicious if for some reason his wife paid attention to his comings and goings. But he didn't think she did.

His fingers tightened around the bunch of cut flowers he'd bought, making the cellophane wrapping crinkle. He went straight to the butcher's block on the counter and took out the pair of left-handed scissors Lily had bought for him and suffered a bittersweet pang. She was such a thoughtful person. He really should make more of an effort to be a better husband, he thought as he cut off the wrapping and took down a vase from the cupboard.

After arranging the flowers in their new home he set the vase on the granite island. Their natural, cheerful beauty only reminded him of how evil he'd become and the plots he'd set into motion. Pushing the thought from his frazzled mind, he strove for a light tone and called out for his wife. "Lil?"

Through the kitchen he heard the noise of the TV. "In here," she called out.

Eased by the sound of her voice, he toed off his shoes and walked through their cozy kitchen to find her. Intent on wrapping his arms around her and holding on tight for a few moments, he froze when he saw her shocked expression, the phone held to her ear.

"Thank you for calling us," she said in Urdu. Ahmed's stomach dropped like a rock. Pakistan, and not good news.

When she hung up he reached for her, automatically drawing her close to absorb the shudder that swept through her. "What? What's happened?"

She raised her head, and her bottomless black eyes were haunted. "It's Mahmoud," she said in a strangled whisper. "He's dead."

His blood went cold. "What?"

A tear trickled down her pale cheek. "He'd been shot through the head. The police found him on a village road near the Afghan border."

Icy tendrils of fear shivered up his spine. His arms tightened around her convulsively. Oh God, what had happened? What had Mahmoud done? Ahmed swallowed. Did it have anything to do with him?

"I'm so sorry," Lily murmured, passing her soft palm over the side of his face, mistaking his expression for grief rather than the gut-wrenching terror it was.

"Thank you." His muscles were tight as steel cables, making his joints ache. My God, what should he do? How could he protect them if Tehrazzi had sent one of his minions after them? The thought of someone harming his beautiful Lily because of what he'd done flooded his veins with terror. "Excuse me," he murmured, pulling out of her embrace.

Empathy and sadness flashed across her face. "Ahmed—"

"I have to go."

Lily ducked her head and wrapped her arms around her trim waist, making him feel even more of a bastard for leaving her when she was hurting.

"I'm sorry, I have to—" He almost gagged, and spun around, then all but ran to the garage. Firing up the ignition, he opened the garage door and backed out, the tires squealing as he put the car in gear and sped off down the darkened street.

His heart raced along with the powerful engine, battling an uneasy fear that he'd left Lily home alone without any protection. He drove aimlessly through his peaceful neighborhood and across the Lion's Gate Bridge with no particular destination in mind, but knew he had to get to the hospital soon.

Not that it mattered where he went. Nowhere was safe now. Wherever he ended up, it would never be far enough away that Tehrazzi couldn't find him.

****

Neveah stepped off the elevator a little past eleven o'clock with the results of Luke's CT images. The attending neurosurgeon was meeting her in Luke's room in a few minutes to discuss the procedure he wanted to perform. Turning left down the hall, she picked up on voices coming from the room at the far end where Luke was. Pausing at the threshold, she knocked before poking her head in. Dec and Bryn were there, along with Emily, Rayne and Christa. Her white bridal gown looked obscenely out of place in the hospital room.

As everyone else backed away to give her room, Luke met her gaze and sat up a little taller. "Well?

What's the verdict?"

She held back a smile. That wasn't bravado oozing from him. That was plain in-your-face stubbornness. You had to admire a man who could face what he was without breaking a sweat. "The neurosurgeon's coming up to talk to you momentarily."

"I'd rather hear it from you."

"You sure?"

"Positive."

She glanced around. "Do you want this in private?"

"No. They're gonna find out anyway. This'll save me a step, and then they can get back to the party."

"Okay then." Stepping to his bedside, she opened the file and held one of the clearest images in the light so he could see it.

Peering at it over Nev's shoulder, Emily leaned over and pointed to the dark occlusion over the visual cortex. "An occipital hematoma."

"Yes," Nev answered in surprise. "You a nurse?" She assumed Emily wasn't a doctor, because she'd asked for one when Luke collapsed.

"Used to be. Geriatrics, mostly."

Why hadn't Emily told her that before?

Sighing, Emily shook her head at her ex-husband. "For God's sake, Luke, do you know how dangerous this is?"

Luke didn't answer her as he stared at the picture. "So what, they're gonna drill a hole in my head and take care of it?"

Nev nodded, raising a brow at his brusque tone. "Basically."

Rayne came closer. "They got a drill bit hard enough to get through his skull?"

Everyone chuckled, except Emily, whom she shared a long look with. As routine as a craniotomy was, this was no laughing matter. "You're real lucky this thing didn't dislodge on you over the past few months."

Luke didn't respond, though she hadn't expected him to.

"The area it covers explains all of your symptoms, but the surgeon will check everything out when he goes in."

He folded his well-developed arms across his muscular chest and regarded her calmly. "So how long will the recovery take?"

She shrugged. "Depends. Anywhere from a few days to a few months. Let's just hope they don't find anything more serious than what's in this image, and that all goes well."

"Any side effects afterward?"

"We won't know that until after the surgery. You still may have some dizziness and blurred vision due to the surgery site. But on the whole you should notice a drastic improvement."

He grunted. "How long until I'm operational?"

"You're in a real damn big hurry," the surgeon said as he entered the room with his clipboard. "Why don't we just take it one step at a time?"

"No time for that, Doc. So let's get this over with."

The doctor's graying eyebrows shot up behind his glasses. "You got something more pressing than taking care of your brain?"

"Yes."

The brows snapped downward. "Just because this is a relatively safe procedure doesn't mean we might encounter something more serious."

"I understand that, but I need to get back overseas ASAP."

The middle-aged man stood gawking at him a moment. "Well, I'll do my best to accommodate that," he said wryly. "I've scheduled the surgery for eight o'clock tomorrow morning. That soon enough for you?"

"If that's the first opening you've got, then yes."

The doctor shot Neveah an unimpressed look before addressing his patient again. "Visiting hours are well over," he reminded everyone, "and whether or not he wants to admit it, Mr. Hutchinson is going to have brain surgery in the morning, so I suggest he gets some sleep."

"I'll sleep when I'm dead," Luke said darkly.

Neveah bit back a retort. Everyone in the room but the other doctor knew Luke wasn't going to sleep. He'd trained his body years ago to go without sleep and food and comfort of any kind, and he was way too vigilant to allow himself to take anything more than what amounted to a combat nap every few hours.

"If you have no further questions, I'll leave you with Doctor Adams," the other doctor finished, giving her a smile. When Luke shook his head, the surgeon looked back at Neveah. "Thanks for your assistance."

"It was my pleasure." As soon as he'd gone, she faced Luke with her hands on her hips. "Well? Anything else I can tell you?"

His deep brown eyes lingered on hers and she could feel the power in him, as fierce and unshakable as the supreme confidence he always displayed. Stubborn man could be dying, and he wouldn't ask for help. Exactly like Rhys. Thank God she didn't have to deal with alpha males like them in her job too often. If she did, they were usually unconscious by the time she saw them. Much easier to handle that way.

"Nope," he answered. "But thanks for sticking around."

His words surprised her. "You're welcome. I'll let everyone say goodbye now, and then I'll come back in the morning to check on things."

"Sure."

Nev said her goodbyes to everyone and stepped out into the hallway where Rhys waited with Dec, their backs to her. On guard, even in the hospital. She withheld a sigh as Rhys swung his head around to look at her. "All good?" he asked.

"Yes. Just let me take this back to the nurses' station." Her shoes tapped on the scarred linoleum floor as she walked down the hall and hung a right. The high heels made her legs look amazing, but they hurt her feet.

Just as she approached the large desk positioned in the center of the ward, the elevator doors slid open and a man stepped off, dressed in a tailored navy suit. He turned his head, and they both froze.

She'd seen him outside her hotel and in Stanley Park.

His dark eyes held hers for a split second before he turned away and strode quickly down the hall in the opposite direction, leaving her frozen in place with her heart drumming loud in her ears.

She threw a quick glance over her shoulder, searching for Rhys. No way could it be a mere coincidence this time. Not three times in two days. Spinning on her spiked heels, she rushed back the way she'd come, and when Rhys saw her, he started forward immediately.

"What's wrong?"

Not wanting to cause a scene, she waited until she was within whisper range to tell him. "I saw someone," she said, leaning into his strength as he wrapped a heavy arm around her shoulders. "I think he's been following me."

"What?" After she explained, he set her away from him with a dark scowl. "Why the hell didn't you say anything until now?"

She waved his anger away. "Because until now I thought it had to be a coincidence." She thought of how her instincts screamed when she saw him. "I just get a really bad vibe from him. I feel like his eyes are always on me."

Rhys took her hand. "Come on, let's go."

She had no choice but to be dragged away. "Where?"

"Back to my hotel, where I know you'll be safe."

Safe? "All I said was that the guy gave me the creeps."

"No, you said you've seen him three times, and that you think he's been following you. Trust me, that gives me every right to be concerned." He continued towing her behind him, the menacing expression on his face enough to make people get out of their way in a hurry.

"Slow down, Rhys, I'm wearing heels for Godsake." Good thing for her she was almost his height with them on, because she had to run to keep up with his long strides.

He slowed fractionally but kept going for the elevator, his whole demeanor advertising the fact he was in operational mode and not to be messed with. When they rounded the corner, they came face to face with Dr. Shirani. His eyes widened, and he stopped there in the middle of the hallway.

"Doctor Shirani," Neveah said. "What brings you here tonight?"

Tearing his gaze away from Rhys's scars, he seemed to shake himself before replying. "I was called to help in Emergency, and heard we had a head trauma patient. I just came up to check on him."

"Do you mean Mr. Hutchinson?"

Shirani blinked. "Yes. You know him?"

"We just came from his room. Doctor Parkes already spoke with him. The craniotomy is scheduled for first thing tomorrow morning."

"Oh." His eyes traveled up Rhys's intimidating frame and back to her. "Is he sleeping, then?"

"Doubt it. His whole family is still in there, and

someone's staying with him until the surgery."

His eyebrows rose. "Really? That's against hospital regulation—"

"His security has already been cleared by the RCMP," Rhys said, still holding her hand tight in his. "He'll have a guard around the clock until he leaves the premises."

"A guard? And the police are involved?"

"They're already here."

The doctor's throat seemed to spasm as he swallowed. "Is there a…a threat against him?"

"It's just a precaution," Rhys said evasively.

Poor Dr. Shirani looked like he was about to choke in alarm. Neveah aimed a glare at Rhys before addressing the surgeon. "I just took his file to the nurses' station if you want to look at it, but there's no need now."

Shirani seemed to come out of his trance-like state and focused on her. Then he raised his hands, almost as though he was warding Rhys off. "No no, that's fine. I'll just continue back down to Emergency then." He gave them a quick smile. "Good night, Doctor Adams. I'm looking forward to hearing your speech tomorrow."

"Thanks. Good night." She glanced over her shoulder at him as he strode toward the staircase rather than the elevator Rhys was taking her to. "Could you be any less friendly?" she demanded, following in his wake. "You scared him so bad he won't even take the elevator down with us."

"Oh well," he said without looking at her. He hit the down button on the wall with a long forefinger and turned her so that he blocked her from view.

"You're being ridiculous. We're in a hospital. Don't you think this is overkill?"

"Nope."

She crossed her arms over her chest and fumed

while they waited in silence for the elevator car to reach them. It pissed her off he'd treated a colleague of hers like that. Her professional image was important to her, and she didn't want anyone thinking Rhys was following her around because she was too scared to be alone.

When the bell dinged Rhys wheeled her around and checked inside first before guiding her inside. His manhandling was not appreciated and she let him know it by narrowing her eyes.

He stared straight back, completely unapologetic.

What was going through his head? Possible attack scenarios? More bullet trajectories? It maddened and frightened her at the same time. What the hell was going on here? Something big, and if it involved her she wanted to know what it was.

She kept her eyes on him while he escorted her to the Escalade. His gaze never stilled, always scanning as he moved her quickly out of the hospital toward the street where he'd parked. Keeping her next to him while he checked the truck over—for explosives, she assumed—he finally unlocked it, settling her in her seat before hustling around to the driver's side and starting the engine. By the time he pulled away from the curb, she was cold all the way to her bones.

She gave him a few seconds after he pulled into traffic, but when he didn't say anything she couldn't keep quiet anymore. "What the hell is going on tonight, Rhys?"

He didn't answer, only checked the rearview and side mirrors as he pulled into the right lane.

So they could turn the corner to escape anyone following them, she realized with a sickening start.

Her fingers dug into her chilled palms. "If you don't tell me, I swear to—"

"Nothing concrete," he said tersely.

Concrete? What did that mean exactly? "Is there a

threat?"

He nodded.

She wanted to scream. Trying to get information out of him was like prying a tooth out with pliers. "Is it against me?"

"Partly."

The blood drained out of her face. She stared at him in disbelief. He was so calm, so composed behind the wheel, as though they were discussing the weather. "Tell me."

He sighed and turned the corner, the headlights of passing cars a blur to her while they sped down the darkened street. "We have intelligence that says Luke, Bryn and you are possible targets."

"For Tehrazzi?"

He didn't answer for a moment, and her vision went hazy. *He's here. Coming after you again.*

"We caught someone earlier," he finally said, his words jarring her out of her head.

At the reception. Holy shit. The air stuck in her aching lungs. "Who?"

"It's all under control now. Don't worry."

She almost laughed, but stifled it because she feared it would come out in a hysterical burst. Biting the inside of her cheek until she found her voice, she struggled with the words. "So that's why you were called to Vancouver." And as Bryn had told her, he'd agreed to come once he'd known she would be in town. He'd arrived with the full knowledge he was protecting her from Tehrazzi, knowing full well what the terrorist was capable of.

"Yes."

Her guts started churning. "Jesus, Rhys, why didn't you tell me?"

"Because of the way you just reacted. I didn't want you to worry."

Well she was more than worried now. "Is the threat against me credible?"

He cast her a sidelong glance. "I'm here, aren't I?"

Shit. "What else haven't you told me?"

He sighed. "I can't tell you everything."

"Then tell me what you can."

"Tehrazzi got his hands on a laptop during the mission when I was wounded. It had intelligence, some e-mails and other things on it. He knew about the wedding and your conference."

She blinked. "But... Wouldn't the files all be encrypted or coded so he couldn't get access? Sam was the communications expert there, and she would have—" The words died in her throat at Rhys's grim expression. "Oh God, she made a mistake, didn't she?" Sam had either lost or left the laptop behind, and Tehrazzi or one of his men had found it.

"Not exactly. There were a lot of extenuating circumstances on that op. It wasn't her fault."

"So that's why they took her away for a debriefing right away in Kabul. They thought it was her fault. Damn, why didn't she tell me any of this?"

"You know she couldn't tell you."

Yeah. Sam worked for the CIA. A lot of what she did and heard was classified. Weird, to think Sam had hidden things from her all this time, but now her phone call after the ceremony made all kinds of terrifying sense.

The engine purred as Rhys slowed to take another turn, and Nev didn't recognize the area. "Where are we going?"

"Police station. Ben's already there, so we'll give the police a description of the guy who's been tailing you and find out if we get any hits."

She stared at him. "Why is Ben there?"

"We had a little incident during the reception that

needed to be taken care of."

Her guts were in knots. "Yeah, I already guessed that, but what kind of incident?" Had someone tried to get in with guns or a bomb or something while she'd been sitting there worrying about Rhys?

"It's all over now, except what Ben's working on. I doubt it's anything serious."

She rubbed a hand over her unsettled stomach. He was lying. She knew it. And he wasn't going to say anything more about whatever had happened at the reception. She was going to have to deal with that somehow. "For the record, I don't believe a damn word of that, but I'm glad I'm finding this out at the end of the evening."

"I'm sorry you found out at all, but in light of the guy at the hospital, I need you to be aware of the risk."

And to think she'd been pissed off at him for frightening Dr. Shirani. She wrapped her arms around her waist. Icy tendrils of fear coiled around her subconscious. The thought of facing any kind of threat to her safety after what she'd been through was enough to make her want to curl into a fetal position and put her hands over her ears. She couldn't go through that again, she'd break into a million pieces.

"I didn't tell you to scare you, Nev," Rhys said, glancing over at her. He reached across the console and took her hand, rubbing his thumb back and forth over her knuckles. "I just want you to be aware, that's all. We've got security in place at the hotel, and undercover agents at all the venues. Plus you've got Ben and me."

"I had a right to know," she argued, growing angry. "How would you like it if I knew something was wrong with you but I kept it to myself so you wouldn't worry?"

"I'd hate it. But then I'd realize you were trying to protect me."

"Yeah, like you'd be okay with *that*."

He kept on rubbing her hand. "So, you still planning to give your speech tomorrow?"

Hell, she hadn't even thought about it yet. "Why, you're saying I shouldn't?"

"Didn't say that. Just wondering how you feel about it now that you know what's happening."

Well, she certainly wasn't looking forward to it like she had been before this conversation, but… No. She was no coward. "I'm still giving it. Terrorists have already taken enough from me, and this is a cause I really care about. I owe it to the men that died in those mountains to stand up at that podium tomorrow and honor their memories."

She couldn't be sure, but she thought he smiled a bit. "That's what we figured you'd say."

"We?"

"Sam, Ben and I."

"So Sam *did* know about this beforehand and she still didn't say anything?" She was totally hurt.

"Even if she did know she couldn't tell you. Of course she suspected something was up, but her hands were tied without being privy to the intel, so she sent Ben along with me." He grinned. "As backup."

The conversation with her cousin the night before she'd flown in from Vancouver came back to her in an insightful rush. So that's why Sam had invited Rhys over for dinner and put him on the phone to her. She was going to strangle Sam when she saw her.

Rhys pulled into the parking lot of the police station and parked near the stairs. He cut the engine and came around to help her out of the truck, holding her elbow like a total gentleman as he led her up the concrete steps and into the building. Inside, uniformed officers were busy at desks or talking on headsets and cell phones. Computers whirred, printers and faxes hummed as they spat out documents.

A female officer looked up from her terminal. "Can I help you?"

"We need to see Ben Sinclair."

"Ben Sincl—oh, the guy with Nate." The woman pushed back from her desk and dropped her pen on the scribbled notes on its surface. "He's in the back. Follow me." She led them through a maze of cubicles to a staircase and up to the second floor. Rhys kept hold of Neveah's arm as they walked down the carpeted hallway, their footsteps hushed on the geometric chocolate and tan designs. For such a big man, he moved quietly.

"Right in here," the officer said, and gestured to the room at the far end.

Rhys knocked once and opened the steel door. The brightly lit beige room smelled of stale coffee and lukewarm Chinese takeout. Ben and Nate both glanced up at them as they entered, poring over what looked like a stack of mug shots while they ate. Containers of barbecue pork and chow mein were laid out on the black laminate surface of the table gracing the center of the room.

Ben set down his chopsticks and smiled. "Hey. What're you two doing here?"

"Just came from the hospital," Rhys said as he pulled out a chair for her.

"And?" Nate said. "What happened?"

"Luke's brain injury finally caught up with him."

"Yeah, I heard he went down in the middle of the dance floor."

"Nev read him the riot act—"

She glared at Rhys. What she'd done was her *job*, and nothing less.

"—and we took him in for some tests. He's got a craniotomy scheduled for first thing in the morning."

Nate whistled, sharing a meaningful glance with

Ben. "Well that must have been a fun moment, dragging his sorry ass to the hospital." His dark brown eyes swung to Neveah. "How'd you manage that one?"

"I reasoned with him."

Ben choked back a laugh. "I'll just bet you did." He looked at his brother. "You could have phoned that in, so I gather something else came up to bring you here?"

Rhys laid a hand on her shoulder and she tipped her head back to see him.

"Tell them," he said.

She didn't like being ordered around, even by him, but she had to admit things were tense right now. With a sigh, she said, "I saw someone at the hospital near Luke's room that I think has been following me."

Two pairs of eyes zeroed in on her, one icy green and the other like black coffee. "Care to elaborate?" said Ben.

"Tonight was the third time I've seen him since arriving in Vancouver. First on Friday morning when I went out for a run with my colleague, Mike. The guy was right outside the hotel, and I noticed him right away, kind of like a sixth sense. I don't know why but I was sure he was watching me, and when he saw me looking at him he left." Ben and Nate regarded her silently. "Then about forty-five minutes later I saw him on the Stanley Park seawall. As soon as he knew I'd seen him, he disappeared again. Then tonight, same thing."

Nate grabbed a pen and paper. "Can you give me a description of him?"

She wrinkled her brow as she thought. "About the same height as me, so around five eleven. Middle Eastern appearance with short black hair, and he had some gel in the front of it. Short, well groomed goatee and dark brown eyes."

"Build?"

"He looked like he was in good shape. Muscular

throughout the upper body." She thought about him for another moment. "Sorry, that's all I can think of to describe him. No scars or anything else I can give you."

"That's okay," Nate said. "Here. See if any of these guys resemble him." He pushed a stack of printed photos over to her.

Damn, the pile was over an inch thick. "Are these all suspects for some crime?"

Ben and Nate both looked at Rhys.

"She already knows the worst of what's going on," he said. "Level with her."

"These are some potential members of local terrorist cells," Ben said evasively. "If you can pick out your shadow, it might give us an edge. That would be a major break for us."

"God, yes," Nate muttered, heading over to fill his paper cup with more stale-smelling coffee as Neveah went through the pictures. Rhys stood behind her. She felt his body heat as he gazed down at the pages over her shoulder.

"What about the kid you brought in?" he asked Ben.

"Gang member, cousin to a bunch of the guys in our list." He jerked his chin at the pile of paper she was looking through.

"So far we can't pin anything on him other than illegally possessing a weapon," Nate put in.

Rhys shifted behind her. "And the 'cousin'? He still in custody?"

"Yeah. I'm giving him another hour or so to think about his options before I go in to question him again."

Neveah scanned the last page and then tidied up the pile. "Nope. None of these guys look familiar."

Nate sighed. "Just once I want my job to be easy."

"Where're you taking her now?" Ben asked Rhys, jerking his chin toward her.

"Our hotel."

Ben nodded. "I'll take Luke's room, since he won't be needing it."

"Thanks."

She hated being talked about like she wasn't even in the room. "I need to go to my hotel first, then," she said, knowing it was futile to argue against staying at the other place. "My speech is first thing in the morning. I need my notes, my computer, my suit and other stuff."

"I can swing by and pick those up for you later," Ben offered.

She shot a glance at Rhys, trying to assess what the danger level was. "Can't we just stop now?"

He considered it for a moment. "I'll go up with you, though."

Of course he would. He was chivalrous enough that he would have done it anyway, but with any kind of a perceived threat against her he'd be even more uptight. So much for a romantic evening alone.

"But right now you're going to stay with Ben while I go back and check out the hospital. I'll pick you up on my way back."

Since she didn't have a choice, she dropped into a chair with a sigh. "Fine."

Chapter Fifteen

After checking the hospital with Dec and increasing security's awareness that Luke might be at risk, Rhys went back up to his boss's room. The door was closed, so he knocked and waited for a reply before opening it, and walked in on a whole lot of awkward tension.

Left in the room with Bryn and Emily after the newlyweds departed, Luke lay on his back with his eyes closed while the women sat next to his bed. It was obvious he wasn't asleep, and equally as clear he wished everyone would leave him the hell alone. Rhys felt for the guy. A man should be allowed to suffer in private after what he'd gone through tonight.

"Someone's coming to relieve Dec shortly," he announced, breaking the tense silence. "But he said he'll stay if you want."

Luke cracked one eye open to look at him, pointedly avoiding his ex-wife. "Naw, but thanks." He shifted his gaze to Bryn. "Tell him I'm good and then go on back to the hotel."

Luke must have figured out Rayne and Christa weren't the only ones in for a night of romance. The way

Dec and Bryn had eyed each other all night made no secret of the fact they'd be spending the night having the kind of sex Rhys was looking forward to having with Neveah. The instant he got her safely into his hotel room.

Luke, however, would be trapped in his hospital bed all night. Talk about rubbing salt into a wound.

Bryn cleared her throat. "Okay, if you're sure."

"Yeah, I'm sure. I'm not so far gone that I can't defend myself if someone tried anything, and I've sure as hell ruined the evening enough for everyone involved without keeping you guys here."

Bryn glanced at Emily. "You ready? We'll drive you out to Christa and Rayne's place."

"All the way back to White Rock? Don't be silly," Emily said, re-crossing her legs for the fourth time since Rhys had walked in. Fidgety and restless, clearly uneasy. Yet she stayed. "It's forty-five minutes in the other direction, and there's no way I'd let you do that."

"Really, it's—"

"If I decide to go back I'll take a cab."

Luke's lids flipped open, and his eyes were clear when they drilled into hers. "Get Ben to drive you."

Rhys shoved his hands into his pockets. Clearly, Luke didn't want Emily taking a cab. He didn't either. There were no trained security personnel in a cab.

Emily's deep green eyes flashed to Luke's. And held. "I think I'll stay for awhile."

Luke's face hardened. "I'm fine. I don't need you to look after me."

Her steady gaze never wavered. *Yes you do*, it said, as clearly as if she'd spoken the words.

Okay…definitely time to leave.

Bryn chewed on her lips, dividing her attention between Luke and Emily, her eyes pinging back and forth like she was watching a tennis match.

Then Luke sighed and rubbed a hand over his eyes. "I'm real tired, Em."

"I know. I can see that."

A spark of temper lit his eyes when he opened them.

Bryn broke the tension by getting to her feet and hugging Emily goodbye, then laid a hand on Luke's shoulder with a friendly pat. "See you after you get out of recovery."

"Sure," he said. "Thank Dec for me."

"Will do." Her dark gaze sought Emily's. "Call us if you change your mind." Hugging Rhys, she left, and when the door closed behind her with a soft click, it felt like they'd all been trapped together in an air lock. Or a vacuum from which all the air had been sucked out. It explained why it suddenly felt so damn hard to breathe.

Rhys rubbed the back of his neck. Shit, he wished he'd left with Bryn. "I'll wait outside until the security is in place."

"No need," Emily said calmly. "You can stay in here."

"Uh, I think—"

"Go back to your hotels," Luke told them both gruffly. "I'm fine."

Emily regarded him coolly for a moment before answering. "You're not fine, but you're going to be. And you and I both know you won't sleep a wink if I go." She settled back in her chair and crossed her arms over her waist, like she was curling in on her body. Comforting herself because she knew damn well she wasn't getting any from her ex-husband.

Rhys withheld a sigh. This was way too damn awkward, and he knew Luke hated him witnessing it.

Emily's tired exhalation made Luke glance over at her uneasily.

"Close your eyes and rest for a while," she said.

"You may not want to look at me, but at least you know you can trust me to watch over you. Let your demons go for a little while, Luke. I won't leave you." Her quiet vow made Rhys wish he was anywhere but in that room with them. Whatever was passing between her and Luke was intense and private. It was obvious Luke didn't want her there. Though he didn't tell her to leave again, either.

Rhys was edging toward the door again when Emily turned her head and put on a smile for him. "Please, stay. It's all right, really."

Yeah, but why couldn't he just wait outside the door? Resigned to feeling like an interloper, Rhys parked it in a chair near the door and eyed his only exit route. He looked at Luke for help, but he'd turned his head away and let his lids drop.

Emily's chair scraped across the linoleum floor as she got up, and Luke cracked an eyelid open to watch her lean over and turn off the dim reading light beside his bed. Plunged into blessed darkness, Rhys relaxed as she returned to her seat until he heard the groan of the plastic chair when she pushed the backrest down. She was turning the chair into a pullout so she could lie down. Which meant she had every intention of sleeping there for the night.

Luke's head snapped around, though it had to hurt him. "Em—"

Okay, definitely time to go. Rhys had no interest in sticking around to watch this showdown.

"I'll be fine," she argued as the sliding closet door groaned open.

She must be looking for a blanket and pillow. While she rummaged around, Rhys seized his chance and slipped from the room, pulling in a relieved breath when it shut behind him and he was able to get a full breath of air. Jesus, those two were intense. Luke was in for a damn long night if she stayed.

When the security agent finally arrived, Rhys checked his credentials and called Nate to verify them, then briefed the guy on the situation. Once the newbie was up to speed, Rhys hesitated outside the door. It was quiet in there, and he sure as hell didn't want to watch the two of them circling each other like wary adversaries, but he wanted to check on Luke one last time before he left. Maybe he could even drag Emily out of there for him.

Tapping softly, he opened the door a crack and peeked in, then pushed it open and stepped inside, careful not to make any noise. The sight before him stopped him in his tracks and made him want to kick himself for coming back in.

Emily had pulled that uncomfortable plastic pullout chair right up to Luke's bedside and was fast asleep, curled up on her side facing him. Luke, however, was wide awake and looking straight back at him. "What's up?" he demanded in a whisper.

"Everything's set," Rhys answered just as quietly. "See you in—"

Emily sighed and shifted in her sleep, suddenly flinging an arm out toward Luke. His expression went from wary to alarmed as it landed on the bed a few inches from him, and he froze in shock when her hand curled around his. He stared down at it like it was a grenade with the pin pulled out. Luke seemed afraid to move, and Rhys didn't blame him.

"See you," Rhys blurted, and got out the door as fast as he could without making any more noise.

Walking out to the truck, he figured chances were good Luke would be awake most of the night, frozen in position so he wouldn't wake Emily. Nev would be pissed if she knew Luke wasn't getting his sleep before the surgery, but Rhys wasn't going to tell her about any of it. What was happening back in that hospital room was Luke's private business. He and his ex might be estranged, but the connection between them was still powerful enough that Emily had reached out for him in her sleep. To Rhys, that said it all.

It made him think about marriage in general, something he'd never imagined doing, but maybe he could someday. He didn't know how far things would go with Neveah, but he couldn't see himself without her in the near future, and that was a shock in itself. He'd never felt this way before. Not even close.

Anxious to see her, he pulled out of the parking lot and turned west toward the police station. Taking one last look at the hospital in his rearview mirror, he found himself hoping Emily would leave her hand where it was.

****

Ahmed parked his BMW next to his wife's Mercedes, climbed out and closed his door with a quiet thud. Since leaving the hospital he'd had the eerie feeling someone was following him, but he hadn't seen anyone. He'd almost decided not to come home in case he was right, but in the end had done it anyhow. He blinked wearily in the flood of the security light above him as the garage door touched the concrete floor and the motor stopped. The sudden silence echoed in his ears.

Suppressing a shiver of unease, he trudged up the steps to the door that led to the kitchen and opened it. The knob was ice cold against his palm as he turned it, but the lack of noise inside brought him up short. No radio, no murmur from the television. Ahmed's heart sped up. It was seven-thirty. His wife was always deep into her reality shows at this time of night.

He glanced up at the ceiling, wondering if she'd

gone upstairs. Was she sick? She hadn't called to say she wasn't feeling well, and as far as he knew, she hadn't left the school early.

"Lily?" he called. She didn't answer.

A whisper of fear crept in. Lily always stayed home on Saturday nights because her favorite show was on. There was no way she'd miss it.

His legs felt weighed down with lead as he went through the brightly lit kitchen. The ingredients for dinner lay out on the counter, and dirty pans and pots filled the sink. Very unlike his tidy wife.

The family room was empty. The widescreen plasma TV he'd had installed over the fireplace was off. His wife's favorite throw blanket lay folded neatly in its place next to her chaise.

She hadn't been here. "Lily!"

He ran up the newly carpeted stairs and down the hall to their bedroom, heart knocking. The solid oak doors loomed before him. Thoughts of what he might find on the other side haunted him. Did he dare open them?

He had to. He had to know she was all right. The blood roared in his ears. *Please just let her be in the bathroom.* Let her be soaking in the tub, and this awful fear would be for nothing.

Battling to keep his breathing under control, Ahmed pushed the heavy wood doors open and hit the light switch with a trembling hand. His heart almost stopped. The carpet was strewn with debris from an obvious struggle. Pieces of broken glass and jewelry lay all over the floor. He stumbled to the cavernous walk-in closet and found more of the same. In the white granite bathroom, overturned drawers met his horrified stare.

Oh God, they'd taken her. Taken her because the first operation hadn't gone like it should have. Because he'd failed to ensure otherwise.

Tehrazzi had warned him about what would happen.

They'd rifled through everything in the room looking for something—phone records? Messages? He'd never be stupid enough to leave clues about his secret life for someone to find.

They hadn't found anything, so they'd taken Lily, an unknowing innocent in this terrible chain reaction he'd initiated.

Staring with hollow eyes at the soaker tub in the corner, his knees gave out and he slid to the cold floor, cradling his head with shaking hands. Nausea swirled in his gut along with the guilt that threatened to suffocate him. He imagined Lily fighting with the men that had taken her, crying and terrified, having no idea what they were talking about. They might have tortured her for information. His stomach lurched. Or…God, maybe they'd killed her.

A strangled moan escaped his raw throat. *Lily*. He couldn't call the police, what would he tell them? They'd eventually find out what he'd done. But he had to find a way to save Lily. He loved her, hadn't meant for any of this to happen.

Think, you asshole, think!

But his brain, always so dependable, was too full of Lily's fearful black eyes and pale face, conjuring up images of her enduring what her captors might do to her.

He didn't know what the hell to do. What could he provide Tehrazzi that would interest him? Money maybe. The cause was always in need of donations. He could do a wire transfer and empty out his bank accounts, his investments, his shares, everything. Whatever it took to keep his wife safe.

In his gut, he knew Tehrazzi would never be satisfied with such a paltry gesture. He'd assigned Ahmed the task and expected it to be carried out. Damn, what could he do to fix this? Whatever it was, he had to buy enough time to take care of Doctor Adams, and then perhaps they'd free Lily.

Bleak as the answer was, it was the only one that came to him.

The phone shrilled from the bedroom. With his heart weighing like a lead lump in the center of his chest, he pushed to his feet and stumbled to the cordless extension, staring at the unfamiliar number on the call display. No choice. He couldn't risk missing a call about Lily. His fingers were almost too stiff to hold the handset he brought to his ear. "Hello?" His voice was hoarse.

"Ahmed!" Lily's fearful cry ripped through him like a lightning bolt.

"Lily." His knees buckled, sending him to the floor with a thud. "Oh sweetheart, thank God—"

"I don't know what they're talking about, Ahmed, please help me!"

He closed his eyes. "I will. I swear to God I'll do anything—"

"That's good to know," a male voice said. The same one that had contacted him with Tehrazzi's number.

Ahmed stiffened. "What do you want?"

"I want you to finish what you started."

Bile rose in his throat. "Be more specific."

"It's too late to get Hutchinson, unless we blow the entire hospital up. Mr. Tehrazzi wants to ensure you won't make the same mistake with Doctor Adams. Shouldn't be too hard to kill one unarmed female civilian, should it?"

He swallowed, his fear for Lily making him half crazy. "I've already hired someone for that."

"Someone different from the idiots you hired for Hutchinson?"

"Yes. He's a professional. A former Force Recon Marine."

The man grunted. "You'd better hope he's a pro. Your wife is depending on it."

Oh God… "Don't hurt her," he pleaded, voice little more than a rasp. "She doesn't know anything about what I've done."

"She does now."

Ahmed bowed his head. If Lily lived, their marriage would be over. No way would she take him back after the things he'd done. She would never understand, let alone condone, the beliefs that had led him to this terrible crossroads. He didn't either. Not anymore. But there was no going back, for any of them. "Please don't hurt her. I'll do anything you want. Take me instead, I'll meet you anywhere you tell me to, but let her go."

"No. She's the best means to ensure you get the job done right this time."

Helpless fury filled him. "I'll make sure this time," he swore, aware he was begging but didn't give a damn. "Just tell me you'll let Lily go when it's over."

A moment of silence filled the line before the speaker said, "We'll know when it's happened from the news reports. Your wife will be delivered to an address we will inform you of once it's finished. It's up to you whether she arrives there alive or not."

The line went dead, the dial tone buzzing in his ear. Ahmed dropped the phone. "Fuck," he cried, covering his face in his hands, letting the tears fall. The life he'd built for him and his wife was over now. He might still be breathing, but he was already dead. Only a matter of time now before his physical being met the same fate as his soul.

I'm sorry, Lily. So damned sorry.

How had he come to this point? He had to kill a woman to save the one he loved. The price was high, enough to damn his soul in eternity, but there was no other alternative. He would do whatever it took to save his wife.

Chapter Sixteen

On the short trip from the station to her hotel, Neveah seemed to make a real effort to put all the scary shit aside for the moment. Which he appreciated.

Rhys parked the Escalade underground and came around to help her down from her seat. She took his hand with a smile that made his blood heat and slid her arms around him when he placed her on the ground. The way she leaned into him and hugged him tight was like a priceless gift.

"Think Luke will take it easy after the operation?" she asked against his shoulder.

He pressed a kiss to the top of her head, appreciating her effort at salvaging what was left of the evening. "Doubt it."

"I swear, alpha males are the worst patients in the whole world."

"No doubt."

"Apart from doctors that is," she qualified. Then she sighed and pulled away, but her eyes were full of shadows. "Take me upstairs and make me forget all this for awhile."

Fuck yeah, he would. "Yes ma'am, just as soon as we get to my hotel." And tonight, he was going to make love to her properly. Not screw her, not fuck her, make love to her. He'd never done that with anyone before. He wanted to know what it felt like.

The prospect probably should have scared the hell out of him, but instead it turned him on even more. He couldn't wait to get her into his room and slide his hands under that dress to find out if she really was naked beneath it. Then he'd lay her out on the soft bed and take his time learning everything he could about her body and what felt good for her.

Even half-blinded by lust, he still had the presence of mind to be vigilant as they got into the elevator with another couple and rode to their floor in silence. Nev pressed close against his right side, her breast not-so-accidentally brushing his upper arm. He shot her a warning glare. If she kept that up, she'd find out quick enough he was more than capable of foregoing manners and the fact that they had two elderly spectators to watch the show.

An impish smile stayed on her lips as the elevator door opened and she sailed out, tossing a challenging look over her shoulder at him. "Coming?"

"Not until after you do, honey. A woman should always come first."

The old lady in the elevator gasped, and Rhys caught sight of her shocked expression in the hall mirror across from the elevator as the doors closed. He grinned and followed Neveah. He loved the deep V in the back of the dress that left most of her back naked, stopping just above the base of her spine and showing off her beautifully curved hips and ass. Damn, she was enough to make his corneas bleed.

A slit up the back of the skirt revealed flashes of her thighs and calves as she walked in those fragile-looking heels. Maybe he'd leave her in those and nothing else, he pondered, imagining them dangling over his shoulders as he pushed into the tight warmth of her body. Oh yeah, that had definite possibilities.

Approaching her door at the end of the hall, Nev pulled out her key card.

"Wait a sec," he said, reaching over her shoulder to grab it.

"I'm perfectly capable of opening my own door," she said with an irritated expression.

"Well, that's not how I do things. I like to be in control, remember?" He knew he didn't need to remind her of why he was being so cautious.

That catlike smile reappeared. "Mmm, and that does have its merits."

Oh yeah. He pulled the card out, and when the little green light flashed, he pushed down on the handle. The door opened soundlessly, revealing an inch or two of space inside. The room was pitch black.

Nev had left a lamp on when he'd come to pick her up. He seriously doubted housekeeping would have turned it off.

The hair on the back of his neck stood up.

"Move aside," Nev said, starting to push past him.

He grabbed her upper arm and instinctively turned her. "Wait—" Jerking her to a halt, he set her against the wall and drew his weapon, ignoring her gasp, and went in fast. No shots, not a sound as he positioned himself, ready to pull the trigger to stop any threat against Neveah. When he was sure no one was in the room he flipped on the light.

The room was in a state of utter devastation. Someone had pulled the drawers out of the bureau and dumped them out, spilling her clothes and books over the floor. Her suitcase lay open next to the closet, its contents strewn on the carpet. The bed was ripped apart, the bedding tossed in a heap at the foot and the pillows lay scattered around beneath it.

"Rhys?"

He ducked his head into the bathroom. All her things were scattered on the floor, bottles and tubes smashed on the granite. Shit. He didn't want her to be afraid, but she had to see this.

As though hearing his thoughts, Neveah pushed the door open and stopped short. Her face paled, eyes going wide at the mess in front of her. "Oh," she whispered, bringing a hand to her long, lovely throat.

"Any idea what they might have been looking for?"

"No." She took a step into the room, eyes locked on the suitcase torn open in front of the closet. "Can I check for something?" Her voice was rough.

He put his weapon back in its holster beneath his coat. "Yeah. Just try not to disturb anything until the cops can get here."

She gave him a look that said she doubted things could be more disturbed than they already were, then went to the suitcase. "My laptop," she explained, bending down to search through the pile of clothes. "I left it in here."

While she searched, Rhys did a more thorough examination, speed dialing his brother and explaining the situation. When he hung up, he noticed something silver sticking out of the crumpled bedding. He pulled back a corner of the comforter. "Here, Nev."

She scrambled to her feet and rushed over to grab the laptop. "Ben coming?" she asked as she opened the lid and fired it up.

"With Nate." Rhys watched her face as the computer booted up and allowed her to search through some files. Her expression filled with acute relief.

"My presentation and speech," she breathed. "They're still here."

"What kind of security do you have on that thing?"

She shrugged. "I don't know…my password."

Figured. "What is it?"

"Samarra."

Not a very secure choice, in his opinion. No way was this a random break in, and whoever had done it would know all about Neveah, including her cousin's name. Hell, their names had both been splashed all over the news networks, including CNN. Didn't take a very high IQ to plug in Samarra as a guess. "Anything on there that someone would be interested enough in to break in here?"

A tiny frown pulled at her brows. "No. Just e-mail, some files for my accountant, my speech. Things like that. Don't you think it's weird they didn't take it? And my jewelry's still here. I mean, why go to all the trouble of breaking in and then not stealing anything?"

He met her eyes and let her make the connection herself.

Her eyes went wide. "You think they wanted *me*?"

Yes and no. They might have a bounty on her head to collect from Tehrazzi's network, or… "I think they wanted something from you, and since you weren't here, they hoped to get it from your laptop."

Neveah set the device down on the carpet and rose to her feet, rubbing her arms. "What do you think it is?"

"About Luke, probably."

Her eyes filled with alarm. "This has something to do with what happened tonight, doesn't it? With those guys you caught."

"I'm not—"

"Don't you lie to me," she snapped, staring holes through him. "Not now."

He let out a deep breath. "Fine. What do you want to know?"

"Did they have weapons?"

"Yes."

Her eyes got even bigger. "What kind?"

"Pistols, an AK-47 and grenades."

For an instant she went completely still, and he was afraid she might keel over, but instead her eyes glittered like shards of steel and she raised a warning finger at him. "God dammit, Rhys, I had a right to know."

He couldn't blame her for being pissed, but there was no sense in letting her get all worked up over something that was already over and done with. Rhys walked over and put his hands on her shoulders. Her muscles were stiff under his palms, but he ignored it and slid his arms around her.

"Don't be scared," he said into the fragrant coil of hair she'd wound on the top of her head. "It's going to be okay. I'm here, Ben's on his way, and we'll get some answers. All right?"

Releasing a breath, she nodded and then melted against him, seeking comfort. Damn, he wanted to get her the hell away from there, but he didn't dare move her without back up. Not now.

She'd been registered here under an alias, so someone had to have followed her from the conference to know where she was staying. The state of the room suggested they'd been in a big damn hurry, and the fact that they'd left all her jewelry and laptop behind meant they either hadn't found what they'd been looking for, or that they'd been alerted to get out before he and Nev arrived. Both possibilities worried him.

Holding her tight, Rhys smoothed a hand over her bare back and spoke softly to her, waiting for Ben to show up. A few moments later a door at the end of the hallway burst open and running footsteps reached them. Rhys left Neveah to look out the door and held it open for Ben and Nate. "Any luck outside?"

"No," Ben answered. He and Nate swept inside,

eyes scanning the wreckage. Ben let out a low whistle.

"Nothing's missing," Rhys told them, draping an arm around Neveah's shoulders. "I wanted you to look at her laptop," he said to his brother.

While Nate took a look around for himself, Ben sat on the rumpled bed and put the laptop on his knees. If anyone could find out if it had been tampered with, Ben could. He was an electronics wizard.

His twin typed in a bunch of commands and checked the hard drive. "Don't see anything suspicious," he said, then glanced up at Nev. "You check out your files?"

"Glanced at them. Everything seems okay, and my speech is still there."

Ben met Rhys's eyes. "Sorry, man. Don't know what else to tell you."

Nate came over from the bathroom. "What were they looking for?"

"Not sure," Rhys answered. "You find out anything from our boys at the station?"

Nate shook his head. "Nothing to link this with whatever his plans were."

Which meant they now had another plot to worry about. "Until we know what's going on, I'm going to move her," Rhys said.

"Yeah, that's for the best." He set his hands on his hips and shook his head. "Damn, I don't like this." Then he waved a hand at them. "Go ahead and take her back to your hotel. I'll get my guys together and see if we can find out anything. If there's a chance this is linked to the cell, I'll call you."

Good enough for now. "Come on," he said to Nev, nodding to Ben. His brother went past him into the hall as Rhys guided his precious bundle out.

"My things," she protested, looking behind her.

"We'll get whatever you need later," he said and

firmly guided her out the door, careful to keep her sheltered between him and the wall.

Ben held the stairwell door open for them. "I'll get the truck," he told him. "Underground or out front?"

"Underground." At least down there they'd have some cover and more than one entrance to come out of if someone was lying in wait. Coming out the front entrance would leave them too exposed.

Ben ran down ahead of them and soon disappeared, leaving nothing but the echo of his treads behind. Neveah kept pace with Rhys, but her steps were impeded by her spike heels. Damn sexy shoes, but not a good choice for getting someplace in a hurry. He consciously slowed his pace and kept his senses open for any hint of danger. Even though he'd gone ahead, Ben would be another minute getting the truck around to them.

"Okay, how worried are you?" Nev suddenly asked him as they hit the third floor landing. "Are you expecting trouble or can I stop panicking?"

"Don't panic," he soothed. "We just want you out of here as fast and quietly as possible in case anyone's still looking for you."

"God, so you *do* think they're still out there."

That's what he'd been trained to do—to expect anything. If he'd gone in to find something and come up blank, he wouldn't leave with empty hands. He'd wait as long as it took to get the job done. He had to assume the people hunting Nev would do the same.

Expect the worst and hope for the best, but don't hold your breath on the last count. "It's all right, baby. Just stay close to me and we'll be out of here in no time."

They finally got to the bottom. Waiting inside a different steel and glass door than the one they'd come in, Rhys put Neveah safely behind him and kept an eye out for the Escalade. He couldn't see anyone else, but he was still uneasy about taking Nev out into the open.

With a squeak of its tires, the Escalade came racing into view and tore around the last corner.

Rhys tightened his grip on Nev's hand. "When I say go, I want you to run straight for the truck, okay?" She didn't reply, so he looked back at her. Her eyes were wide. "Nev?"

"I heard you."

Ben raced up and squealed to a stop as close as he could get to the door they waited behind.

Drawing his weapon, Rhys released her hand. "Go."

He shoved the door open with the heel of his hand and darted out in front of her. She tore past him, head down as she sprinted for the vehicle. Ben reached back to throw the back passenger door open and waited.

Rhys turned his attention away from Neveah for a split second. A puff of air brushed against his cheek an instant before something pinged off the stairwell door and plowed into the concrete wall.

"Down!" he bellowed, diving for Neveah.

She froze at his shout and threw him a panicked look as she started to crouch, her arms coming up to shield her face.

Rhys caught her around the waist and threw her to the ground, taking the brunt of the fall. She cried out when they hit, and he quickly placed his body on top of her to shield her from any more shots. "Stay down," he barked as he lifted off. He dragged her, backing up against the wall and raising his pistol.

The instant his index finger curled around the trigger everything inside him turned icy calm. He gave Neveah a shove toward a parked car, and she scuttled away on her hands and knees to hide behind it. Thankfully she stayed quiet and out of the way. Now he had to deal with whoever the hell was shooting at them.

Rising to one knee behind the concrete pillar he was

using for cover, he paused, slowing his breathing. The shooter had a silencer, and the hole in the rebar reinforced concrete wall told him it was a small caliber round, most likely a 9mm from a semi-automatic pistol.

Whoever it was, he was a piss-poor shot, and too far away to know Rhys was out of range. Jesus, he'd been standing there lit up by the bright lights when he'd grabbed Neveah, all six-foot-six of him, and the asshole had still missed. He had trouble believing Tehrazzi would send an amateur like that after Neveah, but it looked like he was facing their third of the night.

Odds were they'd miss him again when he burst into the open, or at least not hit anything too vital. He didn't want to get shot, especially in front of Neveah, but he had to eliminate the threat and the only way to do that was to go out immediately and prevent any collateral damage.

"Rhys…" Nev's plaintive whisper reached him, full of fear.

He never took his eyes off the far corner of the parking lot where the shot had come from, but spared a fraction of his attention to holding up his right hand to acknowledge that he'd heard her. He pointed toward the ground, telling her to stay put.

"No, don't," she pleaded. "Ben's probably already called security—"

He clenched his teeth and thrust his index finger downward. They didn't have time to wait for security, and even if help arrived, they weren't qualified to deal with this kind of threat. Whoever had shot at them might be acting like someone firing a gun for the first time in their life, but they might still be an assassin sent by Farouk Tehrazzi. Not someone who was going to go quietly. That was fine with Rhys.

All his muscles tensed. His eyes stayed locked on the teal green car in the far corner.

Something moved a fraction of an inch. Stopped. Seconds passed.

He was so done with waiting.

Chapter Seventeen

"Rhys!" Her strained whisper seemed terribly loud as she waited for him to answer her. Ben had wheeled the truck around and thrown it into reverse. The engine revved loud as he sped toward her, leaving Rhys to fend for himself. "*Rhys*!"

He didn't answer her, didn't so much as glance at her, riveted by something across the underground lot that she couldn't see and didn't want to. Her heart was trying to pound its way out of her chest, her muscles so tense they were in knots. About to yell at him, she made a choked sound when Rhys suddenly shot out from behind the pillar and started running.

She screamed his name but he didn't stop, just kept going, using the parked cars for cover. Nev scrambled to her knees, shaking all over as Ben roared up with the Escalade, blocking both her view and any more bullets meant for her.

He shoved the passenger door open and yelled, "Get in!"

Struggling to her feet, she almost fell when her weight landed on the ankle she'd twisted when Rhys had taken her down. She threw a hand out to grab for the inside handle and pulled herself up. Ben's strong hand wrapped around her arm and yanked. She wound up on her stomach sprawled across him and the console as he hit the gas and turned the wheel, slewing the big vehicle around. Pushing up, Neveah wrenched the door shut and fell back against the seat, but Ben grabbed her by the nape and shoved her to the floor.

"Don't move," he commanded, putting the transmission into drive and gunning it.

She lay on the floor, gasping and shaking all over. Rhys was out there, sprinting toward the shooter. She could still see him doing it, the muscles in his thighs stretching his tux pants as he ran, shoulder seams of his jacket straining, gun aimed. "Is he okay?"

"Yes," Ben bit out, turning the corner so sharply the tires screamed, making her grab the door armrest to keep from flying into his legs.

"Shouldn't you help him?" she half yelled.

"He doesn't need my help against this piece of shit. Shooter's a goddamn amateur."

"What?"

Ben cranked the wheel to send them screeching around a corner. "If he was a pro, we'd all be dead right now."

Neveah squeezed her eyes shut and prayed. *Please protect Rhys. Please let him be all right.*

Something cracked into the windshield. She jumped and swallowed a scream.

"Shit!" Ben breathed, jerking the wheel as he ducked. "Lucky shot."

From her vantage point in the passenger side foot well, Nev's horrified gaze went to the hole in the center of the cobweb of cracks splitting the windshield. Her lungs burned from lack of air.

"Get the bastard, Rhys," Ben muttered.

All Nev could do was lie there and pray Ben got to his brother before a bullet did.

Rhys ducked down behind another parked car an instant before a round pinged harmlessly off the rear quarter panel. Bit closer, though. Asshole's aim was finally improving now that Rhys was almost at point blank range. That made nine shots, and none of them had come close. Shooter would be out of ammo in his magazine soon, and he'd better pray he reloaded before Rhys got to him.

Time slowed down as it always did when he was under fire, each second stretching out unnaturally like an elastic. He could feel the air rushing in and out of his lungs and the blood pumping in his veins as his legs ate up the open ground between him and his target.

Wheeling around a back bumper at the end of the row of cars, he squeezed off a shot and managed to hit the culprit's side view mirror. The shooter dropped out of sight, but not before Rhys caught a glimpse of long black hair emerging from beneath a black watch cap.

The driver's door opened and the shooter tried to slide inside. Rhys fired at the passenger window and heard a yelp, the high pitched sound registering over his pounding footsteps and the screech of tires as Ben came after him. Thank God Neveah was okay.

Rhys ran for the next line of cars, but no more shots came. Had he hit the shooter?

Fifty yards from the car now. Almost close enough to get a head shot with his sidearm, but he would only take it as a last resort. He wanted the shooter alive and kicking so they could get some goddamn answers. Rhys kept his gaze pinned to the steering wheel of the shooter's vehicle. No visual.

Then the engine fired up.

Oh no. You're not fucking getting away from me.

Firing twice to shoot out a tire and windshield, Rhys whipped around the hood with his weapon trained, noticing for the first time the spatter of blood on the dashboard. He'd hit them, but he didn't know how badly.

"Show me your hands!" he snarled, ready to go through the shattered window to drag the bastard out.

Two hands came up. One bloody. Both empty.

Sure he was dealing with the only occupant of the car, Rhys went right up to it and stuck his gun through the window, then grabbed his target by the scruff of the neck and lifted their head. When he saw the face staring up at him, he was so surprised he almost let go.

Shit, a woman! A tiny one of East Asian descent, maybe five four and a hundred and ten pounds. "Don't you move," he warned her. He didn't ease up from her as he manacled her wrists in one hand and hauled her out of the door he'd unlocked. The pistol lay on the floorboard at her feet. Her head lolled as he gave her a hard shake. "Who the hell are you?"

Raising her narrowed eyes, she glared up at him with undiluted hatred.

A door shut behind him, and then Ben's voice rang out. "What the *fuck*?"

For once, he didn't reprimand his brother for swearing in front of a woman. "Where's Nate," Rhys growled, all jacked up with no release for it. He couldn't beat an answer out of her, his goddamn moral code wouldn't let him. But he was tempted. Christ, she might be a piss-poor shot, but she could have killed him and Neveah or anyone else unfortunate enough to be in the parking lot with them.

"On his way down. Squad cars should be here any minute."

"Nev okay?"

"Yeah. She's already inside with one of the security

guards."

Rhys clenched his jaw so hard he thought he might crack his molars, and spun the woman around to pin her face first against the car. She gasped but otherwise made no sound despite the ricochet wound in her wrist. He looked at Ben. "Got a zip tie?"

"Fresh out," he said, pulling his tie out of his pocket. "How's this?"

Whatever. He grabbed the thing and tied the woman's wrists together, ignoring her grunt of pain when he jerked the knot tight. "Who are you working for?" he demanded, patience growing thin. Even he had his limits.

She wouldn't answer, merely turned her lips inward and stared straight ahead as though he didn't exist and wasn't towering over her by more than a foot and a hundred thirty pounds.

"I'll take care of this," Ben said, coming up to take his place. "You go get your girl."

Aiming a blistering glare at the woman who'd tried to kill them, Rhys stalked off toward the staircase entrance just as the blare of sirens rose in the distance. About goddamn time, he thought darkly, fighting the adrenaline screaming inside him.

He found Nev in the lobby with Nate and two other officers.

"Rhys," she cried when she spotted him, limping as she rushed over.

He caught her in his arms and held on tight. "I'm okay, it's over," he said, striving to keep his voice calm and mask any aggression he was feeling. She was shaking. He smoothed a hand over the thick fall of her hair. "You?"

"Fine," she breathed against his neck. "Oh God, I was so scared."

"None of the shots came close."

She raised her head and stared at him.

"Trust me, she missed me by a mile," he explained bluntly.

"She?" She gasped, gazing up at him with her fathomless blue eyes. "What the hell were you doing, running toward them—her, like that?"

"Taking care of you."

Her eyes were haunted. "I don't want that kind of protection."

"Too bad."

Before she could respond Nate came up, and Rhys spent the next few minutes giving his account for the record.

Nate's brows shot up beneath his hairline. "A woman?"

"Not something you see every day," Rhys allowed, wanting the hell out of there. They were using female suicide bombers all over Iraq and Afghanistan, so they shouldn't be so shocked. No telling how many more people were hiding in the shadows, ready to take a shot at them. "There has to be someone else. No way Tehrazzi sent someone so inept."

"Yeah, I hear ya." He waved his boys over. "Be right back. Your brother's on his way up."

"We're outta here," Rhys told him, earning a flinty stare. "You've got our statements, and now I'm taking Nev. Luke can contact me later." With that he took Neveah's slender upper arm in his hand and headed for the elevator. She flinched and stumbled when she took a step, so Rhys swung her up into his arms, ignoring her embarrassed protests.

She persisted, pushing at his shoulder. "Let me walk, Rhys. I'm okay."

He set her on her feet, but kept an arm around her shoulders. No way in hell was he letting her out of arm's reach. He bundled her into the elevator. She stayed burrowed in close against him, scrapes and cuts all over her arms from when he'd taken her down on the pavement. She probably had more under her dress. Another surge of anger hit him, but as he caught a glimpse of his expression in the mirrored panel inside the elevator, he forced himself to cool out. Nev didn't need him looking like he wanted to commit murder right now.

Chapter Eighteen

The drive over to the twins' hotel was tense. It should only have been a five minute drive, but Ben took a long, circuitous route to ensure no one was following them. The cracks from the bullet hole had already spread across the length of the windshield.

Ben finally dropped them off at the front door without a word. Rhys immediately came around to lift her out of the Escalade,

"I'm fine," she protested, but he ignored her and hoisted her into his arms. Since she didn't have a prayer of swaying him, she resigned to being carried through the lobby and did her best to ignore the stares people were giving them.

Alone with him in the elevator she relaxed with a sigh. The muscles under her hands and against her breasts were rigid with tension, and his closed expression told her exactly how deep he was in his own head. For the moment, she'd let him be.

Once Rhys got them up to the room and checked to make sure it was secure, he locked and dead bolted the door behind them, then flipped off the lights. The instant he set her down in the sudden darkness Nev dragged the damn dress off and flung it on the floor, leaving her in her bra, panties and high heeled sandals. She would have kicked off her shoes and stomped on the offensive garment that had made getting to safety so hard, but her foot hurt too damn much.

Rhys swung her up off her feet once again and strode to the bathroom. Wincing when he hit the lights in the bathroom, she hung on while he sat on the edge of the tub with her in his lap. He held her so tight the muscles in his arms and chest felt like a vise, but it was exactly what she needed.

Inhaling deeply, she breathed that first precious sigh of relief and burrowed in close, tucking her face into his throat. And just held on. As his warmth seeped into her, she let herself drift in the sensory experience. They could have died tonight. Every second was a gift, every beat of their hearts an experience to savor.

The unspoken fear she sensed in his body made her long to ease him, but she knew if she tried to talk to him about it he'd just close down. Nev tried to let her embrace tell him everything he needed, sliding her hand up to his nape and rubbing gently, then squeezing the too-tight muscles there. He groaned and pressed even closer to her, a shudder running through his big body. Nev closed her eyes against the pain inside her. *Oh, Rhys...*

He was fighting so hard to keep it together, would never give himself permission to let go and show any weakness. He'd never be able to accept that she wouldn't see it as a weakness because she loved him. Things were uncertain enough between them without adding that to the mix, but maybe she should tell him. The thought made her stomach clench.

Against her neck, Rhys exhaled, the warmth of his breath sending shivers dancing over her skin. His big hands splayed across her naked back, his touch changing from possessive to something even more primitive. "I couldn't stand it if anything happened to you," he finally said in a hoarse voice.

Nev raised her head and took his face between her hands to look into his eyes. They were haunted with the terrible knowledge of what could have happened, and she understood it wasn't because he was afraid of dying. Men in the Unit routinely carried their own body bags with them during a mission. No, that deep seated fear was for her.

Helpless, she stroked his back. The strength of her love filled her, rising up until the words crowded her throat, demanding to be said aloud. She swallowed them down. "I'm okay, Rhys."

"That was way too damn close."

Yes. For both of them. And it frightened her that he had charged headlong into danger to protect her, without a thought for his own well-being.

He set her away from him and took her face in his hands, his thumbs stroking the hair at her temples. "You sure you're not hurt anywhere?"

She shook her head. "Just scraped up a bit." A few stings here and there and a sprained ankle were nothing compared to the bullet wound she might have had if things had gone differently.

Rhys lifted her injured foot in his hand, long fingers testing the joint line between her talus and fibula. She held back a wince as he hit the tender spot. He zeroed right in on it, watching her face. "Bad?"

"No. First degree sprain of the anterior talofibular ligament. Most commonly sprained ligament in the body," she added, wiggling her foot back and forth, ignoring the stab of pain. "See? It's nothing." Son of a bitch, that hurt. Maybe it was a second degree sprain.

"You're a really bad liar."

"No, really. I can walk, so it's minor." She sat up.

"Wanna see?"

"No. I want you to sit here so I can check and make sure you're not hiding anything else from me."

She sat very still while he slid her onto the cool porcelain lip of the tub and hunkered down at her feet to begin checking her over. Some of the blessed numbness began to fade away as her endocrine system realized she wasn't in immediate peril and stopped with the norepinephrine barrage. The friction burns on her palms and elbows throbbed along with her ankle, and his fingers found a few forming bruises as they explored her.

Watching his hands as they glided over her, she let him strip her bra and panties off while his eyes catalogued every bruise and abrasion on her body before starting the shower. Once she was naked and he was satisfied she wasn't hurt anywhere else, he reached up and unwound her hair from its knot on the top of her head. The silky weight of it spilled across her back like a sensual caress, adding to the tingles his touch left in its wake. She swallowed, a pulse of need hitting her low in her belly.

Rhys stood and peeled off his own clothes in a distracted way, and the sight of him standing there naked sent a flood of welcome heat through her chilled body. Testing the water, he took her by the arm and helped her over the lip of the tub, then climbed in behind her and pulled the curtain closed, shutting them in a cloud of steam.

Every nerve ending in her body was vividly aware of him standing at her back. Then he lightly touched her shoulders, turning her to face him. Water sluiced over his beautifully defined muscles, from his shoulders and chest down his belly to where his sex stood out proud and straight from his body. Her knees weakened. Heat gathered between her thighs.

His hands were gentle as they swept over her wet hair and body, but his eyes were anything but calm. They simmered with some intense emotion she couldn't begin to name, so hot she could feel them burning her.

Standing motionless under the pounding spray, Nev let him lather her hair and rinse it clean, then watched as he knelt to wash the scrapes on her knees, trying her best to ignore the shocks of erotic power humming through her with each touch. Down her calves and over her feet, back up again, brushing the tender spots behind her knees, his hands made her bite back a whimper of need. His touch electrified her.

When all the scrapes had been cleaned, he slid those beautiful hands up her slick thighs and buttocks to grip her hips, raising his head to press his face hard into her belly where he let out a ragged breath. Frowning, her fingers sank into his wet hair, one hand traveling over his neck and shoulders, offering the comfort he sought. Love for him overwhelmed her, filling every cell of her being.

"Rhys," she whispered unsteadily. He lifted his endlessly blue stare.

The words stuck in her throat. Forcing the fear of rejection and vulnerability out of her mind, she gathered her nerve and said them out loud. "I really love you."

For a split second he went completely still, but then he surged to his feet and pressed her against the cool tile of the shower with his body and kissed her like he'd die if he stopped.

Caught off guard by his sudden desperation, Nev gasped into his mouth and wrapped her arms and legs around him, trying to bring him as close as she could. In response he growled low in his throat and locked an arm around her hips. He lifted her off her feet and pinned her to the wall, his mouth voracious as it devoured her lips, her throat, her breasts.

Crying out at the explosive need throbbing inside her, she nipped at his shoulder and wound her legs tighter around his waist, urging him inside. With a helpless groan, Rhys gathered her against him and pushed the tip of his swollen erection against her sex. She tensed. He wasn't wearing a condom, but they didn't need one if he hadn't been with anyone since being wounded. She'd seen his blood work and knew he was clean. Still, her body resisted the invasion as he pushed harder, not yet ready for him. He began to pull back.

"No," she rasped. They both needed this, especially him if this was the only form of release he'd allow himself.

She bowed backward, easing his way so he slid deeper. God, he was so thick and hot… She bit her lip. It almost hurt, but she'd rather die than deny him this. His jaw was clenched so tightly the muscles stood out. The navy eyes staring back at her glittered feverishly. His fingers dug into her hips. As soon as he was lodged inside her he set in with a rough, urgent rhythm that stole the breath from her lungs. *Oh, Jesus…*

Seized in his unbreakable grip, she could only hold on as he pounded into her, nothing held back, all pretense of control shattered.

My God, he was strong. The raw power of him shocked and aroused her at the same time. It was too much too soon for her, and there was no way she would be able to reach orgasm, but the way he was powering into her still sent an erotic rush through her veins. No one had ever wanted her like this. Needed her like this. Not in her whole life. But here trapped between her lover and the shower wall, every straining line of Rhys's body was testament of his ravenous hunger for her.

His head fell back as he neared his release, teeth clenched and eyes squeezed shut like he was in pain.

Offering all her tenderness and love, she caressed his cheek. Holding him close when he buried his face in the curve of her neck with a guttural snarl, he jerked out of her body at the last moment. Snatching her hand and wrapping it around his slick, pulsing erection, he came all over her belly in hot spurts.

Gasping in the aftermath, he leaned against her as though suddenly exhausted, his whole body trembling. Smoothing her hands over his glistening skin, she soothed him in silence, letting the warm water rush over them until he loosened his grip and allowed her to slide down until her feet came to rest on the bottom of the tub. He was careful to anchor her so she could take the weight off her sore ankle.

After a few minutes, he lifted his head and looked down at her. His eyes were shadowed with concern and maybe even a little bit of fear. Reaching up, he brushed a lock of wet hair away from her temple. “Did I hurt you?”

“Not at all.” Balancing on her good foot, she went up on tiptoe to kiss the grim line of his lips. “Stop worrying.”

“Jesus, I didn’t mean to be so rough.” The reverent hands he slid over her back were full of mute apology.

She smiled against his mouth. “I’m not complaining. Are you all right?”

He broke eye contact. “Yeah. I’m sorry I…” His ribs expanded and contracted as he huffed out a hard breath. “Shit, I’m just sorry.”

“No need to be.” The fact that he swore said how unglued he was about what had just happened. He still had his fist clamped over her hand, wrapped around his softening erection.

As though he’d just noticed that, he let go with a curse. “Christ.” His eyes flashed up to hers. “I’m clean, I swear—”

“It’s okay, I know you are. I am, too, by the way.”

He kept staring at her.

She tried not to smile. "Clean," she explained. "And I've got an IUD, so we're fine."

Rhys let out a relieved breath and picked up the soap to wash the traces of himself off her belly and thighs. He didn't say a word about her breathless declaration of love, and she wasn't about to bring it up. Maybe he didn't love her yet, but he cared about her enough to tackle her to the ground and shield her with his body, fully prepared to take a bullet for her. Add in the way he'd just taken her against the shower wall, and those things told her everything she needed to know for now.

Despite the tense silence that expanded between them, flames licked everywhere his fingers brushed her sensitized skin. Afraid to move or speak lest it break the spell, she leaned back against the cool tiles and basked in the tender consideration he took in caring for her. When he skimmed over her inner thigh to wash between her legs she gasped involuntarily, her body weeping for him. Craving him.

He looked up into her face, read her unfulfilled need and killed the shower. Stepping out of the tub and turning back to her, his deep blue eyes glowed with the promise of ecstasy.

He held out a hand, palm up, and his words were as good as a vow. "Come here."

Guilt rode Rhys hard as he wrapped Nev in a towel and carried her to the bed where he settled her against the pillows. The demons in his soul had torn free and she'd suffered for them. Jesus Christ, he'd pinned her against the shower wall and slammed into her like a goddamn freight train.

He'd never lost control like that. Never in his life, and definitely never with a woman, let alone one he cared about so deeply. He knew his own strength, and unless he was dealing with a bad guy, was always careful to temper it around people.

What the hell had happened to him back there? He knew damn well Nev was afraid of violence and maybe even a little afraid of him. After what had happened at her hotel… Shit, he never should have touched her while he was keyed up like that. He had to have left bruises on her hips from keeping her clamped against him like that. He touched her carefully, disgusted with himself. She probably thought he only did it standing up.

Her skin was like velvet beneath his searching fingertips. So soft, so fragile. How the hell could he have taken her like that, and before she was ready for him? He wouldn't blame her if she kicked him out on his sorry ass and never spoke to him again. At the same time he prayed she wouldn't, because it would rip his heart out. He moved the terrycloth towel over her neck and shoulders, half afraid to meet her eyes. She was watching him. He could feel the weight of her stare.

Face half-hidden in shadows, she lay still while he dried her off, lingering over every dip and curve. When he dragged the towel lower, he couldn't help but notice the way her nipples beaded and flushed. Damned if he didn't feel a glow of arousal building up again. Her small, perfectly rounded breasts rose and fell with her even breaths. A wash of goose bumps covered her skin. He glanced up. "Cold?" The thought of her suffering even that small discomfort bothered him.

Neveah shook her head, her vivid blue eyes almost glowing in the darkness. His hand stopped moving. The towel did nothing to insulate his palm from the sensual curve of her hip.

"Rhys," she whispered, then stopped, closing her eyes as if gathering herself.

Ah, hell, she was hurting. He'd shoved into her and

pounded away until he came, without giving her a prayer of catching up. Worse, he'd gotten her revved up and then left her hanging.

Though he'd behaved like a Neanderthal a few minutes back, she still wanted him. Well he could definitely take away the hurt he'd caused. He'd give her as much of him as she wanted; all night, for as long as he could hold out. That was the least he could do. He needed to show her he could be gentle, that he really did have control over himself.

Eyes on hers, he tossed the damp towel aside, then pulled back the covers and lay down so he pressed up against all her naked curves. She pulled in a sharp breath and rolled into him, wrapping around him like a living blanket. His heart lurched.

He brought one hand up to cradle the back of her head and used the other to trail up and down her spine. Everything about her was a miracle to him. The way she felt in his arms, her gentle heart and her formidable brain. The thought of what she'd suffered in Afghanistan, and that someone had been waiting to kill her tonight made him want to arm up and hunt the bastards down right now.

Her fingers dug into his back as he caressed one round buttock. Hungry. He smiled against her hair. She might be built lean, but she had all the womanly curves a man could ever want. And she fit against him perfectly, her head resting against his shoulder. He was going to take care of her and be the kind of lover she deserved. Patient, attentive and gentle. Until she screamed his name because she needed something more.

Letting his actions speak for him, he kissed her temple and tilted her face up to his. She watched him in silence for a moment, but her eyes drifted closed when he traced over the line of her brows with the pads of his fingers. He followed the dark wings over to one temple and down her high cheekbone, pausing a moment to savor the petal softness of her cheek against his palm before exploring her nose and lush lips. They parted at his touch and though it made his dick miraculously go hard as stone against her abdomen, he traced the same path with his mouth.

She turned into his kisses, angling her head so he could reach the point of her stubborn chin. Hovering a breath away from her lips, he stopped. Nev grabbed his head and brought his lips to hers with a quiet moan.

Her mouth quivered beneath the tender stroke of his tongue, parting to let him inside, one of her legs curling over his thigh to increase the contact between them. Rhys took his time with the kiss, searching out every tender spot, caressing her silky tongue before withdrawing to tease her full lower lip. She came back for more, sighing, wriggling to get closer.

Holding her head, he tipped it back and nuzzled the vulnerable place below her ear next to her jaw. More goose bumps broke out over her skin. Smiling, he pressed a kiss there and swept his tongue across it. She gasped and arched her neck back even further, baring her throat to his mouth. Taking full advantage, he licked and kissed and nibbled that smooth column of flesh until she moved restlessly against him, then traveled lower to her collarbones and finally to the upper swell of her beautiful breasts. He caressed her with his cheeks, careful not to touch the hardened nipples that begged for his attention.

"Kiss me there," she said breathlessly, trying to push his head down.

In answer he bent and gently stroked one ripe nipple with his tongue. Neveah sucked in a sharp breath and bowed her back, and he did it again. And again. Then did the same to the other, until she whimpered. Sliding his hands beneath her back to support her spine, he finally opened his mouth and took her inside, sucking with slow, firm pressure.

"Ohhh," she moaned, fingers curling into his scalp.

So sensitive, he thought as he lingered there, tugging with his lips and rubbing his tongue over her. The muscles along her spine flexed as she lifted for him, begging for more. He switched to the other nipple, lavishing the same attention there and turning so she rolled beneath him. He was careful to keep most of his weight off and not crowd her but immediately her legs came up to wrap around his hips. His aching cock pressed against the damp heat between her thighs. They both moaned. He moved against her in a full body caress, unable to resist, but then stopped despite her whimper of disappointment.

This time he was going to make damn good and sure he gave her all the pleasure she could handle before sliding into her body. He needed to prove she could trust him to see to her needs first. Above all, Rhys wanted her to know she was safe with him, and that he would always take care of her. He needed her to believe that more than he needed air to breathe.

Still suckling her nipple tenderly, he balanced his weight on one elbow and let his other hand wander down her fragile ribcage to her flat stomach. Nev squirmed beneath him, breathing faster as he ringed the delicate indentation of her navel and trailed lower over all that smooth skin to the line of dark pubic hair. The musky-sweet scent of her arousal hit him, making him dizzy. Damn, he wanted his head between her thighs, but it was too soon. He wanted her panting and half blind before putting his mouth to her. His fingers whispered over her mound and over her inner thigh, deliberately avoiding the needy flesh between. He could smell how wet she was, and his mouth watered.

She rolled her hips, lifting until the damp folds of

her sex kissed his abdomen. Against the heavenly softness of her breast, he closed his eyes and fought back the dark tide of sexual need rising within him. He caressed the curve of her inner thigh, down to her knee and back up, switching sides, growling when he finally touched wetness. She was already drenched for him, more than ready for him to touch her there.

Softening the pull of his mouth, he slid the tips of his fingers over her slick folds. Exploring tenderly. Neveah kicked her head back and bit her lower lip, stifling a moan. He released her tender nipple and raised his head so he could see her expression while he touched her. The breath stuck in his throat.

Her eyes were half closed, locked on his and full of such intense heat he could only stare. As he caressed between her slippery folds her eyes closed completely, and her lips parted on a soundless cry of pleasure.

Hell yeah, honey. Show me how good it feels. God, she was so warm and smooth down there.

He slid one finger into her. Slowly. Curled it upward. She arched with a sharp gasp. He rubbed inside the slick heat of her body for a moment before withdrawing, swallowing her cry of protest with his mouth and stealing back inside. In and out, in and out. He teased her for a few minutes before pulling out to glide up over her swollen clit.

"Rhys," she cried, reaching for him.

"Right here," he answered, giving her more of his weight and bending to kiss her tightly clenched lids. "You feel so good, Nev. Melting around my fingers."

"Oh, God…"

He smiled against her cheek and fine-tuned his touch, circling and pressing, watching her face so he knew exactly what she liked best. Then he repeated it over and over, lowering his head to suck one glistening nipple into his mouth. She moaned and writhed in his arms. He loved every second of it, but he wanted more. He needed to taste her, to feel her wild response against his mouth. Holding back a groan, he slid down her body.

Her eyes flew open. "Don't," she gasped, reaching for him again.

She thought he was stopping. He wasn't. Far, far from it. " 'S all right, baby."

When she realized where he was headed, she lay back down and took a shuddering breath. Rhys paused at her navel to dip his tongue inside. The muscles in her belly jumped beneath his lips. His cock pulsed in agony. He ignored it and kissed the top of her mound, drinking in her lush scent. He licked his lips in anticipation.

Sliding one arm beneath the small of her back, he caressed her with his palm in a gesture of reassurance and lowered his head. With as much tenderness as he could give her, he opened his mouth and kissed her soft folds, then let her feel the slow sweep of her tongue over her most sensitive flesh. Her hips jerked up, demanding more.

"Oh, Rhys…"

Mmm, yeah. More.

He licked her carefully, making sure to touch all her sensitive places before focusing on her engorged clit. He stroked softly, slowly, relishing her broken cries. When her hands clutched his head, he closed his lips around the hard bud, sucking gently, flicking his tongue against it tenderly. She whimpered and threw her head back, digging her short nails into his shoulders.

After a minute he slid two fingers into her, rubbing against the upper wall of flesh as he slid in and out, savoring the feel and taste of her, enjoying those incredibly sexy moans coming out of her. Close now. He could feel it in the tremor of her muscles and the way her body clenched his fingers. Damn, he could do this forever.

"Wait," she gasped.

He glanced up in surprise. Was she serious?

"Rhys, stop." Her voice was breathy and her eyes were glazed. Completely at odds with her request.

He backed off reluctantly, fighting the need to go back down on her. "Why?"

Her fingers swept over his hot cheek, her lithe body trembling beneath him. "I want you to be inside me when I come."

Oh, Christ. He almost came all over the sheets at the thought of being buried inside her again, bareback.

"Come up here." Nev held her arms out to him, face soft with pleasure.

He hesitated. He wanted to. God, he was dying to crawl up and plunge into her. But he'd already taken her too hard, too fast. He was too big and rough for her, and knowing how turned on he was right now, he wasn't sure he'd be able to keep control of his baser need to thrust deep and hard until he exploded. So no, being on top wasn't going to be an option. If this was going to work, he'd have to let her do it. And to do that, he'd have to fight his control-freak, dominant nature and hand over the reins.

The thought almost paralyzed him. He'd never given anyone that kind of control over him before. Just thinking about it filled him with unreasoning dread. Making himself that vulnerable to someone wasn't something he was even remotely comfortable with, though he trusted her implicitly. That wasn't the issue.

He struggled to unfreeze his lungs. He wasn't good with words, so he didn't even try to articulate what was happening inside him. Did she have any idea how hard this was for him?

"What's wrong?"

The gentle concern in her voice unfroze him.

"Nothing." He could do this for her. He *would* do

this for her. It was time for him to shove his stupid goddamn baggage out of the way and let her in. All the way in, nothing held back.

Resolved, he slid to the side and stretched out on his back. Her eyes moved over every inch of his body with hungry admiration, then came back to his. And stayed there.

"You don't want to be on top?"

"No." He did. He really did, but couldn't take the risk of losing it and inadvertently hurting her again. Besides, this was his way of showing her how much he trusted her, and proving to both of them he could be trusted in return. His hand swept over the curve of her cheek. "C'mere and kiss me." He needed to get out of his head.

With a seductive smile she crawled up his body and straddled him, taking his face between her palms before leaning down to kiss him. Rhys sighed and opened to her teasing tongue, letting the sensations dim the panic bubbling up in his chest.

"Love you," she whispered, raining kisses over his face.

God. Rhys wound his hands into her thick hair, drinking in her tender affection, shaken by how much the words affected him. He'd never felt like this before. Never let himself need before. Until now, with Neveah. What the hell was he supposed to do with it all?

She kissed and caressed him, her amazingly gentle hands flowing over his shoulders and arms, a soft hum of approval coming out of her as she studied him. He moved into her touch, his body craving it as much as his heart, and waited while she explored him. Her cheek rubbed against his pecs and over his ribs while her hands roamed lower, down the clenched muscles in his abdomen.

"Look at you," she breathed in wonder. "You're so

beautiful, Rhys."

He looked down himself and met her eyes, full of stark hunger, and struggled to breathe. Words escaped him.

Neveah turned her attention back to his body, scooting lower so she could see the swollen, aching erection pulsing against his belly. Her hands slid over his thighs. His quads twitched beneath her trailing fingers. *Hold on*, he cautioned himself. *You can do this.* But damn, she was killing him by not touching his cock.

Her long, dark hair brushed over his thighs and between them, making him quiver. Those soft hands caressed up the inside of his thighs and over his hipbones, framing his cock as it bobbed hopefully under her stare. Then she closed one fist around him, and he couldn't think at all.

His head dropped back on a quick intake of breath. Staring at the ceiling, he fought to hold on while she pumped him, sliding up and down in a torturous rhythm. He clenched his fingers around the sheet beneath him. But when she bent to kiss the swollen head of him he glanced down, and nearly lost it when her pink tongue darted out and licked the shiny drop that had formed at the tip.

Biting back a curse, he brought his hands beneath his head and clenched his fingers together, afraid he'd do something awful like grab her head and force it down on him. He gripped so hard his bones ached.

"I want to make you feel good," she said, rubbing her satiny cheek against him. His hips arched helplessly, his body completely at her mercy. Then her lips opened over him and she took him inside her mouth for that first luxurious suckle.

Shit, oh, shit, he wasn't going to be able to stand it—

She sucked gently, swirling her tongue around him.

He clenched his teeth together to hold back a raw moan.

With a low murmur, Nev took him deeper still. Then her fingers brushed down between his thighs and gently caressed his balls.

"Christ," he barked, unable to stop the word from flying out of his mouth.

She paused, and he almost begged for mercy. "Rhys?"

He struggled to look at her.

"Do you want to come in me, or my mouth?"

Fuck! His cock pulsed, right on the verge of coming. His muscles quivered as he fought it. After a few deep breaths, he was able to unclamp his jaw and respond. "Whatever you want." It sounded like he'd swallowed a load of gravel, his voice was so rough.

She didn't hesitate. Immediately she straddled him, reaching down to wrap her fist around him and hold him up. His stare riveted on the glistening pink flesh between her open thighs, poised above his cock.

She sank down, bringing him to her entrance, and he held his breath. He twisted his fingers together, almost bending the bones, and lifted his hips. Not as far or as hard as he wanted, but enough to slide the thick head into her wet heat. They both groaned. She eased down further with a sigh, then back up, slowly accustoming her body to his. Her breaths were uneven as she finally sank down all the way, taking him right to the pubic bone. His whole body broke out in a sweat.

"Nev," he croaked.

"Shh," she whispered, and began riding him.

Feeling like he was dying, Rhys could only watch, spellbound as she rose up and down the length of him, her perfect breasts bobbing with the motion. She let out a blissful moan and closed her eyes, her head falling back until her hair brushed the tops of his thighs. Mother of Christ she was stunning like this, swaying above him in total abandonment. Even better than he'd imagined.

Her head came up. "Hold me," she panted. "Help me come."

He didn't dare touch her. Not like this. He was so close to the edge.

"Please." Her lips trembled.

No way he could ignore that plea. His hands shook when he brought them out from beneath his head and placed them reverently on the curves of her narrow waist.

If he thought it was torture before, it was a thousand times worse when she slid her hands over her breasts, playing with her nipples. Then she brought one hand down between her thighs to stroke the swollen flesh there. "Oh, God," she whimpered, moving faster. "Rhys, you do it…"

He could hardly breathe or see, but he instantly slid his hand between her legs and stroked his thumb over her wetness. She cried out and closed her eyes as she swayed above him, her expression a portrait of erotic bliss. The feel of her gloving him so tightly and the knowledge she derived so much enjoyment from his cock almost killed him.

Her supple body trembled with helpless, overwhelming pleasure when he caressed her. Sweating and shaking, he gripped her hips with his free hand and helped her with the motion, loving each breathless moan that tore out of her. But he couldn't stay still anymore.

Hanging on to the last vestiges of his control, he thrust up into her depths. Relief slid through him when she let her head fall back on a cry of rapture. He wasn't gentle, but at least the thrusts didn't have his full weight behind them, and she seemed to love it.

Above him, Neveah sobbed and moved faster, up and down in that mind-numbing glide while she played with her beaded nipples. Her soft cries got closer and closer together, all of her muscles drawing tight, her breathing choppy. Then her spine arched tight, her breasts jutting out as her orgasm hit, pulsing through her in waves that he felt in the inner muscles clenched around his cock. Her throaty cries of ecstasy almost took him over the edge with her.

When it was over, she brought her head up and eased down on him with a satisfied sigh. Her thighs trembled on either side of his hips as she gazed down at him, and the love in her eyes made him want to bury his face between her heaving breasts and never let go. Still wedged deep inside her, his cock strained painfully, swollen to bursting.

With a naughty smile, Nev rocked forward. Rhys gasped and clenched her hips, praying he wasn't hurting her. She licked her lips. "You feel so…" Her eyes closed in enjoyment when she impaled herself on him, slick and tight. "Mmm, so good inside me…"

The heavy-lidded, erotic look on her face almost destroyed him. She was still hot with arousal, reveling in it. Ready for more. He wanted to shake his head, beg her to stop, but he couldn't speak for the lump in his throat.

"Don't hold back," she whispered above him, eyes devouring him exactly as they had in his fantasies. She moaned and sank down on him again, obviously loving the feel of his cock buried inside her. "You don't need to with me."

A growl of denial shot out of him. She had no idea what she was saying. He wanted to flip her onto her back and drive into her so bad… Do things that were probably still illegal in most states of the Union.

Don't even think about it, asshole.

She kept rocking, bending down to capture his face in her hands, covering him with kisses soft as the brush of butterfly wings. To his horror, he felt the sting of tears in his eyes as the pleasure killed him.

Fuck, he was losing it, was going to explode. But she kept pumping, filling up every empty place in his soul with her love and tenderness. The orgasm built, pulling every muscle taut, his heart thundering in his chest. Agonizing pleasure intensified with every heartbeat, the friction of her body around his blasting through his restraint.

On a tortured roar, he threw his head back and came in wrenching spasms that went on forever, so hard the tears he'd struggled to hold back trickled from the corners of his eyes.

Completely shattered, he came back to earth and threw an arm over his face to allow himself a few minutes of privacy to collect himself. Nev wasn't having any of it, however, and pulled his hand away from his eyes. Her smile was so full of love and acceptance it made his heart turn over in his chest.

"You are the most amazing man I've ever met in my life."

Rather than risk speaking, he grabbed her and brought her full length atop him, holding her as close and tight as he could without hurting her. She kissed the side of his jaw and sighed sleepily. Within minutes she was asleep, her whole body relaxed.

Savoring the warm weight of her in his arms, Rhys stared up at the ceiling, knowing he was never going to be the same again.

Chapter Nineteen

Early Sunday morning

Nev's eyes flew open in the darkness, heart beating fast. As her gaze focused on the digital clock next to her, she remembered where she was. Oh, in the hotel room, with Rhys's warmth curled around her spine and hips. One of his hands was tucked tightly around her ribs, and the other was stroking the crown of her head. That's what had woken her.

"Rhys?" she whispered, pushing up onto her forearm and turning over. "What's the matter?"

"Nothing." His voice was clear. Without a trace of grogginess, like he'd been awake for a while. Maybe he'd been awake the whole time.

She must have missed him taking a call. "Is it Luke? Did something happen?"

"No, nothing like that."

Her brain was having trouble turning over. "Can't sleep?"

"Don't want to."

Okay. So why had he woken her from a sound sleep then? He must have something on his mind. Rolling onto her side, she shifted so she faced him, their heads resting on the same pillow. “Why don’t you want to?”

His caressing fingers moved over her face and throat. Her body began to heat up, a liquid warmth pooling low in her belly.

“I need to tell you something.”

Alarm rushed through her bloodstream, her heart skipping. “What? Did you get called out while I was sleeping?” She must have been nearly unconscious not to notice he’d taken a phone call.

“No.” His touch remained unhurried, almost reverent, and she felt the smile on his lips as he kissed her. Then he rolled her onto her back and came up over her on an elbow to smooth the hair back from her forehead. In the faint light seeping through the crack in the curtains, his expression was filled with adoration and tenderness. “I love you too.”

Her heart squeezed, then doubled its speed. “Oh…” She couldn’t believe he’d said it. Hearing those words was beyond her wildest hopes because she knew no other man could ever have been so sincere. Even if he’d said them because of everything that had happened, it didn’t matter. He loved her, and he’d been lying there thinking about it all this time.

“Yeah. Thought I’d better tell you.”

A totally sappy smile spread across her face. “I’m glad you did.” Oh, man, she was going to cry… She cradled his face between her hands. “But maybe you should show me, just so I don’t forget.”

His arms slid around her and gathered her up tight against the heavy muscles of his chest. “With pleasure.”

****

A few hours later once they crawled out of bed and got ready, Rhys drove her over to VGH to see Luke. She found him in the recovery room, already awake within twenty minutes of being sent there. He offered a smile when he saw her, the clarity of his eyes assuring her everything had gone well.

"You almost look like you're ready to get up," she remarked, rounding the bed to stand at his shoulder and shake the hand he offered. His grip was warm and firm, but still careful, as though he didn't want to bruise her. Her smile widened. He wanted the world to think he was such a badass, and he was, but few people got to see his softer side. No wonder his ex-wife was still hung up on him. "Your color's good."

"Feel great."

"No blurred vision or dizziness?"

He shook his head. "Nope. Haven't gotten up yet, though." His gaze strayed to the nurses busy doing paperwork over at their station.

Nev tucked her tongue beneath her lower lip for a moment. "Lemme guess. You tried and they gave you shit, right?"

His white teeth flashed, a devilish twinkle in his dark eyes. "Maybe."

"Medical staff can be such a pain in the ass, huh?"

"Except you, of course."

She raised a brow. "Don't you dare try to charm me. I'm immune."

"Is that a fact?" His knowing gaze seemed to probe into her mind, and damned if she didn't respond to his intense stare with a tingle of feminine awareness.

Snickering, she shook a finger at him. "Okay, I'm mostly immune, to everyone but you and Rhys. Don't tell him, okay?"

" 'Course not, sugar. I'm a gentleman."

"You're a charmer, and that's not the same thing." She eyed his bandages. "I hear everything went as well as could be expected."

"That's what the doc said. I'll be outta here in a day or two."

His eyes were already bruising a bit underneath. "So long as you take it easy for a couple weeks after that, they might let you go." His innocent expression made her want to roll her eyes. She glanced over at the nurses. "His vitals are good. You guys okay if I take him back upstairs?"

A young blond nurse waved her hand. "Go ahead. Try and get him to lie still if you can." She returned to her paperwork with a muttered, "Good fricking luck."

Neveah released the brakes and took her place at the head of his bed, then pushed him toward the elevator on the far wall while the wheels squeaked on the linoleum. Rhys had let her come down alone since he had an undercover cop stationed on every floor next to the elevator doors. After what had happened the night before, she was glad to know they were there. "Feeling nauseated at all?" she asked Luke.

"No. I'm good."

She got him into the elevator and punched the number for the neurological floor. An elevator would be an ideal place to hide from a shooter, she decided. Just get the doors closed and take off so they couldn't reach you. Behind the steel doors, a person would be safe enough. Letting that strange thought go, she focused on Luke again. "Dec and Rhys are upstairs. Bryn's going to stay with you."

He angled his head up to see her face. "Where's Emily?"

She might have imagined it, but she thought she detected anxiety in the question. "Ben picked her up to take her to the airport."

"She flying home?"

"I'm not sure. Bryn will know." Tense seconds ticked past while the elevator climbed to the neuro ward.

She didn't know the whole story behind him and Emily, but there was definitely some strong, unresolved emotions there. For both of them. How many women would stay cramped up on a hospital pullout so their ex-husband wouldn't be alone?

The elevator pinged and the doors slid open. Nev swung the gurney around and pushed Luke back to his room, catching a whiff of food as they passed the kitchen. "Looks like we can get you some breakfast if you're feeling up to it."

"Good Christ, no. I'd rather go hungry than eat that crap."

"Oh come on, don't be a baby. Some oatmeal or cream of wheat would taste just fine, and I'm sure you've had way worse than whatever the cooks here can dish out."

Dec and Rhys were talking outside Luke's room and stopped the instant they saw them.

"Hey, look who's back from the dead," Dec said, holding the door open.

Luke held up a good-natured middle finger as they passed by.

Inside, Bryn set down her paperback and greeted him with a bright smile. "You look fantastic! I wasn't sure what shape you'd be in when they brought you up."

"Did Emily fly home?"

Bryn faltered for a moment at the jarring change of subject, and met Neveah's eyes before looking at him again. "Yes. Ben drove her to the airport so she wouldn't miss her flight. She'd already delayed it once because she refused to leave until she knew you were going to be okay. She asked me to give you this back," she added, holding out what looked like a gold chain and medallion in her palm.

Luke went still a moment, then muttered, "Ah, shit," under his breath before taking it from her.

Nev took a step toward him. “What’s wrong?” His expression was almost defeated, as though he’d just lost a battle or something. Obviously the jewelry was more significant than she realized.

“Nothing.” His fingers were clumsy as he fastened the chain around his neck, and he pinned Bryn with a meaningful look. “Is everything okay with her?”

Again, Bryn’s eyes darted over to her, this time for confirmation. “Uh, yeah. She’s fine.”

Nev didn’t know what to say.

Luke’s gaze hardened. “If you know something, Bryn, you’d better tell me.”

Bryn’s spine straightened and her hands clenched in her lap. “She… She had something to take care of.”

Nev processed the words in silence. That didn’t sound good. Not at all.

“Dammit, tell me what the hell’s going on,” Luke practically growled.

Bryn swallowed. “I-I’m not exactly sure. She said something about having her own…demons to face.”

Luke closed his eyes, and Nev’s stomach dropped. Shit, it had to be bad. After the lengths Emily had gone to for Luke’s sake, she would never have left him if it wasn’t serious. What was it? Her health? Someone was threatening her?

God, could Tehrazzi know about her? Nev’s stomach did a slow roll, but then Luke swallowed convulsively and started panting through his mouth like he was about to throw up.

“Whoa,” she said, grabbing a bowl from the table and holding it in front of him. He pushed it away.

“She didn’t seem scared really,” Bryn quickly added, as though that was supposed to reassure him. “Just kind of…sad.”

More sad than she had been? Neveah pondered the possible causes for the hasty departure and the fact that

Emily hadn't even told Bryn the real reason for it.

As the silence thickened and held between Luke and Bryn, Nev became uncomfortable. "I'll just let you two have some privacy," she said, adjusting the IV pole before turning away.

"No," Luke said, meeting her eyes. "Bring the guys in here, will you? I want to get an update."

She exchanged another questioning look with Bryn. One glance at the other woman's face and Nev was certain Bryn knew what had happened to her at the hotel, but an update was the last thing Luke needed right now. Especially if he was stressed out about Emily.

"What?" Luke demanded. "Something happen last night?"

"I'll let Rhys brief you," Nev said, crossing to the door.

"No," Luke snapped when Bryn followed her. "You both stay."

"Fine." Nev opened the door. Dec came in, followed by Rhys who stood almost a full head taller. Dec went over to stand behind Bryn, giving her shoulders a squeeze while Rhys stood against the opposite wall and put his hands behind his back.

Folding his arms across his chest, Luke scowled at them, and when he spoke his drawl was almost nonexistent. "Somebody better come clean here. Right the fuck now."

Completely unfazed by the show of temper, Rhys leaned a muscled shoulder against the wall and regarded him steadily. "Someone tried to off Neveah last night at her hotel when we left here. Hassan's girlfriend, as it turns out. Apparently, the bounty offered made another attempt worthwhile."

Luke's gaze shot to her. "Why didn't you tell me?"

"I'm fine, and I didn't want to tell you in the recovery room. For God's sake, you just had brain surgery."

"Yeah, and my hard drive's good as new." He turned his attention back to Rhys. "What happened?"

Rhys explained everything, then finished by nodding at her and adding, "She's still bound and determined to do her keynote address in a few hours."

Looking at her, Luke raised brow. "You sure about that?"

Her chin came up, the pilot light on her temper igniting. "I'm doing this speech. I will not be intimidated or cowed by people operating under a twisted guise of revenge." She glared at Rhys. "You said yourself these guys were amateurs."

"That's all well and good," Luke drawled, "but in light of the circumstances, maybe you should rethink that decision. You've got lots of security there, and our boys are the best in the business, but you'd still be taking a calculated risk." He nodded at Dec and Rhys. "And so will they."

Dread hit her square in the heart, along with a good measure of guilt. She hated to think she might be placing Rhys or anyone else in danger over this. "Dec's staying here with you. I've already asked Ben and Rhys to stand down, but they both refused."

"Yeah, they're funny that way."

She crossed her arms beneath her breasts and lowered her eyes. How could she make him understand? "I need to do this. They brutally and sadistically murdered two of my colleagues, and would have done the same to Mike and me if not for you and your team." Nev let him see the resolve in her eyes when she looked up at him. "I owe it to them. And to myself. If I stay quiet, they win." Translation: no way in hell was she going to change her mind on this.

Luke held her gaze for a moment before looking at Rhys. "You go over the security plan with Nate?"

Rhys nodded. "Ben as well."

Silent until now, Dec spoke up. "You'd better get her a vest," he advised, absently playing with a lock of Bryn's hair.

"What?" she asked, stepping forward and dropping her arms. "You mean a ballistic vest?"

Luke tilted his head. "Got a better suggestion as to how we can stop a bullet if someone that's not an amateur takes a crack at you? If anyone's still gunning for you, they might not be as incompetent as Hassan's girlfriend."

Her mouth snapped shut and her eyes swung to Rhys, but if she was looking for backup, he didn't give it.

"It'll fit under your blouse, so don't worry," he said. "At least that way most of your vital organs will be protected."

"Unless they use hollow point ammunition," she shot back, angry that he'd do this to her now. If he was so upset about her speech, why hadn't he made his feelings clear before now?

Rhys inclined his head. "True. It's up to you." She made a scoffing sound. "You guys trying to scare me into not speaking?"

"No," Luke answered. "Just doing our job. The initial threat is likely over, but that doesn't mean there's not something in the works we haven't got wind of yet. The leader of the cell is still out there somewhere. Until we nail him, we can't know for sure."

The blood drained from her face at his words, and she fell silent for a moment. Once she'd gathered her nerve, she said quietly, "This is the whole reason I came here." She looked straight at Rhys. "Isn't there some way I can still do the speech?"

He met Luke's dark stare as they both considered the risk level in silence. Finally, Luke conceded with a tiny nod.

Once he had the green light from Luke, Rhys turned his head to look at Neveah. He wanted to take away all the pain she'd suffered, and this seemed the best method for now. "If it's this important to you, yeah. I'll take care of it."

She exhaled and smiled in relief. "Thanks."

Her gratitude and the fact that she trusted him to keep her safe were all that mattered, Rhys told himself. That's why his chest felt so tight. It had nothing to do with the nagging doubt in his gut.

"Would y'all excuse us?" Luke said to the others. "I want to talk to Rhys for a minute."

After everyone else left, Rhys faced him with an arched brow. "What's on your mind?"

"Tehrazzi."

Yeah, well, join the frigging club. "Got something you want to share?"

Rhys almost smiled. "Ben got word early this morning from your sources that Tehrazzi was sighted in Peshawar, headed for the Afghan border." He'd hidden the fact that he'd received Ben's text message from Neveah, and he had no compunction about it. He didn't want her any more worried than she already was.

Luke's face tightened. "Christ, if he gets over it this time…"

They'd have better luck trying to find life on Mars. "Also, a kid by the name of Mahmoud Adir was found dead on a road out of town. Double-tap to the head, time of death approximately matches when Tehrazzi was seen. Soon after we busted the plot at the reception." And the two precise gunshots proved the killer was someone with military training. Tehrazzi had that, taught by the best in the business. Luke.

"Any connection to him?"

Rhys shrugged. "Kid was an IT grad working in Islamabad. He's got relatives here in Vancouver. We're starting with those."

"Nate think it's linked to the local cell?"

"He's not sure yet, but he's working on tracing calls made to Tehrazzi. If the murder in Pakistan is linked, then we still have a big problem." He prayed Nate wouldn't find a connection, but if he did, Neveah was not giving that speech today, or any other day.

"Shit. Well, at least the bastard's using more merciful methods than his bodyguard did."

Yes, but it confused Rhys. "I thought he didn't like killing."

Luke sighed and closed his eyes, suddenly looking bone tired. "He doesn't. That's why he always had his bodyguard do it for him. But since the episode with Assoud, Tehrazzi's probably convinced he can't trust anyone, so he's taking care of things himself."

So he was even more paranoid and dangerous now. Without others to link him with, he'd be that much harder to pin down in the vast landscape of the mountainous tribal regions that straddled the Pakistani/Afghan border.

When Luke lifted his lids, his eyes were grave. "You got all the security you need at the hotel?"

"Yeah." Just a few more hours until he could get Neveah on a flight out of the country. Then maybe he'd take her someplace warm for a few weeks until the cell was cracked.

This thing was almost over. Rhys just hoped nothing else came up for him to worry about.

Chapter Twenty

An hour later, Neveah held her heaping plate away from Rhys when he tried to take it for her and went back to their table. She threw her friend Mike an exasperated look over her shoulder as she walked away from him. He winked, apparently amused by her irritation. "I appreciate the thought," she said to Rhys when he came up beside her, "but I can carry my own food."

"I'd rather you let me do it."

She arched a brow. "Just think of the favor I'm doing you by leaving one of your hands free to pull your gun if need be."

His smile was anything but warm. "Like holding a plate would stop me?"

Rolling her eyes, Nev wound through the other tables to theirs and reached back for her chair, but Rhys had already pulled it out for her. "Thanks," she murmured, amazed again by his manners.

By now she should be used to them, but every time he did something so gentlemanly it touched her. Now if only she could stop the buzzing sensation between her shoulder blades and forget she might still be in danger, she could get through this and go home. Hopefully with Rhys.

He scooted in beside her so he boxed her in between him and the wall, with only her right side open. She didn't miss the wry twist of his lips when she met his eyes.

"Is this seat taken?" a low voice asked.

She glanced up. "Doctor Shirani," she said, standing to offer her hand. "Please join us. This is Rhys Sinclair—you may recognize him from the hospital last night."

The surgeon's gaze went to the scars on Rhys's scalp. "Yes, he'd be hard to forget," Shirani said affably, holding out his hand. Rhys took it and she swore she saw the surgeon flinch. She half expected to hear bones cracking as they shook hands.

She glared at Rhys, warning him to behave himself and sat down to eat. Lifting her silverware, she set about cutting a mouthful of blueberry pancake and accidentally bumped Shirani's arm with her elbow. "Sorry," she said.

"No, my fault. Being left-handed can be awkward sometimes," he said, and scooted his chair another few inches away from her. "Makes it hard to eat at a table full of right-handed people."

Nev smiled and went back to her food, conscious of Rhys's wary vigilance. Switching her attention to something else, she got distracted by the sight of Doctor Shirani sawing through his medium cooked roast beef. The steak knife in his right hand sliced back and forth through the tissue. Bloody juices spilled from the meat with each pass of the blade.

Without warning, the sight and sound of it triggered a vision of a different knife that had killed her colleagues. Her stomach pitched and she set down her fork with a clatter, swallowing hard.

"Maybe you should switch seats with me," Rhys

suggested.

It shouldn't have surprised her that he'd seen her reaction. Forcing her gaze away from the bloody meat, she grabbed her glass and took a bracing sip of ice water. "No, thank you," she murmured between swallows. "I'm fine here." She would absolutely not look like a traumatized loser in front of her peers.

The meal finished quickly after that, and then the luncheon formalities began. Someone from the host committee got up and thanked the staff and volunteers, then introduced the first speaker. When it was her turn, she rose and squeezed Rhys's shoulder. He gazed straight back at her, and she read the unspoken message in his eyes. *Go for it, baby. I'm here.*

Careful to try and mask her limp, she wove through the tables to the podium at the front of the room. Her laptop sat open on top of it, already hooked up. All she had to do was cue it.

She scanned the audience quickly as she set up her power point presentation. Rhys sat at their table against the left hand wall, the back of his chair touching it. She smiled when he looked over at her and gave her a wink that let her know everything was okay. Some of the tension bled out of her.

While she didn't see any security officers in the room, she knew they were around. Maybe they were dressed as wait staff, or maybe they were sitting at tables throughout the room, but they were there.

More of her anxiety drained away, but some remained, a low-grade hum in her gut. Not because of what she was about to do. She was a very good public speaker, and being in front of a crowd didn't bother her. The possible threat hanging over her like a bolt of lightning waiting to strike was responsible for setting her on edge.

She wouldn't let it shake her confidence. This was

what she'd come here to do. She needed to tell her murdered colleagues' stories and do right by them. Her job was to impress upon the crowd that Doctors Without Borders was a critical effort to help the civilian population in Afghanistan and while the terrorists had taken two innocent lives during her captivity, they would not win the war.

Because of people like her and the man she loved across the room, silent and watchful.

One of the waiters approached her, wearing a white dress jacket and slacks. "Are you ready, Doctor Adams?"

For no good reason, her palms grew damp. She put on a confident smile. "Yes."

He nodded and gestured to the conference organizer, already waiting at the microphone. At his hand signal, the lights in the dining room dimmed.

"Ladies and gentlemen," the speaker announced, "it is with great respect and admiration that I announce to you our keynote speaker for today's luncheon, Doctor Neveah Adams."

Amidst the din of applause Neveah stepped up to the podium with the remote for her laptop held tight in one hand. "Thank you, Doctor Williams," she said as she adjusted the microphone to suit her. Stealing one last glance at Rhys, she took a silent breath and began her presentation.

"As most of you know, I recently returned from Afghanistan where I worked as a member of Doctors Without Borders." On the giant screen behind her, a picture of her and the other three doctors came up. "These were my colleagues. Only myself and one other came back alive." She met Mike's eyes from across the room.

The place was so quiet she might have been standing in a soundproof cell rather than a crowded dining room. She had everyone's attention now, each pair of eyes fastened on her.

"I'm here today to honor the memory of those good men, and of those who pulled me out." When she looked at Rhys, the tide of emotion was so strong it raised goose bumps all over her skin. He acknowledged her thank you with a quick incline of his head, and then went back to scanning the room.

As people turned in their seats to look in the direction she had, searching for the mysterious men who had come to her rescue, she hit the button on the remote to move to the next screen in hopes of distracting them. Rhys wouldn't want people to know who he was or what he'd done. "This was our clinic in Kabul."

An image of the one-story beige cinder block building came up. "We were the first Doctors Without Borders team to be sent into the country since the Taliban captured and executed the last one in 2004. The government thought security had improved enough since then to approve our mission, and we got the green light." She paused and let her gaze drift over her captive audience. "If only we'd known how wrong the authorities were about the security situation."

When she knew she had everyone's attention glued on her, she continued. "The need for good medical care in Kabul and the rest of Afghanistan is critical. On our first day we had over eighty appointments scheduled among the four of us. The lineup of people wanting to see us snaked around the building."

The next picture showed a little girl standing with her mother. She was filthy and thin, her eyes way too big for her face. The mother was completely concealed from view by a sky blue burqa, even her eyes hidden behind the mesh veil panel within the hood. "The general public believes Kabul at least has been transformed into a beacon of hope for the citizens of Afghanistan. I can tell you from personal experience that nothing could be further from the truth."

From his position at the rear of the room, Rhys was awed by the power Neveah radiated as she stood in front of the crowd and began her speech. Strength and confidence flowed from every elegant line of her body and blazed out at the audience from her vivid blue eyes. Her voice was strong and clear, filled with the conviction she was doing something important. Something she believed in so strongly she was giving her talk despite the ongoing risk to her safety. He was so damn proud of her.

She commanded respect with her natural poise and her message. The fact that she was before her peers speaking about what she'd survived had a powerful impact on everyone in the room, him included. The picture of the clinic came up. He remembered going there after the fact, looking through the wreckage for clues as to where the militants might have taken their hostages.

A minute into her talk, Rhys's phone buzzed against his hip. Careful not to draw attention to himself, he stepped out into the hall to check the text message. It was from Ben.

Heads up. Cell leader is Ahmed, no last name. Uncle to dead kid Mahmoud.

Shit, then he was linked to Tehrazzi. And Ahmed was a common Middle Eastern name. Due to Nev's speech about her experience in Afghanistan, half the attendees at the brunch were of Middle Eastern or South Asian descent. Was the cell leader already inside?

We're going through a database now. Comms indicate ongoing threat to N. Alert security members. I'm on my way.

Pulse pounding, Rhys deleted the message and

turned to go back inside, but one of the undercover cops named Khan met him outside the door. His lips were pressed into a tight line in the middle of his neatly trimmed goatee.

"What's up?' he asked.

"There's another plot in the works. Get the team briefed and sweep the crowd, seal off the exits." The shoulder holster chafed him beneath his jacket, his muscles tense. He couldn't see many faces in the dimly lit room. He prayed the security search had done its job and that they hadn't missed any concealed weapons.

Still scanning the room uneasily, another text came in.

Be advised, Ahmed linked to hired gun. Be on look out for a male, ex-military…

Rhys's eyes stuck on the last words. *...possibly armed with sniper rifle.*

Couldn't be true. Not here. They'd been thorough. He hadn't seen anything suspicious.

Rhys's hand was unsteady as he keyed his radio to let the team know what to look for. "Seal off all entrances and exits," he finished. If the bastard was already here, he wasn't getting away.

"Sinclair, come back." Khan's low voice came over the radio.

Rhys keyed it again, forcing himself into that icy calm space he operated in so he could do what he had to. Taking a breath, he looked away from Neveah on stage. "Go ahead."

"I'm going through the attendance register, and have three Ahmeds. Two are spouses of attendees, but the other is—"

Whatever Khan had uncovered got cut off by the chorus of shocked gasps that rose from the crowd.

Rhys's head snapped up, and when his gaze focused on the screen behind Neveah, his blood ran cold.

Drawing a deep breath before continuing, Neveah plunged on, detailing how the attackers came through the back door where she'd been working, and hauled her away at gunpoint with the rest of the team members. Her voice remained surprisingly steady for that part, but when she began telling about Gary, her throat closed up. She cleared it, gripping tight to her professional demeanor.

"Doctor Gary Sutherland was a courageous man who deserved a better fate than the one he received. His horrific death will always haunt me, even though I realize there was nothing I could have done to prevent it. Now I can only comfort myself with the knowledge his killer is dead also, shot during the operation in which we were rescued." She didn't specify that Tehrazzi had shot him dead.

A swell of applause rose from the crowd, interspersed with a few loud whistles. She waited for the noise to die down, in full agreement with their reaction.

The next picture came up. "This is Doctor Frank Owens, our resident orthopedic specialist. Those of us who knew him will always remember his kindness and his endearing sense of humor. He wanted so badly to help the people of Afghanistan, especially the elderly who needed but could not afford or access the care they needed."

She glanced down at her notes and flipped to the next card.

The blood drained out of her face. Her lungs seized.

Someone had written on the next card with red ink, over top of her notes.

Do you remember what it was like, Neveah? Do you wake up with their dying screams ringing in your ears?

Her gaze jerked up, whole body tensed, ready to run at the slightest perception of a threat. No one moved.

They all sat staring at her.

Nev tried to slow her frantic heartbeat. Just a sick prank, she reasoned, fighting to hold on to her composure. The ticking seconds seemed like minutes as she stood frozen in front of a roomful of people. Her gaze sought Rhys. He was gone.

Had something happened? Did he know something?

Get a grip, Nev, she told herself sternly. Must have been the people who'd broken into her room and rifled through everything. They'd left the note behind to taunt her.

Or because Tehrazzi had ordered it.

An icy chill shot down her spine at the thought. "Doctor Adams?" The low question from the event organizer jarred her.

She sucked in a breath. "Fine," she rasped, licking her upper lip and tasting the beads of sweat there. Frank was still on the screen behind her. "Pardon me," she told the audience, and hoped they would forgive her the lapse. She hit the button to bring up the next picture.

A collective gasp rose from the crowd.

Tension gripped her chest as she gazed out into the audience. People had their hands over their mouths. Their expressions were horrified. Some of the ladies turned away as though they couldn't bear to look.

She hadn't put anything in the presentation to illicit such a reaction.

Shit... She didn't want to look up at the screen. Couldn't make herself do it.

In her peripheral vision, she caught sight of Rhys on the far side of the room, coming toward her. Which meant he wanted her off the stage.

Cringing instinctively, she turned her head to find out what everyone was gawking at. The remote fell from her numb hand as she too clapped a hand over her mouth and stifled a cry of horror.

She was staring at her nightmare again. Tehrazzi's bodyguard stood in the doorway with Gary's severed head in his fist, holding it by the hair. He was grinning, his white teeth a slash in the midst of his bearded face, yet the scar in the middle of his chin remained visible. His gleeful expression was all the more hideous because of Gary's lifeless eyes and half-open mouth. Forever frozen in a silent scream.

God! She slapped the laptop shut to kill the image, just as the lights went off, plunging the room into darkness. She jumped. What the hell was going on? Several people cried out, and she heard the sound of hundreds of chairs scraping against the floor as the audience rose in alarm. She couldn't see Rhys, but knew he was coming for her. All she had to do was hang on until he got there.

The room seemed to close in on her, suffocating her.

Get out.

The words shot through her mind. Then something brushed past her cheek and hit the wall behind her with a loud *thud*. She shrieked and ducked.

Intuition made her dive to the floor. Her heart threatened to explode. She recognized that sound from the night she'd been rescued. A suppressed shot. A bullet had hit the wall. Someone had taken a shot at her.

Another round hit the podium she'd just been behind. A shower of splinters exploded.

"Down!" She recognized Rhys's distant shout and covered her head with her arms.

Then Mike's voice rose over the noise and confusion in the room. "Someone's shooting! Run, Nev!"

Afraid to move, she whipped her head in Rhys's direction. Where was he? He must be close, still trying to get to her.

Some primal instinct urged her to get off the stage. Her skin crawled, little prickles racing over her body. It was still pitch dark. She couldn't see anything except vague shapes and bodies moving around. Was the shooter going to take another shot at her? Staying still made her an easy target. At least if she moved she would be harder to hit. She kicked off her heels.

Gathering her courage, she jumped to the ground and started making her way toward Rhys, her only thought that she had to get to him. He would keep her safe.

She tripped over something and went down hard on her knees. Flinching at the pain in her sore ankle, she got up and staggered on as fast as she could while the crowd streamed around her toward the exit.

Chapter Twenty-One

Ahmed's heart was in his throat as dim security lights came back on around the edges of the room. People milled about in confusion, but the only thing he was interested was Doctor Adams. His gaze swept over the stage, expecting to find her lying on it bleeding. But she wasn't there. The stage was empty.

He jerked to his feet. She couldn't have gotten away! He looked around frantically, and caught the back of the shooter as he exited the room with the panicked crowd. Had he hit the target or not?

Ahmed's muscles froze when he located Doctor Adams, shoving her way through the crowd away from the stage, her eyes wide with terror.

Dear God, she wasn't even *wounded…*

His throat closed up. Lily. They'd kill her for this. Even though he'd hired the professional and it wasn't his fault the man had missed.

Lily would die because of him.

No. He couldn't let that happen. He could still get to Adams. But how would he do it? He looked down at the table and the knife lying on his plate. It was sharp, the beef he'd eaten was testament to that, and the blade was five inches long. Long enough to penetrate deeply into the body.

Blood roaring in his ears, he reached for it, wrapping his hand about the cold steel handle, and slipped it into his right breast pocket. He searched for his victim, and found her coming his way. Sweat bloomed over his skin. Could he do this? Actually kill her, and in front of all these witnesses?

Security guards were in the room plus that big Sinclair guy who'd been acting like a bodyguard for Adams. Once he pulled out the knife, someone would see him. Then the guards would come after him. Probably shoot him.

In that moment of hesitation, the room faded away. All the noise of the crowd's panicked confusion disappeared into a vacuum of silence. The only thing left was the thudding of his heart. Loud. Frantic.

A terrible sense of grief filled him. He would die if he did this. Wasn't there another way?

He cast a desperate look around the room as everything slowed around him. The shooter was long gone.

The neon red glow of the exit signs beckoned in the distance. He could still run.

You can't! Lily's life is at stake.

Drawing a deep breath, he sent up a prayer. *Allah forgive me for what I'm about to do.*

In slow motion his feet carried him through the crowd, but he could barely feel them. His body was numb. Every ounce of concentration was focused on the grisly task ahead of him, and the knowledge that he and Neveah Adams were taking their last breaths on earth.

God help him, he had no choice.

Scanning frantically about the room, Nev couldn't find Rhys. He must be close and he was so tall he shouldn't be hard to find, so where the hell was he?

The crowd moved around her like a stampede of cattle, blind with fear as they shoved and jostled toward the exit. She spotted Doctor Shirani coming toward her and met his gaze. He was intent on escape and his focused expression set her heart pounding, but she didn't want to leave without finding Rhys first. He would know what to do and he would keep her safe. Dammit, why couldn't she see him? The awful knot in her stomach drew even tighter.

"Neveah!"

She whipped around at the sound of his deep shout, eyes anxiously searching through the crowd. In the weak light she barely made him out, but caught sight of him near the stage, a wall of strength with a deadly black gun in his hand.

"Rhys!" She turned back, intent on getting to him.

Shirani was closer now. She waved him over. Rhys would save them. "Over here!"

"No! Run, Neveah!"

Rhys's barked command made her jump, and when she saw his expression her blood turned to ice. His face was filled with something she'd never seen in him before, not even when he'd been bleeding to death in her arms. Stark fear.

"*Run*!"

Her heart gave a sickening thump. The sharp order confused her, but the urgency on his face had her body swinging around to obey. Then she saw the reason why he'd told her to run.

The man from the park and the hospital was bearing down on her, eyes locked on her with an unnatural light. Fixated. His hand disappeared beneath his jacket, and she knew he was about to draw a weapon.

She wheeled away with a cry, sending one last sidelong glance at Rhys so he'd see her words in her eyes.

I love you…

"Go!" he yelled as he barreled toward her, gun raised like he was preparing to take aim and fire at the man closing in on her.

Stifling a cry, she whirled and ran for the exit. Each pounding step filled her ankle with hot stabs of pain but her sole focus was on getting out the doors and into the hallway beyond.

Her mind raced. Would Rhys really fire his weapon in such a crowded place? He was a crack shot, but how could he possibly hit his target in such a chaotic setting? She kept pushing forward, bracing for the sound of a gunshot and praying everyone but her would-be killer was out of the line of fire.

Where in hell were the other security agents Rhys had told her about? People blocked her way. She shoved and elbowed through them, almost feeling the heat of her stalker's breath on the back of her neck. She expected to feel a bullet in the back at any moment.

Close now. The door was right ahead.

The sour smell of panic swirled through the room, making her dizzy. Air rushed in and out of her starved lungs until she felt faint. She had to get out. Had to.

Nearing the wide double doors, she threw a glance over her shoulder and the breath stuck in her throat. Shirani was closing the gap between them, but the man from the hospital was right behind him.

"Run!" she yelled at him. "He's got a gun!"

A moment's surprise flickered over the surgeon's face, but then grim resolve replaced it and his strides lengthened.

She couldn't waste time trying to help him any further. She had to get to safety first.

Bursting into the main lobby, her eyes locked onto a hallway branching off to the right. She careened into it, catching a glimpse of Shirani running flat out after her. The gunman was a dozen strides behind him, pulling his weapon free of its holster.

No sign of Rhys. Was he all right? She almost stopped, wanting to go back for him. What if he was hurt? She slowed a fraction, the pain in her ankle tearing up her leg.

"Neveah!"

Prickles of fear raced down her spine at the unfamiliar voice yelling her name. She looked back over her shoulder.

"Stop!" the stalker shouted, raising the gun.

"Shit!" she breathed and took off, bare feet slapping against the carpet. People gasped and dropped into defensive crouches when they saw what was coming after her. The elevators loomed ahead at the end of the hallway. Her earlier thought about hiding in one came back to her. She didn't dare take the stairs. If she could get into the elevator and shut the doors before he reached her, maybe she could make it.

Air exploded in and out of her aching lungs. *Halfway there. Keep running.* She kept her eyes locked on the elevator doors, desperate to reach them in time. The glowing call button between the two stalls beckoned like a ray of light in a world of darkness.

"Neveah, stop!"

Like hell. She choked back the whimper of terror and pain locked in her throat, the men's footsteps pounding behind her. Getting closer every second.

A shot rang out, a loud popping noise. Neveah shrieked and instinctively covered her head, expecting to feel the burn of a bullet. Instead she heard someone cry out, and glancing back saw Shirani stumble.

God... She almost tripped over her own feet as she slowed. But the doctor climbed to his knees gripping his right shoulder with his other hand, blood seeping out of the bullet wound.

"Neveah," he said, eyes beseeching her to stop. Before she could move, he surged to his feet and began running again, his gaze locked on her.

"Hurry!" she yelled, lengthening her strides, intent on hitting the call button. She lunged for it and slapped it with her palm, heart racing as precious seconds went by. Her eyes tracked the numbers above the door while the elevator car descended closer. Third floor.

Shirani was almost to her. *Come on*, she begged. *Open!* Second floor.

Footsteps getting closer. Gun rising again.

Lobby.

She swallowed a scream as the gunman raised his weapon for another shot, then the bell dinged and the elevator doors opened. She fell between them with a half-sob and Dr. Shirani was right behind her. The instant he dove inside she frantically hit the button to close the doors and punched the top floor button.

Through the closing doors she saw the assassin's grimace of rage. "No!" he shouted as he ran, still too far away to get off another shot.

The doors finally slid shut, and the relief buckled her knees. Sucking in a shaky breath, she allowed her legs to give way and slowly sank to the floor. Shirani stood slowly, blood dripping onto the marble floor from his shoulder wound.

She forced her chattering teeth to part. "Y-you okay?"

He was breathing hard as he came to his feet, his eyes pinned on her strangely. Was he already in shock?

Forcing aside her own fear, she pushed herself up the wall and removed her jacket so she could tend to his injury. "H-here. Let's g-get th-the bl-bleeding s-stopped."

Rhys was coming for her. She knew that. All she

had to do was wait for him to free her. With hands that flapped like leaves in the wind, Nev offered her wounded colleague the jacket.

Rather than submit to her care, Shirani lifted a hand to the elevator panel and hit the stop button, never taking his eyes off her. The alarm bell sounded as the car jerked to an abrupt halt.

Steadying herself against the wall, she glanced up in confusion at the floor number. He'd suspended them between floors. To prevent the shooter from getting them? Looking back at him, a splinter of alarm swept over her. His expression was too set. Too intense.

Instinct had her backing away. She bumped into the wall.

Holding her gaze, Shirani slid his left hand into the breast pocket of his jacket.

****

Rhys came around the corner so fast he almost plowed into Khan. Dodging him, he skidded to a halt and stared with hollow eyes at the closed elevator doors. God dammit, he'd missed her by seconds.

Five goddamn seconds too late, too slow.

"I couldn't get a shot off," the cop said dully, coming up beside him. "She kept stopping and putting herself in the line of fire."

Rhys had fired once, but he'd failed to make the head shot. He wanted to puke for the terror flooding him.

"She recognized me. I think she thought I was the hit man."

Ah, Christ, it must have been Khan she'd seen following her at the park and hospital— "Is she in there with him?" he demanded.

"Yes."

"Fuck!" He pressed his hands against the elevator,

sick with fear. "Neveah! Neveah, answer me!" Rhys tracked the floor numbers on the display. The elevator was moving up. "Get hotel security to stop the elevator," he said hoarsely and raced to the stairs. The door crashed into the wall when he threw it open and bounded up the steps three at a time. He heard the cop barking commands over his radio when he hit the second floor landing.

His thighs burned from his demand for speed, and though he wasn't tiring, he wasn't moving fast enough.

Third floor.

Move, goddamn you!

"Hotel says they've stopped between the seventh and eighth floor," the cop yelled as Rhys hit the fourth floor.

The reasons for them stopping had Rhys's heart in his throat. He was only halfway to her, and each second cost them time Neveah didn't have.

Chapter Twenty-Two

The look on Shirani's face was terrifying. Eyes wide, Neveah stared at the hand he slipped into his jacket. No. She had to be wrong. The breath hitched in her dry throat. "Wh-what are you—"

The words cut off when he withdrew a wickedly sharp silver knife, like the ones from the dining room. Her eyes flew up to his. Ahmed Shirani… *He* was the one? The one who wanted to kill her?

"I'm sorry," he said quietly.

Her heart shot up into her throat. She shrank back against the mirrored wall, thinking he'd gone crazy.

The blade glinted in the harsh light, cold and lethal. The sight of it paralyzed her.

Horrific memories flooded her. Another knife, dripping with her friends' blood. Agonized screams and strangled cries. The knowledge that she could be next.

Every muscle in her body stiffened as abject fear gripped her. She couldn't die. Not like this. She couldn't bear it. The bite of that cruel blade, slicing into her flesh. The terrible pain and horror. Bleeding to death, weakening with each cut, life draining out of her faster with each terrified throb of her heart. A low whimper escaped through her clamped lips.

His face was stamped with resolve as he faced her, blade gripped in his bloody hand.

She was trapped in here with him. Her heart screamed in denial.

Shirani took a step toward her and she yelled Rhys's name.

"He can't hear you," he said, swallowing. "And even if he could, he can't get to you."

Her eyes misted. He had to get to her. She had no other chance.

Moving carefully, Shirani took another step. Hesitant in his movements.

Her spine was already flattened against the mirrored panel. She had nowhere to go. Her frightened gaze remained on the shiny blade in his grip.

"I…I wish there were another way," he whispered, voice vibrating with regret.

"D-don't," she cried, raising her hands to ward him off. "Please don't do this."

His face twisted with pain. "I have to."

"No, please—there m-must be s-something—"

He lifted the knife, poised to strike. "No. Have to. But I can make it quick. Please…I don't want you to suffer."

She was going to throw up. The bile was right there, ready to come up, her body shaking so hard it hurt her bones. Unable to speak, she shook her head, pleading with him to spare her.

His mouth tightened for an instant as he battled some inner struggle. Then he lunged at her.

Neveah let out a shriek and ducked as he came at her, trying to dart past him. His arm swung down in a sharp arc, the knife catching her high up on the shoulder as she hit the floor. The fiery burst of pain made her suck in her breath. Warmth flowed down her upper arm, the metallic scent of her blood rising up to mix with the choking stench of fear. The hard marble was cold beneath her sweating palms. She shoved upward and spun to ward off the next attack. She had no space to move, no room to maneuver and buy time. Her brain wasn't working fast enough. She couldn't think, couldn't reason because of the thought of what was coming, could only react on pure survival instinct.

The defense course she'd taken. In a knife fight you had to get in close to take away their leverage.

She couldn't do it. She was too afraid. Her instinct to flee was too strong.

Her jacket lay discarded on the floor. She couldn't even wrap it around her forearm to protect her muscles and arteries when he struck next.

He came at her again, this time with a growl, and she lashed out with a forearm to block the downswing of his arm, bracing for the hot burn of the knife in her skin. She made solid contact with his wrist and jammed her knee up at the same time, catching him low in the belly. He gasped and doubled over for an instant, allowing her enough time to scramble away. She faced him, panting with shock and a growing sense of rage.

How *dare* he attack her, feel entitled to take her life after all she'd been through. She'd liked him. Told him about Rhys's neurosurgery. *Trusted* him.

The spike of adrenaline hit her bloodstream, filling her with resolve. She wouldn't go out quietly. If he wanted to kill her, he'd have to do it while she fought and clawed and resisted to the very last.

Pulling in a hard breath, he straightened and looked at her with utter loathing. "Just die, damn you!"

"Fuck you," she snarled back.

He darted forward. Nev doubled her fists and hit him in his wounded shoulder as hard as she could, then spun away. He screamed in agony while the knife whooshed past her ear and sliced through the back of her blouse, narrowly missing her cringing flesh.

He circled her warily now, breathing heavily. Blood dripped from the bullet hole, his entire right arm soaked with it. The floor was wet and slippery with crimson smears that glistened in the overhead lights. The wound in her own shoulder burned like fire, her heart slamming against her ribs like a sledgehammer.

Rhys was coming after her. He would be here any moment. Any second, she told herself. The horrible buzzing of the alarm would stop and the elevator would jerk as it moved, and then the doors would slide open and Rhys would be there ready to shoot the bastard dead.

Hold on, Nev. You have to keep fighting. Just a little longer.

Focusing on that, she squared off with Shirani, hands raised like a prizefighter, praying she'd be fast enough to dodge his next attack and thinking about the most vulnerable points she had to protect. So long as he didn't hit an organ or a major artery, she could buy a few more minutes. But the thought of taking more stab wounds filled her gut with ice. Why hadn't she worn the damn vest Rhys had offered?

Shirani's hand dropped, whipping up hard at her gut. She shrieked and threw herself sideways. The knife slashed against her ribs. The hot blaze of pain tore what little air she had out of her lungs and made her curl in on herself. Tears blurred her vision.

Christ, oh Christ, she couldn't take this. From the corner of her eye she saw the blade flash up again and threw out a hand to catch his wrist. The impact jarred her wounded shoulder and she bit back a cry, muscles straining to hold him back. Shirani grunted and locked his bleeding arm around her throat, squeezing as he forced the knife closer to her throat. Going for her jugular or carotid artery. Severing either of those would kill her in a matter of minutes, if not seconds. She could not lose her hold.

Gritting her teeth, she struggled to maintain her grip on her arm and held on while the pressure around her throat increased. She fought the additional spurt of panic as her air decreased. Both hands were on his frighteningly strong wrist, the muscles in her arms shaking with effort. She couldn't let go to try and pry her arm away from his throat. If she lost her grip on him, she was dead. A raw scream of denial and rage worked up her bruised throat.

In desperation she twisted in his grip, throwing her feet out to brace against the mirrored wall for leverage. She pushed back with all her might, shoving him against the opposite wall, trying to throw her head back and hit him in the jaw. He cursed and jerked his forearm tighter against her. The knife edged closer, quivering as it poised inches above her vulnerable throat. It glimmered in the lights, the instrument of her death, waiting to plunge through the critical vessels in her neck.

Her hands were numb, knuckles white as they maintained their death grip on his wrist, summoning every ounce of strength in her failing body. The loud buzzing of the alarm died away in her ears, replaced by the deafening rush of blood as it raced beneath her skin. Her pulse pounded in her head, blotting out the sound of their grunts and panting breaths, her heartbeat a hollow echo reverberating through her body.

She felt the betraying quiver in the muscles of her arms and legs. Beginning to fail. The edges of her vision grew hazy as the bruising pressure increased around her neck. The blade dipped down another inch, her flesh shrinking from the whisper of the tip against her collar.

No air. Can't breathe.

She sucked in a gasp, hands slipping. Arms and legs

going leaden.

With a scream of anguish, she reared up with her remaining strength, wrenched her head around and latched her teeth onto the wrist holding the knife. Bit him so hard her teeth punctured his skin, filling her mouth with warm, iron-tinged blood.

Shirani let out a bellow and jerked his hand away, the other arm loosening around her throat. She gagged and swallowed, refusing to let go, but he wrenched away.

Gasping, Nev threw her head backward and connected with a sharp crack against his jaw. His head snapped back and slammed hard into the wall, giving her the precious second she needed to fling herself away. Without waiting, she drove her elbow into his wounded shoulder. Goosebumps covered her skin when he howled like a wounded animal and instinctively brought his knife hand up to cover it. She stuck out with her heel at the hand holding the knife, but he swung away and rose to his feet, eyes glittering with rage.

Gasping for breath, she stumbled back and raised an arm as he slashed down with a snarl. The blade sliced deep into her right forearm. She screamed and jerked away, cutting right down the inside from her elbow to her wrist as she moved. With the pain ripping through her flesh he came at her again, but slipped on the blood-slick floor. His arms came out as he fell, grabbing her and taking her down with him. They hit the marble with a bone-jarring thud, her weight landing on his injured arm. His scream almost shattered her eardrums and the knife clattered to the floor, skidding over the slick surface.

Flipping over, she lunged for the knife. The fingers of her uninjured arm closed around the handle and clamped down tight. She brought it up in her fist, whirling on her knees to face him. She swallowed a cry when he launched himself at her, raising the blade even as she shrank back.

Shirani hit her with the force of a defensive lineman, knocking her into the wall so hard the mirror fractured, slamming the air out of her lungs. Her fist made contact with flesh and bone. Pinned beneath his weight, she fought for air and tugged on the knife. It was stuck. Jerking her startled gaze to his, Nev stared up into his wide, shocked eyes.

The blade was lodged deep in the side of his throat, the handle dripping with blood. She'd stabbed him.

Frozen, she watched his hands came up to curl around the handle, his mouth opening in distress. Then he slumped to the side and slid off her.

Scrambling from beneath him, Neveah scuttled away like a crab and curled up against the opposite wall, never taking her eyes off him. Oh Jesus, she'd stuck him right through the jugular. She flinched as he struggled to pull the knife out, withholding her shout of warning. He knew it would kill him. The blade emerged from his flesh inch by inch, then clattered to the floor. The instant it cleared his skin the blood poured out, gushing over his chest and shoulders in a hideous ruby waterfall. Her hands went to her mouth to stifle her cry, her right arm screaming in protest from the throbbing wound there.

His eyes stayed on hers, glassy with panic as he tried to stem the flow with his hands, but the blood poured out despite the pressure he applied. He flipped onto his back with an awful gurgle, still staring at her. "H-help…"

She was shaking so badly she couldn't get her muscles to work. Her gaze darted to the knife. It was within his reach, but he was too badly wounded to use it on her even if he did have the strength to grab it again. He was bleeding so badly his blood covered his clothes and pooled in a spreading lake around him. At the rate he was losing it, he'd bleed out within a minute.

"P-please…"

His choked rasp brought her gaze back to his. The doctor in her couldn't ignore the plea. She couldn't just sit there and let him bleed out, knowing she'd killed him. Her stomach lurched.

Crawling to him despite the pain and her own blood soaking her, she laid a trembling hand over his and used her body weight to add more pressure.

Up close she got a good look at the wound. It was almost four inches across. The knife must have twisted in his neck when she stabbed him. Christ, she'd just stabbed a man to death. Shock immobilized her. Of its own volition, her gaze traveled up his bleeding throat to his face. Staring back at her, his eyes held the awful realization of his own death. A shiver rippled down her spine.

Shirani's trembling fingers curled around hers. She swallowed, resisting the urge to jerk away.

"S-so sorry…"

She glanced away, unable to look into those wide black eyes.

The fingers squeezed. "L-let go."

She shook her head and squeezed her eyes shut. Guilt threatened to smother her, rising up over the protest that he would have killed her. It would have been her bleeding out on the elevator floor if she hadn't done it.

The pressure increased as he tried to pry her hand away. "Allah's…will," he whispered.

Her eyes opened. His were turning glassy, growing unfocused. So much blood. Soaking both of them. He had to have lost several liters of it. His heart would go into ventricular tachycardia, then into ventricular fibrillation. Then it would stop.

Clenching her teeth, she watched him turn paler

with each heartbeat, eyes fixing on the ceiling. The grip on her hand loosened, his fingers growing lax.

His breathing changed from shallow to sparse. His limp hands fell away from his throat. She waited a few more seconds before sliding her fingers up to check his carotid pulse.

Nothing. He was gone.

Falling back onto her heels, Neveah slumped against the wall and stared at their reflection in the blood-spattered mirrored panel. Shirani slumped dead in a lake of blood. She was saturated with it, her face so pale she was almost as white as he was.

In the sudden stillness, the loud buzzing of the alarm pierced her consciousness. The pain in her stab wounds intensified, bringing her attention back to her right arm. Her forearm lay wide open from inside the elbow to just above her wrist, the gap about two inches across and deep. Was that the edge of her radius she saw in the light? Her stomach lurched sickeningly.

As she watched, blood pumped out of the wound in spurts. The brilliant scarlet color made her heart clench. Jesus, he'd hit her radial artery.

She slapped her left hand over the deepest part and squeezed the edges of the wound together to lessen the blood loss, trying to assess the damage. There was too much blood to know how much of it was hers, but judging from what she'd just seen, it was possible she'd lost about a liter of it herself. She'd been too jacked up on adrenaline to notice until now.

The world spun. She collapsed onto her back and stared up at the recessed lights in the ceiling, gripping her forearm as hard as she could and raising it above her pounding heart to slow the bleeding. Her mind spun with what was happening. She had to slow her heart rate. The faster it was, the more blood she'd lose.

Fighting to calm down, she focused on breathing

deep and slow despite the fear clawing at her. What if she'd survived the attack only to bleed to death beside her would-be killer?

No, she told herself sternly. *You will calm down. You're still alive, and Rhys will come for you.*

She called an image of his handsome face to mind and held onto it, struggling to suppress the sobs rising in her chest. Tears trickled down her temples and into her hair, the cloying odor of fresh blood so thick it almost choked her.

Cold seeped through her, so deep it made her teeth chatter, her muscles jerking so hard it hurt. Emotional shock or hypovolemic shock? The fear crept over her like a fog until it was all she could feel. She didn't want to die. She'd fought so hard to live. She had Rhys, and he loved her. She needed to see him.

"R-Rhys… Wh-where are y-you?"

Fighting to hold onto consciousness, she dimly noticed the sudden silence when the alarm stopped and the gentle lurch of the elevator as it began moving.

Chapter Twenty-Three

Rhys was ready to tear the elevator doors apart with his bare hands as he watched the numbers on the display. The waiting fucking killed him. His heart was slamming so hard it reverberated throughout his body.

Beside him, Ben raised his weapon. He needn't have bothered.

Rhys's finger tightened on the trigger. Every muscle in his body was drawn to the point of pain. The instant those doors cracked open he was going to take the motherfucker out, right between the eyes.

His teeth ached from grinding them together. How the fuck had he missed him? The instant he'd known who the mysterious Ahmed was, the guy was a dead man walking. But he'd fucking *missed.* He'd only winged the bastard, then come around the corner as the elevator doors shut Neveah in with a murderer.

His blood ran cold at the knowledge. Was she alive? Had she been able to fend him off long enough? He couldn't accept anything else. Wouldn't, until he saw differently with his own eyes. And if she was dead, he'd…

He couldn't even go there in his head. He'd lose it.

Beads of perspiration broke out over his chest and face as he followed the agonizingly slow movement of the elevator. *Come on,* he urged, ready to scream from the tension. He was lit, ramped up higher than he'd ever been before, liable to break Ahmed's neck with one brutal twist of his bare hands when those doors opened.

The high-pitched ding of the bell seemed to echo in his skull. As the elevator settled before him with a soft thud, the smell hit him.

Fresh blood. Lots of it.

His stomach plummeted like a concrete balloon. "*Neveah*!"

Ben sucked in a sharp breath, but Rhys couldn't tear his eyes away from the seam in the doors. They edged apart with maddening slowness. The instant he could see light in the crack between them, he thrust the muzzle of his weapon in and shoved them apart with his shoulder.

The sight that met his eyes drew him up short. Ahmed was already dead, lying in an obscene amount of blood. Neveah was on her back, gripping her forearm as blood pumped out from between her clamped fingers, the knuckles as white as her face. The bloody knife lay between them on the floor, which was covered with a thick layer of gore. His heart lurched painfully.

"Nev," he croaked, dropping his weapon and falling to his knees beside her. The inside of the elevator looked like a goddamn slaughterhouse. "Baby…" He leaned over her and took hold of her forearm, squeezing hard to staunch the flow of blood. She flinched and whimpered, opening dazed eyes to stare up at him.

Relief had tears burning his eyes. His hand trembled as he brought it up to cradle the side of her face. "I'm here," he whispered, guilt-ridden. He couldn't even think about what she must have gone through in the past few minutes. All he could do now was block her view of Ahmed's body and keep her calm until they could get her to the hospital.

Her gaze focused on him, but the glazed look in her eyes made his guts clench. Her skin was cold as the marble floor he knelt on. "M-my r-radial artery," she mumbled. "He g-got it."

"It's all right," he soothed, holding the pressure steady and keeping his face in her line of vision so she couldn't see her arm and the amount of blood she was still losing.

Ben came up behind him, meeting Rhys's gaze in the mirrored panel and taking in the situation with a single glance. "How bad?"

"Get the truck," he bit out. Ben took off without another word. While Nate and some others came in to survey the scene, Rhys bent over her. "Are you hurt anywhere else?"

"Sh-shoulder. Ribs. Not as b-bad."

His eyes swept over her bloody form and found the other wounds, sick at the knowledge of what she'd faced alone.

She turned her head, but he moved into her line of vision to block her view of the body. A frown creased her brow. "I… I k-killed him." Her teeth chattered, her whole body wracked with shivers.

"Shhhh. Don't talk right now. Just look at me." He waited until her eyes met his, then forced a reassuring smile even though he wanted to throw up. "Everything's going to be fine."

"B-bleeding b-bad."

"You're going to be fine," he repeated. "Ben's gone to get the truck, then we'll take you in for some stitches." The lie rolled easily off his tongue. She'd need emergency surgery to stop the bleeding and repair any damage—

"F-fingers," she complained, mouth bracketed with

lines of pain. "C-can't move."

He glanced at her hand above where he held so tightly. It was pale and bloodless, the fingers curled loosely. Had the knife severed her nerves and tendons as well? "It's just shock, Nev. That's why you're so cold."

She closed her eyes, that little frown remaining. Someone handed him a jacket and he draped it around her with his free hand. Tucking the folds around her, he stroked the blood-matted hair away from her face. His heart ached for her. Goddamn, she'd had to fend the fucker off with nothing but her bare hands because he'd missed the head shot. The pain built inside until it threatened to suffocate him.

A little sob jerked through her. "D-don't let me d-die."

He got right in her face. "You're not going to die," he almost snarled, deliberately making his voice harsh to grab her full attention. "You're going to calm down and keep looking at me."

She blinked as though he'd shocked her, but at least she was focused on him rather than the blood.

"Slow your breathing and relax. I'm here and you're going to be fine. Hear me?"

A shaky nod answered him.

Nate stepped in beside him. "Ben's outside," he said, reaching down to help him lift Neveah.

Rhys blocked the other man's hand before it touched her and instantly scooped her up into his lap.

"Let me help," Nate said reasonably. "You can't lift her and hold her arm."

Rhys bit back the harsh retort, knowing he was right, but hating the thought of anyone except him touching her when she was so hurt and vulnerable. He allowed Nate to take Neveah's forearm while he adjusted her and lifted her in his arms. His heart twisted hard when she turned her face into his chest with a quiet whimper. To him the sound seemed heartbroken.

"It's all right, baby." His voice was rough, his whole body pumped and ready for action. He had to battle the urge to run, shortening his strides to match Nate's so he wouldn't lose his grip on Neveah's wounded arm.

Hurrying through the lobby he barely noticed all the people watching with expressions of sympathy, or the police crowding the place. Every one of his senses was focused on the pale, heart-wrenchingly brave woman in his arms.

Outside, the cold air rushed past him. He gathered Neveah closer against his chest to warm her and headed straight for the Escalade where Ben stood ready with the engine running and the back door open.

Rhys climbed in and took her arm again once she was settled in his lap. Nate stepped back and ran around to the other side while Ben slammed the door shut and jumped behind the wheel. The vehicle tore away from the curb and sped onto the damp street while drizzle coated the windshield and ran down the windows like teardrops.

"How's she doing?" Ben asked, glancing back in the rearview.

"Hanging in there," he answered, cradling her tightly, grateful that St. Paul's Hospital was only a few minutes up the road.

"You check her pulse?"

He checked her carotid pulse, because he hadn't found one in her right wrist. Her radial artery had definitely been sliced. "One-ten." Too fast.

"How much blood you think she lost?"

He aimed a fulminating glare at his twin. She was still conscious, and she didn't need to hear this right now, even if Ben was a trained special ops medic. Goddamn lot of good it did them right now, since he was behind the wheel. "Save it."

"Just trying to help."

"Then fucking drive faster." Nev was white as flour against his shirt, the delicate veins in her eyelids standing out. Her breathing was rapid and shallow. Way deep in shock. Maybe it was for the best though.

A tense silence filled the vehicle as Ben sped south up the hill on Burrard, weaving in and out of traffic. They hit three red lights before the hospital came into view on their right. About fucking time, Rhys thought as they pulled up to the Emergency entrance. Nate jumped out and ran inside while Ben came around and opened up the back door. He reached up to take her arm, his pale green gaze meeting Rhys's.

"I got her," he said quietly, and after a second's hesitation Rhys let go, trusting his twin to keep her from bleeding out.

He climbed out with Nev and together they took her into the hospital. Inside the staff were already waiting, alerted by the police and Nate. Two nurses rushed over with a stretcher and Rhys laid her down gently, Ben following the movement to maintain pressure over the wound in her arm. His brother's hands and forearms were covered in her blood as he gazed at his watch, calculating her pulse rate.

"Pulse is one-twenty, but I don't know her pressure," he told them as they moved toward what Rhys sincerely hoped was an operating room. "Has to be low, though."

"Let's see what we've got," one of the nurses said, reaching for the arm Ben held.

Rhys darted out a hand but Ben had already blocked her with a thick forearm. "If I let go she's gonna lose another quart of blood," he said. "So I'm not letting go until she's been stabilized."

Her annoyed gaze snapped to his. "You need to let

me—"

"I'm a trained Army Ranger medic, and I'm not letting go until you've got something better to get the bleeding under control with and I'm satisfied she's been stabilized."

The woman divided an irritated glance between them but finally let it go. "This way, then. But you'll have to leave once we get her into the OR."

Rhys knew without asking his brother would stay with her until she was ready for the surgery. He wouldn't let go of her arm until he was sure it was safe.

Helpless, Rhys could only watch as they wheeled her away, thankful that Ben was with her. Other than his, she couldn't be in better hands, and Ben had more medical experience than he did.

As if sensing his thoughts, his twin looked back at him. " 'S okay, man. See you in a few." *I got this*. The unspoken reassurance filled the space between them.

Rhys nodded, taking one last glance at Neveah before they disappeared through a set of wide double doors. When the door shut, he ran his bloodstained hands over his shorn hair and let out a hard sigh. An awful numbness settled over him. He should have said something to her before they'd taken her away. Should have at least told her he loved her one more time.

"Here."

He turned his head at Nate's voice. "Better sit down before you fall down."

Trying to get hold of his shredded control, he made it the few steps over to the row of plastic chairs set against the wall and all but collapsed into one. The seat creaked and groaned under his weight as he laid his head back and closed his eyes.

"Rhys?"

He opened his eyes when he heard Bryn's voice, and found her coming toward them.

Her face was filled with concern. “Jesus, look at you. Dec and I were at the hotel when we heard… What happened?”

“Not now, hon,” Nate warned.

Bryn glanced between them and then settled beside Rhys. She laid a tentative hand on his knee, and he had to fight not to throw off her gentle touch. He was a hair’s breadth away from losing it. But she didn’t say anything, merely sat lending her support and maintaining the fragile link between them with the slight weight of her palm.

He closed his eyes again, thinking of how he’d done this same routine with her a few months back. He’d been the one holding her while Dec was in surgery in Basra after the botched op and helicopter crash they’d survived. He’d never dreamed he’d wind up in the same position, scared to death because the person he’d fallen in love with was being prepped for emergency surgery.

He pulled in another slow breath, desperate to hold on. Rage and panic had no place here now. He needed to be calm and clear headed. Nev was going to be fine. Ben was with her, and they’d taken her straight to the OR.

Yet he couldn’t keep from thinking about what she must have gone through in the cramped elevator. It tied him in knots. How the hell was she going to cope with this after all she’d gone through already? No one was that strong.

As long as he lived he’d never forget the sight of her lying in all that blood, just as he’d never forget the sight of her crouched in the filthy room he’d pulled her out of in Afghanistan.

A few minutes into their wait, Nate murmured an excuse and left. A few after that Rhys felt in control enough to curl his fingers around Bryn’s, the only way he could say thank you. Her steady grip made him feel less alone.

If anyone knew what he felt, she did. Years of friendship made it much easier to have her sitting beside him at a time like this. That's what friends did; they had your back when things got rough. But good as it was to have Bryn's silent support, the person he needed most was in the OR with Neveah. Ben might be a smart-mouthed punk, but he knew Rhys better than anyone. Knew the way he thought, and intuitively knew what Rhys was feeling. Their bond was irrefutable.

After a few minutes, Bryn spoke. "Maybe you should go clean up a bit."

Rhys glanced down at himself. His clothes were covered in blood, his arms and hands stained with it. Rusty smears were trapped under his short fingernails. The sight of it made him sick to his stomach. Because it was Nev's.

Sucking in air, he staggered to his feet and stumbled to the men's room as fast as his wobbly legs would carry him. He headed straight for the sink. When he reached for the taps, his fingers trembled. The toilet flushed in the stall behind him. A moment later a sixtyish man came out. He took one look at Rhys and all the blood covering him, and stopped dead. His eyes widened, then met Rhys's in the mirror. Rhys knew he looked like a horror movie, and wasn't surprised the man made a sharp turn and hurried out of the bathroom without washing his hands.

Alone, the numbing shock began to lift. He was breathing way too fast. His nostrils flared on each uneven inhalation. His heart raced.

He was losing it.

Closing his eyes, Rhys leaned his palms on the edge of the stainless steel sink and fought for control, battling the adrenaline crash and the shakes that came with it. The quivers rolled through him like aftershocks of a major earthquake, sharp and debilitating. Thank Christ he was alone so no one would see him this way.

The attack lasted a few minutes, and by the time he'd regained function of his body, a powerful wave of fatigue hit him. Opening his eyes, he raised his head to assess his reflection in the mirror, partially steamed up by the hot water flowing from the tap. His skin was pasty, his pupils constricted, mouth pinched. Streaks of blood covered his neck and the side of his jaw. He washed the blood from his arms and hands, the water turning pink as it swirled down the drain.

All he could think about was Neveah facing Ahmed and that knife, cornered in the damn elevator. Her wounds were all defensive, from fending him off with nothing but her bare hands. His jaw clenched as he splashed water over his face and neck. How the hell was he ever going to look her in the eye after he'd let her down so horribly? She might not be able to perform as a surgeon again, depending on the damage done to her arm.

All because of a fucking *speech*.

No, he corrected, because he'd *let* her give the fucking speech. And then hadn't put the pieces together in time to prevent the attack.

And God, the psychological trauma… Rhys didn't know if she'd ever be able to get over what had happened. And as far as their relationship went? He didn't have a clue what would happen. She had every right to blame him, and he would understand if she did.

It would kill him, though. Losing her now that he'd finally let her in.

A deep sigh escaped him. He'd heard about having a broken heart, but he'd never experienced it before. The tearing pain was almost more than he could bear.

The door groaned open and Ben walked in. Rhys turned his head and stared at him with haunted eyes, heart thumping against his sternum.

"She's under," his brother said. He crossed the floor to lean one shoulder against the wall beside the sink and folded his arms across his chest. "All her vitals are stable, and they're infusing her."

Rhys let his head sag down between his shoulders. God, he'd been so fucking scared she'd been in danger of cardiac arrest.

"Vascular and plastic surgeon are already in there. They figure it'll take a couple of hours, tops."

He nodded, unable to say a single word.

Ben cocked his head. "Doin' all right?"

Swallowing, he found his voice. "Yeah." The word sounded like grinding gears.

"They've got everything under control. She's gonna be fine."

No she wasn't. She'd never be fine again. How could she be?

He shut off the taps, the bathroom filling with the sound of gurgling water for a moment while it drained in the sink. Then silence enveloped everything. Ben handed him some paper towels to dry his hands and face. No sense trying to wash his clothes, since they were unsalvageable. They'd have to be thrown out. He focused on the task of drying off, unable to look at his twin.

"Before you go all hard-ass on yourself, you gotta know this wasn't your fault."

The muscles in his shoulders tensed. But it *was* his fault. He'd been assigned to protect her, had sworn to himself he would keep her safe, and he'd failed.

"Jesus, when are you going to realize you're only human—"

"Do you know how afraid she is of knives?" He could barely get the words out.

A beat passed. "I can imagine."

Yeah, but he didn't *know*. "She still has nightmares

about what Assoud did to her friends. You should have seen her face during the brunch when Shirani was slicing up his roast beef with that goddamn steak knife." He'd been right there in front of Rhys, and still he hadn't connected the dots.

Her fear had been palpable at the table, even in that innocuous moment. To know Ahmed had used the same damned knife against her just minutes later filled Rhys with a helpless rage. "She's a doctor, Ben. Not only did she have to confront that knife alone, but she had to use it against him. Take a life instead of save it." He shook his head. "Christ, I don't know how she managed it."

"Thank God she did."

He met his brother's eyes. Steady, full of kindness. "She should never have been in danger. If I'd done my job properly it would never have happened." The nausea started to twist in his stomach again. "I… I can't handle it," he admitted, voice cracking.

Ben stepped closer and laid a hand on his back. Rhys flinched at the contact but Ben didn't pull away. "Hey. It was *not* your fault. There were plenty of other security personnel in that room and it still happened. You could *not* have stopped it. You're only human, buddy."

Tears threatened. Rhys clamped his jaw tight and blew out a steadying breath, fingers gripping the edge of the sink so hard his knuckles went white. "I should never have let her do it."

"You're feeling helpless right now because there's nothing you can do to help her or make it better. I know how you feel because I sat staring at your ugly mug for almost two weeks without being able to do a damn thing to fix you while you were in the coma. But Nev's going to be fine. You'll see her awake in a couple of hours."

"And what if she can't use her hand again?"

"What if she can?"

Words crowded his throat, confessions that he needed to voice but couldn't let out.

Watching him closely, Ben angled his head. "Spill it."

He couldn't. Couldn't say it out loud.

His brother walked over to the door and turned the deadbolt, locking them in and everyone else out. "Better?"

Rhys nodded.

"Tell me."

He straightened and ran his hands over his head, down his face. He felt so tired. "I knew I wasn't ready to take this on."

"Oh, come on—"

"I knew it and I did it anyhow." A terrible sense of emptiness filled him. "I told myself I was doing it to help protect her, but maybe that's not the whole reason. Maybe I did it to prove to myself that I was back in the game." He swallowed the lump in his throat. "And she paid the price."

"Jesus, Rhys, that's not you. You're a goddamn Boy Scout. If you really questioned your ability that much you would never have come here."

"I don't know if she'll ever forgive me. Christ, I don't know what to tell her."

Ben's eyes searched his. "You love her, right?"

"Yeah. I love her." More than anything.

"Then there's your answer."

Rhys shook his head. "I missed him, Ben. I had a clear shot and I hit him in the shoulder." The admission shamed him.

"If you missed him, then any of us would have."

"You wouldn't have." Nor would Dec or Luke have.

Ben sighed. "Look. I can't stop yourself from doing the mea culpa routine, but before you run out and fit yourself for a hair shirt, you might want to cut yourself some slack." He rubbed Rhys's back. "Look who I'm talking to though," he muttered. "At least do yourself a favor and not play the 'what if' game. You'll drive yourself nuts."

The guilt continued to pile up on Rhys like an avalanche. Smothering him. He covered his head with his arms to save himself. To hide. A sob worked its way up from his chest where it felt like someone was crushing his heart in a vise. He thought he might split apart from the pain.

Ben's hand slid to Rhys's shoulder and tugged. "C'mere."

Rhys flinched and shook his head, hating that he was so weak and out of control. Humiliation crawled through him, mixing with the pain and the knowledge of what Nev had been through because of him.

"Hard-ass," Ben muttered in irritation. "C'mere. This won't kill you." Strong arms pulled him forward, ignoring his resistance and then Ben wrapped him up in a hug. "It's okay. Let it go."

No. It wasn't okay. None of this was okay. Rhys never cried. He'd always been the strong one, the one to hold it together in a crisis. Ever since they'd been kids and he'd become a parent to Ben instead of a brother at age five when their mother had free-based herself into a stupor.

He'd always been the one to step up and take charge, stay cool and clean up the messes Ben got them into. Always. He'd never been allowed the luxury of showing his emotions, let alone cracking under them. Ben did more than enough of that for the both of them.

But those brawny arms tightened further, cradling him like the child he'd never been despite their slight difference in height.

"Just us," his brother murmured, drawing him close.

"It's just us here. No one else will ever know."

Ah, damn, he didn't want to do this in front of Ben, but he couldn't hold on anymore. His body just…crumpled.

As the tears finally came, Rhys had no choice but to let go. Burying his face in his brother's neck, he fisted the back of his leather jacket with both hands, holding on tight while the torrent rushed through him.

Awful, wracking spasms shook him. Tears of grief and fear and loneliness. Tears he'd never let himself shed as a lost and frightened little boy carrying the weight of responsibility on his too thin shoulders. Tears of a man so in love he couldn't bear the thought of facing life without the woman he'd given his heart to.

But how would she ever forgive him?

Ben's hold never lessened. His low voice murmured something, but Rhys couldn't make out the words over the sounds of his own grief. All he knew was Ben had him and he was safe, no matter if he was sobbing like a child in his arms.

When it was over Rhys broke away with a sniff and went immediately to the sink, hiding his reddened face by splashing cold water on it. Coming up for air, Ben held out another paper towel. Rhys took it with a muttered thanks and blotted his skin dry, avoiding eye contact. Shit, he'd never live this down. Not if he lived to be a hundred.

"Better?"

Rhys nodded, bracing for the inevitable ribbing he knew was coming.

Ben didn't disappoint. "See? You lost it and lived to tell about it." His voice dropped to a conspiratorial whisper. "You even survived a man hug." He rounded his eyes in feigned astonishment.

Wiping at his puffy eyes with his fingers, a watery laugh escaped him. "You always were an affectionate little shit."

Ben clapped him on the back. "Yeah. Don't feel bad, though—we can't all have the gift. But don't worry, I think Nev'll straighten you out in that department."

God, he hoped so. He prayed she'd give him the chance. "What time is it?"

Ben checked his watch. "Thirteen twenty-seven. She should be in recovery soon."

"Not soon enough." He glanced at the floor, his shoes, the stark white subway tiles on the walls. Anywhere but at Ben. An awkward silence grew between them.

Ben finally cleared his throat. "You can't see her looking like that, you'll scare her to death. Here, take my shirt." He shrugged out of his much cleaner T-shirt and held it out to him, the mirror reflecting the half infinity symbol and up-pointed dagger tattooed over his left shoulder blade. Rhys's own half of the tattoo tingled as he looked at it. Brothers, by blood and by service. Twins. Separate yet indivisible.

Rhys stripped off his bloodstained button down, still rattled by the knowledge it was Nev's blood all over it. He raised a brow. "Want it?"

"Uh, no, thanks. Ditch it. I'll make do with my jacket."

Rhys pulled his brother's shirt over his head and did one last quick once over in the mirror. Satisfied he wasn't going to make Nev go back into shock when she saw him, he turned away and focused on what he'd say to her when she came out of recovery. "Any word on the security tapes?"

Ben looked away. "All the elevators have security cameras."

Rhys's chest tightened. "So there's footage?"

His twin nodded, and seemed like he was having trouble meeting his eyes. "Yeah. It caught everything."

"I want to see it before she wakes up."

Ben hesitated. "You sure, man? I'm sure Nate could—"

"I want to know what happened. Exactly." Every fucking second of it, whether he was ready or not.

Truth was he was scared shitless of seeing the tape, but he had to know what she'd gone through. He owed her that much, to confront what she had if he was going to help her in the days and weeks ahead. Plus, he'd go certifiable envisioning it in his mind without the tape. The cold hard truth was all that would cut it.

****

Filmy layers of cotton obscured her thoughts. They drifted past in fluffy veils as her brain tried to come back online. When the fog began to clear, she heard voices murmuring in the background and a few mechanized beeps. Her mouth was dry and her eyelids were heavy. Why couldn't she wake up?

Moving her tongue around, Neveah fought to peel her lids apart. Man she was groggy. Squinting in the harsh light hitting her eyes, she focused on her surroundings. *Hospital.*

Her left hand brushed the blanket tucked around her and she saw the IV snaking over the back of it. *Surgery.* Because she'd been wounded in the knife fight.

The breath stuck in her throat as her brain snapped to attention. Her eyes flew to her right arm. The limb was covered in bandages, from her upper arm to her hand. What had they found? Had they been able to fix it? Clammy sweat broke out across her skin.

"Nev?"

She swung her head around at the sound of that unforgettable, deep voice. He walked toward her, his face tense. "Rhys," she choked, reaching out her left hand for him. He gripped it immediately, flooding her cold palm with warmth.

"My arm." Her voice was hoarse and her throat was scratchy, probably from the intubation. "What happened? Was the nerve cut?" Needing to know how bad the damage was, she tried to peel the bandages away.

"Nev, stop." Rhys gently took hold of her hand and wrapped his large ones around it. He stared directly into her eyes. "Slow down, honey. Just breathe a minute. Give yourself a chance to come out of the anesthetic."

"But my arm—"

"Is fine."

Was he lying? She searched his eyes, begging him to level with her. She needed to know.

"You're fine, I swear."

Relief made her lightheaded. She closed her eyes and laid her head back against the thin pillow, suddenly overwhelmed by fatigue. When Rhys stroked the side of her face, she turned her cheek into his palm and looked up at him. "What did they say?"

"The surgeon repaired your radial artery, two tendons, and the median nerve."

Shit. "Was the nerve severed?"

"No, it was still partially intact."

Staring at the thick dressing covering her arm, dread filled her. She couldn't feel anything now because of whatever meds they had her on, but if the median nerve had been damaged, she'd lose at least some motor control and sensation in her right hand. Her dominant surgical hand.

Swallowing, she glanced up at the IV stand. Her stomach dropped. "No more Demerol," she commanded, trying to sit upright. Already she could feel the nausea starting, rolling around like worms in her stomach. She didn't want to throw up right now, especially in front of

Rhys. "No more Dem or morphine."

"Whoa, easy." Hard hands settled on her shoulders and pressed her down.

"Tell them no more—"

"I will." His voice was so calm, so soothing. "Baby, just close your eyes a minute and rest, before they throw me out of here. I promised them you'd feel better with me here when you woke up but if you keep this up they're gonna show me the door."

He was right. With a sigh, Nev tried to relax. "You won't leave, right?" She didn't want to close her eyes in case she drifted off and he left. The idea of being alone filled her with something close to panic. She couldn't handle thinking about the attack and the damage to her arm right now.

For a moment a shadow flickered in his dark blue eyes, but then he took her face between his hands and bent to her. "I'm not leaving you," he vowed, kissing her eyelids closed.

But without visual input to distract her, her brain began to run through what had transpired in the elevator. No matter how hard she willed them away, the images came. The glint of the knife. The gushes of crimson pulsing from Shirani's neck. Her eyes sprang open. "Rhys..."

"What, baby?"

She reached for him blindly and his arms opened up to take her against his hard body. When they closed tight around her, she shuddered in relief. Pressing her face into his shoulder she fought the tears filling her eyes. A sob shook her. The wound over her ribs pulled.

"Ah Nev, *Christ*..." Rhys gathered her even closer. "I want to hold you so tight but I'm scared of hurting you."

"Don't let go," she begged.

He groaned and kissed the top of her head. "I won't.

I love you."

God, she loved him more than anything. Tipping her face up to tell him so, she stopped when a nurse came over and wrapped a heated blanket around her.

"We'll get you up to a private room as soon as it's ready," she said with a sympathetic smile. "I'll draw the curtains around you to give you some privacy, but let us know if you need anything."

Nev nodded. "Th-thanks." The metallic curtain rings made a hissing sound as the nurse drew the fabric panels closed. Neveah laid her wet cheek over the steady throb of Rhys's heart. His big hands stroked gently over her hair and down her back, but her mind was in turmoil. She'd killed a man. Her heart drummed in her ears. "Will… Will the police take me in?"

"No, honey. They'll come here to ask you some questions and take your statement and that's all."

But what then? There hadn't been any witnesses in the elevator. Would she be accused of murder? "I—I didn't want to do it," she whispered. "I just w-wanted him to leave me alone, but he wouldn't stop." Shivers wracked her despite the warmth of the blanket and Rhys's arms around her. God, why hadn't he *stopped*? "He kind of fell on the knife… I don't th-think I s-stabbed him." Or had she? She'd been all instinct in that moment. Maybe she had driven the blade into his neck.

You killed a man today. You know you did.

She wanted to clap her hands over her ears to stop that voice, but she wouldn't let herself. *Think, Nev*, she ordered herself, *think about some way to prove you didn't do it on purpose*. "Are there security cameras in the elevator? So they can see how it was?"

"Yes, but—" His hands pressed against her spine and nape. "Baby whatever happened, you were acting in self-defense. You're not in any trouble with the police."

She raised her eyes to his. "What if the laws are

different in Canada?"

"They're not that different. Everything's going to be fine."

He felt so good against her. Warm and strong and protective. A living shield to stand between her and the rest of the world. "I was so scared, Rhys," she admitted in a small voice.

"Ah, baby, I know. I'm so goddamn sorry…"

The roughness in his voice made her look up at him, and the guilt she saw embedded in his beautiful blue eyes broke her heart. "No," she protested, unwilling to let him blame himself for what happened. She put a palm to his cheek. "You look at me."

"Nev…"

"Rhys, you look at me right now." When he finally raised his gaze to hers she stared directly into his eyes. "What happened to me was not your fault, it was mine. I insisted on doing the damn speech even though you'd all warned me it could be dangerous. I put myself in harm's way along with everybody else. If anyone should be beating themselves up, it should be me. But I think I'm sufficiently battered right now."

Rhys kissed her palm, and when he spoke his eyes were damp. "I came here to protect you, and I didn't."

Her heart squeezed. "Yes, you did. You did everything humanly possible to keep me safe."

"No. I let you give that speech, and I shouldn't have. But I knew how important it was to you so I wanted you to do it…"

"Rhys, I needed to give it. In hindsight I admit it was a stupid risk, but at the time I needed it for myself." She pleaded with her eyes for his understanding and acceptance. "I do not hold you one iota responsible for what happened today."

He bowed his head as he battled with her words and she pressed her cheek to his, wrapping her left hand around the back of his neck. Her voice wobbled. "I knew you'd come for me. Even when he had me in a headlock and that knife was inches from my throat, I knew if I held on long enough you would save me."

"Oh, shit, don't say it—"

She shook her head. She needed to get this out. "I knew you were trying to get to me. So I kept fighting. I kept thinking of how much I loved you, and that I couldn't let him take you away from me."

His embrace was fierce. "I'm so proud of you, Nev. You were so damn brave."

Her heart seemed to stop beating for a moment as insight dawned. "You saw the tape, didn't you?"

He gave a reluctant nod.

Shame and sadness filled her. What must he think of her, after having watched that? Was he going to wind up as scarred as she was inside?

"When I saw you crawl over to help him…" His voice caught. "My heart broke all over again."

She squeezed her lids shut against the memory. "Why did he do it, Rhys? Why?"

"He was part of a terrorist cell, sweetheart. Directly linked to Tehrazzi. We think he had Shirani's wife abducted."

She pulled back, remembering the regret and purpose in the neurosurgeon's eyes. Had he been trying to save his wife? "Is she all right?"

"No one knows yet."

"Tehrazzi set all this up? To get to me?"

"Yeah, he did. From Pakistan. Luke said a team went to his last known location but he'd already cleared out. They tried to track him with a military satellite, but…"

But he'd done another vanishing routine. She shook her head, weary to the bone. "They've got to get him."

"They will. Just as soon as Luke's healthy enough,

he'll be back over there to hunt him down."

"With you?" She hated the thought of him being in any more danger. It had hurt enough before she'd fallen in love with him, but now… How would she deal with that? The idea of him leaving her now when she had all this to deal with frightened her. She didn't think she could handle it without him.

He started up with more of those soft strokes on her back. "I'm not…up for that, I don't think. Not after this."

Yeah, she could totally understand that. And she was glad. A few beats passed. "I don't think I can move my thumb," she said dully, trying to flex her right hand.

Frustrated by the lack of movement, she wondered if they'd put a block in her arm once she was under. She strained to curl her fingers. A gasp tore out of her as fiery pain burned deep in her forearm, like someone had spilled battery acid in her incision and it had trickled down to the bone.

"Don't, Nev," Rhys said, gently capturing her bandaged limb in his hands. He caged it there like he was protecting it from her. "I know you're worried, but you have to give your body time to heal right now. Don't think about the rest yet, okay? It's too soon to know how much function you'll regain."

Besides the attack and the fact she'd stabbed Shirani, the fear that she wouldn't regain use of her hand was like a siren blaring in her head. A flush of perspiration dampened her skin. "What am I going to do if I can't operate again?"

Settling his forehead against hers, Rhys's chest expanded when he took in a deep breath. "One step at a time, baby. I know you're scared, but you're going to be fine. I'm here for you, and I'll do whatever I can to help you. We'll get through this together."

Leaning against him, she closed her eyes and tried

to focus on that. “Okay,” she said. “Okay.”

Chapter Twenty-Four

Massachusetts coast
Two weeks later

The cry of gulls woke her. For a moment she was disoriented, but then she remembered where she was. In a beach cottage on Martha's Vineyard, with Rhys.

On either side of the four-poster bed, late afternoon sunlight spilled in through the white wooden shutter blinds on the tall windows overlooking the rolling blue-green ocean.

Nev frowned and sat up. Where was Rhys? She'd fallen asleep with his warm weight pressed against her back, relaxed after making leisurely love to her. His pillow bore the indentation from his head and his scent clung to the case when she pressed her face into it.

Smothering a yawn, she lifted her arms over her head and stretched, wincing a bit as the muscles in her right forearm pulled. Lowering it, she studied the deep purple surgical scar marring her pale skin from her wrist to her elbow. She'd removed the stitches herself a few days back and though everything seemed to have healed fine, she still didn't have full sensation or movement in her hand. The skin over her thumb and first two fingers was numb, and she had very little strength in those same digits. She could make a fist, but it was awkward, and her fine motor skills were almost non-existent.

If she was going to make it as a surgeon again someday, she had a long road of rehab ahead of her.

Drawing in a deep breath, she caught a delicious scent in the air. Something spicy, like ginger and garlic. Her mouth watered.

Walking around the foot of the bed to the en suite, she ran the faucet and waited for the water to warm while she grabbed a fluffy hand towel from the rack behind her. The hot water felt heavenly on her face, refreshing her tired eyes. She patted dry and brushed her teeth before running a brush through her mussed waves and headed out into the bright, cream wainscoting-covered hallway.

She sniffed appreciatively as she wandered through the pretty living room with its soothing tones of ivory and blue. Near the doorway of the cozy country kitchen, she caught the low tones of Rhys's voice as he spoke. Probably on the phone. Reaching the doorjamb, she leaned against it, heart skipping a beat.

His back was to her, his black shirt stretched taut over the muscles in his shoulders and down either side of his spine. Her eyes followed them down to his hips, where a snug pair of dark jeans hugged his amazing ass and long legs to perfection. His right hand held his cell to his ear, and his left deftly flipped the sizzling contents of their dinner in a sauté pan like a five star chef.

Lord have mercy, he *cooked*? Her knees almost went weak.

Rhys tossed contents of the pan into the air with an expert flick of his wrist, then caught them and gave the works a practiced shake before placing it back on the gas burner and lowering the heat.

"When do you want me?" he said, and her stomach dropped.

He must be talking to Luke. She pressed a hand over her belly. Luke must have asked him to do another mission, and it sounded like he was up for it.

Worry and dread twined inside her. They'd both been through so much already…too much. She couldn't believe Rhys would want to go back.

Yes you can. You've always known what he was and what he did.

She bit her lip. He was a proud, incredibly gifted man who excelled at his work. Of course he would want to go back into the field, especially if it had anything to do with getting Tehrazzi.

"She's doing good," he said into the phone, "but I want to talk to her about this first."

That all too familiar bittersweet pain rose in her heart. He loved her enough to talk about it before he signed on. Problem was, she didn't know if she could be supportive of his decision if he wanted to go. Not that she really had a say. He wasn't the kind of man to let anyone dictate his life to him, but at least he was taking her feelings into consideration. For him, that was a huge statement.

Wrapping her arms around her suddenly chilled body, Nev started to turn away so she wasn't eavesdropping, but he saw her and gave her a warm smile while he held the phone to his ear. She forced one in return and pointed behind her. "I'll just wait in the other room."

"One sec," he said, and laid the phone against his chest as he faced her. "I'll only be a minute. Why don't you go sit out on the patio? I've got the fireplace on, thought we could eat out there."

"Sure. Want some help?"

"No, I've got it."

This time her sappy smile was all too real. Leaving him to finish up, she grabbed a blanket from one of the easy chairs in the living room on her way to the French doors that led to the private patio and stepped outside.

The nip of the air hit her with a rush of salt-scented wind. Once the blanket was tucked securely around her shoulders, she titled her head back and breathed in deeply of the fresh sea air, giving herself a moment to get everything under control.

Rhys was a big boy. He felt strongly about his job and his perceived duty as a former Delta operator. She couldn't fault him for that, because she felt exactly the same way about her role as a surgeon. When the opportunity came for her to go back to work, she knew damned well she'd leap at the chance.

Nev picked her way around the teak table and chairs nestled in the corner. She settled back on the plush cushioned seat of the chaise lounge facing the rolling ocean. The sun nearly touched the gray-green rollers at the edge of the horizon. Already, streaks of pink and crimson set the sky ablaze.

She curled up under her blanket and basked in the warmth of the flames in the rock fireplace across from her. Staring out at the spectacular scenery of the shoreline, she thought of her cousin.

Sam and Ben were back in Virginia in the last stages of planning their wedding. The four of them had spent two days together after she'd been released from the hospital and sent home to New York. Nev had needed that time with her cousin, and felt a secret glow that Sam heartily approved of her and Rhys together.

Dec and Bryn had flown off and eloped on a beach in Hawaii just as she'd said she wanted. Dec was due back on rotation with the SEALs in a couple of weeks. Nev didn't envy Bryn on that count. She just hoped they fared better than Luke and Emily had.

Speaking of Luke, he was back home finishing up his "recuperation" in Baton Rouge, although she'd bet he wasn't taking it easy as directed. Nev hadn't heard anything else about Emily, but in light of what Bryn had said at Christa's place, she had to wonder about the concern she'd seen in Luke's eyes when Bryn had mentioned her going home to face her own demons. She hoped Emily was all right.

Pulling the blanket tighter over her legs and torso, Nev gazed out across the water and let the endless rhythm of the waves soothe her. With Rhys inside and nothing but open beach in front of her, she was at peace for the first time in weeks.

A few minutes later the French doors opened, and Rhys came out carrying two steaming plates piled high with their dinner. He set them down on the side table beside her and then straddled the chaise, facing her as he sat.

Without a word he gathered her up tight against him and tucked his face into the side of her neck, like he was breathing her in. His strong yet gentle hands stroked through her hair and down her back as his warm breath tickled the sensitive spot beneath her ear.

Sighing in contentment, Nev wrapped her arms around his shoulders and slowly rubbed her palm over his short hair, savoring the closeness. Sometimes it startled her, how affectionate he was with her now, but she loved it. It always tugged at her heartstrings because it proved he was comfortable showing how he felt about her. But mostly because she knew how much Rhys needed affection from her in return. He'd lived with emptiness for so long, and Nev was determined to make up for every last bit of loneliness he'd carried with him throughout his life.

When he kissed her temple and drew back, she eyed

the stir fry with its glistening red peppers, broccoli and pineapple served over a bed of noodles. "This looks amazing." And smelled it, too. Garlic, ginger, and orange, if she wasn't mistaken. She glanced up at him and caught the amused glint in his eyes. "I didn't know you could cook."

He shrugged. "I like to when I have the time. Don't get a chance very often."

What other hidden talents did he have that she didn't know about yet? She lifted the plate up so she could get a good whiff. "Mmm. What kind of sauce is it?"

"Orange, honey, soy sauce, allspice, garlic, ginger and a bit of lime. Just sort of threw it together." He smiled at her expression. "What?"

She couldn't wipe the stupid grin off her face. "I'm the luckiest woman in the universe."

"It's just a stir fry."

"Seeing you at the stove flipping that pan has got to be in the top five sexiest things I've ever seen in my life."

He chuckled. "That good?"

"Oh, yeah."

"What are the other four?"

"You're in all of those, too, but with less clothing. God, I could jump you right now."

The grin widened until the hint of a dimple appeared in his left cheek. "Yeah?"

She was seriously tempted.

"I should really go all out next time and cook you pan-seared chicken breasts with a brandy cream sauce. Flame it right in front of you while you finish off a bottle of red wine."

Yup, that would do it. He'd be naked on the floor beneath her in three seconds flat. "Tomorrow?"

Rhys raised a hand and stroked a wisp of hair away

from her face. "Whatever you want."

She took him at his word. "Okay. I'd really like to know what that call was about."

A smile played around his lips, though he had to be getting used to her bluntness by now. "It was Luke."

"Yes, I figured."

"He's going back to Beirut once he's all healed up. Bryn offered him the use of her father's place there as a kind of headquarters. He wants Ben, since he was chief of security there, and for Sam to go too." In case they might be of use in another attempt to nail Tehrazzi, no doubt. "And you." Rhys inclined his head. "And me."

She wrapped her arms around her waist. "Do you want to?"

He dropped his gaze. "You know I'm done with the Unit, but… This is a line of work I'm good at. And I want Tehrazzi wiped off the map as bad as anyone. I trust Luke and the others."

"I don't want you to be in danger."

"I know." Watching her, he exhaled. "Why don't you come with me?"

"What? What would I do in Beirut?"

"You said you wanted to travel with me."

Was he joking? "Yeah, I meant somewhere *away* from militant extremists."

"Ben's got that place wired tighter than the White House. And we could always use your expertise."

"You mean if you got shot up again? God, Rhys—"

He pulled her into a tight hug. "I don't know what I want to do yet, but this is something I want to help with if Luke needs me. Can you understand why I need to see this through?"

Yes, she admitted grudgingly. Along with his honor and integrity, his determination was a big part of why she'd fallen in love with him. And to be honest, the desire for justice burned within her, too. She wanted

Tehrazzi punished for what he'd done, and though she'd rather someone else went in after him than Rhys, she understood why he was motivated to finish it.

His breath was warm against her temple. "I really want you to come with me. Let's spend a few weeks in the sun together, and then we'll see what happens after."

She pulled back. "God, why couldn't you have been an accountant or something?"

His grin was quick and genuine. "Because you wouldn't love me as much."

"Yes, I would, you just wouldn't be quite as sexy." She huffed out a breath, determined to change the subject. "Dinner's getting cold. Let's eat before all your hard work goes to waste."

Rhys's eyes twinkled as he reached behind him. "There's a method to my madness tonight."

She gave him a wary look. "How come I don't like the sound of that?"

From behind his back he brought out two sets of chopsticks and held them up. "You game?"

"God, you're such a slave driver." With a sigh, she took one set from him in her right hand, determined to meet the silent challenge he offered. Her fingers were clumsy as she tried to get them adjusted in her grip, her thumb slow to obey her commands. Even as she tried to cover her awkwardness, she was filled with love for his thoughtfulness.

In his quiet way he always tried so hard to help her in every means possible. There to listen to her if she wanted to talk, holding her tight when she woke up in the jaws of a nightmare; cheering her on during her efforts at physical therapy. The chopsticks weren't instruments of torture, they were a mission for her to complete. Something Rhys had thought of before he'd done the grocery shopping that morning, to help her work on her endurance and dexterity. A new method designed to gently push her.

Holding the smooth polished sticks in her hand, she swallowed the lump in her throat and fought back tears.

Rhys covered her hand with his warm one. "I can get you a fork."

"No. No, it's not that." She fought to get hold of herself before she started blubbering. "It just… It touches me that you're so thoughtful."

His hand went to the back of her neck, his fingers wrapping around it in a gentle squeeze. Nev closed her eyes to absorb the feel of it. Strong. Comforting. Protective. Just like the man before her.

"I want to make you happy, Nev."

She took his hand and pressed a kiss in the center of his wide palm, then stared into his deep blue eyes. Whatever life had in store for her, she wanted it to happen with Rhys at her side, whether it was marriage and kids someday or traveling the world together. All she needed was him. "I love you more than I ever knew I could love anyone."

His eyes darkened and he pulled the chopsticks from her grasp. "Come here."

She melted inside. "But what about dinner?"

He set their plates aside, the erotically charged smile he gave her sending a ripple of heat over her skin. "Life's too short, Nev." Reaching for her, he gathered her into his arms. The tempered strength of them melted her. His seductive whisper brushed against her ear, over her body and straight into her heart. "I say we start with dessert."

—The End—

Dear reader,

Thank you for reading ***Relentless***. I hope you enjoyed it. If you'd like to stay in touch with me and be the first to learn about new releases you can:

- Join my newsletter at: http://kayleacross.com/v2/newsletter/
- Find me on Facebook: https://www.facebook.com/KayleaCrossAuthor/
- Follow me on Twitter: https://twitter.com/kayleacross
- Follow me on Instagram: https://www.instagram.com/kaylea_cross_author/

Also, please consider leaving a review at your favorite online book retailer. It helps other readers discover new books.

Happy reading,
Kaylea

Acknowledgements

NY Times and USA Today Bestselling author Kaylea Cross writes edge-of-your-seat military romantic suspense. Her work has won many awards, including the Daphne du Maurier Award of Excellence, and has been nominated multiple times for the National Readers' Choice Awards. A Registered Massage Therapist by trade, Kaylea is also an avid gardener, artist, Civil War buff, Special Ops aficionado, belly dance enthusiast and former nationally-carded softball pitcher. She lives in Vancouver, BC with her husband and family.

You can visit Kaylea at www.kayleacross.com. If you would like to be notified of future releases, please join her newsletter:

http://kayleacross.com/v2/newsletter/

Complete Booklist

<u>**ROMANTIC SUSPENSE**</u>

Vengeance Series

Stealing Vengeance

Covert Vengeance

Explosive Vengeance

Toxic Vengeance

Crimson Point Series

Fractured Honor

Buried Lies

Shattered Vows

Rocky Ground

DEA FAST Series

Falling Fast

Fast Kill

Stand Fast

Strike Fast

Fast Fury

Fast Justice

Fast Vengeance

Colebrook Siblings Trilogy

Brody's Vow

Wyatt's Stand

Easton's Claim

Hostage Rescue Team Series

Marked

Targeted

Hunted

Disavowed

Avenged

Exposed

Seized

Wanted

Betrayed

Reclaimed

Shattered

Guarded

Titanium Security Series

Ignited

Singed

Burned

Extinguished

Rekindled

Blindsided: A Titanium Christmas novella

Bagram Special Ops Series

Deadly Descent

Tactical Strike

Lethal Pursuit

Danger Close

Collateral Damage

Never Surrender (a MacKenzie Family novella)

Suspense Series

Out of Her League

Cover of Darkness
No Turning Back
Relentless
Absolution

PARANORMAL ROMANCE

Empowered Series

Darkest Caress

HISTORICAL ROMANCE

The Vacant Chair

EROTIC ROMANCE (writing as ***Callie Croix***)

Deacon's Touch
Dillon's Claim
No Holds Barred
Touch Me
Let Me In
Covert Seduction

Printed in the USA
CPSIA information can be obtained
at www.ICGtesting.com
CBHW021306171024
16008CB00022B/118